KT-151-409

Please return/renew this item by the last date shown
on this label, or on your self-service receipt.

To renew this item, visit **www.librarieswest.org.uk**
or contact your library

Your borrower number and PIN are required.

Libraries**West**

4 4 0155351 3

Also by Brenda Jackson

The Westmoreland Legacy
The Rancher Returns
His Secret Son
An Honorable Seduction
His to Claim
Duty or Desire

Westmoreland Legacy: The Outlaws
The Wife He Needs
The Marriage He Demands

Also by Joss Wood

Murphy International
One Little Indiscretion
Temptation at His Door
Back in His Ex's Bed

South Africa's Scandalous Billionaires
How to Undo the Proud Billionaire
How to Win the Wild Billionaire

Discover more at millsandboon.co.uk

WHAT HE WANTS FOR CHRISTMAS

BRENDA JACKSON

HOW TO HANDLE A HEARTBREAKER

JOSS WOOD

MILLS & BOON

First Published in Great Britain 2021
by Mills & Boon, an imprint of HarperCollins*Publishers* Ltd
1 London Bridge Street, London, SE1 9GF

www.harpercollins.co.uk

HarperCollins*Publishers*
1st Floor, Watermarque Building,
Ringsend Road, Dublin 4, Ireland

What He Wants for Christmas © 2021 Brenda Streater Jackson
How to Handle a Heartbreaker © 2021 Harlequin Books S.A.

Special thanks and acknowledgement are given to Joss Wood for her contribution to the *Texas Cattleman's Club: Fathers and Sons* series.

ISBN: 978-0-263-28310-5

1121

WHAT HE WANTS
FOR CHRISTMAS

BRENDA JACKSON

To the man who will always and forever be the love of my life and the wind beneath my wings, Gerald Jackson, Sr.

Wishing everyone the best of the holidays.

To all my readers who love the Westmorelands and Outlaws. This book is for you.

With thanks to Diaminique Watson and Mahogany Mitchell for sharing information on North Pole, Alaska, and Fairbanks, Alaska. Your time and the information were greatly appreciated.

Judge not, and ye shall not be judged: condemn not, and ye shall not be condemned: forgive, and ye shall be forgiven.

—Luke 6:37

One

Sloan Outlaw whipped his head around. He would recognize that voice anywhere. There were some things he'd never forget, like the sound of the woman who had broken his heart ten years ago.

He couldn't stop his eyes from scanning the crowd of people, who, like him, were attending the wedding celebration for Tyler and Keosha. Within moments, he had spotted her.

Leslie Cassidy.

There she stood, regal, sophisticated and as beautiful as ever with her bedroom brown eyes, mocha-colored skin, a pair of full lips, high cheekbones and short hair. He blinked. Short hair? What happened to that glorious mass of dark brown curls that used to flow around her shoulders? The same hair he'd loved running his fingers through whenever they made love? Whenever she'd cuddled in his arms, whenever they did just about anything? The curls were gone. However, he would admit the short style looked cute on her. Sassy and chic. It showed a degree of maturity and modishness that defined her strikingly gorgeous features. He couldn't help but think the short style made her look even sexier.

His gaze raked down the rest of her. She still possessed a body that made men take a second look. Those legs were the most gorgeous pair he'd ever seen on a woman. He could clearly remember how she would wrap them around him tight whenever they made love. The sexiness of her above-the-knee dress not only showcased those legs but also emphasized every single curve she possessed.

Leslie had always been an attention grabber, and from the number of guys he saw checking her out, it seemed nothing had changed. He should have known she would be here. After all, like him, she was friends of both the bride and groom from their college days at the University of Alaska at Anchorage. And yet he honestly hadn't thought about running into her. He had deliberately blocked her from his mind over the years. He would always have an issue with her believing a lie about him, when she of all people should have trusted him beyond any doubt.

Instead, she hadn't given him a chance to defend himself. She'd left the university, only sending him an email, the contents of which still burned when he thought about them. The first line had read, *I hate you.* It hadn't taken long for him to find out why—she had believed the lies of her roommate. The same woman she'd thought was her best friend. The same woman who'd tried coming on to him behind Leslie's back. If anything, his mistake had been in thinking he could handle the situation and not involve Leslie by telling her of Sarah Olsen's behavior. Had he told her, then Leslie would have been prepared for the woman's lies. But he hadn't, and in the end, Leslie had believed the worst.

More people had arrived at the wedding celebration. The ballroom of the hotel in Juneau was crowded, and now his view of Leslie was obstructed. Just as well. Still, Tyler should have warned him she was coming. He intended to give his frat brother and good friend a piece of his mind for not doing so.

As Sloan stood there nursing a glass of champagne, he knew he was ill-equipped to deal with seeing the one and only woman he had ever loved.

"Well, have you seen him yet?"

Leslie Cassidy turned and looked into the face of her best friend, Carmen Golan. When Leslie had left the University of Alaska at Anchorage, she had transferred to Howard University in DC to be close to her aunt Ella, her father's only sister. At least that's the reason she'd told everyone. Carmen had been her roommate at Howard and was one of the most positive people she knew. Her friend's optimism had helped Leslie get through some rough times after her breakup with Sloan.

"No, I have not seen him, and I'm not looking for him, Carmen."

"Well, you should. You owe him an apology."

There were days Leslie wished Carmen had not been with her that night three years ago when they'd taken a girls' trip to LA. At a nightclub they had run into Sarah Olsen, of all people, the woman who'd been Leslie's roommate while at college in Alaska. It was obvious Sarah had had one too many drinks, and in a drunken spiel she had bragged about how her plan to deliberately break up Leslie and Sloan had worked.

She'd even made fun of Leslie in front of everyone for being gullible enough to believe Sarah's lies. That was when Leslie realized all those things she had believed about Sloan had not been true.

"I will eventually see him, Carmen, but I don't intend to go looking for him. There're over a couple hundred guests here."

What she wouldn't mention to Carmen was that the phone call she'd gotten from her attorney before leaving the hotel was weighing more heavily on her mind than an apology to Sloan right now.

"I would help find him if I knew what he looked like."

She was glad Carmen didn't know, because there was no doubt in Leslie's mind that Carmen would go looking for Sloan. "He might not have come."

The disappointment in Carmen's eyes made Leslie feel bad for even suggesting such a thing. Her friend believed in taking any opportunity to right a wrong. Carmen was also a hopeless romantic. That's one of the reasons Leslie had asked Carmen to attend the wedding with her as her plus-one. Weddings were right up Carmen's alley. Carmen had flown to Alaska to spend Thanksgiving with Leslie, and her best friend had then also agreed to attend the wedding because it would be the perfect opportunity for Leslie to apologize to Sloan.

Leslie knew Carmen was also hoping she and Sloan could reconcile a relationship that should not have ended in the first place. Leslie had told Carmen countless times that ten years had passed. These days, saving her company from the clutches of Martin Longshire weighed more heavily on her mind than reuniting with Sloan.

"Didn't the bride tell you that she'd gotten Sloan's RSVP saying he would be attending?"

Yes, Keosha had said that. "Yes, however, something could have come up."

A part of Leslie knew that no matter what she'd just said to Carmen, somewhere in this crowd of attendees was Sloan Outlaw. He was here. She could feel his presence.

Sloan knew it would be close to impossible to grab even a minute of Tyler's time since he was the groom and taking wedding pictures. That sent Sloan in search of Redford St. James.

Sloan could forgive Tyler for not mentioning Leslie's attendance to him, since he'd probably had a lot on his mind in preparing for the wedding, but there was no excuse for Redford. If Tyler knew, then so had Redford. During their college days, the three of them had been thick as thieves, and although they now lived in different cities in Alaska, they still found time to get together twice a year.

Moving in and around several people—some he knew, others he did not   Sloan figured that even in this crowd he would have no problem finding Redford. All he needed to do was figure out the best place an amorous couple could engage in a quickie. That sort of thing was what Redford had always been good at, even when they were in college. Storage closets, empty classrooms, underneath the stairs—those were just a few places that easily came to mind.

Sloan left the ballroom and headed down a side corridor toward the back. When a woman rounded the corner and quickly walked past him while trying to straighten her outfit and hair, Sloan knew Redford St. James had struck again. His friend had a problem with keeping his pants zipped.

When Sloan reached a cracked door, he slowly opened it and entered a small meeting room. Redford had his back to him, putting on his jacket.

"I thought I'd find you in here, Redford."

Redford jerked around and then glared at him. "Damn, Sloan, you almost gave me heart failure. I thought you were that woman's boyfriend."

Sloan lifted an eyebrow and then crossed his arms over his chest. "Boyfriend? When did you start trespassing on another man's territory?"

Redford gave him a smooth grin. "When she looked my way a few times and deliberately licked her lips. I figured someone wasn't taking care of her properly, and I got the message. The opportunity was too good to pass up."

"Whatever," Sloan said, closing the door behind him. "So why didn't you tell me Leslie would be coming to the wedding?"

Redford rolled his eyes. "Did you honestly think she wouldn't be invited? Leslie and Keosha were good friends in college."

"I didn't know they'd stayed in touch over the years."

"No reason they wouldn't, Sloan. You're the only one who considered Leslie an enemy. In fact, if you recall, you forbade me and Tyler to even mention her name around you, so we didn't. Hell, man, we told you what you should have done after that time Sarah came on to you. She was just trouble waiting to happen."

"Okay, maybe I should have said something about it to Leslie, but regardless, Leslie should have trusted me and not believed Sarah."

"Well, that was a pretty convincing lie, and Sarah had proof to back it up, Sloan."

"Regardless, Leslie should have known I was not texting or calling Sarah behind her back, no matter what Sarah's phone records showed."

"I still say you should have warned her about Sarah, so you share the blame as well."

Sloan didn't like it that Redford's thought mirrored his brothers'. They had liked Leslie and felt he should have told Leslie about Sarah, even though Sarah had promised it wouldn't happen again.

"I guess you heard about her father," Redford said, breaking into his thoughts.

Sloan lifted a brow. "No, what about her old man?"

"He died three months ago."

Sloan hadn't known. "I'm sorry to hear that. Was he ill?"

"It was a sudden heart attack."

He could just imagine how hard that must have been on Leslie. She and her father had been close. Her mother had died years ago when Leslie had been in her teens. "Who's running the company?" Leslie's father had been founder and CEO of Cassidy Cosmetics, an Alaska-based company whose products were sold directly to stores in the state.

"Leslie's in charge of things now, but I don't know how long that will last."

Sloan frowned. "What do you mean?"

"I'd rather not say, because you have no reason to care. Look, Sloan, we need to go back or Tyler will wonder where we are."

"So now you're worried about being absent from the wedding celebration? Tyler won't care where we are since he's all wrapped up in Keosha, so what's happening with Leslie that I have no reason to care about, Redford? What aren't you telling me?"

Redford sighed, giving in. "Martin Longshire plans to take over her company. He and Leslie's father were long-time enemies, and since her father is dead, he plans to make Leslie pay. Two weeks ago, I slept with a woman who works for Longshire, and she told me. Apparently, the people who work for him can't keep a secret—or the man doesn't give a damn who knows what he plans to do to Leslie."

"Did you tell her?" Sloan asked.

"No, not yet. But I did tell Tyler and Keosha. Keosha said she would warn Leslie about it, but I doubt it will do any good. Everybody knows Martin Longshire is a bas-tard. If he did have a beef with Leslie's father, then he has no problem making her suffer because of it."

Sloan didn't say anything as he and Redford returned to the ballroom. He silently told himself anything dealing with Leslie was not his business.

"I'll be back, man," Redford said. "Telling you what

Longshire plans to do to Leslie has left a bad taste in my mouth. I need a stiff drink." He then quickly walked toward the bar.

As Sloan watched his friend leave, the hairs on the back of his neck stood up. He immediately knew who was standing behind him even before she spoke.

"Hello, Sloan."

He turned to stare right into Leslie's face.

Two

"How are you, Leslie?"

Leslie knew the man towering in front of her was every bit of six two, and her five-foot, eight-inch height didn't reach his chin even in her stilettos. But his height wasn't what had her heart pounding and pulse racing.

Ten years ago, Sloan Outlaw was considered extremely handsome. By today's standards he was that ten times over. And he wore a suit better than any man she knew. He'd always been a sharp dresser, even in college, when he'd had the preppy style down to an art form. Even now his jacket embraced a pair of masculine shoulders while covering the broadness of his chest. Her gaze lowered to the zipper of his pants, and she recalled all the times she would ease it down. He loved whenever she undressed him, and she had loved it as well. She had never regretted sharing his bed… except for when she thought he'd betrayed her with Sarah.

After Sarah's drunken boast, Leslie had thought about contacting Sloan to apologize. Locating him would not have been difficult, since his family's freight line was a successful one in Alaska. However, considering how she'd broken things off between them, leaving town without letting him know where she'd gone and then sending him a nasty email, Leslie had figured she was the last person he would want to hear from, even if it was to apologize.

She had looked him up on social media. In addition to being the handsome man he'd always been, Sloan Outlaw was now successful in his own right. Not only did he work in the day-to-day operations of his family's multimillion-dollar business, he was involved with several of his own companies, including a foundation he'd established a few years ago. He gave of his time and money, which meant Sloan was still the generous and caring guy she had known and fallen in love with at nineteen.

Leslie noted that he also gave of his time to the opposite sex. He'd been captured in a number of photos with beautiful women on his arm while attending several high-profile events. But he hadn't married yet. She found it hard to believe that someone hadn't snatched him up by now. Just looking into the darkness of his chocolate-colored eyes and seeing those well-defined lips was making it hard to breathe. He'd had that impact on her from the first.

"I'm fine, Sloan. You look well," she finally found her voice to say.

She didn't miss the way his gaze drifted over her. The same way hers had done to him. "And so do you."

Electricity sizzled through her veins just from hearing the sound of his voice. Now was not the time or the place, but was she really surprised when Sloan had always had this sort of effect on her?

"I'm happy for Tyler and Keosha," she said, not able to break eye contact with him, although she knew she should.

"Hell, it took them long enough."

Leslie fought back a smile, because he was right. Tyler

and Keosha had been high school sweethearts who'd refused to go to different universities like their parents had suggested. Instead, they had ended up together at University of Alaska at Anchorage.

They'd dated all through college and had been the perfect couple. After college they had returned to Juneau and worked for their families' corporations, satisfied to live together. They saw no rush in getting married, to the dismay of their parents. Tyler and Keosha always said they loved each other and didn't need a piece of paper to prove it. Now they were ready to start a family and felt they should do so as husband and wife.

The couple had refused to give in to the pressures of both sets of parents, who wanted a huge, over-the-top wedding. The bride and groom had preferred a small wedding. When the planning of the large wedding was getting on both their nerves, Tyler and Keosha had taken matters into their own hands and eloped to Vegas just days ago.

Those who'd showed up today discovered they would be attending a wedding celebration instead of a ceremony.

"Well, I guess you can say they got married when they felt the time was right. Just look at them now."

Their gazes traveled across the room to the couple, who were smiling brightly while taking pictures. "They are happy," Sloan said, returning his gaze to her.

The moment their eyes reconnected, she recalled how it felt being touched by Sloan's strong hands. Being stroked by them. Caressed in places that could take her breath away.

She felt a tightness in her throat. "Yes, they are," she agreed. She needed to say what she needed to say before Carmen returned from the dance floor. "I need to talk to you, Sloan."

She saw his face tighten when he said, "You're talking to me now."

She swallowed deeply. They were standing off to the side, where it wasn't crowded. That afforded them some privacy, at least. "I ran into Sarah three years ago, and she told me the truth."

"And what truth was that, Leslie?"

She drew in a deep breath, knowing he would not make this easy for her—and frankly, she couldn't blame him. "The truth that you had not slept with her behind my back."

"I would have told you that if you'd given me the chance."

Yes, he would have, but she had left town without letting him know where she was going, and she had forbidden her father from telling him as well. When she had reached her aunt's house in DC, the first thing she'd done was send Sloan that email, and it hadn't been nice. And then in anger, she had deleted his replies without even reading them as well as blocking his calls.

"I owe you an apology, Sloan."

"Yes, you do." The gaze holding hers was hard, unwavering, and she saw the snarl that curled his lip.

"I apologize."

He didn't say anything for a moment, then he said, "Apology accepted."

His features were hard and unyielding. The one thing she knew about Sloan was that he didn't forgive easily. For him, forgiving did not mean forgetting, excusing or reconnecting. He was a man who loved deeply and cherished friendships until trust was destroyed. By not believing in him, she had destroyed his trust in her beyond repair.

"Thank you for accepting my apology." She felt compelled to say it, although she knew his words had merely been lip service.

"I heard about your father. I offer my condolences. I liked him," he said, propelling the conversation to another topic.

There was no need to tell him that Lester Cassidy had liked Sloan, too. In fact, when she told her father what happened, he had strongly suggested she hear Sloan's side of the story. She hadn't, and now she wished she had taken her father's advice.

"How is your family?" she asked to change the subject. She had met his father, four brothers and sister when he had invited her to his home for Christmas one year. They had all been nice people, although his father had acted sort of reserved.

"Everyone is fine. Garth and Cash are married, Maverick is still happily single, and Charm is still Charm. Jess is a United States senator."

"I know, I voted for him."

He lifted a brow. "You've been back in Alaska for a while?"

"Yes. I moved back to Wasilla two years ago to help Dad run the company."

He nodded and glanced at his watch before looking back at her. "It was good seeing you again, Leslie. I need to let Redford, Tyler and Keosha know I'm leaving. I'm flying to the lower forty-eight in the morning for Thanksgiving."

She noted he didn't tell her which state. It wasn't any of her business. "It was good seeing you again, too, Sloan."

She watched him walk over to where Redford St. James was talking to a group of guys. She was glad she'd gotten the chance to apologize to Sloan. Although that meant closure, it also meant accepting that some things were never meant to be.

"What's wrong with you, Sloan?"

Sloan glanced up at his brother Garth, the oldest of his siblings. He and his family had returned to the office today after spending Thanksgiving at his brother Cash's ranch in Wyoming. This year they were joined by their cousins, the Westmorelands.

"What makes you think something is wrong with me?"

Garth leaned back in his chair and smiled. "The meeting ended a few minutes ago. Everyone has left the conference room, but you're still sitting here."

Sloan glanced around the room. Yes, he was. He then glanced back at Garth, gave him a cocky grin and said, "So are you."

"Only because I figured you might want to talk."

Sloan lifted a brow. "About what?"

"Anything. I noticed you weren't your usual chipper self over Thanksgiving, either. Is everything going okay with your new position within the company?"

Cash's marriage to Brianna had caused a shifting of job duties at the family's multimillion-dollar company, Outlaw Freight Lines, which was located here in Fairbanks. To accommodate Cash's permanent move to Black Crow, Wyoming, they had established a satellite office of Outlaw Freight Lines on Cash's ranch. Cash now handled the company's expansion into various other states in the lower forty-eight.

Sloan, who had been in charge of international sales and marketing, had replaced Cash in the office to assist Garth in the day-to-day running of the operation. His youngest brother, Maverick, had been more than happy to take over Sloan's former position in charge of international sales. Their brother Jess had been the company's executive attorney until he'd decided to run for political office two years ago. Now as Senator Jessup Outlaw, he lived most of the time in the nation's capital. Twenty-five-year-old Charm was their only sister. As far as what Charm's duties were at the company, the jury was still out on that one. At the moment they'd given her a job mainly to keep her out of their hair.

"No. I like my duties just fine."

"Glad to hear it. You know if there's ever an issue with anything, you can talk to me about it. That includes any problems with Bart."

Sloan chuckled. He and his siblings knew their father, Bart Outlaw, could be a handful and usually was. The reason Garth was now running the company was because Bart had been forced into retirement. It was either that or be ousted by the board.

It was no secret that Bart had been married five times and that each of his sons had different mothers. It also wasn't a secret that some of those wives had been full-fledged gold diggers. Somehow Bart had managed, and quite manipulatively and underhandedly, they figured, to obtain custody of all five of his sons from his ex-wives. Things had been a little different with Charm's mother, Claudia. To this day, Claudia was the only woman Bart had ever truly loved. And she'd been the only one Bart had not married…but not for lack of trying on his part. Hell, he was still trying.

Bart hadn't known Claudia was pregnant with Charm when their six-month romantic fling had ended and she had taken off for parts unknown. Fifteen years later, Claudia reappeared with Charm in tow, telling Bart that Charm was his child and Claudia couldn't handle the sassiness of the daughter he hadn't known about. She'd given custody to Bart and told him he could deal with Charm now. Bart's idea of dealing with Charm was spoiling her rotten. It had taken the brothers, especially Garth, to let Charm know they wouldn't tolerate her unruly attitude. Charm quickly fell in line and now adored the five older brothers she hadn't known she had.

"Sloan?"

He glanced over at Garth. "What?"

"You're daydreaming again."

Had he been? Probably so. Sloan paused but then decided to discuss with Garth what had been on his mind since he had spoken to Redford at the wedding. As much as he wanted to dismiss it from his mind, he couldn't, so he definitely could use someone else's perspective.

"I saw Leslie Cassidy at Tyler and Keosha's wedding celebration."

Garth nodded, then asked, "How did that go?"

He knew why Garth was asking. Everyone knew how much he'd cared for Leslie and how badly he had taken their breakup. "It was fine. She finally found out the truth and apologized."

"Better late than never, I guess."

"Yes, better late than never."

Garth studied him. "I take it there's something else."

Sloan nodded. "Have you ever heard of a businessman by the name of Martin Longshire?"

Garth shook his head. "I can't say that I have. Who is he?"

"A bastard."

Garth chuckled. "Will you tell me how you really feel, Sloan?"

Sloan chuckled as well. "I just did."

"Then maybe you ought to tell me why you feel that way."

Sloan told Garth about the conversation with Redford. He could tell by his older brother's facial expressions that he didn't like what he was hearing.

"Did you get a chance to talk to Leslie about it when you saw her at the wedding reception?" Garth asked.

"No. I figured it wasn't my business."

"Like hell" was Garth's quick reply. "If what Redford told you is true, then that's alarming. No man should deliberately target a woman just because of a beef he had with her father. You're right. Longshire is a bastard."

A smiled spread across Sloan's lips. "So tell me how you really feel, Garth."

Garth didn't say anything for a minute and then he asked, "Cassidy Cosmetics is still headquartered in Wasilla, right?"

"Yes, what of it?"

"Nothing. I was just asking." Garth paused. "You still plan to take December off?"

Since Sloan hadn't taken any time off this year, Garth had suggested he take off the entire month of December. Normally this time around the holidays would be the freight lines' busiest, but thanks to Cash's satellite office, road transportation was doing great, since the weather in the lower forty-eight had been pretty good this year. All the domestic freight trucks were delivering ahead of schedule for the Christmas season.

"Yes, that's the plan. I'm looking forward to spending a week or two at the cabin on Kodiak Island before joining everyone in Westmoreland country for Christmas."

It still amazed Sloan how their Westmoreland cousins, whom they'd met only a few years ago, could be such an intricate part of their lives now. The Westmorelands and the Outlaws enjoyed getting together as if to make up for that period of time they hadn't known about each other. "Those plans can be changed if you think I'm needed here, Garth."

Garth shook his head. "No, you won't be needed here. However, considering what Redford told you about Leslie's company, I'd think you might be needed elsewhere."

Sloan held his brother's gaze, knowing what Garth was alluding to. "Why should I even care what happens to Leslie or her company?"

Instead of answering him, Garth stood and walked out of the conference room. Sloan didn't have to wonder why his brother hadn't answered. In Garth's mind, Sloan's question didn't dignify a response.

Three

Leslie glanced up from the papers on her desk when she heard the buzzer. "Yes, Beverly?"

"Mr. Longshire is here to see you, Ms. Cassidy."

Leslie scowled. That man was the last person she wanted to see. Just that morning, Stan Middlebury, her company's attorney, had given her an update, so she knew everything Martin Longshire was up to. The man was intent on taking her company away from her.

She was still catching up on paperwork that had piled up when she'd been out of the office attending Tyler and Keosha's wedding celebration. Carmen had left yesterday to return to DC, and Leslie was missing her already.

"I don't recall Mr. Longshire having an appointment, so I'm unable to meet with him today, Beverly."

"I will let him know."

Before Leslie could go back to reviewing the documents she'd been reading, she heard Beverly's loud voice say, "Wait just a minute. You can't just barge into Ms. Cassidy's office." Her door flew open, and Martin Longshire stood there, looking like the monster Leslie thought him to be.

"Do you want me to contact security, Ms. Cassidy?" asked a flustered Beverly Neal, who'd also been Leslie's father's personal assistant for years.

Leslie stood and came around her desk. "No, Beverly, that won't be necessary. I can handle Mr. Longshire."

Beverly gave her a look that said she wasn't sure, but she nodded anyway. She was about to turn to leave when Mr. Longshire barked at Beverly, "Start cleaning out your desk. When I take over this company, you will be one of the first people I fire."

Instead of responding to what the man said, Beverly walked out, but she did not close the door behind her. Martin Longshire angrily slammed it shut. He then turned his attention back to Leslie. "So, you think you can handle me?"

"Don't you ever talk rudely to my employees again, Mr. Longshire."

The man had the nerve to smirk. "I do whatever the hell I please, and they won't be your employees for long. Like I just told the woman, I'm taking over this company, and there's nothing you can do about it. I'm sure you've heard of my plans by now."

Leslie drew in a deep breath. She had to believe there was something she could do. She didn't have the capital to fight him. As a last-ditch effort, her company attorney was working with several banks to see if one would be willing to give her a loan or extend the ones she had.

"You will never own my company," she said with a lot more confidence than she actually felt.

"We shall see. In the meantime, enjoy the holidays, because they will be the last you'll have here at Cassidy Cosmetics." He turned and walked out of her office.

On weak knees, Leslie made it back around her desk to

sit down. She held her head in her hands, but she refused to cry. Her father had taught her to be stronger than that. The last time a man had made her cry had been when she had believed Sloan had betrayed her. At the time, unknowingly, she'd been crying for nothing because he'd been innocent.

"Are you okay, Leslie?"

She glanced up and saw Beverly standing in the doorway with deep concern in her features. She sat up in her chair. The last thing she wanted was for her employees to think she didn't have things under control, although, honestly, she didn't. Because of his intense dislike of her father, Martin Longshire wanted to destroy her.

"Yes, Beverly, I'm fine. And I regret that Mr. Longshire talked to you that way."

"He doesn't scare me any," Beverly said. "As your father's personal assistant, I've had my run-ins with Martin Longshire before." She paused. "Is there anything that I can do?"

Leslie shook her head and forced a smile. "No. What I need is a Christmas miracle."

Beverly nodded. "Well, tomorrow is officially the first of December, so we're going to hope we get that miracle. We have a month." Beverly left, closing the door behind her.

Leslie leaned back in her chair. In reality, they had less time than that. Keeping with the tradition established by her father years ago, Cassidy Cosmetics closed for the holidays on the seventh of December every year and didn't reopen until the second week of January. December ninth had been her mother's birthday, and January fourth had been her father's. All the employees enjoyed the time off with pay. Now according to Mr. Longshire, neither she nor her employees would have a company to return to, since he'd made it known he planned to fire everyone.

Her employees knew the dire straits of the company,

but for some reason they believed she would fight and win. After all, she was her father's daughter, and he'd been in sticky situations before and managed to get the company out of it. However, this was more than just a mere sticky situation. This was a hostile takeover by Longshire Industries.

Needing to switch her mind off Martin Longshire, she thought of Sloan Outlaw. At least she had apologized for believing Sarah's lies, and she felt good about that. A weight had been lifted off her chest.

So why had she been thinking about him a lot since the wedding? Well, one reason could be that seeing him again had made her realize what not trusting him had cost her. Being in his presence had pushed a lot of her passion points, ones she'd thought dead and gone. His look alone had made heat settle all through her. Now she felt her stomach flutter at the memory.

But she couldn't indulge in fantasies. Knowing she had plenty of work to do, Leslie turned her attention back to the documents on her desk.

Sloan entered the building that housed Cassidy Cosmetics. The first time he'd come here had been to meet Leslie's father. It had been her first year at the university, and her father had asked her to come home to accompany him to a benefit being held in her mother's honor.

She'd told him on the plane flight from Anchorage to Wasilla that her mother, who had passed away of cancer when Leslie was fourteen, had been active in a number of community and charitable events, and the city of Wasilla would be giving her the recognition she deserved.

By the end of the weekend, he'd mentally compared Leslie's father with his own and seen how vastly different the two men were. Where Bart had a brash countenance, it was easy to see Lester Cassidy had been a people person, and he had made Sloan feel right at home. He'd even made Sloan comfortable while being interrogated. The older man had wanted to get to know Sloan since he would be a part of his daughter's life.

As Sloan stepped into the elevator, his thoughts shifted to his first job at Outlaw Freight Lines—a company researcher. He'd put his skill to work to investigate not only Longshire but also Cassidy Cosmetics. He'd wanted to come up with the best plan to protect Leslie's company against Martin Longshire's hostile takeover.

The proposal he would offer Leslie was a fair one. But would she accept it with the condition he'd attached? Bottom line, he wasn't giving her a choice in the matter if she wanted to save her company. Besides, she owed him. She might have forgotten about it, but he hadn't. And if she had forgotten, now was a good time to refresh her memory.

He got off the elevator on the fifth floor, and it seemed he had walked straight into a Christmas wonderland. The lit tree was beautifully decorated, and there were candy canes hanging from the ceiling. A huge replica of Santa was surrounded by nearly life-size reindeer. All eight of them. Santa was carrying a huge silver case that advertised Cassidy Cosmetics. The display was right on point for the holidays and the company's seasonal promotions.

From the research he'd done, it appeared Leslie had done a good job of handling things since taking over. Her employees loved and respected her. It seemed her only problem was Martin Longshire, who was making an ass of himself. Sloan doubted Leslie was aware of all the underhanded things the man was doing. Well, Sloan was prepared to throw a monkey wrench in those plans if Leslie agreed with his proposal. The decision would be hers.

"May I help you?"

He smiled at the older woman sitting at the desk. "Yes. I'm here to see Leslie Cassidy."

"And who are you, sir?"

"Sloan Outlaw."

The woman studied him curiously, and Sloan had a feeling that just like Helen, their personal assistant at Outlaw Freight Lines who'd worked for them for years, this woman had also taken on the role of guard dog. "Please have a seat, Mr. Outlaw. I'll see if Ms. Cassidy is free to see you."

Sloan nodded and took a seat in one of the chairs across the room. His gaze stayed glued to the woman as she picked up the phone and began speaking. Before she could disconnect the line, the door with Leslie's name flew open. A look of total surprise was on her face. "Sloan?"

He stood. "Yes?"

His gaze traveled over her. If he thought she'd looked good when he'd seen her at the wedding celebration, she looked doubly so now. She was wearing a midi-length green dress with a belt that hugged her small waist. The hem of her dress swished around a pair of black suede boots when she walked. His gaze went back to her short hair again. The more he saw the style on her, the more he liked it.

"What are you doing here?"

Sloan was about to answer, but he glanced over at the woman sitting behind the desk, who wasn't even pretending not to listen to their conversation. He then looked back at Leslie. "I need to speak with you privately."

She held his gaze for a long moment before nodding. "Please come into my office."

He followed her, noticing the sway of her shapely backside. Some things couldn't be helped, and he'd always had a thing for Leslie's ass. But then, he'd adored the entire package, including that mind of hers. Pushing the memory away, he knew he had to stay focused. The only reason he was here was because he knew it was the right thing to do. Whether she saw it that way would be up to her.

Closing the door behind them, he glanced around, not surprised to see that she had her very own decorated tree in her office. And it wasn't a small one. But then, he shouldn't be surprised. Christmas had always been Leslie's favorite holiday.

"So, what's this about, Sloan?"

He glanced over at her and saw the questioning look on her face. She had to be wondering why he was there. After all, they had gone ten years without seeing each other, and then they had run into each other at a wedding celebration and now he was here, in her city, her territory, her space. She had to know how far he'd traveled to get here. It wasn't like Fairbanks and Wasilla were in close proximity.

"May I sit down?" he asked her.

"Yes, of course."

He watched her move around her desk to sit in the chair behind it. Then he eased down in the chair across from her.

She placed her entwined hands in the middle of her desk and looked at him expectantly.

"It was good seeing you at Tyler and Keosha's wedding celebration."

"It was good seeing you, too, Sloan, but I'm sure you didn't travel to Wasilla just to tell me that."

No, he hadn't. "I'd think my being here would be pretty obvious, Leslie."

She tilted her head the way she always did when confused about something. "Sorry, Sloan, but I have no idea why you're here."

He leaned back in his chair. "I know about your problems with Martin Longshire."

He saw surprise light her eyes. "And what does that have to do with you?"

Good question. Every once in a while he asked himself that same thing. He would tell her the answer he always came up with. "I always liked your father, and I refuse to sit by and let Martin Longshire destroy the company he worked so hard to build."

"So, you're here because of my father?"

He didn't say anything for a minute. Then he decided to be totally honest with her. "Not entirely. You and I were friends once, Leslie. In fact, there was a time when we were more than friends, and I want to help."

She released what sounded like a frustrated breath. "I doubt there's anything you can do at this point, Sloan. I talked to my company attorney a few hours ago, and the picture he painted for me is pretty grim. It seems Mr. Longshire has been working on his revenge since even before Dad died. He's scared off my lenders, and my distributors are beginning to freak out as well. Sales are down because several stores that normally carry our products are not doing so."

All of what she said had been revealed in Sloan's research. What he hadn't found out was why. What was motivating Martin Longshire to destroy Cassidy Cosmetics? "What sort of beef did Longshire have with your father that makes him so determined to take over Cassidy Cosmetics, Leslie?"

She gazed into his eyes for several long moments before saying, "My mother."

Sloan lifted a brow. "Your mother?"

"Yes. Martin Longshire was the man my maternal grandparents selected for their daughter to marry, but my father, a man considered not part of an upstanding social class, was the man she loved. One night, a few months before the wedding was to take place, she eloped and married my father instead. As a result, there was a scandal. For years my grandparents disowned my mother, and Martin Longshire despised them both. I'm not sure he ever loved my mother, but he saw her as a possession he wanted. Was entitled to have. According to my father, the scandal lasted for a while, and it was embarrassing to Mr. Longshire. He moved out of the country to head up his family business in Paris for a few years. He returned fifteen years ago and has been causing my father grief ever since."

Sloan recalled her telling him years ago that her maternal grandparents had died when she was a little girl of ten. He further recalled her saying she'd had a close relationship to them. "Because you and your grandparents were close, I assume they finally accepted your parents' marriage."

"Yes. They saw how happy Dad made my mother—and how mean Martin Longshire turned out to be—and were glad Mom hadn't married him." She paused then added, "That's why Longshire wants to destroy the company my parents started together. He sees doing so as the ultimate revenge."

Sloan shook his head. "The man sounds demented."

"Yes, that may be the case. He's been planning it for a long time, and with Dad's death, he sees the opportunity."

Drawing in a deep breath, she pushed back from the desk. "In fact, I'm getting my employees together later today to prepare them for the worst. When this office closes for the holidays on Friday, there's a possibility it might reopen in January under new management. Right now, I'm doing all I can to make sure their pensions are protected, since Longshire plans to fire them all."

He lifted a brow. "And how are you going to protect their pensions?"

"With all the insurance money, investments and such that Dad left me, as well as the trust fund established for me by my grandparents."

Sloan stared at her. Did she not know that doing such a thing might take care of her employees but could leave her penniless? Sloan leaned forward in the chair and tried to fight back his anger that Martin Longshire had placed her in such a predicament. "Like I said, Leslie, the reason I'm here is because I want to help, and I believe that I can."

She lifted an eyebrow. "How?"

"By coming on as your business partner."

Leslie was sure she had not heard Sloan correctly. "My business partner?"

"Yes. By doing so, I'll provide you with unlimited resources to continue doing what you need to keep your business operational. As you've indicated, because of Longshire, most of the major banks have put a freeze on loaning you any money."

"And?"

"Well, they wouldn't dare do that with me as your partner. If anything, my investment will let them know your company is financially sound."

"But Mr. Longshire has launched a hostile takeover, Sloan. How can you stop him?"

Sloan's lips thinned in anger. "Stopping him isn't as hard to do as you think. Longshire has been so busy trying to take over your company that he's neglected to protect his own."

"Meaning?"

"He's left his own company vulnerable to another hostile takeover. I have no problem adding Longshire Industries to my portfolio of assets, and I plan to let him know that."

Leslie sat up straight in her chair. "You would take over his company?"

"In a heartbeat if I have to, but I don't feel it's necessary. All I need to do is make sure he knows that I can."

She stared at him, remembering the conversation she'd had with Keosha after Sloan had left the wedding celebration. From what Keosha told her, Sloan was even wealthier than Leslie had thought. In addition to being an executive in his family's business, he had a stake in several business ventures, including his brother Cash's dude ranch in Wyoming, a horse-breeding business with some newfound cousins living in Denver, a security company with some more cousins in Montana and North Carolina, and a film production company in Los Angeles. All of which were doing quite well. That meant Sloan had the financial means to do what he'd suggested. However, she needed to know why, after all these years, he would want to step in and help save her company. Also, she wasn't sure if she could afford him as a business partner. How much of a percentage would he want? Seventy-five percent of her company? Even more than that?

"How much?" she asked him.

He raised a brow. "How much what?"

"What are the partnership terms? Specifically, the percentages?"

Sloan held her gaze. "Seventy-five/twenty-five."

So, he did want seventy-five percent of her company? That meant her company would literally become his. "Are those terms negotiable, Sloan?"

He gave her questioning look. "I think those terms are more than fair. You get seventy-five percent and I get twenty-five percent."

Leslie's mouth nearly dropped open in shock. "Not the other way around?"

"No. And the partnership is only in effect for a year, granted Longshire is no longer a threat. After that time, I will remove myself as your partner and the company will again be yours, free and clear."

Leslie tried to wrap her mind around Sloan's offer. What he was proposing was too good to be true. But she couldn't get all giddy just yet. She had a feeling there was a catch. There had to be. Anything that sounded too good to be true usually was.

That made her ask, "What's the catch, Sloan?"

"What do you mean?"

Oh, he knew just what she meant. It might have been years, but she could still recognize certain Sloan Outlaw habits. Like the way he would flex his fingers when he was up to something. And usually it was something he knew would not make her happy.

"I mean what's in this for you other than a measly twenty-five percent?"

He stopped flexing his fingers and leaned forward in his chair as if to make sure he had her complete attention. The gesture was wasted, because he'd had it from the moment he had walked into her office, wearing a tailor-made business suit and looking the epitome of a wealthy businessman right off the cover of *GQ* magazine.

"There's not a catch, Leslie, but there is a proposition. It's an agreement between us that won't appear in any of the documents, but one you must agree to. I will take your word for it."

"And just what is this agreement?"

"An assurance that I will get what I want for Christmas."

There was something about the way he was looking at her that made the pulse flutter in her throat. "And what exactly is it that you want for Christmas, Sloan?"

"You, Leslie. I want you for Christmas. In my bed."

Four

Sloan knew what he'd just said had probably shocked her, but she should know just how straightforward he was known to be. While she was sitting there, staring at him as if she thought he'd lost his mind, he decided to say, "After seeing you at the wedding celebration, it quickly became apparent that even after ten years, I'm still attracted to you. Then I remembered that you owed me something."

That got her to talking. "I owe you what?"

"A week. If you recall, you left town at the beginning of spring break, after we'd made plans to spend that week together at my family's cabin on Kodiak Island. It would have been our last time together by ourselves before graduation." He had been scheduled to graduate from college in a few months, although she'd had another two years to go.

What he wouldn't tell her was that he'd intended to give her an engagement ring that week. There was no way he would have graduated, leaving her behind at the university, without putting a ring on her finger. Leslie was a beauty, and too many guys would have been all over her the moment he'd left campus. The thought of waiting two years for them to marry hadn't bothered him, just as long as she'd known how much he loved her and that they were promised to each other.

However, that never happened, because she hadn't shown up on Kodiak Island. He had waited for an entire day at the only airstrip on Kodiak. Then he'd gotten the email telling him to go to hell and that she didn't want to ever see or talk to him again. He had tried calling, but it had gone straight to voice mail.

It had taken him an entire day to get off the island due to a massive rainstorm, but he'd left the moment he could and headed to Anchorage. Once he'd reached her apartment, it was Sarah who'd told him Leslie had packed up and left. She'd then happily told him why. If she couldn't have him, then Leslie wouldn't, either.

Sloan had contacted Leslie's father, who'd told him he had to honor his daughter's wishes and could not tell Sloan where she'd gone. However, Mr. Cassidy did tell him it was somewhere in the lower forty-eight.

Sloan had returned to Kodiak and spent the week alone, drinking booze and regretting the day he'd allowed Leslie into his heart. It had been Garth who'd found him in that pitiful state and talked some sense into him. His oldest brother reminded him that he had months before graduation, and that's what he needed to focus on. Afterward, he'd promised to help Sloan find Leslie, even if he had to hire a private investigator to do so.

By the time Sloan had graduated, Garth was ready to keep his end of the bargain by hiring a PI. However, by then Sloan's heart had hardened. He refused to love a woman who had not trusted him. So instead of wasting time and money looking for Leslie, he returned to Fairbanks and began working at his family's business, deter-

mined to forget her and pledging never to give his heart
to another woman again.

"What you're suggesting doesn't make sense, Sloan!"

Her sharp words snapped him out of his reverie. He
needed to leave. All those memories were getting to him.
Standing, he said, "That's your opinion, Leslie. I suggest
you think carefully about your options. When you do, I'm
sure you'll discover the one I'm offering isn't so bad."

He placed his business card on her desk. "You've got
until noon tomorrow to decide."

Sloan turned and walked out of her office.

Several hours later, an angry Leslie paced her apartment floor while she talked on the phone to Carmen. "Can
you believe the nerve of Sloan Outlaw? Just who does he
think he is?"

"Um, he sounds like a man who wants you for Christmas."

Leslie stopped pacing. "This isn't funny, Carmen."

"And you don't hear me laughing. I wish some man who
looked like Sloan wanted me for Christmas. I would wrap
myself up to be put under his tree anytime. Then I would
wait patiently for him to unwrap me."

Leslie rolled her eyes. "Will you stop being a romantic for once?"

"No. Someone is offering you a chance to actually live
the life while I'm just dealing with fantasies."

"Listen, Carmen, the man wants me in his bed."

"So? It's not like you've never been there before."

Leslie dropped down on the sofa. "Those times were
different. We were in love then. We aren't now. All he
wants is revenge for what I did to him ten years ago. That
makes him no better than Martin Longshire."

"Isn't he? Mr. Longshire wants to destroy your company. Sounds to me like Sloan Outlaw is trying to help

you save it. Think about it, Les. He's offering you a temporary partnership that even you said was too good to be true. All you have to do is something you probably want to do anyway."

"Carmen!"

"Just keeping it real. Are you going to try and convince me that you haven't once wondered if he's still good in bed? And according to you, he was good. 'Testosterone on legs' is how you described him to me, and he's all you used to talk about. In fact, you admitted he's the reason you never could sleep with another guy, because he'd spoiled you for anyone else. I bet he doesn't know you haven't slept with another guy since him."

Leslie frowned. "That is none of his business."

"True, but I still say being his Christmas present would be your present, too. It's either enjoy his bed or lose your company. For me it's a no-brainer."

Leslie thought about everything Carmen had said. She glanced at her watch, knowing she needed to jump on a call with her company's attorney. "I need to go, Carmen. My attorney will be calling in a few minutes."

"When do you give Sloan your decision?"

"By noon tomorrow."

"Okay. I know after sleeping on it you'll wake up tomorrow and make the right one."

She knew in Carmen's mind, the right one was agreeing to Sloan's proposal. "I'll talk to you later, Carm."

"Okay, but just so you know, Sloan's offer pretty much sounds like that Christmas miracle you mentioned you've been hoping for. Bye, Les."

Later that night, while Leslie lay in bed, all kinds of thoughts were going through her mind. According to the phone call she'd had with Stan, the bank would not give her the extension on the loan. That left her with no options on the table other than Sloan's.

Like Carmen, her attorney thought Sloan's offer was a godsend, almost too good to be true, and that made Stan suspicious of Sloan's motives. Of course, she didn't tell Stan about the condition Sloan had attached to his proposal. However, to arrest Stan's concerns, she explained that she and Sloan had dated in college and what he was doing was a favor. That had satisfied Stan, and he'd even said she was lucky to have a friend who would come to her aid.

Such a friend…

She had known the old Sloan, the one who didn't have a ruthless bone in his body. Granted, the Sloan Outlaw who'd shown up at her office today still had charm and impeccable manners, but she knew he'd changed. And so had she. Considering how they had broken up and the lies she had believed about him, she was surprised he was willing to help her at all. And why would he want them to sleep together, of all things? To her, it didn't make sense, because they'd always made love and not just had sex. To them, there had always been a difference. Evidently, he thought that now there wasn't a difference.

But still, she needed to talk to him, because there were questions that needed answering before she could make a final decision.

Easing out of bed, she pulled his business card out of her purse. It was just a little past ten, but he used to be a night owl. Was he still? Was he even in Wasilla or had he gone back to Fairbanks? She would find out soon enough, she thought, as she punched in his number.

"Hello?"

"Sloan, this is Leslie."

"Yes, Leslie?"

She swallowed deeply. He still had a sexy phone voice. "There are a few things I need to know about your proposal before I can make a decision."

"What do you need to know?"

She nibbled on her bottom lip. "It's about my week at your cabin, if I decide to do it."

"What about it?"

"Will we sleep together just one time?"

"Would we have slept together just one time ten years ago, Leslie?" was his quick comeback.

She frowned. "Things were different then, Sloan."

"I'm aware of that. What I want is the week I didn't get. I would not have forced myself on you then, and I won't do it now. I will leave it up to you if or when we make love."

"Oh?" She was surprised to hear that. "And what if I decide that I don't want to make love to you at all during that week?"

She heard his soft chuckle, and it sent warm shivers through her body. "I'm not worried about that happening."

"I'm not the same person, Sloan."

"Neither am I. We might find it interesting to discover what those differences are."

"Are you still in Wasilla?"

"Yes. I plan to be in town until you make a decision. If you accept my proposal, then I need to hang around to make sure Longshire knows I mean business." He paused. "I know your company shuts down for Christmas this Friday. I'd like you ready to go to the cabin with me the following weekend. We'll stay for a week."

She frowned. "What if I've made plans for that week? What if I have a boyfriend?"

"Have you? Do you?"

As much as she now wished she could say yes to both questions, she truthfully couldn't. "No, I'm not dating seriously at the moment, and as far as my plans for the holidays—"

She paused when she felt the thickness in her throat. She tried not to think about the fact that this Christmas she would be all alone. "With Dad gone, I didn't have any plans," she finally said. Then to change the subject, she asked, "What about your job?"

"What about it?" he countered.

"Don't you have to go to work?"

"No. My vacation started the first of December. I'm off until after New Year's."

"I see."

"Any more questions?"

"Yes. Will you involve yourself in the day-to-day operations of the company?"

"No. There's no reason that I should. Handle your business just as you would if I wasn't involved. And just so you know, the twenty-five percent that I would get will be going directly to my charities."

That was another surprise. Drawing in a deep breath, she said, "I'll call you tomorrow with my decision. I need to sleep on it. Good night, Sloan."

"Good night, Leslie. Pleasant dreams."

She quickly hung up. Saying "pleasant dreams" was how he would always end their calls at night, because he'd known her dreams would always be of him…and they would always be pleasant. Did he assume that now? Putting her cell phone back on the nightstand, she snuggled under the warm covers.

What bothered her more than anything was knowing she *would* have pleasant dreams of him tonight. How could she not when Carmen and Stan were right? Sloan had become her Christmas miracle. With that thought in mind, she settled in bed and closed her eyes. The reality of the situation was that Sloan Outlaw was back in her life, and she honestly wasn't sure how she felt about it.

The next morning Sloan woke up around seven, showered and got dressed while thinking about his conversation with Leslie last night. After the call had ended, he'd tried turning his attention back to the murder mystery he'd been watching on television but found that he couldn't. He'd always thought she had a sexy voice. This older Leslie's voice was even sexier, which pretty much agreed with the rest of her.

He had tried not to let it annoy him that she had to sleep on his offer. Although she had apologized and admitted she now knew Sarah had lied, he couldn't get past the fact that she had believed her roommate in the first place. Was that why she was having a problem trusting him now? Even with his generous terms, did she think he wanted to take her company? If she did, then she'd classed him in the same category as Longshire.

Sloan hadn't wanted to take Leslie's actions personally. Any competent businessperson knew not to make hasty decisions. She was merely following the rules, and he would expect the same of anyone he did business with. But then, he'd never intended to sleep with any of his business associates. That made this entire situation with Leslie different.

He'd meant what he'd told her last night. He had never forced himself on her before, and he wouldn't be doing it now. However, if she thought they could stay together at the cabin and not share a bed, then she would only be fooling herself. Whenever they were alone for any period of time, they were spontaneous combustion just waiting to explode.

Although they'd been apart for ten years, he'd picked up on the strong sexual attraction between them at the wedding reception. Even Redford said he'd noticed it from across the room, which was why he hadn't come back to join them when he'd seen them talking.

Sloan had picked up those same vibes yesterday in her office. Even when they had been discussing something as important as the possibility of her losing her company, whenever their eyes met, desire had flowed between them—whether they wanted it to or not.

There was no doubt in his mind it had been a mutual attraction both times. For that reason, he could understand her call last night to clarify a few things. She of all people knew what potent sexual beings they used to be and still were.

And why he had held his breath at the possibility that she was seriously involved with someone. Although after intense questioning, Redford had said he'd not heard she was dating anyone. But still, Redford's information might have been wrong. Would it have mattered? Yes, it would have. Unlike Redford, Sloan had never encroached on another man's territory, and he didn't intend to start now.

He was about to leave his hotel room for breakfast when his cell phone rang. Before going to bed, he had added Leslie's phone number to his contact list and had even given her a special ringtone. He didn't want to analyze the reason he'd done that.

He clicked on the phone. "Yes, Leslie?" He immediately wished he could bite off his tongue. Now she knew he had her name in his phone.

"I've made a decision, Sloan."

He paused a moment. "And what is your decision?"

"That you and I become temporary business partners."

Why was he releasing a relieved breath? He didn't want to admit that the alternative was one he would not have been able to accept. The only reason he had gotten involved was because he refused to let a man like Martin Longshire think he could get away with being a bully.

"Okay. We need to meet tonight and plan our strategy. Let's do dinner at six."

"Dinner?"

"Yes, dinner. You know, that meal people usually eat at the end of the day."

"Yes, smart-ass, I know it."

Sloan couldn't help but chuckle. Now this was the Leslie he knew. The one who could hold her own against anyone, including him. He had a feeling Martin Longshire had begun breaking her down when she hadn't been able to see a way out. Now Sloan was giving her one and she could go back to being herself again. The woman he used to...

He blinked, knowing he couldn't go there. He would never go there with her again. "Okay, since you know what it is, will you be free at six?"

"Yes, but why wait until then? You can come to my office at five."

"No, I can't. There's a business call I need to be on at four."

"I thought you were off work from Outlaw Freight Lines for the rest of December."

Was she questioning him? Would there always be an issue of trust between them? "The meeting has nothing to do with Outlaw Freight Lines. Will you be able to do dinner or not?" he snapped.

"Yes, just tell me where to meet you," she said in a brusque tone.

"My hotel."

"Excuse me?"

Sloan rubbed the back of his neck, getting more agitated by the second. "I said my hotel, Leslie, not my hotel room. There happens to be a nice restaurant, the Elderbrae, located in the Ghanis Hotel."

"I know where it is. In fact, it's right around the corner from where I live."

He'd known that from his research and had chosen his hotel for that very reason. "In that case, there won't be a problem in you finding it," he said.

"No problem at all."

"Good. I'll see you at six."

Five

Leslie walked into the Ghanis Hotel and glanced around. She shouldn't have been surprised that Sloan was staying at the most elegant hotel in Wasilla or that he would want to dine at one of the most exclusive restaurants. She had dined at the Elderbrae a few times with her father, who claimed nobody could cook a steak to perfection like they could.

Pausing, she took in the hotel's Christmas decorations. A huge Christmas tree stood in the middle of the lobby. It had to be at least twenty feet tall, was beautifully decorated and surrounded by more than a hundred beautiful red poinsettias. On both sides of the ring of poinsettias were life-size polar bears on their hind legs. The bears looked so real she instinctively took a step back.

"I promise they won't bite."

Looking over her shoulder, she saw Sloan was walking toward her. She then glanced back at the display. "They look so real."

"Yes, they do. I saw them when I checked in and wondered if it would be safe to stay here."

His comment made her laugh, because if anyone should be used to bears it was Sloan. His family owned that cabin on Kodiak Island, and everyone knew there were more bears on that island than people. Not polar bears but grizzlies, and they were the worst kind.

"I've only heard good things about the food served here, so I hope you're hungry," he said as they headed over to the restaurant.

"Whatever you heard is true. Dad and I ate here a few times, and the food was fantastic."

When they reached the entrance, they were met by the smiling maître d'. Within minutes they were shown to their table that provided a picturesque view of snowcapped mountains. She knew tables on this side of the restaurant went for a premium, but the view was worth it. "That view is beautiful," she finally said, glancing over at him.

"I think so, too," he said, looking at her. He hadn't been looking out the window when he'd said it, but she dismissed the possibility they were talking about different views.

"I'm surprised you're not staying in Anchorage since it's only a short drive away."

He chuckled. "I had no desire to drive the forty minutes back and forth when my business is here in Wasilla."

His business? Did he think of the situation involving her as "his business"? A part of her should have been glad he did, even if it sounded so impersonal.

At that moment a waitress appeared to take their drink order and presented them with menus. When she left, Leslie looked up from her menu to find Sloan staring at her. Lifting a brow, she asked, "Is anything wrong?"

He smiled, and she wished he hadn't. Sloan Outlaw had

the kind of smile that could make a woman weak in the knees even while they were already sitting down.

"I was just noticing that you haven't changed much."

If he thought that, then he was wrong. "Of course I've changed, Sloan."

Although he might be referring to physical appearance, she was referring to her emotions. Leaving school in Anchorage the way she had and dealing with pain and heartbreak for nearly seven years had broken her. And then to discover it had all been a lie, and for Sarah to have the nerve to gloat about it in front of others, had been another kind of pain within itself. Probably the worst thing to ever happen to her.

No, losing Sloan because of that lie was the worst thing to ever happen to her.

"I've grown an inch taller, Sloan," she said proudly. "You probably can't tell since I'm always in heels."

"Trust me, Leslie. I've noticed all your changes."

It wasn't what he'd said but how he'd said it, in a low and intimate voice that gave her pause. They needed to change the subject, and she decided to take the initiative to do it. "So, Garth and Cash are both married now?"

A genuine smile touched his lips. "Yes. I'm sure you remember Garth's wife, Regan. Her father had been our company's pilot for years."

"Yes, of course I remember Regan. I met her when I visited your family one Christmas. I liked Regan."

"Well, she and Garth got married. Cash fell in love with someone he met when he went to Wyoming for the reading of his mother's will. He and his wife, Brianna, live in Wyoming. She's pregnant and having twins in a couple of months."

"Twins? Wow! That's great."

"We all think so, too. Cash will make a wonderful father."

"I can't believe he moved from Alaska."

"I know, and that took getting used to. But he loves the huge spread he inherited there, and I've never seen him happier."

"Does he still work for the company?"

"Yes, he operates a satellite office on his ranch."

At that moment the waitress returned to take their order, and they both decided to try the steak. "You still like your steak burned, I see," he said when the waitress walked off.

She smiled over at him and said, "And you still prefer yours half-cooked."

"Some things never change."

She took a sip of her wine while thinking that most things did. "So, Sloan, now that I've agreed for you to become my business partner, what is your plan regarding Longshire?" No need to beat around the bush when his whole purpose for taking her to dinner tonight was to discuss business.

"The plans are already in place. By midnight he'll know things are not going as he expected, and he'll be quite upset about it. If he shows up unannounced, I suggest you have security escort him off the premises."

Leslie nodded as she studied Sloan. She had a feeling there was something he hadn't told her. "Is there anything else I should know about?"

Sloan leaned back in his chair. "To let him know I meant business, I took one of his companies from him."

Leslie nearly choked on her drink. "You took his company?"

"Not his major company, Leslie. It was a company he took over last month. I happened to find out about them when I did research on what he was doing to your company. Like your father, he had some kind personal vandetta against the family. Evidently Longshire is a man who holds grudges."

"What kind of company is it?" she asked.

"It's a family business that's been around for generations. It's run by an older couple and their offspring. All toy makers."

"Toy makers?"

"Yes. I understand that for years they'd been quite successful, but for the past year, sales had been declining, and then they were dropped by their distributor. I discovered all of it was Longshire's doing, just to get back at the family."

"Why on earth would Longshire need a toy manufacturing company?"

"He doesn't. Just like he doesn't need a cosmetics company. He's doing it because he knows he can, and he evidently likes to make people's lives a living hell. Like I said, he holds grudges."

"What an ass."

"Yes, and the sad thing is that he has no plans for the company. He just wants to ruin it. After doing my research, I decided that in the right hands the toy making company would be a good investment. The first thing I plan to do is hire the family back and put them in charge. It would boost their local economy."

She nodded. What Sloan hadn't said, but what she'd figured, knowing Sloan like she did, was that unlike Longshire, he would sell that family back their company once he'd made it financially sound for them. Leslie took a sip of her wine and said, "Longshire is going to get even more upset when he finds out you're giving that family back their company."

Sloan lifted a brow. "What makes you think I'll be giving that family their company back?"

Leslie shrugged. "A hunch." When he didn't say whether her hunch was right or not, she asked, "Where's this place? Is it here in Wasilla?"

"No. The North Pole."

"North Pole, Alaska?"

"Yes."

Leslie chuckled. "An older couple whose family makes toys in North Pole, Alaska. That's interesting."

He smiled. "I think it's interesting as well. I plan to fly there to meet them this weekend."

"You've told me what to expect of Martin Longshire, Sloan. Now I need to know what to expect of you."

Sloan glanced up from his meal and met Leslie's direct gaze. Instead of answering her, he pointed to her glass. "Need more wine?"

She frowned, and he thought she looked cute when she did so. "Why? Is that your way of saying what you're about to tell me will make me want a drink?"

He chuckled. "No. I just noticed your glass was half-full."

She nodded. "Thanks for your concern, but I'm fine. Now, if you will please answer my question."

Sloan shrugged. "There's really nothing else to tell you, Leslie. I think I made it clear yesterday what my expectations are. I want you for Christmas. Why are we having this discussion, anyway? You agreed to my terms."

"Yes, but I need you to clarify a few things."

"Things like what?" he asked, cutting into his steak.

"What do you have planned for us that week?"

"Other than hoping we make love every day, every hour, using every position known to man and then some that few men know about yet?" Sloan knew he had, for the second day in a row, shocked Leslie speechless.

"You're basing your agenda for that week on the assumption I will fall at your feet."

"No, I'm basing my agenda on the assumption that you'll share my bed." He drew in a deep breath. "Look, Leslie, we can hash and rehash the issue all we want, but it won't get us anywhere. You have your mind made up about not sleeping with me, and I have my mind made up that you will. Let's just see how things turn out. However, the one thing you need to do is trust me."

"Trust you?"

"Yes. There was a time you trusted me, but then, through no fault of mine, you stopped."

Her spine stiffened. "How can I trust a man who has told me he wants me in his bed?"

"There was a time you appreciated my honesty. Would you prefer I not tell you?"

"I prefer you not to want *me* for Christmas."

That made him ask, "What is it that you want for Christmas, Leslie?" He couldn't help being curious. Now she was nibbling on her bottom lip in a way that had blood rushing straight down to his groin.

She stared into her drink instead of at him when she said, "I haven't thought about Christmas much, Sloan, since it will be my first without Dad. We would always spend the holidays together. The only exception was that year I spent Christmas with you and your family."

Leslie then looked up at him, and that's when he saw it. The deep sadness in her eyes. "Even while I lived in DC, Dad would either come there to spend the holidays with me and Aunt Ella, or I would come home here. With Aunt Ella and Dad both deceased, this will be my first Christmas alone. So the only thing I want for Christmas will be the ability to get through the day."

Sloan didn't say anything as he took a sip of his drink. He recalled the holidays only had come to mean a lot to him because of her. Christmas had been her favorite holiday, and she'd let everyone in her inner circle know it. For him, his brothers and sister, it hadn't had the same meaning.

The Outlaws had discovered their differences when Sloan had taken Leslie home with him during their college holiday break. First, she'd been aghast that they had not planned to put up a tree or any decorations. It didn't take long for her to whip the Outlaws—Bart excluded—into shape. By Christmas Eve they had gone out and bought a live Christmas tree and had it decorated with newly purchased ornaments. She had been a novelty, and his family had fallen in love with her immediately. After her visit, the Outlaws never failed to put up a Christmas tree again.

The thought of her spending time alone on Christmas bothered him. After their week at the cabin, what would she do for those remaining days before Christmas? What about the week after Christmas that led into the New Year? He shouldn't care, but he did.

He could invite Leslie to spend Christmas with his family this year. As they'd done for the past few years, the Outlaws would spend the holidays in Denver with their cousins the Westmorelands. They would remain through New Year's Day, since the annual Westmoreland charity ball would be held on New Year's Eve.

However, a part of him didn't want to include her in his life that way. He didn't want to give his siblings any ideas that there was more than a business arrangement between them. But there was another part of him that could not forget their history and didn't want her to spend the holidays alone.

Six

The next day, Leslie looked up from the document on her desk upon hearing the commotion outside her office door. Stiffening, she recognized one of the voices just seconds before her office door flew open and Martin Longshire stood there. Anger radiated not just from his features but also his stance.

"You won't get away with this," he snarled. "You're a fool if you think an ex-boyfriend can save your company."

She wondered how he knew about her and Sloan's past relationship. Standing, she crossed her arms over her chest, but before she could say anything, Beverly moved from behind him and asked, "Do you want me to call security, Ms. Cassidy?"

Leslie switched her gaze from Longshire to Beverly. "If he hasn't left in five minutes, then yes, call security."

Beverly glanced over at Longshire with an expression as if she wasn't convinced leaving Leslie with him would be a good thing to do.

"I'll be fine, Beverly. Five minutes and he will be gone."

"Like hell I will!"

Ignoring the man's outburst, Leslie said, "Five minutes, Beverly. If it makes you feel better, alert security to be on standby just in case."

Beverly smiled and said, "I think that's a good idea." She then swept past Longshire to leave but left the door open. Like before, he slammed it shut, but at least he hadn't given Beverly a smart-alecky remark like he had the last time.

Leslie turned her attention back to Longshire. "State your business and leave. Now you have four minutes."

He strode over to her desk, and for a minute she thought he would reach out and grab her, but he didn't. Instead, he said, "You've made a mistake by bringing Sloan Outlaw into this. And he's made a mistake by taking one of my companies from me. Neither you nor Outlaw will get away with it. Now I will destroy you both."

Longshire then turned and walked out of the office. When he'd opened the door, Leslie had seen two members of her security team standing by Beverly's desk to escort him out of the building.

She drew in a deep breath as she sat back down in her chair. Beverly stood in the doorway. "Are you all right?"

Leslie nodded. "Yes, I'm fine."

Moments after Beverly left, she pulled her phone from her purse to call Sloan. Before they parted ways after dinner last night, he had told her to call him if Longshire showed up today.

"Yes, Leslie?"

She felt an intense pull in her stomach at the sound of him saying her name. Last night over dinner, although they'd disagreed on a number of things, the physical attraction between them had been mind-boggling. "Martin Longshire just left, and he made threats."

"Against you?" Leslie could hear the anger in his voice.

"Against both of us, Sloan. He said he will destroy us both. Something else he said surprised me."

"What?"

"He knew you were my ex-boyfriend."

"Um, I wonder how he knows that?"

"I'm not sure," she said. "I guess he did research after wondering why you'd come to my aid the way you did."

"Doesn't matter. He's gotten the message that he's wasting his time trying to take away your company."

"How long will you be in town?" she asked him.

"I'm flying out Saturday."

"Oh." She wondered why hearing that he was leaving Wasilla was somewhat of a downer.

"Cassidy Cosmetics closes for the holidays on Friday, right?" he then asked her.

"Yes, why?"

"How would you like to fly to North Pole with me to meet those toy makers?"

Leslie lifted a brow. "You want me to go with you?"

"Why not? I'm only going to be there a couple of days. And before you get bent out of shape, let me go on record to say I will make sure we get separate rooms at the hotel. I recall you've never been…unless that has changed over the last ten years."

"No, I've never been to North Pole."

"You've always wanted to do so, now here's your chance, Leslie. Of course, if you don't trust yourself around me, then I understand."

She frowned. "I do trust myself around you, Sloan."

"Does that mean you'll go?"

Leslie recalled when they'd met, he couldn't believe she had never visited North Pole. He'd figured every Alaskan had done so at some time during their childhood. She had explained that although she'd always wanted to go, there was never time to do so. Her parents had worked long days making the company a success, and they rarely traveled too far from Wasilla. Now Sloan was giving her a chance to go there. With him. Should she?

Why not? Hadn't she just told him that she trusted herself around him? What they'd once shared was over. She'd blown things years ago, and they'd both moved on. Besides, wouldn't they be spending a week together at his cabin in a week or so anyway? "Yes, Sloan, I would love to go. Thanks for inviting me."

"I'll pick you up Saturday morning at six."

"All right. You'll need my address. I'm no longer living in my father's house. I sold it."

"I know where you live now."

Leslie frowned, bothered that it seemed both Sloan and Martin Longshire knew too much about her.

"You're up early, Sloan."

Sloan chuckled as he walked out of the hotel to his rental car. "I'm on my way somewhere, Cole."

Sloan's cousin Cole Westmoreland was a former Texas Ranger who had married Dr. Patrina Foreman. The couple lived in Montana and had three kids. When Cole retired as a ranger, he joined forces with another cousin, Quade Westmoreland, who'd worked for a special services unit to protect the president, to start a network of security companies.

"So where are you headed?" Cole asked.

"The North Pole."

"You're kidding, right?"

"Nope," Sloan said as he loaded his luggage into the trunk of his car. "I bought a toy company there."

"Yeah, right. The next thing you're going to tell me is that it's run by an older couple named the Kringles."

Sloan smiled. "It's run by an older couple, but their last name is Yule."

"Whatever."

Sloan shook his head, knowing his cousin probably didn't believe him. There was no need to tell him the man's first name was Rudolph. "The reason I'm calling is because I have a job for you."

"What?"

"There's a person I want you to investigate by the name of Martin Longshire."

"Anything in particular I need to look for?" Cole wanted to know.

"Not sure. I screwed up his plans to take over a couple of companies, and he's known for getting revenge. I want to be ready if he tries."

"I'll dig to see if there's something in his past we could use as leverage if it comes to that."

"I'm sure if there's something out there on Longshire, you'll find it. You're good at what you do."

Cole laughed. "If you have so much confidence in my abilities, then let me take a crack at finding out why your old man refuses to claim the Westmorelands as kin. That's rubbish when you can't deny these strong Westmoreland genes."

Sloan knew that was the truth. Not only did all the male Westmorelands look alike and favor the male Outlaws, but their cousin Bailey and his sister, Charm, looked similar as well. "Charm's mother, Claudia, persuaded us to not look into it. She felt it was an invasion of Dad's privacy and felt when he got ready to tell us why he was so opposed, then he would."

Sloan and his brothers had agreed not to let their father's refusal to accept their Westmoreland kin have any bearing on their willingness to do so. Over the past years, the Westmoreland and Outlaw cousins had formed a close bond.

"Will you be flying that toy plane of yours to North Pole?" Cole asked.

He chuckled. "Yes, one day I'll let you at the wheel."

Sloan knew Cole had his pilot's license. In addition to the security company, Cole owned a helicopter service that provided transportation between the various mountains in Bozeman, Montana, to the people who lived on them. Cole's father was one such person who lived on a huge mountain they called Corey's Mountain.

After disconnecting the call, Sloan thought about the woman he would be seeing in a few minutes. The same one who'd occupied his thoughts most of the night. He was trying to keep a level head where Leslie Cassidy was concerned. Once burned, you never wanted to experience such pain again. However, the thought of her being alone for the holidays was outweighing any desire to keep his distance.

Sloan couldn't imagine such loneliness, because he'd always had his siblings. They all knew, although Bart would never admit it, that their father had loved having a full house, and they'd been content living on the Outlaw compound. However, when they got older and Bart began trying to manipulate them, they'd each moved into their own places. All except for Charm. She adored the old man and managed to see past his faults. Besides, like her mother, Claudia, Charm knew how to handle Bart.

Pulling into Leslie's yard, Sloan saw that even more snow had fallen overnight in the area where she lived. He hoped there wouldn't be a delay in getting his plane off the ground.

Flexing his gloved hands a few times and tightening the scarf around his neck, he got out of the car. There was no way you could live in Alaska and not be used to the cold and snow. To them it was a way of life, but as far as he was concerned there was no other place he'd rather live. He had traveled to most of the states in the lower forty-eight, and although some had been nice to visit, there was no place like Alaska.

As he shoved his hands into the pockets of his long coat, he glanced around. There had to be at least three feet of snow, possibly more. But it was beautiful.

Sloan liked Leslie's home. It sat in a cul-de-sac with four others, all spaced a nice distance apart. He was glad she hadn't asked how he'd known where she lived. Had she done so, he would have had to confess to researching any personal information he could find.

She had moved out of her father's house a month after he'd passed away. Sloan recalled the house had been massive, much too large for one person. The size of this house was perfect for her.

He also gathered from his research that since returning to Alaska, she had rolled up her sleeves and worked hard beside her father. The bulk of Cassidy Cosmetics business was in Alaska. The businessman in him wondered why Lester Cassidy never expanded into the lower forty-eight.

Ringing her doorbell, Sloan was surprised when she opened the door immediately. His gaze automatically moved over her from head to toe. Why had he forgotten how beautiful she could look first thing in the morning? He was suddenly filled with a hefty dose of desire. To a degree he didn't want or need.

"Good morning, Sloan. Come on in. I just need to grab my travel bag and coat," she said, walking off.

Sloan nodded, unable to do anything other than that. She wore a pair of skinny burgundy corduroy pants, a light gray pullover sweater and knee-high black boots.

Leslie had such a gorgeous body, he couldn't help but stand in the doorway and stare. Just watching her ass in motion was an arousal waiting to happen, and seeing her small waist and all those curves had him transfixed.

Glancing back over her shoulder, she stopped and

turned back around, a questioning look on her face. "Is anything wrong?"

He drew in a deep breath and decided to play dumb. "What makes you think something is wrong?"

She shoved her hands in the pockets of her pants. "You're standing there with the door wide-open, letting out the heat."

"Oh," he said, entering her home and quickly closing the door behind him.

When she continued walking toward an area that he figured was her bedroom, he glanced around, not wanting to think about where she slept. She had decorated for the holidays and had a nice tree. He moved closer as an ornament caught his attention. It was the same one he'd given her years ago. He was surprised she still had it.

"I'm ready."

Sloan turned around. He'd forgotten how she dressed warmly from her head to her toes. Cold Alaska weather was never going to get the best of her. She looked cute in her fur hat and knitted face mask with a scarf to match. Then there was her heavy wool coat. There was no doubt in his mind it was totally lined.

"Okay, let's go," he said, taking her overnight bag.

Seven

"You can stop holding your breath now, Leslie."

She glanced over at Sloan and couldn't hold back her chuckle. She'd never liked small planes, and although he knew how to operate one, she couldn't help the nervousness floating around in her stomach.

He'd told her years ago that the Outlaws' corporate pilot had taught them all to fly. Now Sloan had his personal plane, a Cessna, and according to him it took him wherever he needed to go in the United States.

"It wasn't snowing when we took off, but it is now," she said.

"It's light, and this baby can handle it."

Why at that moment did she recall him saying that same thing to her the first time they'd made love? She had been a virgin, and the moment she'd seen him without clothes—especially that part below the waist—her expression must have said it all. He'd strolled over to her with his sexy walk, touched her between the legs and said, "This baby can handle it."

"Leslie?"

She glanced over at him. "Yes?"

"I asked if you slept well last night."

Leslie figured he'd asked the question while her mind had been preoccupied with memories from the past. "Yes. It was the best sleep I've had since Dad died. It felt good knowing my company won't be taken from me. I'm grateful to you for making that possible."

"I don't want your gratitude, Leslie."

She didn't say anything, because she knew what he wanted. He'd told her plainly. He wanted her…for Christmas…in his bed. Deciding to change the subject, she said, "Is it true your family located relatives you didn't know you had in the lower forty-eight?"

He glanced over at her. "Who told you that?"

There was no way she would tell him that Keosha had told her. Then he would know she'd asked about him. So she said, "I think during one of our conversations you mentioned it."

He nodded. "Yes, but we didn't find them, they found us. The Westmorelands had evidence leading them to believe their great-grandfather Raphael Westmoreland fathered an illegitimate child. They hired a private investigator to determine if it was true, and the man's investigation led them right to our doorstep."

"And you're sure they are your kinfolk?"

"You wouldn't ask me that if you'd ever seen us together. We share some strong Westmoreland genes. Practically every Westmoreland has an Outlaw cousin who looks almost identical to them. The resemblance is so uncanny that Cash swapped places with Bane Westmoreland in a government sting operation."

"So, there's a Westmoreland who looks like you?" She couldn't imagine another man having similar sexy features.

"Yes. Derringer Westmoreland. We honestly do favor, but I'm sure you'll be able to tell us apart."

Leslie thought about what he'd said. Had he just hinted there was a chance she would meet his cousin one day? She honestly didn't see that happening. "You've gotten to know these Westmorelands?"

"Yes, and it's the oddest thing. Although we only met around five years ago, we act as if we've known each other all our lives. There are a lot of Westmorelands living in Colorado, Texas, California, Montana, Georgia and North Carolina. You ever heard of Thorn Westmoreland?"

"Of course. He's that celebrity who builds and races motorcycles."

"Yes, and he's a cousin. And do you recall reading a few years back when an American woman married a sheikh from the Middle East?"

"Yes. There was a huge spread about it in several magazines. I believe she was a doctor."

"Well, that was Delaney Westmoreland, Thorn's sister. Now she's a queen, since her husband, Jamal Ari Yasir, has become king. She won't be visiting this year since she's expecting."

"She is?"

"Yes, twins. They have two older kids and waited years before deciding to have any more. I heard they always wanted at least four, so now they will get them."

He paused a moment to move one of the controls. "I also noticed you had a Rock Mason novel on your coffee table."

"Yes, what about it?"

"He's a cousin as well. His real name is Stone Westmoreland."

"Honestly? I went to a Rock Mason book signing at Howard. I still have that autographed book." She then asked, "How does your father feel about all these new relatives?"

"Bart is pretty much in denial. He refuses to believe his grandfather was adopted and claims we're Outlaws and not Westmorelands."

She lifted a brow. "Even after seeing the resemblance in all of you?"

"Yes, even after that. It's the strangest thing how he refuses to accept them as kin. But it doesn't matter if he accepts them or not, because we do."

"There has to be a reason he feels that way."

"Maybe there is and maybe there isn't, or it could be Bart is just being Bart. You've met Dad, and I would tell you all the time how ornery he is. Bart likes controlling every situation, but he can't control this one. My siblings and I are adults who refuse to let Dad tell us what to do."

Sloan chuckled. "Doesn't really matter since most of his time these days is spent courting Claudia."

"Charm's mom?"

"Yes. She's the one woman who refused to marry him."

He reached up to adjust a control near the top. "We'll be landing at the Fairbanks airport in less than thirty minutes."

She knew they would get a rental car from the airport and drive to North Pole. "How far is North Pole from Fairbanks?"

"Twenty minutes. And just so you know, the landing might be a little rough, since there's a lot of snow. The runway has been deiced, so we should be okay."

She glanced over at him and drew in a nervous breath. "Okay, Sloan. I'll take your word for it."

A couple of hours later, Sloan and Leslie had checked into the hotel in North Pole. The landing of the plane was just like he'd warned her it would be, but she hadn't complained. A rental car had been waiting for them, and they'd driven to the only hotel in town.

Just like he'd told Leslie, they had separate rooms; however, his room was next to hers. Her expression had been unreadable when he'd told her they would join the Yules for dinner at five. Other than lifting a brow at the older couple's last name, she merely nodded before entering her hotel room.

Moving over to the window, he looked out with his hands shoved in his pockets. Although a thick blanket of snow covered nearly everything, it was easy to see that North Pole, Alaska—population of a little more than two thousand people—was a beautiful small town. One of his fondest memories was visiting here around the holidays as a kid with his classmates. He recalled the huge gift shop located in Santa's House that had some of the neatest items.

Moving away from the window, he went to his duffel bag to unpack. He was excited to share North Pole with Leslie. And little did she know that having her sitting next to him in the cockpit had placed temptation solidly at his feet. For starters, she had worn that perfume he liked so much. He also noted she liked keeping the conversation going whenever she was nervous about something. He figured what had her anxious had been them flying in bad weather.

Was that the reason he had shared more about his family than he would normally have done to someone who was not a close friend? Granted, she had met everyone years ago and had been considered a close friend of the family then. He didn't consider her one now. However, how should he refer to a woman he'd traveled over three hundred miles to help?

A woman you've been thinking a lot about since running into her again?

Every time he looked at her mouth, he recalled how

sweet her lips could be. Whenever he saw her hands, he remembered her touch and how he had taught her to stroke him in certain places. Whenever they'd made love, it had propelled him to a level of ecstasy he'd never been to before and, to be honest, hadn't been to since her.

He had dated a lot of women over the years, but none had come close to fulfilling his needs, wants and fantasies like Leslie. But thanks to her he had learned a valuable lesson—to never give his heart to a woman or she was liable to crush it.

He rubbed his hand down his face. Leslie meant nothing to him now, and he hadn't done any more for her than he would have for someone else in her predicament. The Yules were a prime example of that fact. But on the other hand, he didn't want the Yules for Christmas. He didn't go to bed thinking of them and wake up doing the same thing. It hadn't been the Yules on his mind during the flight here, and his anticipation of five o'clock had nothing to do with meeting the Yules and everything to do with seeing Leslie again.

Every muscle in his body tensed. He had to stop this right now before his attraction to her got out of hand. He had to remember the pain she had caused him when she'd left without a trace. Left because of a lie she had believed. How had she honestly thought he could have betrayed her the way Sarah had claimed? Hadn't his words of love, his actions, proven anything? Obviously not.

He glanced at his watch. He would rest awhile. Hopefully by dinnertime he would have reclaimed complete control of his senses.

"How are things going with you and Sloan?"

Leslie sat on the edge of the bed. "Why do you have to make it sound as if we're a couple, Carmen?"

"A little wishful thinking on my part, maybe."

"Let's not go there."

"Well, you did fly to North Pole with him. I never knew there was really such a place. I thought it was made up."

Leslie smiled as she got up to walk over to the window. "I'm sure a lot of people think the same thing, but the town does exist. This is where all those letters to Santa end up, which is why their post office is the most popular in the world. I imagine it's pretty busy this time of the year."

"I'm going to add that place to my bucket list."

"You do that, and the next time you come visit me in Alaska, I'll make sure we come here. It's a beautiful little town, and it's so Christmassy. I'm looking out of my hotel window, and it's so picture perfect. Even with all the snow."

"Please take pictures," Carmen begged.

Leslie chuckled. "I will."

"For you as an Alaskan, I'm surprised it's your first time there."

Carmen recalled Sloan had said the same thing when they'd met years ago. He'd teased her and said he would take away her Alaska card. "Dad was always too busy, and the drive to North Pole from Wasilla is over three hundred miles. There was no time. When we did take vacations, we went to check on Aunt Ella."

"And just think, it's your first time and you're doing it with Sloan."

Leslie frowned. "You're trying to make us into a couple again, Carm."

"I can't help it. How did your employees react when you told them you wouldn't be losing the company?"

"They were happy. Some have worked for my parents since the time they started this company over thirty years ago."

"I'm glad things turned out the way they did, Leslie. You should be forever grateful to Sloan."

"And I will be. Can we change the subject?"

"I thought we had. Not my fault that all the talking points, regardless of the conversation, come back to Sloan Outlaw."

Leslie glanced at her watch. "I want to take a nap before dinner."

"Okay. When do the two of you leave for Sloan's cabin?"

Carmen would have to remind her of that. "A week from today."

"You're going to enjoy yourself."

Leslie rolled her eyes. "How would you know?"

"Because Sloan is a nice guy."

"You've never met him, Carm."

"I saw a glimpse of him before he left that wedding reception. Besides, as far as I'm concerned, he proved just how nice he truly is by saving your company. And another thing, Les."

Leslie knew Carmen was on a roll, although she wished otherwise. "What?"

"There's something you tend to forget."

"And just what do I tend to forget?"

"That you hurt Sloan when you believed that woman's lies. He didn't hurt you, you hurt him. So the way I see it, he's entitled to be a little salty about it. I'll talk to you later."

Eight

Sloan knocked on Leslie's hotel room door, and when she opened it, he tried not to show any reaction. Doing so was difficult. Why did she have to look so darn good in that red velvet pantsuit? The blazer seemed tailor-made and flowed over her slacks precisely. And that color was perfect for this holiday season. He thought the dangling earrings complimented her hairstyle and gave her a sexy look.

Only when he was certain he had retained control of his senses did he say, "You look nice."

"Thanks. I just need to grab my coat."

Although she didn't invite him in, she left the door open, so he remained in the doorway and watched her grab her wool coat off the bed. The same bed she would be sleeping in tonight. He could envision her in that bed, sleeping on her side, which was her favorite position. It was a position he'd liked for her as well, especially whenever they slept spoon style with her backside resting smack against his groin.

"I'm ready, Sloan."

She'd come to stand in front of him while his thoughts had been a million miles away. Well, in truth, they had been only as far as the distance to that bed. After closing the door behind her, they walked side by side, in sync, toward the elevator. "Where are we dining?" she asked him.

"I told you earlier, with the Yules."

She glanced over at him, and the moment their gazes met, he felt a stirring in the pit of his stomach. "I didn't mean with whom, but where?"

"We're dining in their home."

"Oh."

"Do you have a problem with that?"

"No."

"Like I told you, they're an older couple, and I understand Mrs. Yule loves to cook and wanted to prepare a meal for us."

"That was nice of her," Leslie said as they stepped into the elevator.

They said nothing during the short ride down to the first floor. Just as well, Sloan thought.

"I got a call from my attorney around an hour ago," she said as they stepped outside.

He glanced over at her as he held the door. Their four hours of daylight had ended hours ago, and it was dark outside. At least for the time being, it had stopped snowing. "And?"

"And he said the paperwork your attorney sent to him looks good. It included everything you said it would."

"Did you think it wouldn't, Leslie? I only wanted to help you, not take your company from you."

"I know that, Sloan. I wish you wouldn't dissect everything I say and make it an issue of trust."

When they reached the car, he opened the door for her

and said, "If I am making it one, maybe you need to ask yourself why."

"And maybe you need to act like you accepted my apology like you claimed you did."

Sloan didn't say anything. Instead he waited for her to get in and snap her seat belt in place before closing the car door.

"Welcome to our home."

"Thank you." Leslie could not help staring at the white-bearded, hefty man who opened the door wearing a pair of overalls. Her eyes widened, immediately thinking that he looked just like…

"I know what you're thinking," Rudolph Yule said with a huge grin on his face. "The reason I look so much like Santa Claus is deliberate. This time of year, I pretend I'm the jolly ole guy himself here at North Pole. So did my father, grandfather and great-grandfather. And one day I figure my oldest son will do it as well. I guess you can say it's been a tradition in the Yule family for generations."

"Who was Santa here twenty-three years ago?" Sloan asked. He stood beside her, and when he accidentally brushed against her, a tremble ran through her body.

"That was Dad. He passed away twelve years ago."

"I'm sorry to hear of his passing. I took a picture with him as Santa at that gift shop in town when I was ten. I still have the picture we took together," Sloan said.

Rudolph Yule gave a hearty laugh, one Leslie thought actually made his belly shake. "Probably you and a million other kids. You wouldn't believe the number of adults who took photos with Dad or Granddad and now bring their kids back for photos. Both Dad and Granddad left big shoes for me to fill. Come to the living room and sit by the fire. My wife is happy you're here for dinner."

"We're happy to be here," Sloan said, placing his hand

at the center of Leslie's back. Her heart skipped, and when she glanced over at him, she knew he'd felt something, too. Yet he didn't remove his hand.

The huge room had what Leslie thought was the largest fireplace she'd ever seen. It made the entire area feel warm and inviting. What really caught her attention was the massive, beautifully decorated Christmas tree that sat on one side of the room. It had to be over fourteen feet tall, with thousands of twinkling lights.

"That tree is gorgeous," Leslie said.

"One hundred school children from all over Alaska get to come here on a field trip the week before Thanksgiving to help me decorate Santa's Christmas tree," an elderly woman said, coming into the room.

The older woman gave both Leslie and Sloan hugs, showing she was just as friendly as her husband. Leslie thought she looked just like anyone would envision Mrs. Claus to look…if there had been a real one. She was wearing a red dress with a white apron, and her round face and high cheekbones seemed to make her gray hair glow.

"I hope the two of you are hungry," Mrs. Yule said.

"We are," Sloan replied. "Something smells good."

"It's my moose stew."

"I love moose stew," Leslie said as they followed the Yules into the dining room. "My mother used to make it all the time."

There was a long table that seated at least twenty people. That prompted her to ask, "You have a large family?"

The older woman smiled. "Yes, we do. Rudy and I have ten children and six grands. They all work in the toy factory and are looking forward to meeting the two of you tomorrow when you're given a tour of the factory."

Leslie smiled. "I look forward to meeting them."

Always the gentleman, Sloan pulled out the chair for her before taking his own. Dinner was served immediately, and the food was delicious. Mrs. Yule had baked yeast rolls that were so good they practically melted in Leslie's mouth. Even the wine, which had been produced in a neighboring town, was delicious. The after-dinner dessert was a Christmas cake.

Because this was a business dinner meeting, the Yules sat down and thanked Sloan profusely for coming to their rescue and saving their company. A company he had yet to see. They admitted they hadn't known about the hostile takeover attempt by Martin Longshire until it was too late to do anything about it.

That made Leslie say, "I understand he went after your company for personal reasons."

Mrs. Yule glanced over at her and nodded. "That's true. He did it to get back at Merry."

"Mary?" Sloan asked.

"Yes, Merry, and that's M-e-r-r-y, and not M-a-r-y. She's our oldest daughter and the only member of the family who doesn't work in the family business. She always wanted to develop her skill as an artist, and years ago she got the chance to attend an art school in Paris. While living over there, she met Martin Longshire. He was living there as well, running his parents' business."

Mr. Yule then took up the story. "He saw Merry at some party and wanted her, although at the time she'd met Paul and the two of them were serious. It's my understanding that he even tried breaking them up, but he failed. Merry eventually married Paul. They still live in Paris and have three beautiful adult children."

"And you think that's the reason he wanted to take your company?" Leslie asked.

"Oh, we know that's the reason. After the takeover had gone through, he contacted Merry and told her what he'd done and why. He would have tried destroying Paul's company but couldn't. Paul's family is just as wealthy as

Longshire. Paul would have helped us out but like we said earlier, we hadn't known about the hostile takeover attempt until it was too late to do anything about it."

The older woman then looked over at Sloan. "That's why we're glad you came along, Mr. Outlaw."

Sloan smiled. "I'm Sloan, remember." He then assured the older couple that he would work with them to improve their business and expand their market.

Leslie had never seen the business side of Sloan and had to admit that because of her mistrust, she'd been leery of his offer at first. But listening to him explain the ways he could help the Yules made her see him through the older couple's eyes. They saw his offer for what it was—a genuine desire to help someone in need. The Yules were gracious and had not questioned his motives the way she had. It was obvious they appreciated his help, especially after dealing with the likes of Martin Longshire.

It was fascinating to hear how the Yules and their family manufactured toys all year long, stockpiling the merchandise to have the items ready to ship out beginning the week before Thanksgiving. It seemed they had a good routine going, and she listened while Sloan made a number of suggestions. His vast knowledge of various business models and the way he was able to recommend several he felt would be ideal for them was amazing.

While Mr. Yule showed Sloan his train set collection, Leslie offered to help Mrs. Yule clear the table. The kitchen was just as massive as the other room, but Leslie figured when so many kids once lived there, you would need a lot of cooking space.

"I think you and Mr. Outlaw make a stunning couple. The two of you will have beautiful babies."

Leslie nearly missed her step. She then quickly corrected the woman. "Oh, it's not like that. Sloan and I aren't a couple."

The woman only smiled and said, "If not, then you should be. Do you know what I see when I see the two of you?"

"No. What do you see?" she asked, curious to know.

Mrs. Yule smiled. "I see forever."

Forever? Leslie wasn't sure how the woman could see something like that, but she decided not to ask. Instead, she changed the subject by inquiring about some of the places to tour while in town. The first place Mrs. Yule suggested was Santa House, where there was a gift shop that sold their toys.

As Leslie continued to help the older woman clear the table and put things away, she couldn't help but think about what the woman had said about her and Sloan.

"So, what do you think of the Yules?" Sloan asked as they left the older couple's home.

"I like them. They certainly appreciate you saving their company from Longshire. And to know he went after their company for the same reason he went after mine—because years ago, a woman he wanted hadn't wanted him—is truly sad. How can one man be so despicable?"

"I have no idea. He definitely takes holding grudges to a whole other level, that's for sure." Sloan then glanced up into the sky. "It's a beautiful night, isn't it?"

She looked up as well. "Yes, it is. The sky is so bright, and you can see the stars so clearly. It's like you can reach up and touch one."

"According to Mr. Yule, tonight will be the best time to see the Northern Lights in this area," he said.

"Is it really?"

Sloan smiled upon hearing the excitement in her voice. "Yes," he said, opening the car door for her. "Do you want to see them? Mr. Yule gave me directions to the best observation point in town." Most Alaskans knew Fairbanks and North Pole were the best places in the state to view the Northern Lights, since both towns were located inside the Auroral Oval.

She glanced at her watch. "What time will it appear?"

"A little after midnight?" That meant they would be sitting together in a parked car for an hour. That was something they hadn't done since their college days.

Leslie finally nodded and said, "We only get a glimpse of the lights in Wasilla, definitely not what you can see in this section of Alaska, and I really would like to see it from here. Besides, I'm sure a number of others will be parked at that observation point as well."

Did her latter comment mean she had a problem being parked alone with him? In that case, Sloan wouldn't mention that the location Mr. Yule had suggested was a very private one and there wouldn't be others around.

"I can't wait to see the place where the toys are manufactured tomorrow," he said, changing the subject.

"I can't, either. Thanks for inviting me along, Sloan."

A part of him wished she wouldn't thank him for everything he did. But how would he feel if she didn't show her gratitude? He knew Leslie, and one of the reasons he had fallen in love with her was that she never took anyone's kindness lightly.

As they drove through the streets of North Pole, she commented on how it appeared every street had a Christmas theme. There was Mistletoe Road, Snowman Lane and Kris Kringle Drive, just to name a few.

When he thought things had gotten too quiet between them, at a traffic light, he glanced over at her and said, "There's a place I visited a few years back in the lower forty-eight called Christmas, Florida."

She lifted a brow. "Is that a real city?"

He chuckled. "Yes. It's small, but a city nonetheless. It's located not far from Orlando. There's this huge Christmas tree at the entrance to the town that's kept decorated all year round. Some of the residents even keep their homes lit with Christmas lights all year."

"I bet that can get expensive," she said.

Sloan glanced back at the road when the traffic light changed. It was good timing, too, since he hadn't been able to *not* look at her mouth and remember the number of times he'd kissed it. "I'm sure it can be, but I would hope the electric company gives them some kind of break for promoting the town's theme."

"I would hope so, too."

He made a turn off the only main road in town and headed into a more rural area. "I've never been somewhere so dark at night."

Sloan chuckled. "Missing streetlights already, are you?"

"Yes, I'm a city girl, so I'm used to them."

"And that's another reason why you don't get to see the Northern Lights as well as we can in this section. This is a rural area. Not much of that in Wasilla," he said.

"True." She leaned in to look out the windshield at the sky. "It's even more beautiful out here."

A few minutes later, he made the last turn Mr. Yule had instructed him to make. It was so dark, he had to hit his high beams to see in front of him. He then brought the car to a stop. "We are here."

She glanced around. "Where are the others?"

He glanced over at her. "What others?"

"You said this would be a good night to watch the Northern Lights and this was the best observation point."

"It is."

"I assumed other people would be parked here."

"No, there aren't any others. This is private land, and we're all alone."

Nine

They were all alone...

Leslie wondered why that thought bothered her when it shouldn't. They had been alone on the flight coming here, but that was different. They hadn't been in a parked car in the middle of nowhere in years. Total blackness surrounded them.

However, they did have a full moon in the sky that provided some light in the interior of the car. Out of the corner of her eye, she saw Sloan's head tilt back against the headrest. She sighed. Sharing a parked car on a secluded lot with Sloan Outlaw was not a good idea.

She was about to suggest they forget about seeing the Northern Lights when he asked, "Have you ever thought about expanding your business beyond Alaska, Leslie?"

Sloan's question made her realize whatever sexual chemistry she felt was one-sided. The only thing on Sloan's mind right now was business. She should have been grateful for that, but she couldn't help feeling a little let down.

There was a time when being in a parked car with him automatically meant only one thing. Was he letting her know those days were long gone?

"I haven't had time to think about it. Dad was contemplating it, though. He'd thought about testing the market by doing an exclusive line in Hollywood."

"Hollywood?"

"Yes. There are several makeup artists there who only use our brand. We ship it directly to them." After shifting in her seat, she said, "Why do you ask?"

"I was just wondering. Like I was telling the Yules over dinner, companies that are just doing business in Alaska are missing out on bigger markets."

Leslie nodded. "I'll eventually get there. After Dad died, my main concentration was holding on to the company. I got wind of what Martin Longshire was up to the day after Dad's funeral. Unlike what he did with the Yules, with me he wasn't keeping his plans a secret."

She then recalled that she'd never asked how Sloan had known Cassidy Cosmetics was under a hostile takeover. "How did you know what Longshire was up to with my company, Sloan?" He switched on the car's heater. She appreciated that and figured her occasional shivers had given her away.

"It was a conversation Redford shared with me at Tyler and Keosha's wedding. Evidently he slept with one of Longshire's employees, who shared the plan."

"I see."

When the car got quiet, she decided to keep conversation going and asked, "So what are your plans for Christmas?"

Sloan figured it would not be a good idea to tell her that his plan for Christmas was her. She knew he wanted her for Christmas. Now he couldn't dismiss that things went a lot deeper than that. Even after they spent a week together at the cabin, she would still be alone for the holidays.

For days he'd been battling with the thought that he didn't care, only to finally accept that he did. As absurd as it might sound, he wanted her to spend the holidays with him even after the time they spent at the cabin. It would be her first Christmas without her father, and he didn't want to think of her hurt and all alone.

Why he even gave a damn he wasn't sure, but he did.

Knowing she was waiting for his response, he said, "I told you about my cousins, the Westmorelands."

"Yes."

"Since getting to know them, it has become a habit to spend the holidays with them."

She lifted a brow. "Why?"

He wasn't surprised she asked, because she knew how, thanks to Bart, their family used to be considered unsociable and unfriendly years ago. "We have a lot in common and enjoy spending time with them. Besides, their charitable foundation holds this huge event every year around the holidays. It's a meaningful time together, and it's also fun. We consider it family bonding time." He hoped she would get to see firsthand how meaningful things were for the Westmoreland family, a family the Outlaws were now a part of.

All of a sudden, he heard her sharp intake of breath. He followed her gaze and saw what had caught her attention. The Northern Lights. Prisms of color flooded the skies in a brilliant display. He thought now what he thought every time he saw it—it was a powerful thing. While growing up, he'd always felt fortunate that the state where he was born could claim this beauty in a way others could not.

"I have to get out of the car," Leslie said, opening the car door.

Following her lead, Sloan got out as well. Outside, it

seemed as if the sky was right there on top of them. Mr. Yule had been right. Sloan had seen the Northern Lights from several sites over the years, but he thought this particular location was the best.

He and Leslie were standing side by side in front of the car. When he felt her shiver, he turned to see her tighten her coat and scarf around herself while still looking up into the sky. "Beautiful."

Sloan had to agree. However, he was not looking up at the sky but at her. She was as beautiful as the Northern Lights. In fact, the sky's prism seemed to highlight her features in a way that brought out her beauty even more.

"Yes, it is beautiful," he said and looked up into the sky. The last thing he wanted was to give away what he was thinking.

He then decided to tack on, "Mr. Yule was right. This is the best place to see it." When she shivered again, he instinctively wrapped his arms around her to share his heat. Wordlessly, they stood together, looking up at the sky.

Sloan wasn't sure how long they stood there, but the temperature had dropped even more, and they needed to get back inside the car. He was about to tell her that when he saw her staring at him.

At that moment, something happened that he hadn't expected. He momentarily forgot that she was the reason for his first heartbreak. That she was the reason he refused to fall in love again. Instead, he was remembering other times when they had gone to a secluded area, gotten out of the car and stood beneath an Alaskan sky. Usually, they would kiss.

They had never shared a kiss under the Northern Lights. Why did he want to do so now? He mentally told himself to release her and step back, suggest they get in the car and leave. However, for some reason he couldn't do that.

Instead, he gave in to temptation and leaned in to capture her mouth with his.

The moment their mouths touched, the taste he'd thought he had forgotten renewed itself in every part of his being.

Ten years ago, he and Leslie had been a lot younger, carefree and in love. Now they were older, serious-minded and no longer in love. But that didn't stop his gloved hands from moving over her shoulders while his mouth feasted on hers. And when his hands lowered to her back, he could feel her heat even through his gloves and her coat.

She was kissing him back. That let him know she was enjoying the reunion of their mouths as much as he was. When his tongue took hold of hers, he tried to convince himself he wasn't retaking a claim. He was merely enjoying the moment. Relishing her taste. However, a part of him knew he was doing more when he began sucking on her tongue with a hunger he felt right in his groin. Wrapping his arms around her tightly, he nearly groaned when even with the thickness of their coats, he could feel his solid, hard erection pressed between her thighs.

There was no telling how long they would have stood there kissing in the freezing cold beneath the Northern Lights if they hadn't heard the sound of a moose call. One that was too close for comfort.

Breaking off the kiss and releasing her, he said, "I think we better get back in the car, Leslie."

When she released a long sigh and then nodded, he escorted her back to her side of the car and opened the door for her. "Thanks."

"You're welcome," he said.

After getting back inside, he started the engine to warm up the car. He also wanted to warm her up. Thoughts of pulling her across the seat and into his lap to kiss her again, while his hands opened her coat to touch her everywhere, filled his mind.

She squashed that idea when she said, "I'm ready to go back to the hotel now, Sloan."

He wasn't surprised that she regretted their kiss and was ready to bring this night to an end. Obviously that kiss had shaken her up as much as it had him.

"All right."

"And, Sloan?"

He glanced over at her. He figured this was when she would tell him their kiss had been a mistake. "Yes, Leslie?"

"Thanks for sharing the Northern Lights with me," she said in an almost whisper. "I enjoyed it."

A part of him was tempted to ask if she'd enjoyed sharing a kiss with him as well, but he thought better of doing so. "Don't mention it."

While putting the car in gear to leave the observation point, he knew he would be carrying the memory of the kiss they'd shared under the Northern Lights around with him for a while.

Ten

Was Sloan staring at her more than usual? Specifically, her mouth? Leslie couldn't help pondering that question when they'd arrived at the Yuletide Toy Factory the next morning. He had just opened the car door for her, and now his gaze seemed to be glued to her lips.

The same thing had happened earlier over the breakfast they'd shared at the hotel. More than once she had looked up from her meal to find him staring at her. Namely, her mouth. Had he been reminded of the kiss they'd shared last night?

It had been a kiss she hadn't expected, but she wasn't surprised she'd gotten wrapped up in it like she had. Sloan had been a great kisser, and it was obvious nothing had changed. If anything, he was better at it.

He was older, more experienced, and the lips that had taken her mouth last night had contained a fire she hadn't known back then. The intensity of the way their mouths mated was the reason she hadn't been able to settle into a peaceful sleep when they'd returned to the hotel. Instead, she had lain awake most of the night reliving it.

As she walked beside Sloan, she wondered if he'd had a hard time sleeping like she had. Probably not. She was certain he had kissed a lot of women since her. That made her wonder how she compared.

She also wondered about something else. Had their kiss reminded him of how things had once been for them? Did he now regret kissing her? If that was the case, then he could only get mad at himself, because he had initiated it. Not her. But she'd gone along with it. Honestly, what had he expected? She'd always been putty in his arms, especially when it came to his kisses.

However, his touch was another weakness of hers, she thought, when he touched her arm to escort her to the door of the building. "This place is huge," she said when they reached the entrance. Before she could stop herself, she took a quick look over at him. He looked handsome this morning. But then, Sloan always looked handsome.

"Yes, it is."

Sloan knocked, and immediately the door swung open and a jolly-looking Mr. Yule stood there with a huge grin on his face. "Welcome to Santa's workshop," he said, moving aside to let them in. The moment she walked over the threshold, Leslie took it all in. Although there were no elves, just regular people busy stocking boxes, it still reminded her of what Santa's workshop should look like. It might have something to do with the fact that everyone was wearing red Christmas hats with white cuffs. There was another decorated Christmas tree and a group of life-size reindeer that seemed to be looking on the process with their approval.

"This is the packaging area. Next, I want to show you where everything is manufactured," Mr. Yule said excitedly. "All our toys are made of wood," he told them.

She raised a brow. "No plastic?"

"Not a bit," Mr. Yule said, opening a huge door. They followed him in. "Wood lasts longer and is more durable," the older man said. "However, because wood is heavier in weight, that has always been a major problem for us when it comes to shipping costs."

"Not anymore," Sloan said, scanning the area where the toys were being manufactured.

Leslie looked over at him. "Why will it no longer be a problem?" she asked.

Sloan glanced at her. "Since my family owns a transport company, the cost of shipping will no longer be a major issue."

She nodded. "I see." In a way she saw more than Sloan probably wanted her to. Just like she'd suspected, he was setting up the company for success and making sure they would be able to hold their own if Longshire ever got the mind to come after them again.

Mr. Yule looked at his watch. "I need to leave to get on my post as Santa at the Santa House. Make sure you two stop by to visit me there. My oldest son, Garland, will continue on with the tour."

Leslie lifted a brow. "Garland?"

Mr. Yule laughed. "Yes, Garland. I also have sons named Cane, Kris, Nicholas and Sleigh. We told you about our daughter Merry last night. There's also Holly, Star, Noel and Angel."

Garland, a man in his fifties, who was smaller in stature than his father and whose beard wasn't as massive and white, led them through the rest of the building. They watched toys being made and then, in another section, watched as toys were hand-painted.

At the end of the tour, Mrs. Yule prepared lunch. That's when Leslie and Sloan got to meet the other adult Yule children and grandchildren, who all worked at the factory and who all had names connected with Christmas. They were appreciative of Sloan saving the family business.

When she and Sloan were back in the car after leaving the toy factory, he asked, "So what do you think?"

She glanced over at him. "I think it's a tidy operation, and although most of the employees are related, they seem to work well together."

"I noticed that as well and think of it as a positive," Sloan said. "It's obvious they take pride in the products their family produces."

She thought so as well. When neither seemed to have anything else to add, she thought it would be a good time to bring up a subject she knew they'd been avoiding—their kiss. Although she didn't regret it, she knew it was something they should not do again. "I think we need to talk about that kiss, Sloan."

"What about it?"

"It shouldn't happen again."

He released a smooth chuckle. "It will happen again, Leslie. However, if it will make you feel better, I will let you initiate it next time."

"Then I don't have to worry about it happening again."

"Okay."

Okay? "What is that supposed to mean?"

"Okay means I don't agree or disagree. Whatever happens will happen."

When he pulled into the parking lot of Santa House, he switched off the car and said, "We're leaving early in the morning."

She lifted a brow. "I thought our flight didn't take off until noon."

"It doesn't. I need to do a pit stop in Fairbanks for some papers."

Leslie nodded. "At your office?"

"No, at my home." He turned in his seat to face her. "Do you have a problem with that?"

"Should I have a problem with it?"

He shrugged. "I don't see why you should when we'll only be there for a few minutes."

There was no need to tell him that a lot could happen behind closed doors in a few minutes. As if he'd read her thoughts, he said, "This time next week, we'll be spending a week together in seclusion at the cabin on Kodiak Island. I hope you're not nervous about being alone with me."

She rolled her eyes. "I am alone with you now, Sloan. I was also alone with you on the flight here and will be alone with you on the flight back."

Sloan smiled. All kinds of sensations flooded her stomach. Drawing in a quick breath, she broke eye contact with him and turned to unlock her door.

"I've got that," he said, opening his own car door to sprint around the front of the car to open the door for her.

"Thanks."

"You are welcome," he said, taking her hand to help her out.

The moment their hands touched, she felt heat, even though they were wearing gloves. It had snowed heavily last night and was snowing now with temperatures below zero. Regardless of the fact that it was cold as the dickens on the outside, some kind of fire was consuming her on the inside. It didn't take a rocket scientist to know she was in trouble with Sloan.

She may have bitten off more than she could chew.

Sloan glanced around Santa House. It seemed a lot larger than he remembered as a child, and when he asked their tour guide about it, the young lady said that over the years, due to remodeling, it had nearly doubled in size.

He noticed a lot of parents and their kids were headed to

where he knew Mr. Yule was holding court as Santa. Leslie headed to the gift shop, and he instinctively followed her.

"I want to buy one of those wooden train sets for Elan."

He lifted a brow. "Who is Elan?"

"Carmen's nine-year-old nephew."

That told him nothing, since he had no idea who Carmen was, either. Evidently seeing the bemused look on his face, she added, "Carmen was my roommate at Howard, and someone I consider my best friend. She was my plus-one at Tyler and Keosha's wedding."

He nodded. "She lives in Alaska?"

"Heavens, no. She hates cold weather, but I managed to talk her into spending Thanksgiving with me. No easy feat, I assure you. Even with the weather, we got to spend ten fun days together while she was here." Leslie smiled. "She claims she hasn't thawed out yet."

There had always been something about Leslie's smile, and he was convinced that smile was what had captured his interest from the first. "And she has a nine-year-old nephew?"

"Yes. He's her sister's son. I think he will love the train."

When they reached the shelves, he saw there were only two left, and he quickly pulled one off the shelf for Leslie. "Got it."

"Thanks," she said as they headed for the checkout counter. "I think it's great that they'll ship it for me, too." It didn't take long for her to pay for the item and complete shipping papers.

"Now," he said, taking her hand, "let's go see Santa. I am dying to know if you've been good this year."

She threw back her head and laughed. "You, who once admitted to always getting into trouble as a child and whose last name is Outlaw, are curious as to whether *I've* been good this year?"

He couldn't help laughing as well. "I guess that does sound rather amusing."

"Yes, it does."

While standing in line waiting their turn for Santa, a curious little girl standing in front of them, who looked to be about five years old, asked, "Where is your little boy or girl?"

Leslie smiled down at her. "We don't have one. I'm here to see Santa for myself."

"Oh. You've been bad?" the little girl asked, and Sloan thought the expression on her face showed she was trying to figure out what bad deed an adult could do to sit on Santa's lap and ask for forgiveness to get a toy.

"No, I haven't been bad," Leslie said, and Sloan had to cough to smother a laugh.

The little girl was about to ask Leslie another question when the child's mother gave Leslie an apologetic smile and shushed her daughter. "Kids still like you, I see," Sloan whispered.

"And I still like them," she said.

He didn't say anything as he recalled the number of times he'd thought about them sharing those children. Had things worked out the way he'd wanted them to, the way he'd assumed they would, she would have been the mother of his babies by now.

He quickly pushed that thought from his mind. It was a dream that had been destroyed and would never be resurrected.

That night before going to bed, he called Leslie to tell her he had changed his mind about making a stop at his home in Fairbanks. What he hadn't told her was that while spending time with her today, he had experienced emotions he didn't want to feel. Emotions she seemed to elicit from him effortlessly.

The best thing to do was return Leslie to Wasilla. He

needed to prepare mentally for their week together on Kodiak Island. Besides, there were a few behind-the-scenes things he needed to take care of regarding both her company and the Yuletide Toy Factory.

And there was Martin Longshire.

Already Sloan had gotten a call from Cole letting him know Longshire was digging into Sloan's affairs. Because he'd contacted Cole when he had, safeguards against tampering had been put in place. However, Sloan intended to track every move Longshire made. He would remain in Wasilla and work out of his hotel room instead of returning to Fairbanks. It really didn't make sense to go back and forth when he would need to return to Wasilla at the end of the week for Leslie.

He was determined not to have any contact whatsoever with Leslie this coming week. Putting distance between them for a few days would definitely help him get his head together where she was concerned. The strong attraction he'd felt toward her was something he could deal with as long as he kept things in perspective.

The one thing he refused to do was let Leslie Cassidy tangle with his mind ever again.

Leslie glanced over at Sloan when he parked the car at the airport. Since leaving the hotel, he'd said very few words to her. It was, she decided, a definite change compared to yesterday, when he'd been in a more talkative mood. Actually, she had picked up on his change of moods yesterday evening when he'd brought her back to the hotel.

"Thanks," she said after he opened the car door for her. Already he was moving away, toward the office where flight papers had to be filed.

Last night, he hadn't invited her to join him for dinner, which was just as well. She had ordered room service while watching a holiday movie on television. Afterward, she had showered and gotten in bed. That's when Sloan had called to tell her he wouldn't be stopping at his home in Fairbanks after all. She hadn't asked why he'd changed his mind, and he obviously hadn't felt the need to tell her.

It didn't take long for him to complete the necessary paperwork for them to take off. Unlike their earlier flight, when they'd engaged in a steady stream of conversation in the cockpit, the silence between them lasted through the entire flight.

More than once she found herself staring over at him while he maneuvered the plane through the less-than-friendly skies. It was snowing harder now than when they had arrived in North Pole, and she could tell Sloan's concentration was on piloting the plane through the rough weather.

When the plane took an unexpected dip, she drew in a sharp breath. He obviously heard it, and that's when he glanced over at her to ask, "You're okay, Leslie?"

She nodded, trying not to remember that's what he would ask her after they'd made love. It had always been important to him to know that the intensity of their love-making had been all right with her and that she had enjoyed it as much as he had. "Yes, Sloan, I'm okay."

He resumed looking ahead, and she continued watching him, unable to look away. At that moment she felt a deep loss, a sense of extreme regret. It wasn't the first time she'd felt this way since discovering the truth, but it was hitting her harder today than ever before.

Why? Could it be the time she'd spent with Sloan over the past several days had made her realize just what she'd lost? Then there was the kiss they'd shared. She drew in a deep breath, definitely feeling the impact of knowing a man who'd once loved her as deeply as she'd loved him was lost to her forever.

Refusing to look over at him any longer, she thought

about the plans for next week, when she would spend time with him at the cabin. Unlike the last time he'd asked her to spend a week with him, when she'd been all happy and excited about doing so, now she was dreading it.

Because he had invited her for one reason and one reason only: closure. Sleeping with her, if that's what happened, would be closure for him. He had loved her once. She knew Sloan. He had gotten over her like he'd said he had, but they needed a final chapter. There would not be a happy ending, just an ending.

Sloan had shared with her that closure was how he had dealt with his mother, too, after he'd discovered how much of a gold-digger Barbie was.

Bart hadn't had to take Barbie to court for custody of Sloan. Instead, he'd given her enough money up front to keep her living in style for the rest of her life. Unfortunately, she hadn't known how to manage her finances. Sloan had heard from her a number of times over the years. Somehow, she had managed to reach out to him without Bart knowing about it. But she hadn't called because she was interested in Sloan's well-being. The only time she'd call was when she wanted him to hit Bart up for more money. When Sloan had refused, she cursed him out and told him she was glad he wasn't a part of her life.

Sloan had told Leslie how he had gone to see Barbie during his first year of college, after finding out where she was living. He had given her a check that had represented every last cent he'd had in his savings account—which had been close to fifty thousand dollars—and had told her he didn't want to see her ever again. Seeing his mother that day had been about closure.

Now Leslie figured she was just another closure he had to deal with. However, little did he know, but she needed closure as well. It was only when she got it that she could move on with her life.

Eleven

On Saturday morning Sloan arrived at Leslie's home just as he'd told her he would.

In the time since they had parted ways on Monday, he had thrown himself into his work, putting cautionary measures in place in case Longshire made a move in retaliation. He'd also met with members of his board to give them his take on the Yuletide Toy Factory and his recommendations for next year. He'd come up with a number of ideas, including one that would take the toy manufacturing company global.

Even with enough to keep him busy, he still had managed to think about Leslie. Not just a little, but a lot.

Tightening his coat around him, he rang her doorbell and remembered he'd stood in this same spot and at the same time last Saturday morning. How could a woman he hadn't had any dealings with for ten years become a regular feature of his life now? Luckily for him, she was temporary. After their week together, she would go back to being out of sight and out of mind.

The door opened. "Good morning, Sloan."

Before he could respond, Leslie stepped out, and he instinctively moved back. "You're ready?" he asked, watching her lock her door.

"Yes." Then she headed toward the car, with a duffel bag on her shoulder and pulling a piece of luggage behind her.

He quickly followed her and then opened the trunk to place her luggage next to his before opening the car door for her. "Thanks."

"You're welcome," he said, closing the door.

Sloan slowed his pace as he walked behind the car to the other side, trying to pull himself together. He'd thought he had everything under control, and basically, he had—until she'd opened that door. Seeing her had done something to him, but he wasn't sure what. All he knew was that his heart had begun beating rapidly in his chest. It still was.

Opening the door, he slid behind the wheel and glanced over at her. She looked good. She smelled good. "You have everything?"

"Yes."

She was staring straight ahead, refusing to look at him. However, he couldn't stop looking at her. What was there about her this morning that had claimed his attention? That had desire flowing through his veins?

Like before, in deference to the cold weather, she was covered from head to toe. Wool coat, gloves, boots and a furry hat on her head. So what was there?

While he sat struggling with the dilemma, she glanced over at him. "Is something wrong?"

The only thing wrong with him was that he had missed her.

"Sloan?"

"No, nothing is wrong. I was just thinking about something."

"What?"

He broke eye contact with her to start the car. "Nothing."

Sloan backed out of her driveway. This coming week might be more of a challenge than he'd figured it would be.

Leslie watched Sloan as he drove.

They would be spending an entire week together, and if for one minute he thought he was going to ignore her like he'd done on the trip home from North Pole, then he was mistaken.

"I'd like a tree, please. A small one will work," she said when he brought the car to a stop at a traffic light.

He glanced over at her. "What kind of tree are you talking about?"

She smiled and didn't care that he didn't smile back. "A Christmas tree, of course. I can't imagine spending a week in a place not decorated for Christmas."

"I thought you said you wouldn't be celebrating it this year," he said, breaking eye contact with her and moving the car forward.

She shook her head. "I didn't say that. I told you this would be the first one without my father and I hadn't made any plans. I believe that Dad would want me to still enjoy the holidays, so I intend to do just that. Does this cabin have internet?"

"Yes, it has internet. We have our own tower, since this section of the island is pretty secluded. Walker's place, Hemlock Row, is about twenty miles away, so we share it with him."

"Walker Rafferty?"

"Yes. You remember Walker?"

She doubted any woman could forget the former Hollywood actor. When she'd accompanied Sloan home for

Christmas that time, she had met Walker briefly. "Yes. How is he?" She remembered his wife and son had been killed in a car accident, which was the reason he had left Hollywood and returned to Alaska.

"Walker is fine. He remarried and has a set of twins."

"That's wonderful. Who did he marry?"

"Bailey. She's one of my Westmoreland cousins from Denver."

Leslie settled in her seat, listening to him tell her how the two had met and the beautiful family they had now. She thought it was a wonderful love story, one she knew she would never experience. It had been a long time since the thought of that bothered her, but it was bothering her now.

"This place is awesome, Sloan," Leslie said, entering the cabin and turning around in the huge living room. "It's definitely a lot larger than what I imagined."

Sloan entered after bringing in their luggage. She had removed her coat to reveal a pair of jeans and a choco-late-brown pullover sweater that clearly defined her curvy body. "Ready for a tour?" he asked.

"Yes."

He took her around the huge five-bedroom, four-bath-room cabin that was located deep in the mountains and backed up against the Shelikof Strait, a beautiful water-way that stretched from the southwestern coast of Alaska to the east of Kodiak Island.

Each bedroom had a huge stone fireplace, and the cabin had been built in such a way that the waterway could be seen from every bedroom. There was a huge kitchen, din-ing room and a massive family room.

Sloan figured what had impressed Leslie more than anything was the movable wall that led to an underground tunnel. Like he'd told her, he wasn't sure why his grand-father had built the secret passageway or why there was a gun case that held probably every type of weapon ever manufactured.

He went on to tell her that he and his siblings had their ideas. The repeating of those suspicions had pissed off their father so much he had ordered that they get rid of all the artillery. Unknown to him, they hadn't.

Sloan glanced at his watch. "Before we start losing daylight, I want to bring in more wood for the fireplace."

She nodded. "Do you need any help?"

"No, I got this."

It took him a few trips to fill the wood box inside before he got a sniff of something cooking. They hadn't talked about what they would be eating, although he'd told her about calling days ahead to make sure the refrigerator and freezer were fully stocked before they arrived. Sloan knew how much Leslie liked cooking and just how good she was at it.

"Something smells good," he said, coming into the house with a load of wood in his arms.

"I checked out the refrigerator and cabinets and saw there was everything I needed to make a pot of chili, a salad and some yeast rolls. I was listening to the weather report and heard it's supposed to start snowing tonight."

"That wouldn't surprise me." Kodiak Island was known not only for its bears but also for harsh weather.

"I took the bedroom across from yours, Sloan."

He glanced over at her, figuring that was her way of letting him know they wouldn't be sharing a bed tonight. "That's fine, Leslie. You can sleep in any bedroom you like."

"They're all beautiful."

Sloan chuckled. "I'm surprised you think that, since they were all decorated for the men in the family. All except Dad, since he hasn't been here in years."

"What about Charm?" she asked.

"Charm rarely comes here. She finds the place too secluded to suit her. The farthest she'll go whenever she visits Kodiak Island is Walker's ranch. She visits them often enough. She and Bailey forged a close relationship, and Charm has fallen in love with Walker and Bailey's twins. Charm hasn't been around a lot of babies before."

He glanced out the window. Unlike Fairbanks, which usually only got four hours of daylight, Kodiak got six to seven hours. Now they had gone, and it was dark. "It's snowing already and coming down pretty hard," he said.

"Do you think we'll lose power?" she asked.

"There is always that possibility, but we have a fully operational generator. We're good."

What he'd told her was true, they were good, and before he left here, he intended to show her just how good together they could be.

"You've gotten quiet on me, Leslie."

She glanced across the dinner table at Sloan. Funny he should say that. When he had picked her up from her house, he'd barely said anything to her. But she'd been determined not to let him ruin what she'd decided would be a good time at the cabin, even if she had to entertain herself. Ignoring his brooding attitude, she had kept up a steady stream of conversation, even when his responses had been a nonchalant grunt.

His less-than-friendly attitude had begun thawing out when they had landed on Kodiak Island. Once settled in the rental car, he had told her about the time the cabin had become a stronghold against domestic terrorists, who'd been determined to kidnap his cousin Bane's wife. And while driving, Sloan had taken what he'd referred to as the scenic route that showed the beauty of the island with its abundance of hemlock trees. That had been the extent of what he'd said since picking her up.

And now he wanted to keep the conversation going?

"I've talked enough for today, Sloan. Didn't want to wear out my welcome, since you've been in a less-than-friendly mood."

He nodded, as if he accepted her accusation. "I apologize for that. I had a lot on my mind this week business-wise, which is why you hadn't heard from me."

It hadn't bothered her when she hadn't heard from him. In a way, she was glad she hadn't. She'd needed time to unwind her brain and put everything in perspective. So whether he knew it or not, he'd done her a favor. "Did you get a lot accomplished?"

"Yes. I wanted a plan that could help the Yules. They run a tidy operation, but I've come up with other ways to make it grow."

She nodded. "I'm sure they will appreciate that. I like them. They are nice people."

"Yes, they are."

When he got up from the table and walked over to the counter to refill his coffee cup, she couldn't help but notice how good he looked in his jeans. When he'd been kneeling in front of the fireplace, she'd appreciated the way those same jeans stretched tight over his muscular thighs. Thighs that she remembered well. They would ride her hard while making love to her.

She'd always thought he looked good in pullover sweaters, since they captured the broadness of his chest so well. A chest she'd licked a number of times from top to bottom. He definitely looked good in the one he was wearing now. The tan color enhanced the darkness of his eyes. There was a lot about him that had changed physically. He was more built, and hard muscled, and solid, and—

"Would you like a refill on your coffee, Leslie?"

He had glanced over his shoulder to look at her. More than likely he had caught her staring. "No, thanks, I'm fine."

He smiled. "Yes, Leslie, you most definitely are."

She wished Sloan didn't have the ability to seduce her with just words alone.

"So what do you plan to do the rest of the day?" Sloan asked, coming to sit back down at the table.

"Read. I brought my e-reader, and it contains a number of books that I haven't started yet. And I am hoping we can get a tree tomorrow."

He nodded. "That shouldn't be a problem if the snow lets up. There are quite a few Fraser firs on this property."

She couldn't help but smile at that. "Then we need to go out early."

"And we will, granted it's not snowing." He took a sip of his coffee and then looked over at her in a way that made sensuous shivers race up her spine. "There's something I need to ask you, Leslie. Information that will be vital when we make love."

When we make love? Leslie wondered what part of *I will not sleep with you this week* he did not understand. He'd said he wanted her for Christmas, in his bed. She had explained to him, quite clearly, she'd thought, that the only thing he would get from her this week was companionship. "Need I repeat myself, Sloan? I will not be sleeping with you."

He smiled in a way that made more shivers race up her spine. "Then humor me and let me ask my question anyway."

Feeling frustrated, yet at the same time curious as to what he wanted to know, she asked, "What's your question?"

"When was the last time you made love with a guy?"

There was no way she would tell him that the last time had been with him. "Why do you want to know such a thing?"

She wondered if the kiss they'd shared had given her

away. Could he tell that she kissed the same way she had ten years ago?

"Leslie?"

Instead of answering, she stood. "Even if I had agreed to sleep with you this week Sloan, the answer to your question would be that it's not any of your business. I'm not asking you about the last time you made love to a woman."

"You can if it interests you."

"It doesn't." After loading her dishes in the dishwasher, she turned around and said, "I'll see you in the morning, Sloan."

She could feel the heat of his gaze on her back when she walked out of the kitchen.

Twelve

Sloan leaned against one of the tall hemlock trees as he watched Leslie walk around several Fraser firs looking for what she'd said was the ideal Christmas tree. When he had awakened that morning, a part of him had hoped she had canned the idea of a Christmas tree. It didn't take long to see that she hadn't. She'd been up, dressed and had even prepared breakfast by the time he'd walked into the kitchen.

The breakfast of pancakes, bacon and eggs had been delicious. However, he didn't want her to assume that he expected her to do all the cooking, so he'd told her they would be sharing cooking duties. She told him she didn't mind cooking since she enjoyed it so much, and since her father died, she had no one besides herself to cook for.

Now here they were, on a part of the property where Christmas trees grew. She had checked out at least five but hadn't made up her mind about which one she would take. He recalled her saying she would settle on a small tree, but none of the five were what he considered small.

Like usual, she was dressed for the cold weather, but that didn't stop him from imagining what all she had on underneath that wool coat, boots and fur hat. He would give just about anything to be able to peel all that clothing off her when they got back to the cabin.

Last night, after watching the sway of her hips when she'd made her exit from the kitchen, he hadn't heard a peep out of her the rest of the night.

He had remained up for hours, enjoying a glass of wine while watching cop shows on television. When he had retired to his room, he had seen a light on under her door, which let him know that although she'd been quiet, she was still awake. Since he hadn't heard the sound of the television in her room, he figured she was reading.

Glancing at his watch, he looked back at her now and said, "How much longer will it take you to make up your mind about a tree, Leslie?"

She glanced over at him and smiled. He hadn't expected that smile, and it warmed him to the core. "Too cold out here for you, Sloan?"

"You know better than that."

She of all people knew how much he enjoyed cold weather. The colder the better. However, leaning against this tree with his gaze trained on her, he remembered another time he'd taken her to a Christmas tree farm. It had been a Sunday, and few people had been about. He'd come close to tempting her to engage in a quickie behind the branches.

Thinking of that day made him recall the first time they'd met. It had been an extremely cold day in Anchorage when he and Redford had been headed to class. Leslie had sprinted across the yard in her haste and had bumped into them. Literally. She would have lost her footing and toppled over if he hadn't reached out and grabbed her. That would have been that, and he and Redford would have continued on their way, if she hadn't taken off that furry hat she'd been wearing to smile, apologize for bumping into him and thank him.

The moment he had looked into her eyes, he was convinced he had fallen in love right then and there. After thanking him, she had rushed off before he could get any information from her, including a name. He had thought of her constantly. Her eyes and smile had invaded his dreams. Just when he was convinced that he would never see her again, he had.

Her face had been on a campus flyer advertising her organization was accepting donations to help buy toys for disadvantaged children. Not only had he made a donation, but to spend time with her, he had joined her group. At first, he'd figured his attraction to her was merely sexual. But the more time he spent with her and the more he had gotten to know her, he'd accepted it was more than that.

"Okay, Sloan. This is the one I want."

Her words pulled him from the past and back to the present. He wasn't surprised that the one she'd finally settled on was the one he'd liked the best. "Are you sure that's the one?"

She smiled brightly. "Yes, I'm sure."

He nodded and picked up the saw by his feet, not believing she would spend time decorating a tree just to have it up for one week. He then thought of something. "We don't have any ornaments here," he said.

"No problem. I brought my own."

Sloan shook his head. Honestly, he wasn't surprised.

Leslie stood back as Sloan erected the tree near the window in the cabin's living room. It was beautiful and just what she needed to brighten her mood. Yesterday after dinner, she had taken a shower and gotten into bed but hadn't gone to sleep. Instead, she had pulled up her e-reader. From the sound of the television in the family room, it had been easy to guess Sloan was still a fan of cop shows.

And she'd known when he had decided to call it a night and go to bed. Although he'd tried to be quiet, she had heard him walk down the hall to his bedroom. She had held her breath, hoping he wouldn't knock on her door. He hadn't.

When she'd awakened to find it wasn't snowing, she had wanted to hurry and dress and get a tree before snow began falling again. When Sloan still had not awakened, she decided to go downstairs and prepare breakfast, convinced the smell of bacon would do the trick. She knew how much he loved bison bacon. That had worked. He had walked into the kitchen, fully dressed but still with that sleepy-sexy look.

"Are you sure this is where you want it?"

She blinked, recalling other times, during their lovemaking, when he would tease her relentlessly. He would rub his erection all over her, between her legs. Then as he entered her, he would teasingly ask, *Are you sure this is where you want it?* By then she would be nearly out of her mind. She would push upward to hold him inside her tightly, to show him that she'd known just where she wanted it.

"Leslie?"

From the look on his face, he was waiting for her to answer. There was no indication he had made a connection between what he'd asked now and the other times when he'd asked that same thing. "Yes, that location will work. I like that it's sitting in front of the window."

He rolled his eyes. "Need I remind you that we're out in the middle of nowhere, miles from civilization? The only person who might notice blinking Christmas lights are the bears."

"Thanks for reminding me, Sloan."

He threw his head back and laughed even though she honestly didn't see anything funny. He had told her the property surrounding the cabin was bearproof. In addition to the electric fencing, bear sensors were installed that not only emitted scents that bears detested but also blared music that bothered their eardrums. Besides, most bears hibernated during winter.

"Now that the tree is where you want it, I'm going to sit back and relax with a beer," he said.

"You're not going to help me decorate?"

"Nope. You can do a better job at it than I could. So, knock yourself out while I observe."

Leslie wasn't sure how she felt about him sitting there drinking beer, watching her. Knowing Sloan's eyes would be on her was not a comforting thought. He could look at her in ways that would make her feel naked even while she was wearing clothes. "Not sure I like the idea of you just sitting there observing. Don't you have anything better to do?"

"Yes."

"Then do it."

A smile curved his lips, and she had a feeling there was an ulterior motive behind it when he said, "I can't."

Why now of all times was she intensely attracted to him? She'd almost forgotten how he could seduce her with his eyes. "And why not?" she asked.

"Because what I really want to do is you, Leslie."

When Sloan left the living room and headed for the kitchen to get his beer, he couldn't help but smile at Leslie's expression. He had told her the truth—he wanted to do her, but he would settle for just sitting there and drinking his beer while watching that body in action. He had popped the top off his beer bottle when his cell phone rang. He recognized the caller. Garth. Pulling his phone out of the back pocket of his jeans, he clicked on.

"Yes, Garth?"

"I take it you made it to the cabin."

"Yes, I'm here. Arrived yesterday."

"Did you stop by Hemlock Row to visit with Walker and Bailey before you got there?"

Sloan took a swig of his beer. "I didn't have time. I wanted to get here and get settled before dark."

"That was a good idea."

At that moment Sloan heard Leslie call out to him to bring her a beer as well. Without thinking, he answered her in a loud voice, "Sure thing."

"I take it you're not alone, Sloan."

Garth's comment made Sloan realize his mistake. But then, he was a grown-ass man who could invite anyone he wanted to join him here. "No, I'm not alone." And because he knew from past experience that Garth had a way of finding out anything he wanted to know, Sloan decided to save him the trouble. "I invited Leslie to join me."

"Leslie Cassidy?"

"Yes, Leslie Cassidy," Sloan said, like there would be any other Leslie he would invite here.

"Does that mean the two of you are—"

"No!" Sloan said in a firm tone, squashing the assumption his oldest brother was about to make. "Leslie and I are not getting back together. I know how much she enjoys Christmas, and with her father's death, she has no family left to spend the holidays with. I saw no reason not to ask her to join me at the cabin this week."

Sloan knew the silence on Garth's end meant his oldest brother was analyzing what he'd said. So that Garth's thoughts wouldn't be headed in the wrong direction, Sloan added, "I could never love Leslie again."

"So, the two of you are merely friends."

Sloan frowned. *Friends? Not hardly.* "In all honesty, Garth, I can't rightly say I even consider her a friend. She is nothing more than my business partner. Not the first time I've invited a business partner to the cabin."

"Yes, but the others were business partners who were also relatives, like Cole, Quade and the other Westmorelands. No woman has spent time with you at the cabin before, Sloan."

"How would you know?"

"I just do. Are you denying it?"

It was times like this when he wished his brother didn't know him so well. "There is nothing between me and Leslie, Garth."

"If you say so."

"I do say so, and there's no reason I shouldn't," Sloan said, ready to end the call.

"I hope you know what you're doing."

"Trust me, Garth, I know exactly what I'm doing."

"I just hope whatever plan you've concocted doesn't backfire on you."

Sloan lifted a brow. "Meaning what?"

"That you fall in love with her all over again. I know how much you loved her before."

Yes, of all people, Garth would know. He'd been the one to pull Sloan out of the pain and misery when Leslie had left. "Trust me, it won't happen. There is no way I can or will love her again."

"Possibly, however, I think you have forgotten something."

Sloan frowned. "What?"

"You should have told Leslie that her friend had come on to you, Sloan. Had you told her, there's a good chance she would not have believed the lie that woman told her. As far as I'm concerned, you share the blame for what happened."

You share the blame...

A short while later, Sloan was thinking about the words Garth had spoken as he sat on the sofa, slowly drinking his beer while watching Leslie decorate the tree. She was deliberately ignoring him, but he didn't mind, because he definitely wasn't ignoring her. Far from it. He was sitting with his legs stretched out in front of him, and he couldn't take his eyes off her. He was tuned in to every movement she made as she decorated the tree.

She wasn't trying to draw his attention. In fact, he would bet money she would have preferred he was someplace else, instead of sitting there, with a front-row view of what she was doing. Especially when he wasn't saying anything but pretending to listen to the Christmas music playing on her cell phone while she went about her business hanging ornaments on the tree. Where in the world had all that stuff come from?

"You're frowning, Sloan. Don't you like how the tree is taking shape so far?"

He blinked upon realizing what she'd said. "The tree is looking good," he said, as if the tree and not her had been holding his attention all this time. "I was just wondering where all this stuff came from. You had all this stuff left over after decorating your own tree?"

"No."

"Then you went out and bought all this stuff." It was a statement more than a question, since it was the most logical one.

"That's precisely what I did. And my suitcase was mostly filled with decorations."

"You didn't mention anything about having a tree until

we were on our way to the airport yesterday. What made you think I would go along with it?"

"I saw no reason why you wouldn't."

Yes, he could see her thinking that way. In the past he'd been known to give in to anything she'd wanted. It wasn't that she'd asked for much, and most of the time she asked only to help others. But whenever she did ask, he would move heaven and earth to give her whatever she wanted. That was then. So why would she think it would be the same now?

"The least you can do is flip the switch since I'm all finished now," she said, breaking into his thoughts.

She was staring up at the tree with a huge smile on her face, as if she was pleased with what she'd done. His gaze shifted off her to the tree. It looked good. "I assume you'll be taking this tree down before we leave here," he said, standing to move toward the light switch on the wall.

"Of course, but I don't plan to take all this stuff back to Wasilla with me."

He stopped walking and glanced over his shoulder at her. "What do you intend to do with it?"

"Leave it here. If someone else in your family decides to spend time here around the holidays and wants to put up a Christmas tree, then they will have the decorations to do so. It's my donation."

He couldn't see that happening but decided to let her think whatever she wanted. He flipped the light switch and watched as an even wider smile spread across Leslie's face when the tree came to life.

The tree wasn't overly done. Every ornament she'd selected was in the right place, and the lights seemed to illuminate the tree in a way that made his breath catch. At that moment, he wished more than just the bears could see her handiwork. There was no way anyone who saw this tree wouldn't eagerly anticipate the approaching holidays.

"It's beautiful, isn't it, Sloan?"

He shifted his gaze from the tree to her. The blinking lights seemed to say, "Look at me." And he was looking. Ten years ago, he had loved her to distraction, had wanted to make her a permanent part of his life, and now...

"The one thing I didn't get is a timer."

He lifted a brow at her comment. "A timer?"

"Yes. That way I could program the tree to come on and go off at certain times. Now we'll have to do it manually."

He shrugged. "That's not a problem."

"Glad you feel that way. I'm assigning you that job since you didn't help decorate."

He was about to tell her that anything dealing with the tree was her job since it was her idea, but he didn't want to ruin it for her. "Do you want me to prepare dinner, or are you still keen on the idea of doing all the cooking this week?" They had eaten leftover chili for lunch, and he'd told her more than once just how good it had been. But then, breakfast had been good as well.

"I'd like to prepare dinner if you don't have a problem with me doing so. However, if you ever want to spend time in the kitchen with me or without me, please let me know," she said.

She didn't have to worry about that happening. Had he been here alone, Sloan would have been just fine getting by on easy meals he could prepare quickly. But he wasn't here alone, and Leslie loved to cook and had a way of turning an easy meal into a masterpiece.

A short while later, he was back to sitting in front of the Christmas tree, watching the blinking lights while his ears picked up the sound of Leslie moving around in the kitchen as she prepared dinner. He didn't want to think that if things hadn't ended between them ten years ago, this could very well be the same scenario...with them here spending Christmas at the cabin. He'd like to think they would have had at least two or three kids by now. Maybe she would have a position in Outlaw Freight Lines or he a position at Cassidy Cosmetics. Hell, there was no reason they would not have been able to manage both.

While dating, they had never talked about marriage. He'd just assumed it was a foregone conclusion and figured she'd thought so as well. Proposing to her at this cabin would have been a surprise to her, but it was something he'd wanted to do for a long time. He had seen forever in their future. Not only had he seen it, but he had wanted it with a yearning that went down to the very core of his existence.

Sloan drew in a deep breath, trying to regain control of his thoughts and accept that none of those plans happened. He'd never gotten the chance to propose, and there was no forever for them. A part of him wished he could forget about their past and handle her like he would handle any other business partner. Just like he'd told Garth, Leslie wasn't the first business partner he'd invited to the cabin.

But Garth had been right as well when he'd said it wasn't the same. Sloan and Leslie had history. Personal history. He didn't want to think of what Garth's reaction would be if he knew why she was spending a week here, and the stipulation Sloan had placed on her to save her company.

You share the blame...

He rubbed his hand down his face, feeling like an ass. He'd had hopes for how this week was supposed to pan out. Granted Leslie had said she wouldn't be sleeping with him, but he'd felt the attraction that was still there between them, and he was banking on her feeling it, too.

Garth was right. Sloan did share the blame for their breakup. Just like she should have trusted him, he should have made her aware of the situation when that trust might be challenged.

Standing, he began pacing, deep in thought. After a short while, he knew there was only one thing to do. Over dinner he would tell her to pack up her things tonight so he could fly her back to Wasilla in the morning. He would no longer hold her to the proposition that had been part of his plan to settle a score. A vengeance he'd refused to acknowledge until now.

But what about him not wanting her to spend the holidays alone?

At that moment he decided Leslie spending the holidays alone was better than her spending them here with him for all the wrong reasons.

Thirteen

Leslie glanced across the table at Sloan. She had cooked baked salmon with cabbage, rolls and slices of Yukon Gold potatoes. She'd even made a berry pie for dessert. Although he seemed to be enjoying the dinner she'd prepared, he wasn't saying much. Something was up and she could sense it, but she had no idea what that something was. She knew better than to try to figure out Sloan or his mood.

After decorating the tree, she felt good. The last thing she wanted was for Sloan to put a damper on her own mood. She definitely had no plan to ruin it by engaging in any type of verbal sparring with him. After dinner she would do what she'd done last night, what she intended to do every night, which was to go into her bedroom, shower and then curl up with her e-reader.

"I made a decision about something an hour ago, Leslie."

She looked up from buttering her bread and held his gaze. "A decision about what?"

"It was a decision about you. I will no longer hold you to the stipulation that you be here this week."

What exactly was he saying? "Meaning what, Sloan?"

"Meaning you need to pack tonight, because I'm taking you back to Wasilla in the morning. Nothing will change as far as my being your business partner, but I will now admit what I asked you to do here was unfair."

Yes, it had been, and she couldn't help wondering what had made him realize it. "Like I told you, Sloan, I wasn't going to sleep with you anyway."

"I had hoped to seduce you."

Leslie frowned at him. He sounded so confident, as if he believed he would have been successful in doing so. Back in the day, when she was his girlfriend, he'd never had to seduce her into anything, because she'd always been willing and ready to share his bed. That was then and this was now. And now he wanted her gone, so she would never know the extent of his seduction skills.

"I'll start packing tonight and will be ready to leave in the morning," she said, standing. After walking over to the sink to place her dishes in it, she then walked out of the kitchen.

Deciding to take a shower before packing, she began stripping off her clothes. She liked this cabin, and although leaving here was the last thing she honestly wanted to do, maybe it was for the best. Sloan obviously thought so.

In the privacy of the shower, while water cascaded down her naked body, she closed her eyes and remembered those times when she and Sloan would shower together. Recalling how he would touch her all over, fill her with an intensity of sexual longing and desire she hadn't felt in years.

Showering with him was something she'd always looked forward to doing. The last time it had been in a hotel room the night before he was to fly out to prepare the cabin for their upcoming spring break week. The reason she hadn't left when he had was because of an exam in one of her classes.

Because Redford and Tyler had been Sloan's roommates at his apartment, and Sarah had been hers, the only time they'd had any privacy was when Sloan reserved a hotel room for them. He'd done that a lot because he'd said he wanted them to spend as much private time together as possible.

Although her father had been disappointed in her decision to spend spring break with Sloan instead of coming home, he had understood. He'd known how much she loved Sloan, and after meeting Sloan, he was convinced Sloan loved her, too.

Getting out the shower, she dried off while thinking Sloan would never know how hard it had been to decorate that tree with his eyes on her the entire time. She had tried to ignore him, had refused to look over at him, but she had been conscious of him sitting there, his masculine scent and the vibes she'd felt emitting from him.

Had he felt the strong sexual chemistry between them, too? Was that why he'd decided to take her away? Had he seen seducing her as a double-edged sword? Would he be tempting himself as well?

It truly didn't matter what had made him change his mind. He no longer wanted her here, and she didn't want to be here.

But, as she slipped into her nightgown, she knew that was a lie. She had begun looking forward to spending time here this week. She loved the cabin, she loved the tree, she loved being able to clear her mind of Cassidy Cosmetics business and do something she hadn't done in a while, which was read for pleasure.

She didn't want to think about returning home to spend the rest of the holidays alone. It was the new normal, and one she needed to get used to.

Leslie pulled her luggage from underneath the bed and then she heard the knock on her bedroom door. She wondered if Sloan had changed his mind and had decided not to wait until morning but to take her home tonight. "Just a minute."

Grabbing her bathrobe off the bed, she quickly put it on and tightened the belt around her waist before opening the door. Sloan stood there, frowning.

"What do you want, Sloan?"

"Forget about packing. There's no way I can take you home tomorrow."

She crossed her arms over her chest and frowned back at him. "And why not?"

"I just got a call from Walker. In case I hadn't been paying attention to the weather reports, he wanted to let me know about the severe snowstorm headed this way. It's the worst this area has seen in years."

Sloan figured Leslie wouldn't be happy about the forecast, but instead of disappointment in her expression, he saw concern.

"Is there anything we need to do tonight, Sloan? Are you sure the generator will work? Do you have any idea how long the snowstorm is expected to last? Do we have enough chopped wood for the fireplace? Do we—"

"Whoa, Leslie. Slow down. We'll get through this. Yes, the generator will work. Not sure how long the storm will last, but I'm hoping it will blow over in a few days. Yes, there's plenty of chopped wood, and yes, there are a few things you can help me do to get prepared."

"What?" she asked, and he could hear the eagerness to help in her voice.

"I'm going outside to put the car in the garage and to cover everything that needs to be protected. I'd like you to go around and gather the candles and matches. There's also batteries and mobile phone chargers in the closet at the end of the hallway."

"Okay."

"And since it's best not to run a generator overnight, we'll need to sleep in front of the fireplace for heat. That means we need to grab sleeping bags and blankets from that hall closet."

"Separate sleeping bags, of course."

"Of course," he said, somewhat annoyed she'd think he would take advantage of the situation.

"Give me a few minutes to get dressed and I'll get to everything right away."

An hour later, Sloan had done all the outside chores that needed to be done and had also brought in more wood for the fireplace. He'd noted that snow had already begun falling, and there was an increase in wind coming off the strait. He'd weathered harsh snowstorms before. You couldn't live in Alaska without having experienced a few; however, he had a feeling the one headed their way was a doozy.

As he bent down to add more wood to the box next to the fireplace, he could hear Leslie moving around in the kitchen. He couldn't help thinking about the fresh-showered Leslie who'd opened her bedroom door earlier. She had smelled good and had looked even better in her robe. First time he'd ever seen her in one. There was a time when she'd been comfortable wearing very little around him or nothing at all after a shower. He'd noted during one of his wood-toting trips into the house that she'd changed into a pair of jogging pants and a sweatshirt. She looked good in that, too.

"I pulled water bottles out of the cabinet and loaded them into one of the coolers filled with ice, Sloan."

He glanced up to see the subject of his thoughts standing beside him as he knelt in front of the fireplace. "That's a good idea," he said. "Glad you thought of it."

"Can you think of anything else you need me to do?" she asked.

He broke eye contact with her to poke at the fire. "I can't think of anything at the moment."

His phone rang, and he stood to pull it out of his back pocket. "Yes, Garth?"

"Regan and I are looking at the report on the weather channel. Sounds like pretty bad weather headed your way. You're ready to hunker down for a while?"

"Ready as we'll ever be, Garth. Leslie and I will be just fine." He saw the lifting of Leslie's brow. Did it bother her that Garth knew she was there with him?

"Well, take care and I'll check on you guys tomorrow," Garth said, reclaiming Sloan's attention.

"The wind is pretty high outside. If you can't reach us, it might be the result of too much wind near the towers."

"Okay, I'll keep that in mind. I'll call and check on Walker, Bailey and the twins now. Tell Leslie hello."

Sloan ended the call with his brother and put the phone back into his pocket. "Garth says hello."

"He knows I'm here?" Leslie asked.

"Yes. Is there a reason why he shouldn't?"

She shook her head. "No, there's no reason. I'll make us some hot chocolate."

He nodded, appreciating that she remembered how much he liked the stuff. "Thanks. I have a feeling it's going to be a hot chocolate kind of night."

"I have that same feeling," she said, and then he watched her turn and walk off toward the kitchen.

Sloan rubbed his hand down his face. A turbulent Alaska snowstorm was headed their way, and of all things, he was stranded here alone with Leslie.

Fourteen

The sound of doors opening and closing brought Leslie awake. She lay there a moment and recalled the night before and how they'd prepared for the oncoming storm. Jumping out of bed, she raced to the window. A thick blanket of snow covered everything, and it was still coming down hard. She could barely see past where she knew the detached storage shed was. There was no doubt in her mind the temperature had dipped a lot lower than it had been when she'd finally gone to bed.

After pouring cups of hot chocolate for her and Sloan, they had then worked together to prepare things. She had followed him to the underground tunnel…at least that's what Sloan had called it. To Leslie it looked more like a man cave, with living quarters that included a flat-screen television, wet bar and a wall filled with a collection of bottles of wine.

To not overwork the generator, they had removed all electrical items that had been plugged in and made sure the doors were secured. Then they had carried more blankets and sleeping bags from one of the closets to the fireplace.

It had been close to two in the morning before they'd said good-night and gone to their individual bedrooms. She was certain that as soon as her head touched the pillow, she'd fallen asleep.

Moving away from the window, she returned to the bed and picked up her cell phone off the nightstand. She was glad it was still working. Sloan had warned her that even with the tower that had been installed, they might lose reception due to the strong winds. So far they hadn't, although it was taking longer than usual to make a connection to the weather app. The temperature had dropped ten degrees from where it had been when she'd gone to bed.

When she heard another door opening and then closing, she knew Sloan was already up. Glancing over at the clock, she saw it was almost nine and then realized she had forgotten to set the alarm. Her goal had been to be up by seven.

Moving quickly, she made the bed and then rushed to the bathroom for her morning shower, hoping Sloan had the coffee going.

Sloan's plan had been to return her to Wasilla today. Now they were stranded and had no choice but to make the most of it. Since the cabin was ready for the worst, he would probably start ignoring her. She noted he hadn't had a lot to say last night, even as they'd worked together to get things prepared.

A short while later, she had showered and dressed and was halfway to the kitchen when her nose picked up the aroma of coffee. Entering the kitchen, she saw him leaning against a kitchen counter sipping a cup. "Good morning, Sloan."

"Good morning, Leslie. I got your oatmeal ready."

"You didn't have to do that."

"I figured it was the least I could do since you prepared such a delicious breakfast yesterday. I recalled how much you like the stuff."

She went to the cabinet to grab a bowl, trying not to notice how good he looked in a pair of sweatpants with a matching sweatshirt that advertised Outlaw Freight Lines. He'd given her an OFL T-shirt years ago. It had been two sizes too large, and for years it had been the perfect sleep shirt. "You got up early."

"I doubt if I even slept. I lay there remembering stuff I should have done. So I got up and filled the tubs in the other bathrooms with water and went outside a few times to make sure the pipes were sufficiently covered."

"I see," she said, going to sit at the table after filling her bowl with oatmeal and grabbing a box of raisins. She was surprised when Sloan joined her at the table after refilling his cup.

"You started a trend with my siblings with that, you know."

She lifted a brow. "Oatmeal and raisins?"

"Yes. To this day it's Charm's favorite breakfast meal. She even has the old man eating it."

Leslie couldn't help but smile. "It's a good meal to add to anyone's diet. You even liked it yourself."

"Only because you liked it. There was a time I liked anything you liked."

She didn't know what to say to that, so she said nothing. Sloan in turn sat across from her and drank his coffee. He definitely appeared in a better mood this morning than he had been last evening.

As tempted as she was to glance over at him, she didn't. She couldn't. Nothing looked sexier than Sloan Outlaw when he needed a shave. Just thinking about tracing her palm across that bearded jaw had warmth seeping between her legs.

"Why didn't you return to Alaska after completing your studies at Howard, Leslie?" he broke into her thoughts to ask.

His question did make her look up. Did he really want to talk about that time in their past? If so, why? But since he'd asked, she would give him an answer. Even if it was the one she'd convinced herself she believed.

"Aunt Ella was getting up in age, and after she had a nasty fall that required months in rehab, Dad felt having me there with her was far more important than returning home."

There was no need to tell him that even after her aunt had fully recuperated, Leslie hadn't rushed back to Alaska because she'd still been suffering from a broken heart. It was only after she'd discovered the truth of Sarah's lies that she had given thought to returning home. She'd known at some point she couldn't move on without seeking Sloan out and apologizing for believing the worst about him.

He took another sip of his coffee and then asked, "Did you enjoy living in the nation's capital?"

She shrugged. "It was interesting and definitely different. It always amused me when the first drop in temperature caused people to panic. And their major snowstorms weren't anything compared to ours, that's for sure. But there were more nice days than not, and it's a beautiful place."

After taking a sip of her own coffee, she added, "I'm sure now that you have a brother who's a United States senator, you've visited there a lot."

"Not a lot, but enough. Jess has a nice place on the Potomac. And I agree about the weather. I also like its proximity to New York."

He didn't say anything for a while, and the room was quiet except for the howling of the wind and the rustling sound of snow falling. It wasn't even lunchtime yet, but the amount of snow falling made it appear dark outside, robbing them of their few hours of daylight. She was about to stand and take her empty bowl over to the sink when Sloan's next words stopped her.

"I need to know something, Leslie."

She could tell from the tone of his voice that whatever he needed to know was serious. Drawing in a deep breath, she asked, "What is it that you want to know, Sloan?"

He held her gaze. "How could you have thought I betrayed you with Sarah?"

A part of Sloan wanted to bite off his tongue for even asking, when he'd told himself over the years that he hadn't given a damn. He still didn't, but he figured at the moment, anything was better than his mind being preoccupied with that phone call he'd received from Cole before daybreak this morning, detailing new developments about Martin Longshire.

Just as Sloan had suspected, the man was trying to go after several of Sloan's companies with hostile takeover attempts. All it had taken was Sloan to make a couple of calls to his attorneys to turn the tables on Longshire once again. This time Sloan had left no doubt in anyone's mind, especially Longshire's, that compared to Sloan's wealth, Longshire was a pauper. Fearing Sloan would retaliate with a countertakeover, the stockholders of the Longshire Industries had demanded that Longshire step down as CEO immediately and take early retirement. It was basically the same type of ultimatum the board at Outlaw Freight Lines had given Bart.

"At the time it all seemed pretty clear," Leslie said, intruding into his thoughts. "You weren't returning my calls. And Sarah had what I thought was proof that you were texting and calling her and not me. The text messages she let me read were supposedly from you, begging her not to tell me what happened that night between the two of you, that it had been a mistake I didn't need to know about. I saw the text messages, Sloan. What was I supposed to believe?"

He tried to keep the anger from his voice when he said, "You should have believed that no matter what those text messages said, there was no way I could have slept with her."

"Even when you didn't return my call, I refused to believe it…until she provided proof."

"Those text messages and documentation of phone calls weren't proof of anything. Anyone can assign someone's name to a contact in their phone. Although it said the person making the calls and sending those text messages was me, it could have been made up."

"You think I didn't know that? That's why I tried calling you. But I couldn't reach you."

"The reason you couldn't reach me was because there was no reception at the cabin. That's why I didn't get your call." He rubbed his hand down his face and said, "But then, I can't fully place the blame solely on you, Leslie, since I should have told you."

He saw the confusion in her eyes. "You should have told me what?"

Sloan hesitated and then said, "That Sarah made a couple of passes at me before."

"What! And you didn't tell me about that?"

"I didn't tell you because I thought I had handled the situation. The first time she did it, I thought it was just her being flirty."

Leslie leaned over the table. "What exactly did she do?"

"She copped a feel of my ass. It happened at that birthday party Keosha gave for Tyler. I figured Sarah had had one drink too many. But then one day I stopped by your apartment and you weren't there. She invited me to come in and wait for you, claimed you had just made a quick trip to the store. That's when she tried coming on to me again. This time she was sober."

Leslie crossed her arms over her chest. "And just what did she do?"

He wished when she'd placed her hands across her chest the action didn't reveal a pair of full breasts he used to enjoy sucking.

"Sloan? What did she do?"

Bringing his focus back to her question, he said, "She tried to kiss me. It pissed me off, and I told her in no uncertain terms I didn't appreciate it and not to ever do it again. She began crying and apologized and said she wasn't sure what had gotten into her and promised it wouldn't happen again. She asked me not to mention it to you because she didn't want to lose your friendship."

Fire appeared in Leslie's eyes. "Well, she would have definitely lost my friendship. I could see you ignoring that time she was drunk, but not the time she tried to kiss you. You should have told me, Sloan."

He rubbed his hands down his face. "I told you why I didn't tell you. She started crying and apologized, Leslie. She said it wouldn't happen again, and I believed her. I saw her a number of times after that whenever I came to see you, and she never tried anything else. In fact, she went out of her way to avoid me. I had no reason to think she would have done it again or anything else remotely as devious."

"But she did, didn't she?" she snapped. "You should have told me. If you had told me, at least I would have been prepared for the lies. Thanks to you, I wasn't, and you had the audacity to get mad because I believed her?"

"Yes, I still felt you should have trusted me."

"But there was no reason for me not to believe her, Sloan. She probably felt emboldened knowing you hadn't told me about the incident, just like she'd asked you, which was why she decided to carry things further. Those text messages alone weren't what made me break things off with you and leave school. What hurt me more than anything was finding those panties."

Frowning, he sat up straight in his chair. "What panties?"

"*Her* panties. According to Sarah, that weekend I went out of town with the debate team, you offered her a ride home when you stopped by the café where she worked at closing time. Instead of taking her straight to our apartment, you took her somewhere for drinks. She claimed the two of you had a little too much to drink and decided to sober up in the parking lot instead of immediately driving home. She said one thing led to another, and the next thing she knew the two of you were making out in your car, right there in the parking lot."

"And you believed that?" he asked incredulously.

"I didn't until she told me where to find her panties. In your car. And I did find them, Sloan. They were just where she said they would be—stuffed under the cushion in the back seat."

Sloan stared at Leslie. This part about Sarah planting a pair of her panties in his car was news to him. How could she have done that when she'd never ridden in his car before? When he'd left for the cabin, he had left his car with Leslie. She had driven him to the airport and three days later was to use his car to drive herself there. She was to leave it parked at the airport when she caught the plane to join him in Kodiak. "If that's true, I have no idea how they got there. You had the car while I was gone. Did you ever give her a lift somewhere?"

Leslie shook her head. "No."

"Then she apparently got the keys without you knowing and put them there."

He watched her draw in a deep breath. "I guess that's what she did, Sloan. All I know is that night when I ran into her in LA, she'd been drinking, and that's when she told me the truth. She wanted me to know the text messages and panties had been used to deliberately break us up, and she even seemed pretty damn happy about it. Sarah showed no remorse at all and didn't say why she'd done it. I wish you had told me about her coming on to you. You didn't, and I was blindsided."

"You didn't have to leave town without telling me where you'd gone, Leslie. You could have confronted me about Sarah's lies when you saw me at the cabin."

She didn't say anything for a minute. "I felt I had to leave, Sloan. Sarah claimed the only reason she was finally leveling with me about what the two of you had done was because she'd missed her period, and if she was pregnant, the baby was yours."

"What!"

"Yes, that's what she told me. And just the thought of her having your baby was something I couldn't handle. I refused to stay around to find out if she was pregnant or not."

Sarah's lies had been deeper than he'd known. All this time he had assumed Leslie had left because of fake text messages and phone calls. "When did you find out she didn't have my baby?"

"I figured it was a false alarm when Keosha never mentioned anything whenever I talked to her."

"Did Keosha know the full extent of Sarah's lies?"

Leslie shook her head. "No. I never told her about anything but the text messages and phone calls. I made Keosha promise not to bring up your name in any of our conversations."

Sloan rubbed his hand behind his neck, feeling tension building there. He'd made Tyler and Redford promise the same thing about Leslie. The kitchen got quiet as she stood, and he watched her carry her bowl to the sink and rinse it out before putting it in the dishwasher. Then, without even looking at him, she walked out of the kitchen.

Sloan opened his mouth to call her back but then clamped it shut. She was right, and he couldn't argue the point. He should have told her about Sarah coming on to him. Because he hadn't, she hadn't known just what a vile person Sarah Olsen truly was.

Hell, he hadn't known. He'd honestly believed Sarah had regretted her actions. In the end, he'd been wrong. Sloan knew he couldn't fault Leslie for being taken in by the woman, because in the end, he had been fooled by her as well.

Fifteen

Leslie entered her bedroom, closing the door behind her, and began pacing the floor. She was upset knowing Sarah had come on to Sloan and he hadn't told her about it. Granted, that first time might have been due to her over-drinking like he'd assumed, but that second time should have set off red flags. Flags he should have told her about.

She glanced toward the door when she heard the knock. Knowing it was Sloan, she took her time moving to the door, not sure she wanted to see him. Opening the door, she raked her gaze over him as he stood with his hands shoved in the pockets of his jeans.

"What is it, Sloan?"

"Now it's me who owes you an apology, Leslie. I apologize."

She actually heard regret in his voice, and as she studied his features, she saw regret there as well. A part of her didn't want to accept his apology, but then, hadn't he accepted hers? And she couldn't dismiss the fact that he hadn't known about the panties or Sarah's claim of a possible pregnancy. Now that he did, she hoped he understood why she had been hurt to the point of needing to put distance between them. Why she had left school the way she had and forbidden her father to tell him where she'd gone.

Drawing in a deep breath, she said, "I accept your apology, Sloan. It seems we both could have handled things differently."

They hadn't, and it had cost them ten years. But then, maybe it hadn't been meant for them to be together for the long haul. Maybe it was only meant for him to be someone who would occupy her heart for a short while. That time had come and gone, and she knew it could never be recaptured again. She figured he knew it as well.

"Do you honestly accept my apology, Leslie?"

Leslie narrowed her gaze at him. "Just as much as you honestly accepted mine at the wedding."

It was easy to see her words had hit home, which let her know she'd been right. Although he'd told her he had accepted her apology that day, and while he'd reached out to her to help save her company, he'd still intended to exact his form of revenge as well. That made her wonder if helping to save her company had been as honorable as she'd assumed. Was there an ulterior motive for that as well?

She dismissed the thought. He might have not truly accepted her apology, but she believed getting her to sleep with him again was as far as he would have taken any retaliation he might have implemented. Nothing could convince her that helping to save her company wasn't aboveboard. He would not have taken things that far.

"Now, if you don't mind, there's a book I'd like to finish reading."

He nodded. "Do you want to cook dinner today, or would you prefer I take care of it?"

"I'll prepare something later."

"All right."

He walked off, and she closed the door. Leslie had barely made it across the room when the lights flickered and then they lost power for barely a minute. When the lights came back on, she knew the generator had kicked in. But like Sloan had told her, the generator had to be turned off at night. That meant to preserve heat, they would be sharing a spot in front of the fireplace tonight. She wasn't sure how she felt about that.

Leslie hoped the weather would improve by tomorrow and then she could be on her way. She didn't want to spend any more time than necessary with Sloan, and she was certain he felt the same about her.

Sloan looked up when Leslie entered the living room. "I see that we've lost power," she said.

"Yeah," he replied, following her gaze out the window. The high winds were causing sheets of ice to hit against it. It was like something out of a bad movie. He'd been expecting bad weather, but not to this degree. "I'm surprised the power lasted as long as it did," he said.

"Any idea how long this storm will last?"

He shook his head. "I don't have a clue. Even the tower isn't working, which means we can't send or receive calls. Last weather report I saw indicates we haven't been hit with the worst of it yet. To preserve the generator, we need to turn it off around seven."

"Then let me start dinner."

"And while you're doing that, I need to go outside and check around to make sure things are still covered."

"You're really going out in that, Sloan?" Leslie asked him in an incredulous voice, placing her hands on her hips.

He tried not to notice how good she looked standing there in her jeans and sweatshirt. "Yes. The wind is so high it might have blown something off, and I need to check while there's still a little daylight." He walked over to the hall closet and grabbed his coat, hat and gloves.

"How long will you be gone?"

Sloan was sliding into his coat when he met her eyes. "Probably no more than twenty minutes. I'll be back before you know it."

"Please be careful."

Was that concern he heard in her voice? He smiled at her, hoping that would assure her he would be fine. "I will," he said, putting on his gloves. "Do me a favor and have a cup of hot chocolate ready when I get back."

"I can do better than that. I'll also make sandwiches to go along with the hot chocolate."

He gave her a thumbs-up as he headed for the door, bracing himself against the wind that had gotten stronger over the past hours. One of Maverick's bright ideas had been to place heated planks in front of the door. That way snow wouldn't block the opening or closing of the door.

The moment he stepped outside, the freezing temperature cut him to the core. Shouldering his body against the snow and winds, he headed toward where the pipes were located to make sure they were still properly covered. It was cold as the dickens, and he figured if he thought about Leslie—specifically, how good she looked and how nice she smelled—it would warm up his insides somewhat.

After checking the pipes as well as several pieces of machinery to make sure they could continue to withstand the wind and snow, he was headed back toward the house when he noticed that a huge tree limb had blown to the ground, too close to the generator to suit him. Deciding to move the limb out of the way, he began tackling the job and discovered the limb was heavier than he'd thought. It ended up taking a lot longer than planned, but he had finally dragged it back to what he considered a safe distance.

He was about to head back toward the cabin when another huge tree branch came flying toward him like a missile. While ducking, he slipped on a patch of ice, and fell flat to the ground, the wind knocked out of him. It took him a few minutes to regain his strength enough to pull himself up to his knees. That's when he felt a pounding pain in his head and figured he hadn't moved quick enough. A part of the tree branch had struck the side of his head.

He was determined to get back to the cabin, though his head was hurting even more. Forcing himself to stand, he felt somewhat dizzy. When he felt himself getting lethargic, he pushed himself to continue walking as snow thickened even more around him.

Sloan knew the cabin should be close. If he could just ignore the cold and the pain, he would be fine. It was getting dark, and he wasn't even sure he was going in the right direction. The falling snow made it nearly impossible to see in front of him, but he had to keep moving and hoped he was going east and not west.

At that moment he wasn't sure of anything other than he was freezing cold and needed to get warm fast. He then thought of Leslie. The thought of never seeing her again shifted the pain from his head to his chest and close to his heart. He wasn't sure why, but it had.

He pushed his way forward, shivering from the inside out, yet determined to find his way back to Leslie.

Leslie stopped pacing long enough to check her watch. The house was quiet except for the sound of the sleet hitting the windows. It was getting dark. Sloan had said it wouldn't take him any longer than twenty minutes and he'd been gone close to an hour. Why hadn't he come back yet?

She glanced over at the cups of hot chocolate and the two sandwiches wrapped in cellophane. The hot chocolate had gone cold, and when he returned she would have to make some more. There was no problem if she had to do that, she just wanted him safe. Leaving the kitchen, she went to the living room window and practically pressed her face against it. She could barely see past the porch for all the snow that was falling. Glancing at her watch again, she decided to give Sloan ten more minutes. If he wasn't back by then, she would go looking for him. The wind had gotten louder, and the snow was falling more heavily.

Leslie began pacing again, getting more worried by the minute, especially when the wind outside sounded even more fierce. Deciding not to wait any longer, she went to the hall closet and pulled out her boots, coat, hat and gloves. She also grabbed a flashlight.

She was met with freezing temperatures the moment she opened the door, and she was tempted to go back inside. She could barely see beyond the porch, but she refused to turn around. To get her bearings for a moment, she huddled in the corner near the porch swing before pushing herself forward.

She called out for him but soon discovered her voice was drowned out by the sound of rushing winds. She hesitated before stepping off the porch, holding on to the rail as she did so. The wind was so strong she was convinced it could sweep her away easily, and the snow was coming down even more.

The flashlight helped. She wished Sloan had taken it with him. Since it had still been daylight when he'd left the cabin, he hadn't done so. Now it was dark. She stopped walking when she thought she heard a sound.

What had Sloan told her about bears? He claimed his property was bearproof and that most bears hibernated during the winter months. Even if the sound she'd heard wasn't a bear, it could be some other kind of animal. Like a moose. A very unfriendly moose. Or an even larger bison.

Refusing to give in to her fears, she began walking

again, or else her feet would get frozen in place. Taking a chance, she called out to Sloan again in the loudest voice she could. Her eyebrows went up when she thought she heard a deep groan coming from the direction where she'd heard the sound earlier. She had a feeling what she'd heard wasn't a bear or any other animal but was Sloan. She called out to him again, and when she didn't hear anything, she braved the weather to move in that direction.

Moments later, she found him, leaning against the side of a tree. When she shined the flashlight on his face, she saw a bruise near his left eye. "Sloan! What happened?" she asked, reaching him.

"I got hit in the head with a flying branch and then I slipped and fell," he said in a shivering and slurred voice. "I need to get to the cabin. I'm almost frozen."

She saw that he was, and that wasn't good. "Lean against me, and we'll go back together."

"I'm too heavy, Leslie."

"No, you're not, so do what you're told, Sloan."

It must have been the tone of her voice. All she knew was that when she wrapped her arms around him, he leaned against her, and when they began walking, she slowed her pace to keep up with his steps. She then led him toward the area from where she'd come. She supported his weight and he supported hers as together they slowly moved toward the cabin.

"Are you sure we're going in the right direction?" he asked in a voice that shivered.

"Positive."

"Did you throw down bread crumbs?"

Leslie couldn't help but smile. In college, more than once, she'd gotten lost on campus while walking from one building to another. Jokingly, Sloan had suggested that she throw down bread crumbs to find her way. "Not this time."

Moments later, she said, "We're here."

"We're here?"

She could hear the surprise and gratitude in his voice. "Yes, Sloan, we're here."

Once they walked through the cabin door, Leslie knew her work had just begun. First thing she needed to do was get Sloan warmed up and then check his injuries. He had been out there a long time, and she needed to look for hypothermia and frostbite. She was grateful she'd been a Girl Scout back in the day.

They made it to the sofa. She checked the knot on his head and then raced to the kitchen for the first-aid kit. She made sure he took a couple of aspirin for the pain and determined there was no frostbite. But she needed to get him warm.

He assisted her in removing his wet clothes, and then she quickly removed hers. There was no time to be modest, since they'd both seen the other naked a number of times, although not recently. The important thing was getting dry as quickly as possible to share body heat.

Luckily for them the fire was blazing in the fireplace. Wrapping themselves in a sleeping bag and blankets, they lay down in front of it. She wished she could ignore the naked body plastered to hers that was shivering profusely. Hopefully, their bodies' heat would stop any hypothermia. She had taken a quick look at the knot on the side of his head. She needed to watch for any signs of a possible concussion, which meant waking him up periodically.

The feel of his hard body pressed against her back and his arms across her waist felt comforting. She didn't want to think of what the outcome could have been if she hadn't gone looking for him. From the way he was shivering, he was still cold, but the body pressed against hers was beginning to feel warm.

His arms tightened around her, and his body shifted slightly to whisper in her ear, "Thank you, Leslie."

The huskiness of his voice made certain parts of her tingle. "Don't mention it, Sloan."

She lay there, cuddled in his arms inside the sleeping bag, as they continued to share heat. She was facing the fireplace, and for the longest time she watched the blazing wood, trying to recall the last time she'd slept naked in his arms. It had been the day before he was to leave to come here and prepare this same cabin for their week during spring break. They had made love most of the night and again that morning before she'd taken him to the airport. That had also been the last time she'd seen him until she'd run into him at Tyler and Keosha's wedding.

Leslie thought about all they'd discovered about what happened ten years ago, since being here. Lies she thought he'd known about, only to discover he hadn't. Their one accomplishment was realizing they both had contributed to their breakup. They had played right into Sarah's hands, and she felt herself getting angry just thinking about it.

As for Sloan, she had no idea what he was thinking. Was he also remembering the last time their bodies had fit this snugly? When she heard Sloan's even breathing, she knew he had drifted off to sleep, which meant he wasn't thinking at all.

Leslie wished she could say the same about herself, but she was thinking and doing a lot of it. What if she hadn't gone looking for Sloan? What if he'd been injured far worse than he had? What if he'd gotten frostbite and needed extreme medical care and she couldn't give it to him or expect anyone to come out in this weather? What if…

She closed her eyes, not wanting to think about all the things that could possibly have gone wrong. Instead, she focused on all the things that had gone right. He was back in the cabin and safe.

They might have been apart for ten years, but she

knew some things hadn't changed. And that included her love for him.

Yes, she still loved Sloan, and it had taken almost losing him to make her realize that. She also knew he'd seen her leaving him ten years ago as no different than the way his own mother had deserted him. He had shared with Leslie how he'd felt about his mother's desertion, how it had affected him, although he knew he'd had a better life without her.

And Leslie knew he couldn't trust her after what had happened ten years ago. More than anything she wished she had more time with Sloan, but she knew that wouldn't be the case. There was no doubt in her mind, when the weather cleared up he would be taking her back to Wasilla as planned. She knew it, and although she wished otherwise, she accepted it. She'd appreciate having him here with her for as long as the weather lasted.

Sixteen

Sloan slowly opened his eyes as his gaze skimmed over the woman who slept snuggled beside him in the sleeping bag. She lay pressed close to him in the spoon position with one of his legs thrown over her thigh. She smelled good and was very much naked. But then, so was he. How did this happen when Leslie had made it pretty damn clear they would have separate sleeping bags? More importantly, how could he have slept naked with her all through the night and not…

Suddenly, memories of the day before flooded his mind. Leslie had awakened him periodically due to a possible concussion. He even recalled her shoving more aspirin and water down his throat each time she did so. And then he'd dozed back off.

Clearly his mind had been fuzzy for him not to fully realize Leslie was sleeping with him naked. He knew the sharing of body heat was the best way to ward off hypothermia, but he honestly would not have thought she would have gone that far. But she had. The proof was that she was sleeping in his arms without a stitch of clothing on.

Forcing that thought from his mind, he glanced across the room to look out the window. From the sound of it, the wind was still howling, and it seemed snow was still coming down hard. The timer had kicked on, and the generator was back on for the next twelve hours.

"You're awake."

He looked down at Leslie, and all kinds of sensations floated around in his chest. He'd forgotten how sexy a just-waking-up Leslie looked. "Yes, I'm awake."

She shifted to face him. "How do you feel? Does your head hurt?"

Before he could answer, she reached up to place the back of her hand against his forehead. He recalled that was something else she'd done a number of times during the night, to check his temperature. As far as how he felt, it wasn't *this* head that was pounding, but the one between his legs pressing against her. There was no way she couldn't feel his leg or his erection...with the both of them being naked and all.

"No, I'm fine. Actually, I'm feeling a lot better," he said, trying to sound convincing.

"It's time for more aspirin," she said, reaching to grab the pill bottle off the coffee table, along with a bottle of water. Her movement shifted their bodies, but he still managed to keep his leg over hers. And it seemed his erection was determined not to go anywhere, either.

Shifting his body somewhat, he took the aspirin and water, downing both while holding her gaze. He handed the glass back to her. "I guess I'll live," he said, grinning.

"You better. Now I'll go fix that hot chocolate you didn't get to enjoy yesterday. I trashed the sandwiches but will be glad to make you an omelet."

Forget about whatever meal he'd missed yesterday. His

thoughts were on what he could enjoy this morning. Right at this moment. "Can you wait on the hot chocolate and omelet a minute? There's something I need to ask you."

A wary look appeared in her eyes. Did she honestly think he would ask her for sex? If she recalled, whenever they made love, it had been because the sexual chemistry between them had been overwhelming. He was attracted to her now, and the sexual chemistry was strong. However, he wasn't sure it was mutual.

"What do you want to ask me, Sloan?"

He drew in a deep breath. "I need to know what made you come looking for me last night."

She broke eye contact with him and glanced out the window, not saying anything for a moment. "You were gone longer than you said you would be. I got worried. It was either go see what was taking you so long or pace the floor worrying even more. I chose the former."

"But the weather had turned into a blizzard, Les." He then realized he'd called her what he'd normally called her while they'd been together. She had been Les and not Leslie.

"I know that. I also knew you were out there in it. I tried to convince myself that you could take care of yourself, but I also knew with the amount of wind blowing and snow coming down that anything could have happened."

She paused again before saying, "Chances are, you would have made it back to the cabin, but I couldn't risk the chance you would not have."

He tried not to concentrate on the sadness he heard in her voice and saw in her eyes. Instead, he concentrated on her mouth and in doing so was reminded of just how it tasted. "Not sure if I would have made it back. My head was hurting, and it was getting harder and harder to make my body move because I was so cold. Hell, I wasn't even sure I was going in the right direction. I regret you put your own life at risk, but I'm damn glad you were there when I needed you."

"Just like you were there for me and my company when I needed you, Sloan," she said softly.

Her words made him realize that they'd been there for each other when it had mattered the most. He didn't want to think what would have been the outcome if he'd been at the cabin alone as originally planned and the snowstorm hit. Nor did he want to think what would have happened to her and her company if Redford hadn't told him what was going on. The potential outcome of either made him shiver.

"You're still cold. I'd better go and get that hot chocolate going," she said, shifting to get up and reaching for her clothes.

"Don't go yet," he said, not ready for any distance to be put between them or their bodies.

She glanced over at him. Their gazes held and then, as if she'd just noticed his erection pressing against her thigh, she said, "You do know the only reason why we're naked in this sleeping bag together, right?"

He nodded. "Yes. Because I needed your body's heat last night." He inched his mouth closer to hers and then said, "Only problem is, I still need your body's heat, Les. But now I need it for a totally different reason."

And then he leaned in and kissed her.

Leslie knew she should break off the kiss, pull herself out of Sloan's arms and put on clothes and head for the kitchen. But on the other hand, she didn't want to do any of those things. All she could think about was that she could have lost him. She forced the thought from her mind that she really didn't have him, because that didn't matter. No matter how he felt about her, she knew how she felt about him, and that was what mattered to her.

So instead of pulling away, she settled into the arms

holding her while he was giving her one hell of a hot, deep and thorough kiss. It was a kiss that had her sliding her arms around his neck and kissing him back like her life depended on it.

Every muscle in her body seemed to come alive beneath the onslaught of his mouth. It was different than the kiss they'd shared in North Pole under the Northern Lights. There was something more seductive about the way his mouth took hers, gliding his tongue over hers like he thought it belonged to him. She then felt the tightness of his arms around her as the kiss blazed heat into her.

Somehow during the kiss, they had wiggled their way out of the sleeping bag and were naked on top of it. When she felt his palm caress her nipples, she couldn't hold back her whimper. In the deep recesses of her mind, she thought about all the other times they'd made love, but then she pushed them away. This was a different time. Same man. What she felt now was even more powerful. Sloan was kissing her long, he was kissing her hard. He had her heart pounding in desire so strong she felt herself drowning in it.

Last night, she'd accepted the realization she still loved Sloan. And now in the brightness of a new day, she knew she had never wanted Sloan Outlaw more than she did at that very moment. She wanted him and she needed him. It didn't matter that there was no future for them, or that whenever the weather cleared, he would still be taking her home. At that moment, she needed the ultimate in sexual pleasure that only Sloan could give her.

Panting heavily, she broke off the kiss, and their eyes locked while they both fought to get their breathing under control. The eyes staring back at her were dark, hot and filled with more yearning than she'd ever seen in them. This Sloan was ten years older, which meant over the years his desire, wants and needs had changed. Could she handle this more experienced Sloan? A more important question to ask was…would she be enough for him?

He took her wrist and brought it to his lips to place a kiss there. Still holding her gaze, and as if he'd read her thoughts, he said, "I want you, Leslie. I want you more than I've wanted any woman. That hasn't changed."

His words managed to calm her rattled nerves and appease her unsettled mind. Yet heat flared through her. Was she imagining things, or were their heartbeats in sync? She could tell him that she wanted him more than she had any other man, and that since him there had been no one else. But then she figured that was something he didn't need to know right now—or possibly ever.

"Are you sure, Sloan? You said you wanted me for Christmas, but we both know when you said it, it was for all the wrong reasons."

"I still want you for Christmas, but now it's for all the right reasons. What I should be asking you is whether you want me. Do you, Les?" he asked while trailing the tip of his finger down her jaw to her throat.

His touch generated a hunger deep within her, and the eyes staring back at her were expressing a desire that was making her heart rate increase. Why was he calling her Les? Did he not know doing so brought back memories of a time when just the sound of him calling her that would send her body into a tailspin of longing?

"Les?"

"Yes, I want you, Sloan."

"And not because of the near trauma of last night, right?"

What was he asking her? Just what was he trying to get her to say? Maybe she should be the one asking him that, given the feel of the huge erection pressing against her thigh. "Do you want me because of last night?" She needed to know the answer to that as much as he did.

He shook his head. "No, that's not what this is about for me, and I don't want it to be what it's about for you, either."

She nibbled on her bottom lip, nearly too afraid to ask, but she did so anyway. "Then what should it be about?"

His fingers reached up to gently stroke her chin, and his touch nearly sent her over the edge. It increased the heat spreading through her body. "It's about two people who once cared a lot for each other, who allowed someone to destroy what they had. It's about them still desiring each other and wanting each other for the right reason."

She thought on his words and noted he wasn't making any promises of anything after today. "And what reason is that, Sloan?"

"Now that we both know the truth of what happened ten years ago, that truth has set us free."

Sloan meant the words he'd spoken to Leslie. They were now free of lies, anger and resentment. However, from the way she was staring at him, he could tell she didn't fully comprehend the magnitude of what that meant.

He saw the guarded eyes staring at him. The only way he knew to help her understand was to show her, and it would be a demonstration that removed any doubts—on both their parts—as to where they would go from here. Hopefully, by the end of the storm, they both would know.

His gaze swept over her, and he could actually feel the whoosh of blood racing through his veins. He glanced back at her when he heard the change in her breathing. At that moment he knew she felt as drawn to him as he was to her. Holding her gaze, he asked, "What do we have to lose by trying, Les?"

He swooped his mouth down on hers. He took his time, savoring her, enjoying the taste it had taken him years to get over. Now he wondered if he really had.

Angling his head to explore her mouth the way he

wanted, he moaned when her tongue met his. They explored each other's mouths with an urgency that was overwhelming yet at the same time welcoming. He felt her hand touch his back, and the warmth of it soothed him yet at the same time felt hot. He disengaged their mouths for a quick breath and then latched back on to her mouth, returning for more.

By the time he broke off the kiss again, the room seemed to vibrate around them, and she quivered. He felt somewhat dizzy, and it had nothing to do with the blow to the head he'd received last night. It had everything to do with Leslie. Only Leslie. Her mouth had the ability to send a strong man keeling over with need.

Sloan drew in a deep breath, and when he did so, it included her scent, one that was uniquely her. He'd missed it. He breathed her in again, while holding her gaze with his. When he saw her nibble on her bottom lip, he knew what she was doing and why. Initially she'd been reluctant to tell him what she wanted whenever they made love, but over time she had gotten bolder. Now it seemed she didn't feel quite comfortable doing so. He intended to remedy that.

"How bad do you want me, Les? I need to know if it's as bad as I want you."

Her expression turned serious, and when she swallowed, he saw how fast the pulse was moving in her throat. "How bad do you want me, Sloan?"

He reached out and brushed the pad of this thumb against her cheek. "I want you so bad that I ache for you all over, especially in my groin."

He saw the flare of heat in her eyes. Instead of nibbling on her lips, she swiped her tongue across them before saying, "And I want you so bad that I ache for you, too. Especially between my legs."

It wàsn't what she'd said but rather how she'd said it—in a tone of voice he hadn't heard in years. It was a tone filled with a desire he'd come to recognize and appreciate because it had always been just for him. Recognizing that tone had him easing up on his knees to open a secret compartment to the coffee table to pull out a condom packet.

At one time there had been five sexually active Outlaw brothers, and most didn't come to the cabin alone. It was understood there would be times when they might not make it to the bedroom, and it was always better to be safe than sorry. With Garth and Cash married off now, that meant it was up to Sloan, Jess and Maverick to replenish the supply whenever needed.

Although Sloan had never brought a woman here, he'd had no problem donating to the cause to make sure there were always plenty on hand. Now he was glad he had. He knew Leslie's eyes were on him while he sheathed himself. She'd once told him she loved seeing him do this part and would often get turned on by it. He wanted her more than turned on. He wanted her hot, eager and filled with need.

Sloan then returned to her, placed his body in position over hers while leaning on his elbows to stare down at her, totally overjoyed at what was to come. "I'm still a foreplay kind of guy, Leslie. You know what that means, right?"

She nodded and licked her lips again before she said, "Yes, I know."

He smiled and whispered, "So enjoy me like I plan to enjoy you."

Seventeen

There was so much desire in Sloan's eyes that it would have given her pause if Leslie thought it wasn't a mirror of her own. She didn't want to entertain all the questions that were bombarding her mind. The main one continued to be, just where would this lead?

At the moment, the only destination was pleasure. One part of her knew she needed to put a stop to this madness when she didn't have answers, but another part of her knew she was too swept away to do anything about it. She hadn't been consumed with this much passion in years. Ten years, to be exact. Now she was ready, and there was no doubt in her mind that Sloan Outlaw would deliver. She had watched him. She had seen the size of his erection when he'd donned the condom. It was hard and primed, and he wanted her.

She had been tempted to reach out and touch it, encircle her hands around it to show him just how much she wanted him, too. It no longer mattered to her that even after they'd made love, nothing would change between her and Sloan. When the weather improved, he would still take her home. The only difference was that she would be taking memories of this time with her. A day of pleasure in his arms, at this cabin and in front of a warm and inviting fireplace.

All thoughts suddenly left her mind when she felt him gently caressing her womanly folds, then spreading them open. She closed her eyes when she felt one finger, then another, ease inside her. He began stirring around inside her to the point where she couldn't hold back a moan even if she'd wanted to.

Leslie moaned when his mouth spread hot, wet kisses along her inner thighs. And then when the tip of his tongue massaged her, she instinctively moved her hips. He grabbed her hips to keep her in place when his tongue penetrated her and then consumed her with a greed that rocked her to the very core. Passion speared through her entire body, making her fully aware of what he was doing, how he was doing it and how much she had missed him doing it.

She felt him nudge her legs farther apart as his mouth and tongue continued to drive her over the edge, taking her breath away. He was behaving worse than the last name he bore. *Outlaw.* He was more like a desperado, a bandit of the most merciless kind.

He must have felt her body getting ready to explode, because he moved his tongue in such a way that her muscles tightened just seconds before she cried out his name.

"Sloan!"

Opening her eyes, she stared at him, and from the look in the eyes staring back at her, she knew he wasn't through with her yet. He proved her right when he began licking her body, moving up toward her chest, stopping briefly to pay homage to her navel. She knew where he was headed and tried bracing herself for the impact of how it would be when he got there. However, nothing could have prepared her for the feel of one of her nipples being sucked into his mouth. What he was doing to her breasts swamped all her senses, almost making her come again. Didn't he remember how sensitive her breasts were?

There was no doubt in her mind that he remembered, and he was letting her know he not only remembered but also planned to take advantage of that fact. He proved her right when he latched on to a nipple and she released a deep groan. The wet heat from his tongue devoured her. He acted as if she was the best thing he'd had in his mouth in a long time.

Thrumming sensations started at the soles of her feet and began moving upward. Recognizing the feeling for what it was, she strained her inner muscles to keep it from happening and discovered there was no use. She couldn't hold back. After inhaling a deep gulp of air, she cried out his name again, but he didn't let her go until the final moan had escaped her lips. Leslie was convinced Sloan was trying to kill her, but if she died it would be a pleasurable death.

"The best is yet to come, baby," he whispered, covering her body with his. "Open your eyes and look at me, Les."

Leslie opened her eyes and looked at him. That's how it had always been whenever they made love. He'd wanted them to be looking at each other the moment he entered her. The thought that he wanted to do things the same way filled her with so much pleasure. She fought back telling him that she loved him. It would not serve any purpose, since he didn't feel the same way. The last thing she wanted was for him to regret what they were sharing. No promises had been made. She was getting what she wanted and so was he.

"Are you concentrating on us, Les?" he asked as he sank into her, going deeper than she'd known him to ever go before.

"Yes, I'm concentrating on us," she whispered.

"Good."

He began moving, thrusting in and out. Slow at first and then faster. When she pushed her hips up to meet his downward thrusts, he pounded into her harder and deeper. The only sound in the room, other than the logs crackling in the fireplace, was their rapid breathing as he continued to drive harder and harder into her. And if that torture wasn't enough, he leaned close and licked her face, starting with her cheeks and ending on her bottom lip.

When she opened her mouth to let out a scream, he captured it with his lips at the same moment his hands grabbed her hips to rock deeper inside her. When he finally released her mouth, she screamed as another orgasm ripped through her. He didn't stop but kept going, thrusting as if he hadn't gotten enough and didn't intend to stop until he did.

When he cried out her name, the sound thundered in her ears louder than the sound of a building being blasted to smithereens. Numerous spasms racked their bodies while their cries of pleasure mingled, lengthened. Yet he didn't let her go. Although he shifted his body so his weight wouldn't hurt her, he continued to hold her while still filling her completely.

She felt satisfied and didn't mind him holding her close. At that moment she couldn't think of anywhere else she would rather be.

The snowstorm wasn't letting up. But then, Sloan thought, neither was he as he slid into Leslie's body again. Making love that first time and enjoying the experience of lying there with their bodies still intimately connected had only fueled his desire. He'd wanted more, and he was getting it.

Earlier they had taken the time, finally, to go into the

kitchen for lunch, since they'd made love through break-fast. Then afterward they had returned to their place in front of the fireplace to make love all over again. Watching her undress had nearly brought out the beast in him, and he'd ended up licking every inch of her body, determined to satisfy a different kind of hunger.

Gazing deep into her eyes as he thrust hard inside her, establishing that perfect rhythm their bodies seemed to know and accept. It seemed to be an agreement not spoken aloud that they might as well continue through the rest of the day and well into the night. There was no reason for them not to when the desire was strong and condoms were plentiful.

So here he was, between the most gorgeous pair of legs to walk this earth, while he held tight to her perfect little ass and thrust hard into her with long, measured strokes. Gazing into her eyes told him she was feeling everything he was feeling. More than anything, he wanted her to know just how much he needed what she was unselfishly sharing with him.

As he stared into her dark, intense eyes, memories flooded him of other times they'd made love. They'd been young, probably hadn't known what they'd been doing most of the time, but now, with every downward thrust into her body, he knew exactly what he was doing. He was in a perfect place. Inside her. Feeling her inner muscles clench him, trying to hold him hostage while he stroked in and out. Hell, he could even feel his erection inside her getting larger. Her moans meant she felt it, too.

Leaning closer, he broke eye contact to kiss her neck, licked her there, rubbed his nose against her, loving her scent, the taste of her skin, every single thing about her.

"Sloan..."

He lifted his head to look into her eyes again, not missing a beat, not a single stroke, as he continued to thrust hard into her body. Hers seemed to stretch for him, taking all he had, and that made his erection harden even more. Made the magnitude of his arousal for her that much stronger.

Sloan could feel it about to happen but refused to let it. He wasn't going over the edge unless Leslie went with him. He increased the pace and knew the minute she came; he heard it in her scream, felt it in her body as it jerked and quivered beneath his. It was only when she came that he let loose inside her. He felt her. He felt so damn good. Great. Totally satisfied to the nth degree.

When the tremors eased from both their bodies, he leaned in and kissed her, needing her to know how much he'd enjoyed making love to her and how good he felt. Easing off her, he drew her naked body into his arms and enjoyed the feel of her cuddled with him. Wrapping his arms around her waist as if he'd never let her go, he closed his eyes to sleep.

Eighteen

"It's finally let up," Leslie said as she stood at the window looking out. The wind had died down, and it was no longer snowing.

"After nearly three days of nonstop snow, it's about time, don't you think?" Sloan said, coming to stand beside her.

She looked over at him. Those snow days had been wonderful for her. Not just the time they'd spent either in bed, making out in front of the fireplace or in the shower, but the time they spent together, talking over hot chocolate or their meals, or just curled up together on the sofa.

He told her about several of his business ventures and the plans he had for them. He also told her about the call he'd gotten three days ago concerning Martin Longshire, and what Sloan had to finally do to show the man he meant business. Although she regretted it had to come to Longshire being asked to step down, she knew over time he would have gotten worse. The man didn't know the meaning of cutting losses and moving on. Sloan also told her more about his Westmoreland cousins and through him she got to know them better. The one thing they hadn't talked about, and what she wasn't sure about, was what would happen with them.

"Now that it has stopped snowing, does that mean you're ready to take me back to Wasilla, Sloan?" she asked, wanting to know, since as far as she knew his plans hadn't changed.

He turned to face her, reaching out to hold her around the waist. "Do you still want to leave?"

Leslie raised her chin. "If I recall, my leaving was your idea. You couldn't wait for me to be gone."

"But that was before…"

When his voice trailed off and he didn't finish what he was about to say, she decided to finish it for him. "Before what? Our two-day sex marathon?"

He frowned. "It was more than that, and you know it."

"Do I, Sloan? I don't recall you saying it was more."

"Well, I'm saying it now," he said, turning to walk off.

That wasn't good enough for Leslie. "Tell me how it was more than that, Sloan."

He stopped walking and turned to her. "Why do you want to get into this now, Leslie? Why can't we continue to enjoy the moment?"

She bit her bottom lip to hold back saying what she really wanted to say. Instead, she said, "I guess there's no reason we can't, Sloan."

"Good."

Leslie doubted he knew how much his words hurt. There were a number of reasons why they couldn't continue to enjoy the moment without them deciding where things went with them from here. His words basically let her know that what she'd assumed was true. Over the past couple of days, they had been making up for all those years they'd been apart, but with no real plan in place to move forward together beyond this week. All she'd been was a bed partner for him during the storm. She'd suspected it, but she had hoped he'd eventually see things differently. Although he'd admitted he was just as much to blame as she was for their breakup, he wasn't ready for a reconciliation. The only thing he was ready for was sex.

"Now that the roads appear clear, I need to drive over to Walker's. I talked to him earlier, and he has an extra fuse that I need for the electric box in the underground tunnel. Will you be okay here until I get back?"

She plastered a smile on her face. "Yes, of course, I'll be fine."

Twenty minutes later, Leslie stood in front of the window and watched as Sloan drove away. He hadn't even bothered inviting her to go with him. It wasn't like she and Walker had never met. Besides, she would have loved to have met Walker's wife and seen their twins. Evidently Sloan didn't consider Leslie worthy of doing either.

At that moment, she knew what she needed to do. Grabbing her cell phone off the table, she was glad it was working again. It didn't take long to arrange a car service to take her to the airport. A part of her refused to think that she was doing the exact same thing she'd done ten years ago, which was to run away without confronting him. In a way that might be true but this time it wasn't about a lie she believed. It was about the truth she knew. She loved him but he didn't love her.

Accepting that truth, she had to pack and be ready when the car arrived and hope she was gone by the time Sloan returned.

It was obvious that he wasn't ready to say one way or the other if she meant anything to him, so she had to assume she didn't. Ten years ago, the only way she'd gotten over him had been to make a clean break. To protect her heart, she had no choice but to leave him once again.

Sloan entered the cabin. He'd been gone way longer than expected, because part of the roof on Walker's barn had collapsed from the weight of the snow. Sloan had helped with temporary repairs until the roofer could get there tomorrow.

He noticed that although it had gotten dark outside, there were no lights on inside the cabin. Was Leslie in her room reading now that power was fully restored? He'd sent her a text message letting her know he would be delayed because he was helping Walker with the roof.

Bailey had raked him over the coals for not inviting Leslie along, saying she would have loved to have met her. When he'd told Bailey he hadn't brought Leslie because there was no reason for the two of them to meet, it had suddenly occurred to him what his words had meant.

Those words hadn't been true, and he'd known it.

When he'd left for Walker's, he'd been deliberately running away from emotions he hadn't been ready to face. Emotions Leslie had forced him to face. He couldn't help but recall bits and pieces of their conversation earlier...

Does that mean you're ready to take me back to Wasilla, Sloan?

Do you still want to leave?

If I recall, my leaving was your idea. You couldn't wait for me to be gone.

But that was before...

Before what? Our two-day sex marathon?

It was more than that, and you know it.

Do I, Sloan? I don't recall you saying it was more.

Well, I'm saying it now.

Tell me how it was more than that, Sloan.

Sloan hadn't told her because at the time he couldn't. Instead, he had found an excuse to leave. To escape by putting distance between them—that had given him a chance to think and accept a few things.

Now he could tell her what he should have told her during those two days they'd been making love. What he should have told her when she had confronted him earlier before he left the cabin to go to Walker's. He could tell her that making love to her was more than just a sexual marathon, because he loved her.

She had made him realize that he hadn't stopped loving her. That's what had made him protect her from the likes of Martin Longshire. What had made him want to spend time with her at the cabin. And what had gotten him to finally see that those plans he'd had for bringing her to the cabin had been made for the wrong reasons, what had made him see that taking her back to Wasilla was the right thing to do.

Now he needed to tell her why taking her back to Wasilla was *not* the right thing to do. He needed the rest of the week to show her their time together meant more to him than sex. It was about loving her unconditionally. Wanting a life with her. Sharing everything with her. Having children with her. He smiled at the thought of a little girl as beautiful as her mother.

He was about to head down the hall, eager to see Leslie, when he realized Leslie had removed all the Christmas decorations and had placed them in a box beside the tree. Why had she done that now when they had two more days to spend at the cabin?

The hairs on the back of his neck stood up as he moved toward the tree. When he got closer, he spotted the note hanging on one of the branches. Snatching it off, he read it.

Sloan, I am returning to Wasilla. Thanks for a won-
derful time at the cabin. I hope you got what you
wanted for Christmas.
Leslie

Sloan crumbled the paper in his hand as he headed for his bedroom to pack. If Leslie Cassidy thought she could take off and run away from him a second time, then he intended to prove her wrong.

He was in the middle of packing when his cell phone went off. He quickly pulled it out of the pocket of his jacket, hoping it was Leslie, but sighed in disappointment when he saw it was Cole. "What's going on, Cole?"

"Calling for two reasons. First, I wanted to make sure you're okay. We all heard about that massive snowstorm and were concerned when we couldn't get through to you, Walker and Bailey."

"We survived," he said, deciding not to mention his accident. Just thinking about it made him once again appreciate that Leslie had been there with him.

"Good to hear it. The other reason I'm calling is about Martin Longshire."

Sloan stopped packing and released a frustrated sigh. "Please don't tell me Longshire has refused to step down and I have to take away his company."

Cole chuckled. "No, that's not it. I understand that, although he's not happy about it, he will retire and has plans to move back to Paris."

"Good riddance. So, what's up with the man?"

"While checking him out, I came across a few things that warranted further digging. There's something I found rather interesting, and I'm not sure you know about it."

"And what's that?" Sloan asked as he resumed packing. He placed the call on speaker so he could move around as he threw items into his luggage.

"Did you know that a few years ago, Longshire was some young woman's secret sugar daddy?"

Sloan continued packing. "Why would that be of any interest to me, Cole?"

"Because the woman was Sarah Olsen, Leslie Cassidy's roommate."

Sloan went still. "Damn."

Nineteen

"You deserted Sloan Outlaw a second time, Leslie?"

Leslie rolled her eyes. Leave it to Carmen to get dramatic. "Trust me, he got just what he wanted from me. If you recall, he wanted *me* for Christmas."

She wouldn't bother mentioning that she'd gotten what she'd wanted from him, too, even when she hadn't realized she had wanted it or needed it. All it had taken was a day in Sloan's arms to make her realize just what she'd missed the past ten years. To be honest, she hadn't gotten enough of him.

"And what if he comes after you?"

"He won't, since he has no reason to do so. Besides, it's been almost two days and I haven't heard from him. Not even a phone call." She had received a text message on the day she'd left letting her know he would be returning to the cabin later than expected, because he was helping Walker. She hadn't responded to the text because she'd been busy packing.

"You know what they say, Carmen. Out of sight means out of mind. I figure since he is my business partner I'll eventually see him at some point after the office opens in January."

"And you're okay with that?"

She opened her mouth to lie and discovered she couldn't. This was Carmen. Her best friend. The woman who knew all her secrets. Most of them, anyway. Carmen knew how much Leslie had loved Sloan before and probably suspected she loved him now. "It doesn't matter. Sloan made it clear all we were sharing was sex this time."

"But you said he told you it was more."

"Yes, he did say that, but he couldn't tell me how it was more, so what he said doesn't count, Carmen."

"Well, at least the two of you know the extent of Sarah Olsen's deceit."

"Yes, now I know what he didn't know."

"I wonder how Sarah can live with herself after what she did."

Leslie rolled her eyes. "You saw her at that nightclub, and you heard how she bragged about it. She might have been drinking, but she didn't have any remorse then and I doubt she has any now." Leslie glanced at her watch. "Look, Carmen, I need to go finish up my laundry."

"All right. And you still haven't made any plans for the holidays?"

"Nope," she said, looking at the Christmas tree. "I plan to spend quiet time here."

"You know you're welcome to join me in Atlanta at my sister's. She would love seeing you again. And Elan received that package you sent to him. He can't wait to open it on Christmas Day."

"I'm glad he got it. Thanks for the invite, but I'll be okay."

A few hours later, she had finished laundry and taken a

bath. She had changed into her Christmas pj's she'd gotten from Carmen last year. She'd even taken the time to make Christmas brownies and a batch of sugar cookies. The house was filled with the aroma of baked goods, and she liked it.

Leslie headed for the stairs to grab her e-reader and finish the book she'd begun reading at the cabin when she heard the doorbell. She went still, having an idea who was at the door. There was a reason her body was beginning to tingle all over.

Deciding to ignore the bell, she was about to go upstairs as heavy knocks sounded on the door. Frowning, she decided to answer it to see what Sloan could possibly want. When she snatched the door open, a bouquet of red roses stared her in the face, but she recognized the hand holding them. "What do you want, Sloan?"

He lowered the flowers and said, "Now that's a loaded question, Les."

Her frown deepened. "No, it's not, and the name is Leslie to you."

Instead of addressing what she'd said, he asked, "May I come in so we can talk?"

"Why?"

"I think we need to clear up a few things. Besides, it's cold as the dickens out here."

"So? You like the cold."

He shrugged. "I *liked* the cold. That episode at the cabin has changed my mind about that. Now can I come in so we can talk?"

Deciding she didn't want to freeze while standing in the doorway talking to him, she moved aside to let him in.

He glanced over at the tree. "Nice tree."

She crossed her arms over her chest. "You've seen it before, Sloan."

"Yes, I have." He sniffed the air. "Something smells good. You're baking?"

"Yes." She needed him to say whatever he'd come there to say so he could leave. Seeing him standing in her foyer, looking yummy enough to eat, wasn't good.

"Do you mind if I remove my coat, Leslie?"

Deciding not to be impolite, especially when he'd called her by her full name, she said, "You can give it to me and I'll hang it up. I'm sure whatever you have to say won't take long." After putting his coat in the closet, she walked off toward the living room, and he followed.

Leslie offered him the wingback chair, and she sat down on the sofa. "So what do you want to talk about, Sloan?"

He leaned forward, and when he did so, his jeans tightened across thighs she remembered riding. "First, I have a question for you about Sarah Olsen."

She frowned, wondering why he would bring her up. "What about Sarah?"

"Did you know that while the two of you were roommates, more specifically, during the time you and I were together, that Sarah and Martin Longshire were involved in an affair?"

She knew her expression must have shown her shock as she leaned forward in her seat as well. "Are you kidding me?"

He shook his head. "No, I'm not kidding you."

"Do you think he had anything to do with aiding and abetting our breakup?"

Sloan held her gaze. "I know he did. I paid Sarah a visit, and she confessed to everything."

"Was she sober?"

He nodded. "Yes. She was also desperate to save her job but was fired anyway."

Leslie leaned back in her seat. "I don't understand."

He leaned back in his chair as well. "You know the old saying what comes around goes around?"

"Yes."

"After discovering Sarah was involved with Longshire, I had Cole research her. Imagine my surprise to find out that she's living in LA and had a real cushy sales and marketing position with a film company where I'm a silent partner. Imagine *her* surprise when she walked into the conference room to find me sitting there."

"And?"

"And she confessed to everything she did to break us up and said Longshire paid her to make sure we ended our relationship. He figured hurting you was a way to get back at your father and your deceased mother."

Leslie stood, too angry to sit, and began pacing. "I had nothing to do with what happened between my parents and Longshire. He had no right to go after me."

"No. Just like he had no right to go after the Yules because their daughter rebuffed his advances. He did so anyway. The man is demented. Sarah was apologetic and hoped, since her involvement happened a long time ago, that I could forget about it and move on."

"What did you say?"

"I honestly didn't feel any sincere remorse from her. So I told her there was no way I could forget and move on, and that a person with her tendency for deceit was not anyone my partners and I would want working for our company. I fired her on the spot."

Leslie went back and sat down on the sofa. A part of her wanted to feel bad for Sarah, but all she could remember was how cruel Sarah had been at that nightclub. "I'm sure she'll get another job."

"Not in LA. However, I suggested she follow her ex-boo to Paris. According to Cole, now that Longshire had to step down as CEO, that's where he's moving."

Sloan watched Leslie stand up and begin pacing again. Even in her red-and-green pj's with designs of Santa, reindeer, Christmas trees and candles, he thought she looked cute. He also thought, like he always did, that she had one hell of a figure.

Just looking at her in motion made him want her all over again, but he knew there had to be more to their relationship than lust. There *was* more. Now he had the important task of convincing her of it.

She suddenly stopped pacing and turned to stare at him. "I should have suspected something. If you recall, I mentioned to you that when Longshire came to my office, he knew you were once my boyfriend. We both wondered how he had known that when you and I hadn't been in contact in ten years."

"Come to think of it, considering what you told me about Longshire's relationship with your parents, it makes sense that he went after us all those years ago," Sloan said.

"How so?" she asked.

"He was engaged to your mother, but she eloped and married your father, right?"

"Yes."

"Then what better revenge than to have something similar happen to her daughter?"

When he saw that Leslie was no longer following him, he said, "It was my plan to ask you to marry me that week at the cabin during spring break."

"What! It was?"

"Yes," he said, seeing surprise on her face. She hadn't known. "That was my plan. I even bought the ring. I figured we would get married after you graduated."

"You wanted to marry me?"

"Of course I wanted to marry you, Leslie. I loved you and believed that you loved me. I figured marriage would be the next step for us."

"B-but you never mentioned marriage. We never talked about it. I had no idea you wanted a future with me."

He leaned forward again, to make sure she understood. "That's apparently another mistake I made in not making sure you knew how I felt. However, in my defense, you told me plenty of times that you loved me, and I told you numerous times that I loved you. I figured that although you might not have known about my pending marriage proposal, you knew I wanted our relationship to continue beyond graduation. I had no intention of giving you up, Leslie. No intention whatsoever."

"But how did Sarah know you were going to ask me to marry you? Did you tell her what you planned?"

"No. I was so happy about it, though, I told Keosha, Tyler and Redford. I especially wanted Keosha to know so I could have an idea of your ring size."

He shifted his position on the sofa. "I spoke with Keosha yesterday and she admitted that in her excitement, she had mentioned it to Sarah. At the time she'd had no idea of Sarah's duplicity. When Sarah told Longshire, he probably thought it would be the ultimate revenge to hurt the daughter of his enemies the way they had hurt him."

Leslie nodded. "Evidently. And even after that worked, he still wasn't through with me and wanted even more revenge after Dad died." Suddenly, a huge smile spread across her face.

Sloan raised a brow. "What do you find amusing?"

"No wonder Martin Longshire was beside himself with anger that day he came to my office after finding out the identity of my new business partner. Taking my company away from me was supposed to be the ultimate revenge. The finale, so to speak. How do you think he felt knowing the man who ruined those plans was the same man he stopped me from marrying ten years ago? The same man Longshire assumed I would never be with again."

Sloan stood and crossed the room to stand in front of Leslie. "And that's where he made his mistake, Leslie. Because no matter how things ended between us, there was no way I could have stayed away when I found out you were in trouble. Undoubtedly, the man doesn't know the first thing about true love."

Leslie tilted her head back to stare up at him. "But you do?" she asked.

"I think so. I believe that even people in love make mistakes. And when they do, they should own up to those mistakes, admit they were wrong and apologize. I was wrong to leave you at the cabin without asking you to come with me to Walker's, and I apologize for doing it."

"Why did you?" she asked softly.

He broke eye contact with her for a minute. When he looked back at her, he knew he needed to try and explain how he felt. "Leaving me the way you did ten years ago hurt deeply, Leslie. It took me years to recover, and there were days when I wasn't sure I had. But I knew I had to help you out when I found out what Longshire planned to do. However, to protect my heart, I convinced myself I was doing it for my own kind of retribution. That's why I made that stipulation that you spend a week with me at the cabin."

He shoved his hands into the pockets of his slacks and said, "As you know, things didn't work out the way they were supposed to."

"We did sleep together, Sloan," she said. "That's what you wanted."

"Yes, but I was supposed to remain emotionally detached, and I couldn't do that. When we made love, I knew."

"You knew what?" she asked.

"That I still had deep feelings for you. That I still loved you. Discovering that made me feel vulnerable. I left the cabin to go visit Walker as a way to put distance between us and give me a chance to deal with what I was feeling. When I came back, you were gone."

In a soft voice, she said, "I couldn't stay at the cabin any longer, Sloan. Making love with you made me realize I still loved you as well. But I suspected it was one-sided and knew I had to protect my heart. I thought all we shared was a sex marathon."

"I told you there was more."

"Yes, but you never defined what 'more' was, Sloan, and I needed to know."

He squatted down and boxed her in with his arms on both sides of her. "Then let me define it now, Leslie. More means not just being a bed partner with you. It means you knowing that you are the woman I love, the only woman I could ever love. The woman I want in my life forever. More means sharing a life with you, having a family with you and you wearing my name. All the things I wanted to give you ten years ago, I still want to give you and with the promise that I will love you forever. It might be ten years in the making, but I believe we deserve our happy-ever-after."

Leslie fought back tears at Sloan's words. He loved her and ten years ago he'd intended to ask her to marry him. He *still* loved her.

"Leslie?"

She knew that now was the time to let him know just how she felt. "I do love you, Sloan. Even those years when we were apart and I believed you had betrayed me, I still loved you. That's why I could never become involved with another man. In all this time, you're the only man whose bed I've shared."

She saw the surprised look on his face. He straightened up to his full height. "Are you serious?"

"Yes, I am serious. The thought of another man making

love to me was a total turnoff. That's probably why I was all in when we made love almost nonstop for two days. I was making up for lost time."

"And did you? Make up for lost time?" he asked as a smile touched his lips.

Leslie returned his smile. "Let's just say I tried." She stood and wrapped her arms around his neck. "I love you, Sloan. I love you so much."

She pressed her mouth against his. Tightening his arms around her, he deepened the kiss. The hard erection pressing against her middle said it all.

When Sloan finally broke off the kiss, she said, "Just think, Martin Longshire's plan failed, and we are back together. In the end, love won."

Sloan caressed the side of her face as he stared into her eyes. "Yes, sweetheart, love won. Our love won."

Leslie watched as Sloan took a step back, lowered himself to one knee and reached out for her hand. "I am about to do what I intended to do ten years ago. Will you marry me, Leslie?"

She threw her palm over her heart, shocked speechless. But it didn't take her long to recover. "Yes! Yes! I will marry you."

"And you won't make me wait, right?" he asked, sliding a ring on her finger.

She was in awe at how beautiful it was. "No, I won't make you wait."

"Good. And the reason it took me two days to get here is because in addition to flying to LA to confront Sarah, while I was there, I went shopping for your ring. I decided I could afford a more expensive one than the one I'd planned to give you ten years ago. I still have it and will give it to our daughter on her sixteenth birthday."

Leslie threw her head back and laughed. "Our daughter at sixteen? You are definitely thinking ahead, aren't you?"

"Yes," he said, wrapping his arms around her. "I would love to have a little girl who will grow up to be just as beautiful as her mother."

She shook her head, grinning. "If you say so."

"I do, and I can't wait to announce our engagement to the family. Most are headed for Denver this weekend to spend the holidays with our cousins, the Westmorelands. I'd like you to go with me. Will you go meet my relatives and spend Christmas and New Year's with me, Leslie?"

"I'd love to, Sloan. And you know what else I would love?"

"What, baby?"

"For you to make love to me."

Sloan then swept Leslie into his arms. "Which way to your bedroom, sweetheart?"

"Upstairs. The first door to your right."

And then, holding her tight, he took the stairs two at a time. Trembles rippled through her when he placed her on the bed.

He glanced around as he sat on the side of the bed to remove his boots. "Nice bedroom. You're still into yellow, I see."

"Um," she said, running the tip of her finger along his jeans-clad thigh. "Right now, Sloan Outlaw, I am into you, and more than anything, I want you into me. Literally."

"I am glad to accommodate you," he said, standing.

He quickly undressed and then returned to the bed to remove her pajamas. Heat flared all through her as he studied her naked body. She drew in a deep breath when he cupped her breasts.

"Sloan…"

She breathed out his name as he leaned in and began trailing kisses down her jaw and along her neck.

"Later for the foreplay. I need you inside me now, Sloan."

Leslie had dreamed of him every night since leaving the cabin, although she hadn't wanted to do so. And those dreams had been off the charts.

"I'll accommodate you now, but you know how I feel about foreplay."

Yes, she knew. He called it foreplay, but she thought of it as sensual torture. She watched him reach for his pants to retrieve a condom packet and then sheath himself, admiring his hair-covered chest and the trail that led down to his pelvis. She had accepted years ago that Sloan Outlaw was friggin' hot and overtly male. And from the look in his eyes, and the huge manhood between his legs, he was definitely aroused.

"You're going to owe me a whole lot of foreplay, Les."

Hearing him shorten her name made her loop her arms around his neck. "I have no problem with that, Sloan."

"Good."

No, *this* was good, she thought as she placed butterfly kisses around his mouth. He then lowered her to her back and eased into position on top of her while simultaneously opening her legs wider with his knee.

His manhood rubbed against her center, and the throb there made her eyes flutter closed.

"Look at me, Les. I want you to see me as well as feel me."

She fully opened her eyes to stare up at him, and what she saw in the dark depths of his gaze nearly took her breath away. She saw love, as deep as it could get, and she knew her own eyes displayed the same thing.

Then he entered her slowly, as if he needed to feel every inch as he made his way inside. His tight, hair-roughened stomach pressed against hers as he continued to go deep, and deeper still, until their bodies were locked together so tightly there was nothing that could get between them.

She smiled, and he smiled back. Then he slowly thrust

in and out as she moved her arms from around his neck to his shoulders, sinking her nails into his skin. If her action caused him pain, he didn't show it. Instead he picked up the rhythm, faster and harder.

That's when he leaned in and captured her mouth, kissing her in a way that had their tongues tangling nearly out of control. Each time she lifted her body, he plunged down, gripping her hips as he pounded into her.

She let out a scream at the exact moment he released a deep, guttural growl, and she knew this was only the beginning of forever.

Twenty

"Are you going to sleep in all morning, baby?" Sloan whispered close to Leslie's ear. He glanced out the window and saw it snowing. No surprise there. This was Alaska, after all.

He looked back down at Leslie and watched as she slowly opened her eyes. When she stretched her lips in a smile, he felt hunger stirring in the pit of his stomach.

"I'm exhausted," she said, closing her eyes again.

He didn't doubt it. After all, other than eating dinner, they had remained in bed and made love all through the night. He caressed the side of her face as love for her flowed through every bone in his body. "You want me to make you some oatmeal?"

She opened her eyes with a stern look on her face. "Stay out of my kitchen, Sloan Outlaw."

He chuckled. "Why? What harm could I do?"

"I'm not willing to find out." She glanced out the window. "It's daytime."

"Yes, and we only have four hours of it. I thought we could make some calls. I can't wait to tell everyone that I am marrying the most beautiful woman in the world."

"Oh, Sloan."

She wrapped her arms around him, and he pulled her closer in a long, drugging kiss. With her cradled beside him, Sloan took his cell phone and began making calls. With such a huge family, all he had to do was call specific individuals who would get the world out. Of course, it was Charm who asked the most questions. He couldn't help but smile. "Yes, Charm, Leslie and I are back together, and you're right. It is about time." He nodded. "I'll tell Leslie how happy you are to have another sister and that you welcome her to the family."

Glancing over at Leslie, he knew she was listening to his words, and he could see her fighting back tears. She might have lost her father, but she had gained a huge family who would adore her and love her as much as he did. When he finally ended the last call, the one to his cousin Dillon, he placed his phone aside and eased down in the bed.

"Tell me what you're thinking, baby." He saw the tear that fell from her eye, and he leaned in to lick it off her cheek.

"First you help save my company, then you want me as your wife and now you share your family with me. You make me feel so special, Sloan."

"That's because you are special. If nothing else, I think being apart as long as we were has taught us not to take anything for granted. You mean so much to me, and I intend to spend the rest of my life showing you how much I love you."

He bent his head and kissed her, thinking he would never be able to show her often enough just what she meant to him. Since they were already naked, it didn't take him long to grab one of the condom packets he'd placed on the nightstand and prepare himself to make love to her.

They had decided they would start trying to make babies after the wedding. And since they intended to have a June wedding, when the weather wasn't as cold, that meant this time next year they would be making babies.

He'd already told her that she was what he'd wanted for Christmas this year, and he'd let her know what he wanted for Christmas next year. He wanted her pregnant.

He began kissing her, starting at her mouth and continuing down her body, making stops to tug on the hardened tips of her breasts and feast on her navel. She trembled beneath every area his tongue licked. Just tasting her skin had desire pumping through him. And when he made it to the area between her legs and buried his head between them, an intense hunger spread through him. His greedy tongue showed her just how much he wanted her, and it didn't take long for her body to respond with one hell of an orgasm.

"Sloan!"

He made his way back to her mouth, taking it with an urgency that he felt all the way to his toes. Then, releasing her mouth, he held her gaze as he slid inside her. "You still owe me a lot of foreplay, and I plan to collect, Les."

Her inner muscles clenched him as he began thrusting into her. "I love you, baby."

"And I love you," she said, running her hands over the muscles of his back.

Her touch made him thrust harder, and from the sounds she was making, he was doing it right. He broke eye contact with her to lean up and trail hot, moist licks along her neck and shoulders, her chin, and finally her lips. Pleasure erupted between them with a shared orgasm that rocked him to the core. She clung to him as much as he clung to her, and he knew at that moment he had definitely gotten what he wanted for Christmas.

A beautifully wrapped package named Leslie.

"Well, what do you think?" Sloan asked, pulling Leslie aside after he had introduced her to everyone. At least to those relatives she hadn't met yet.

"You were right. You and your cousin Derringer favor a lot, but I was able to tell you guys apart."

"There was no doubt in my mind that you would."

"I hope you don't expect me to remember names. This is a large family, and you are blessed to be a part of it. Everyone is so kind, and they are truly happy for us."

"Of course they are. Another Outlaw will be single no more."

Leslie glanced around the ballroom that was hosting the Westmoreland Charity Ball, not believing the number of people here. Most had arrived the day before Christmas, like they had, and everyone stayed on Westmoreland property. There were plenty of rooms. She and Sloan were staying at the Westmoreland B&B. It had been a ranch that Jason Westmoreland's wife, Bella, had inherited and turned into a bed-and-breakfast. Leslie liked Bella, but then, she liked all the women in the family, those who were born Westmoreland or who'd married one.

Sloan's brother Garth and his wife, Regan, had announced they would be having a baby in the spring but assured them the baby would arrive before Sloan and Leslie's June wedding. Last night they'd gotten word that his cousin Delaney had given birth to twin boys.

However, the highlight of the night was when his cousin Bane and his wife, Crystal, announced they were expecting. And if the doctor's prediction held true, Bane and Crystal would be having their second set of triplets. They would be the first Westmoreland couple who'd managed such a feat, and they honestly seemed overjoyed about it. According to Sloan, the couple wanted a big family.

Everyone loved Leslie's engagement ring and thought she and Sloan made a beautiful couple. Leslie had to agree.

"Did I tell you today that I love you?" Sloan said, reclaiming her attention.

"Yes, but you can always tell me again," she said, smiling up at him.

"I love you, Leslie Cassidy, soon to be Leslie Outlaw."

She couldn't help but beam. "And I love you."

Not caring that they had an audience, Sloan pulled his future wife into his arms for a kiss.

Epilogue

A June wedding

With family and friends looking on, Sloan accepted the wedding ring from Garth, who was his best man. He then turned to his future bride to slide the ring on her finger while repeating the words the minister had instructed him to recite. "With this ring, I thee wed."

Once the ring was in place, he lifted her hand to his lips, sealing his vow with a kiss. He didn't care if what he was doing wasn't part of the program. He was a man who made his own rules. However, he did behave when she slid the wedding band on his finger. He noted she was wearing his wedding gift to her, the vintage aurora borealis bracelet with colorful crystals and diamonds. It looked good on her wrist and was a reminder of their time under the Northern Lights. Deep emotions hit him that he was finally marrying the woman he'd always loved.

He was ready for the part of the ceremony that pronounced them as husband and wife so he could kiss his bride. He would kiss her the way he wanted, and nobody better stop him. He thought she looked too beautiful for words in her bridal gown of white satin and lace.

His heart had nearly stopped when she entered the church on Mr. Yule's arm. The two had stayed in touch and formed a close friendship over the past six months. In addition to operating Cassidy Cosmetics, Sloan had brought her on to assist him in the running of his other businesses. For the time being, they had dual residences in both Wasilla and Fairbanks. She was grooming one of her junior executives to eventually take on more duties, since the cosmetics line was being expanded to the lower forty-eight.

"And by the powers vested in me by this great state of Alaska, I now pronounce you husband and wife."

Sloan didn't wait for the minister to give him permission to kiss his bride. He reached for Leslie and pulled her into his arms, giving her the only kind of kiss they would ever share. Long, thorough and possessive. Nobody interrupted, and he only released Leslie's mouth when he was good and ready.

He glanced over at the minister, who didn't seem the least bothered by Sloan's strong show of affection. In fact, Reverend Cross was actually grinning as he proceeded to announce, "I present to you, Sloan and Leslie Outlaw."

Among claps and cheers, Sloan swept Leslie off her feet and carried her out of the church. Once outside he placed her back on her feet and pulled her into his arms.

When he released her lips, she whispered, "You're so bad, Sloan Outlaw."

He grinned down at his wife. "Possibly, but I am also yours. Totally and completely, Mrs. Outlaw." He then pulled her into his arms for another kiss.

* * *

"Sloan definitely likes kissing you, girlfriend," Carmen leaned over to whisper to Leslie at the end of the wedding party's photo session.

Leslie couldn't help but smile. "And I love kissing him."

"Obviously. The two of you can't seem to keep your lips to yourselves," Carmen said, glancing around.

Leslie followed her friend's gaze and saw just where it had landed—right on Redford St. James, who was now being corralled by the photographer as Sloan took pictures with his best man and groomsmen. A sense of panic stirred Leslie's insides.

She had known Redford for as long as she'd known Sloan, since she'd met both guys the same day on the university's campus. Redford had been known around the university as a womanizer, and according to Sloan, Redford hadn't changed. If anything, he'd gotten worse.

"Carmen, I think I need to warn you about Redford," Leslie said, hoping it wasn't too late. She'd noted how taken her best friend had been with Redford last night at the wedding rehearsal.

"I know all about him, Leslie, so you don't need to warn me. However, you might want to put a bug in Sloan's ear to warn Redford about me."

Leslie lifted a brow. "Why?"

A wide smile covered Carmen's face. "Because Redford St. James is the man I intend to marry. Your hubby is on his way over here, so I will see you at the reception."

Leslie watched Carmen walk off toward where Redford was standing. *Marry? Redford?* She hoped her friend was not biting off more than she could chew but had a feeling that she was.

"Are you okay, sweetheart?" Sloan asked, wrapping his arms around her.

She smiled up at him. "Yes, I'm fine." She decided

to give him the warning from Carmen later. Right now, the only thing she wanted to do was concentrate on this man. Her Outlaw who would give her plenty of little Outlaws. It seemed she'd married into the right family. Not only was there a pregnancy announced practically every other month, but the Outlaws and Westmorelands had a knack when it came to multiple births. Garth and Regan had given birth to a little boy, and Cash and Brianna had twin sons. Sloan had jokingly told everyone he and Leslie would give Bart the first Outlaw granddaughter.

"You ready for your monthlong honeymoon to begin?" Sloan asked her.

She couldn't help but smile up at him. "Are you sure you want to do all that driving?"

He chuckled. "I am sure."

They would first take a road trip from Alaska to the lower forty-eight through Canada, which was something they had always talked of doing while in college. When they reached New York, they would switch the rental car for a private jet. From there Sloan would fly them to Belize, where they would spend the remainder of the month.

"Are you ready to leave for our wedding reception?" she asked. "Things won't get started until we arrive."

"They can wait a minute," he said, and then he pulled her into his arms for yet another kiss.

* * * * *

HOW TO HANDLE
A HEARTBREAKER

JOSS WOOD

One

He's here.

Hayley Lopez scowled at the text message on her phone from Bubba Conor and knew the "he" was the bullying billionaire Jackson Michaels. Michaels, Royal's most successful real estate developer, had been harassing her client for the past month, demanding he sell his well-situated parcel of land on the edge of Stone Lake so that he could build a mixed-use estate on the edges of Stone Lake.

Well, technically, Bubba wasn't her client. He was just a lonely old widower she periodically checked on in her official capacity as one of Royal's sheriff's deputies. She had another year of law school until she could officially have clients but, until then, she was faking it to make it and dispensing the little legal advice she could.

She had a ton of work and didn't have time to visit Bubba's property to have a chat with Jackson Michaels. But Bubba, mild-mannered and shy, needed a representative, and Hayley could tell Michaels, forcefully, that Bubba had no desire to sell his smallholding.

Maybe then Jackson Michaels would get the message.

She'd also tell him that Royal didn't need a mixed-use development spoiling the serene and tranquil lake. Families camped at the lake, fished there. Lovers—young, old and sometimes illicit—made out there. At a recent community meeting, the residents of Royal made it clear that they weren't keen on any developments at Stone Lake. The developer, damn his stubborn soul, had yet to back down.

Hayley loved Stone Lake. Her grandparents were once Bubba's closest neighbors. She'd spent most summers in her swimsuit on the water, fishing and swimming and canoeing. She loved the peace of the area and hated the idea of a multistory hotel and cottages, all generic and boring, on the edge of the lake.

Ugh. Hayley pulled on her seat belt, jammed her sunglasses over her eyes—designer and a gift from her older brother for her birthday—and headed out of town. She appreciated the gift because there was no way she could afford a pair on her cop salary; between feeding herself and paying for law school, making ends meet was enough of a challenge as it was.

You can always run home to Daddy...

Hayley scoffed at her inner voice, knowing she had more chance of falling pregnant by celestial intervention—as she wasn't currently enjoying a red-hot affair—than of her running home to Mom and Dad.

Juan Lopez, a billionaire oil baron and complete control freak, would love that and she had no intention of falling into line like her three older brothers. No, like her father, she preferred doing things her way. The hard way, her mom told her, but if hard meant her freedom, then she'd take it over being dictated to.

"You are too ambitious..."

"You are too up-front..."

"You are too independent..."

Remembering the words frequently lobbed at her by her parents, and her older brothers, Hayley scowled.

"You are never going to find a man, settle down."

Hayley released a snort. Now there was a sentence her brothers never heard. No, her two single brothers—her eldest sibling was married with kids—were encouraged to play the field, to sow their wild oats. From cars to curfews to chores, there was one set of rules for her brothers, another set for her. They'd been allowed to study what they wanted at college, encouraged to chase their business dreams and to be as ruthlessly ambitious as they could be. In her brothers, ambition and drive were positive attributes but her parents expected her to settle down and marry to make babies instead of making a difference. Be protected instead of being the protector. Hayley tapped the butt of her Glock. Screw that. She wouldn't stand on the sidelines of life, waiting for some man to put a ring on her finger and to, supposedly, make her happy.

She was happy already. Okay, reasonably content. *Busy* was a better description. Crazy busy.

But at least she was master of her destiny.

Hayley swung into Bubba's driveway, taking it easy through the potholes and over the bumps in the road. As she approached the house, her heart stopped when she noticed the astonishingly expensive, limited-edition Ford 150 pickup lording over Bubba's battered Jeep. The matte black pickup was the latest of her dream cars, the one material object she lusted over...

If there was one thing that could tempt her to return to the family fold, it would be the ability to buy luxury vehicles. In fact, her father had tried to bribe her to return home with the offer of a new car, anything she wanted, no expense spared.

If she'd acquiesced, then a truck like this would be hers. But, when weighing her freedom versus a new set of wheels, freedom always won, hands down.

Hayley parked, exited her patrol car and pushed her sunglasses up onto the top of her head. Unable to resist, she ran her hand down the sleek line of the truck's hood and stood up on her tiptoes to look inside the interior.

"It has heated seats, an eight-inch touch screen, a Wi-Fi hot spot, and wireless device charging." A deep voice rolled over her and raised goose bumps on her skin. But while she appreciated the deep and dark tenor, the fact that he'd assume that she could only appreciate the pretties on his truck annoyed her.

"I'm more interested in the 450-horsepower twin-turbo V6 engine and its ten-speed automatic transmission," Hayley replied, her back still to him.

"A girl who likes cars. I'm impressed."

A girl? She might be young—she'd be turning twenty-four in a few months—but she wasn't a *girl*, for God's sake! Holy crap, could he sound more patronizing if he tried?

Hayley spun around, intending to nail him with an "it's Officer Lopez to you, dirtbag" look but, on catching a glimpse of all his golden wonderfulness, her tongue disconnected with her brain. Jackson Michaels stood in front of her, looking sinfully sexy in a black crew neck sweater and gray chinos, trendy trainers on his feet. Thick hair, the color of sunlight dancing on a cornfield, was expertly cut and styled. Someone with no imagination would call his eyes *blue* but it was such an insipid word for the various shades she saw in his eyes. *Sea blue* would be closer but on looking closer, she saw the hint of purple and decided they were the color of ripe blueberries, picked off the bush. Maybe they were the color of Texas bluebonnets… Whatever their shade, thick eyebrows and dark lashes complemented the blue.

Hayley, still trying to fill her lungs, took in his slightly hooked nose, his sexy mouth and the thick stubble over his strong jaw.

Jackson Michaels was, undeniably, hot.

Hayley, very reluctantly, pulled her eyes off his tall, muscled, athletic-as-hell body and looked past him to see Bubba scowling at her from his rickety porch. Right, she was here on business…

Best to remember that.

"Mr. Michaels, I am Officer Lopez," Hayley told him, trying to put a decent amount of frost into her voice. She had to remember that this man was trying to force Bubba off his land, to convert a pristine area into a pimped-up office block and residential estate with a golf course. *Ugh*.

"Yeah, Bubba said I was trespassing and that he called you."

He didn't look even a little intimidated. Damn him.

"Are you going to lay charges against me, Bubba?" Jackson asked, his eyes not leaving Hayley's face. Hayley resisted the urge to check whether her waist-length hair was still in its severe bun, whether any strands had come loose. She felt like she was under a microscope and she didn't like the sensation, not one bit…

But she could easily imagine him looking at her like that when she was naked… Now, that would be hot.

For God's sake, Lopez, get a grip.

"No, I'm not going to lay charges. Hayley, please tell him that I don't want to sell," Bubba demanded, the tip of his walking stick hitting the wooden planks on his porch.

"Mr. Conor doesn't want to sell, Mr. Michaels," Hayley said, keeping her voice bland. "Please stop harassing him."

Those eyes cooled a little… "I think *harassing* is too strong a word, Officer."

"You've made the offer, he's declined—" Hayley made a shooing gesture with her hands "—so you can leave."

Jackson grinned and Hayley knew he wasn't leaving anytime soon. "Is the crime rate so low in Royal that they are now sending officers to mediate civil disputes?"

Ah, this was always a tricky question to answer. Technically, she shouldn't be here and if Sheriff Battle heard that she'd made a stop at Bubba's, he'd rip her a new one. She had work to do and Bubba, fit and healthy, wasn't high on the list of his priorities.

Hayley wrinkled her nose, trying to find an explanation that would fly. Before she could speak, Bubba jumped into the conversation.

"Hayley is my lawyer."

Hayley winced. That wasn't, technically, true. It wasn't true at all. She was a sheriff's deputy studying for her law degree and she had no right to issue advice. But the undeserved, unseen and neglected citizens of Royal needed a champion and she couldn't stand by when they needed help. In fact, they were why she'd decided to study law. She wanted to become a Legal Aid lawyer, someone they could turn to when life became legally overwhelming.

Yeah, she'd inherited her father's protective nature but, unlike him, her "clients" had to ask for her help. She never assumed they were incapable.

"A lawyer and a cop," Jackson drawled, looking amused. "Quite the combination. How do you find time to do it all? Do you keep your Superwoman cape in the trunk of your car?"

Now he was just mocking her. Or was he? The light in his eyes suggested he was teasing but Hayley couldn't be sure. Besides, she was the law. She should be above being teased. She had a goddamn Glock on her hip and a shield on her belt.

But, because she *was* the law, she couldn't misrepresent herself. "I haven't taken the bar yet, and I make suggestions, I don't give advice. And if I did hand out advice, it would be unofficial."

Remembering her father's advice to her brothers—always portray confidence and show no fear—she refused to drop her eyes from his, not for a second. And, let's be honest here, why would she want to look away? He was gorgeous and a balm for her very tired eyes.

A lazy smile crossed his face. "What did the lawyer name his daughter?" He waited for a beat before hitting her with the punch line. "Sue."

A lawyer joke that was so corny she almost cracked a smile. She tipped her head to the side. "Have you seen the size of my weapon, Mr. Michaels?"

"It was an awful joke but not so bad to warrant a threat of violence." Yep, definitely amused.

"I didn't threaten violence. I asked you if you noticed my weapon. It's big, and spurts out big bullets that make big holes," Hayley tartly responded, watching Bubba slip back into his house.

His laugh danced on the cool November air. He peered at her name tag. "What does the *H* stand for? Helga? Hesta? Honoria?"

Honoria? Really? Hayley was still very tempted to pull out her gun and shoot him. But the paperwork would be a bitch and jail inconvenient. Decisions, decisions…

"I don't have time to spar with you, Mr. Michaels," Hayley said through gritted teeth. "Bubba doesn't want to sell, and you can't make him. From what I understand, his land is essential to your project so why don't you give up this idea of developing the area around Stone Lake and find somewhere else to spoil?"

Jackson remained slouched against his car. "I'm beginning to think you don't like me, Officer Harriet Lopez."

She did like him...no, wrong. She liked looking at him. His smart mouth? Not so much. Well, she wouldn't mind kissing that mouth...

Oh, God.

Hayley, just leave...

Hayley pushed her shoulders back and lifted her chin. "I'm asking you, nicely, to leave Bubba alone. He doesn't want to sell. Deal with it. Do not make me come out here again."

"Oh, I might. If I'm bored and I want some entertainment, Officer Hanna—"

Entertainment? She was his *entertainment*?

"Are you normally this patronizing and annoying, Mr. Michaels?"

Hayley felt her temper inch up at his blatant disregard for her and the work she did. How dared he assume that she had time to waste. That the most important part of her day was meeting him.

Jerk.

"I have more important things to do than trade inanities with you!" Her words felt hot leaving her mouth and she knew that, with just the slightest provocation, she might lose her shit.

Sheriff Battle would not be amused. He and her temper were old friends and he'd cautioned her, on more than one occasion, that it would one day get her into trouble.

Chill, Hayley.

"Do you know how busy I am, Mr. Michaels?" Hayley asked through gritted teeth.

"How busy are you, Helen?"

Hayley narrowed her eyes at Michaels, desperate to wipe that smug smile off his face. "Did you hear about the

baby that was abandoned on the trunk of Cammie Wentworth's car in the Royal Memorial Hospital parking lot?"

Jackson nodded. "Of course I did. Cammie is a good
friend of mine."

How good a friend? Were they sleeping together? Were
they involved? She could see it. Cammie Wentworth was
the daughter of Tobias Wentworth, a Texas Cattleman's
Club stalwart and billionaire oil and cattle rancher. Jackson's father had been, apparently, Wentworth's best friend
and after his son, Rafael, left Royal after falling out with
his father, Michaels became Wentworth's de facto son.

Cammie and Jackson made perfect sense. But she'd
seen Cammie with Drake… Honestly, keeping up with
Royal gossip was exhausting.

Annoyed and jealous, and irritated at feeling annoyed
and jealous, Hayley slapped her hands on her hips. "I
have been working twelve-to-fourteen-hour days trying
to find out who baby Pumpkin belongs to and you know
how far I've got?"

"How far?"

"Nowhere! I've checked local birth records, have pe-
rused reports of missing infants and checked on whether
any accident victims had a baby. I'm running out of ideas."

Jackson looked like he was about to speak so Hayley
nailed him with an if-you-talk-you-die look. "I haven't had
a decent night's sleep in a month and if my parents insist
on introducing me to another man they think I should
marry, I will throw up."

"Uh—"

"I have to study, I have assignments coming out of
my ears and I'm falling behind. I'm not the falling-be-
hind type."

"I'm sure—"

She wasn't done. Not until he understood why she
didn't have time to waste. "I can't even use my crazy life

and insane schedule to get out of going to the TCC gala next week—"

"Not your thing?"

"The primping and the preening? God, *no*. And I don't have a dress so I have to make time to find one!"

"So, don't go to the gala," Jackson suggested on a casual shrug.

That would be first prize but impossible. "Real estate moguls can blow off important events on the town's calendar and not suffer any reprisals but, as an underpaid, almost broke cop who has been ordered to be there by her boss, I can't."

Humor flashed in his eyes again. "Is Sheriff Battle expecting violence to break out on the dance floor?"

"Funny." Hayley tipped her head up and looked at the blue Texas sky. She'd begged Nathan to let her off the hook, telling him that galas were her wealthy and socially active family's thing, not hers. She far preferred to drink a beer and shoot pool at Bert's, a bar on the outskirts of the town. Sheriff Battle listened to her impassioned plea before telling her to find a dress, get her hair done and not to be late. And if she ignored his order, she would be riding a desk for the rest of her life.

A TCC gala ball or desk duty? Both were equally tedious.

"Are you one of the first responders being honored for your work during the COVID-19 pandemic?" Jackson asked, looking curious.

Hayley sighed. At the gala ball, various first responders from fire and emergency services, as well as hospital workers, were to be inducted as honorary Texas Cattleman's Club members for their heroic service through the two worst disasters in recent Royal history—the tornado that ripped through the town in 2013 and the COVID-19 pandemic. Hayley had zero interest in joining the TCC and the idea of being lauded for doing her job made her feel deeply uncomfortable.

Hayley wrinkled her nose and refused to look at him. "I don't know who came up with that stupid idea. I was just doing my job. I don't need anyone to make a fuss." Releasing a frustrated sigh, she forced herself to meet his eyes.

"Anyway, I hope you now understand why I don't have time to waste, Mr. Michaels, so don't make me come back out here, okay?" Hayley scowled at him. "Next time I might not be quite as nice."

The smile Jackson handed her was as wide as the Texas sky above and Hayley saw the deep dimple in the left side of his cheek, and his eyes deepened to purple. His open, laughing face made her want to touch his lips with hers, to bury herself in his arms, to soak in some of his vitality and to roll around in his deep, sexy laugh.

Damn. Not good.

"This is you being nice?" Jackson asked when he stopped laughing.

Yeah, well, it had been a few tough weeks.

Jackson lifted his hand and Hayley held her breath, thinking he was about to touch her. Every hormone Hayley possessed sat up and quivered, hoping he would. But then his hand fell and he incinerated her with a hot look instead.

You're on duty, Lopez.

So?

"You need to get back to work, Harper Lopez. You need to find that baby's mama."

Hayley shook her head, a wave of tiredness and despair rolling over her. She was stumped and more than a little despondent. "I don't know if I can."

Why did she let that slip? And why in front of him, of all people? There were just a few people she opened up to and an arrogant man she met fifteen minutes before did not qualify.

Jackson cleared his throat and Hayley forced herself to look at him. All traces of amusement were gone and her breath caught at the intensity of his expression.

"You can. And you will," Jackson told her. There was no equivocation in his voice and Hayley found herself nodding, suddenly a little more energetic and optimistic.

"It's been—" he hesitated, as if looking for the right word "—interesting meeting you, Officer Lopez."

Same.

Not wanting him to leave without a solution to her Bubba problem—hell, not wanting him to leave at all—she waited until he was behind the wheel of his big-ass truck before tapping his window. He hit the button to the electric window and when it was down, she put her hand on the open window. "So, do I have your word that you will leave Bubba alone?"

Jackson flashed her another of his amazing smiles. "Not a chance, Hortense."

Hortense? Really? She sighed. "My first name is Hayley."

She wondered how long it would take him to do the computation and arrive at the right conclusion.

Five seconds passed before comprehension dawned. He was quicker than most. "Juan Lopez's only daughter? The one he's desperate to find a husband for?"

She still found it strange that everyone in town knew her father didn't approve of her moving out of the family compound—the roots of the family business were in Royal but the family relocated to Dallas over fifteen years ago—into a small apartment in town, that he was horrified at her being a cop and couldn't understand why she wouldn't stay home and play the pampered princess. He'd worked hard to give his children everything, yet his youngest and most stubborn child was determined to throw his generosity in his face.

She didn't need his generosity or his patronage. She'd make it on her own, dammit. Unlike her brothers, she refused to allow another person, even if that person was her father, to write the story of her life. She'd wield the pen, thank you very damn much.

Jackson stared at her, his expression inscrutable. "Well, that explains a lot."

He started his engine—God, it sounded good—and accelerated away.

Hayley slapped her hands on her hips and scowled at his departing truck. And what, exactly, did that mean?

So that was Hayley Lopez.

Jackson had heard of her. Few in their uber-wealthy circles didn't know about the headstrong youngest child of Juan Lopez, who'd walked away from the family to follow a career as a public servant. But he hadn't realized she was a cop or that she was so incredibly gorgeous...

Or so damn young.

Driving back to Royal, Jackson rested his wrist on top of his steering wheel and scowled into the midday sun. He'd lost his sunglasses again, the third pair this month. He was an intelligent person but keeping track of his sunglasses was beyond him. Anyone would think he was sixty-three and not thirty-six.

Thirty-six. God. Where had the years gone?

And Hayley Lopez couldn't be more than twenty-three, twenty-four? There had to be a baker's dozen years between them and that was why the thoughts he was having—what she looked like under her ugly cop uniform and whether her long hair hit her spectacular ass—were wildly inappropriate.

But there was no denying that she was hot.

With brown-black eyes that flashed fire, she had the longest eyelashes he'd ever seen and hair that was long, thick and, he suspected, a little curly. Her amazing attributes didn't stop there: cheekbones that could cut glass, a straight nose, sexy lips and a stubborn chin. And God, that body. Hayley was tall, with legs that went on forever, and on the skinny side of slim. She did, however, have amazing curves that could make lingerie models weep.

Heading back to his offices in Royal, Jackson tried to shift his attention from the sexy cop to his in-peril development but he couldn't get those flashing eyes and her obvious irritation out of his mind. Her reaction to him amused him. Most women, on meeting him socially—and it never mattered whether they were single or not—went directly into flirt mode. Hayley Lopez, probably because she had three very macho brothers and a father who took no shit, wasn't even remotely impressed by him.

Jackson wasn't sure whether to be pissed off or pleased.

Jackson heard an incoming call on his car's Bluetooth system and, scrunching his eyes up as he drove into the sun, tapped his steering wheel to answer the call.

"Michaels."

"Jackson, darling, it's Thea Bowen-Hardy."

When was he going to learn to check the display before answering calls? "Thea, I'm on another call so I can't talk."

He wasn't but he wasn't in the mood for Thea's inane conversation.

"I was wondering if you'd like to be my date for the TCC gala ball next week?" Thea asked in a breathy, baby-doll voice. No doubt about it, he far preferred Hayley Lopez's take-no-prisoners (literally, in her case) voice. "I appreciate you thinking of me—" no, he didn't "—but I already have a date."

"Ah, well, I'm sure I'll see you there."

Not if he could help it, Jackson thought as he said good-bye and disconnected the call. Thea was the last in a long line of women asking him to be their date to the TCC function. Normally he refused without an explanation so what made him tell her that he was bringing a date? And Jackson did not doubt that Thea had already texted ten of her girlfriends and her mother with the news that he, the guy who went to most functions alone—why create more chatter?—had a date for the year's most prestigious event. Jackson sighed. Knowing Royal's penchant for gossip, he'd be engaged by nightfall and married by morning.

He'd boxed himself into a corner, Jackson reluctantly admitted. If he rocked up at the gala without a date, he'd have a crapload of women pissed off at him…

He'd have to find a damn date. And that was going to be a pain in his ass. He instructed his phone to call his oldest friend and smiled when he heard her harried hello. "Why don't we have any chemistry?" he demanded.

"Hello to you, too, Jackson," Cammie drily responded. "Care to explain that out-of-the-blue statement?"

"Well, if we had chemistry, we could be married already and I wouldn't have to find a damn date for the damned gala."

Cammie laughed softly. "I'm so sorry that our lack of chemistry has inconvenienced you. Besides, I'm with Drake now and he wouldn't appreciate me ditching him to be your date."

His oldest friend had recently reconnected with her first love, Drake Rhodes, and Jackson smiled at the happiness in her voice. Cammie deserved to be loved and in love and if Drake hurt her again, he'd kick his ass. But Drake seemed to be as much in love with Cam as she was with him but he'd keep an eye on him.

Nobody was allowed to hurt the people he cared about.

"I stupidly told Thea that I had a date for the gala ball,"

Jackson told her, scowling when Cammie responded with a chuckle.

"You moron! You do know that she won't keep that news to herself and the world will want to know who you are taking?" Cammie asked him, pointing out the obvious.

"I'm aware," Jackson sourly replied.

"Just say yes to the next woman who asks you to the ball," she suggested.

"I'd rather shoot myself in the foot," Jackson muttered.

"Did you go out to Bubba's this morning?" Cammie asked him, changing the subject. "Is he still balking at selling?"

"He is. And Hayley Lopez is giving him legal advice, advising him of his rights and encouraging him not to sell, as if she were a real lawyer and not still studying toward her law degree," Jackson grumbled as he swung into the parking area adjacent to his office building. A lot of his colleagues found it strange that the headquarters of Michaels International, a phenomenally successful real estate development company his father started forty years ago, was based in Royal but he had satellite offices all over the world and spent most of his time on the road.

"I can't develop the area around Stone Lake without his property, so if he doesn't sell, the whole development is a nonstarter."

"Community opposition to your proposed development is growing, Jackson," Cammie told him.

Jackson cut his engine and shrugged. If he had to kowtow to the people who hated his developments, he wouldn't have built anything in the last decade. Opposition came with the territory.

He didn't march to the beat of the collective drum.

"Jackson?"

"Yeah?"

"You said you were going to call Rafe and try to persuade him to come to the gala ball. What did he say? Is he going to come?"

He'd been waiting for and dreading her question. Jackson pushed his index finger and thumb into his eye sockets, thinking of how to tell her about his and her brother's tense conversation.

It was all so damn complicated...

His father and Rafael's father had been best friends and he and Rafe grew up together. He'd watched the proud and ambitious Rafael butt heads with Tobias, partly because Tobias was demanding and controlling, partly because Rafael always felt like an outsider in his own family. He was the son of Tobias's long-term mistress and when she died, Tobias took Rafael in and gave him the Wentworth name. But his new stepmother, Cammie's mother, hated the bastard child sharing her daughter's inheritance and made his life a living hell. Jackson couldn't blame Rafe for leaving Royal but desperately wished he and Tobias could find a way back to each other.

He'd give anything to spend more time with his dad. His mom? Not so much. Jackson pushed thoughts of his family away, preferring to keep his focus on the Wentworth family. Recently he'd noticed changes in Tobias, brought on by the death of his beloved third wife, Danae. He seemed softer, less combative and abrasive. And his quiet announcement a few weeks back, telling just him and Cammie that he would be announcing, at the upcoming TCC gala, that he would fund the college expenses for all the children of the emergency service honorees, floored him.

Tobias's generosity was a side to the man he'd never expected to see. If Tobias Wentworth, proud, stubborn and ornery, could change, Jackson thought anyone could.

And maybe if Rafe saw Tobias 2.0, they'd manage

to repair the Rio Grande–sized rift between them. And Cammie could have a relationship with her older brother.

So Jackson had called him yesterday, Rafe answered and Jackson asked him to attend the gala. Rafe didn't reply for the longest time before responding with a two-sentence zinger.

"My father has you as his bonus son. Does he need me there?"

That was pretty close to a no, so Jackson didn't want to give Cammie any false hope. "I don't think so, honey. I'm sorry."

Jackson heard her disappointed sigh and, wanting to change the subject, he steered Cammie away from the thorny subject of her family. "How's baby Pumpkin? I still can't believe I was out of town and missed all the excitement."

Cammie was looking after the newborn who'd been left on the hood of her car a few weeks before. The authorities—and Hayley Lopez in particular—were desperately trying to chase down his relatives.

"Good, lovely," she responded and he heard the smile in her voice. "I'm so enjoying fostering him. Did Hayley say anything about whether she was any closer to finding his mother?"

He thought back to his conversation with the firecracker, remembering her black eyes filled with fire and her kissable mouth. And body.

Too young for you, Michaels. Way too young.

"Just that she's working on it," Jackson said, exiting his vehicle. He heard the beep of another incoming call and explained that he had to go.

"It's probably another sexy single wanting to invite you to be her date for the ball," Cammie told him.

She wasn't wrong.

Two

"Morning, Mom."

Hayley, on her way out of her house, yawned and tucked her phone between her ear and her neck. Only her mom would call her shortly after first light, before she'd managed to snag a cup of coffee from the Royal Diner.

Only her mother was that brave.

"Hayley Sofia, you did not call me yesterday. How am I supposed to know that you are not dead in a ditch somewhere?" Inez demanded.

Hayley, getting into her patrol car, decided not to remind her mom that if she were hurt or missing or dead, Sheriff Nate would've called them as soon as he heard. But, since it was way too early for a fight and because she was caffeine deprived, Hayley decided to let it go. There were some arguments she would never win.

Hayley settled herself in her car and scowled at her home as she backed down her drive. Another of those no-win battles was to get her landlord to renovate the Victorian cottage she rented. Painted in shades of bright lilac and purple, it was a cookie of a house and didn't suit the tough-cop image she liked to project. But, since her landlord cut her a deal on her rent in exchange for picking up her groceries and walking her overweight bull mastiff, Peppermint, Hayley tried not to nag her.

But purple...*seriously*?

Slapping on her sunglasses, she turned right and headed into town. "How are you, Mom?"

"Fine. Your dad is fine, your brothers are fine but you, *you* don't have a date for the TCC gala!"

Oh, God, this. *Again.* Hayley turned onto Main Street and headed straight for the Royal Diner. She needed coffee, intravenously injected. Stat.

"Are you coming to the gala?" Hayley asked, trying to duck the question. "I thought you and Dad are heading for Europe next week."

"We are but Luis and Miguel will be there to represent the family and watch you get your award."

"And are Miguel and Luis bringing dates?"

"Well, no."

Ah, the usual double standard. Irritation flashed through her, as hot and as bright as a supernova. Matias was married, with kids. Luis and Miguel were still sowing acres of wild oats but Inez nagged only Hayley about her single status. It was okay for her siblings to be ambitious, to be proud, stubborn and intractable—those were traits that her parents admired but only in their boy children—but she was expected, as the baby and the girl, to be dependent. In her parents' eyes, her being ambitious meant snagging a wealthy, successful man and then producing more much-wanted grandchildren.

She was a constant disappointment, but she couldn't change for them, wouldn't change for anybody. She would never allow anyone to dictate the terms of her life, ever.

And because that was her universal truth, a cornerstone of her personality, Hayley knew that the chances of her finding a man who could love a headstrong, forthright, kick-ass-and-take-names Latina boss-girl were slim to none. Sometimes the thought made her sad, but mostly she was happy to be single, doing what she wanted when she wanted, answerable only to herself. Sure, she occasionally wished she had a pair of muscular arms to step into, a hard chest to lay her head on, a masculine mind to bounce her ideas off, but if the cost of love meant losing herself, then she'd pass, thank you.

"Chiquita..."

And that was the problem. She'd always be a little girl to her mother.

Hayley listened to her mom tell her about a distant aunt who was in the hospital having a tummy tuck—and this was important, why?—and inspected Main Street, still empty but for the occasional jogger and cyclist. The lights were on in the Royal Diner and even if it wasn't open, she knew that someone inside would give her a cup of coffee.

Hayley said goodbye to her mom and was about to pull into one of the many empty parking spaces outside the diner when she looked down the street and saw a low-slung sports car—holy shit, was that a Bugatti Chiron?—do an incredibly fast and highly illegal U-turn at the traffic light a block away.

Coffee or compliance? Hayley sighed, cursed her ability to let things go and backed out of the parking space.

If she chased the Chiron and the driver hit the accelerator, there was no way she'd be able to catch up with one of the fastest cars in the world. But it would be a stupid move for the driver as only a few people in the country owned a Chiron so she'd easily track him down.

And then she'd throw the book at him.

God, she needed coffee.

Hayley sped down East Street, flashed her lights and saw the Bugatti slow, then pull into an open space next to the RCW Steakhouse. Good deal, she thought, the driver wasn't a fool.

Getting out of her vehicle, she slowly approached the driver's door and watched as the window slid down. Damn, it was hard not to run her hand down the car's sleek body, to not feel a little envious of whoever it was who was privileged enough to drive this car-rocket. It was a masterpiece of car engineering and, yep, she was envious. God, she'd love to take it for a spin, to push it to its three-hundred-miles-per-hour top speed.

But maybe not. She wasn't sure she had the balls to go that fast.

Hayley radioed Dispatch, told them she was making a traffic stop on East and kept her eyes on the driver's hands. Nice hands, she realized, broad and masculine with long fingers and neatly clipped nails. "License and registration, please."

"Officer Lopez, you are a lovely sight first thing in the morning."

Hayley bent down to look into Texas bluebonnet eyes and sighed. Jackson Michaels. Of course it was...

"Mr. Michaels, you did a U-turn back there."

"I forgot some important papers and there wasn't a car on the road."

Ah, the old "the road was empty so the rules don't apply" argument. Hayley looked down, saw that he was holding an overlarge, Texas-size coffee mug and reminded herself that she wasn't allowed to appropriate anyone's coffee. Dammit.

Hayley stepped back as he opened the door and exited his stupidly expensive vehicle, coffee cup in his hand. She wasn't sure what to focus on, his clean-shaven face, his big body in a dark gray, Hugo Boss suit or his fabulous car.

For the first time, she wished she wasn't wearing her cop uniform, that her hair wasn't scraped back into its usual bun and that she'd remembered to swipe on some lip gloss or some mascara.

She liked her uniform, liked the authority it gave her, but it wasn't sexy. For some asinine reason, she wanted Jackson Michaels to look at her as a woman and not as a law enforcement officer.

But a law enforcement officer she was. And would be until she passed the bar exam.

Jackson snapped his fingers in front of her face and Hayley blinked, trying to remember where she'd lost the conversation. Had she asked him for his documents yet?

"Are you still half-asleep, Hayley?"

She should tell him to call her Officer Lopez but she didn't have the energy. "I was up until about two studying and I've run out of coffee at home so I'm not firing on all cylinders yet," she admitted.

Jackson held out his mug to her. "I'm happy to share."

She shouldn't, it wasn't professional, but coffee was her happy, make-her-human juice. "You're not going to get out of a ticket by peddling my favorite drug, Michaels."

Jackson's laughter heated her from the inside out and made her lady parts sit up and pay attention. "It never occurred to me."

Liar, Hayley thought, taking his big mug. She lifted it to her mouth, tipped it and sighed when the rich, dark taste rolled over her tongue and slid down her throat. She liked her coffee sweet and rich with cream but this was black and dark. And extraordinary. She pulled it away from her mouth and looked at the cup. "Oh God, this is sensational. What is it?"

"The beans are grown on the slopes of Mount Meru

and Mount Kilimanjaro in Tanzania," Jackson replied, watching her as she sipped his coffee. He leaned back against his Chiron and crossed his ankles and his arms, looking tough and sexy and amused and sexy…all at the same time.

"You have brilliant taste in cars and coffee," Hayley told him.

"I know," he replied. He crooked his fingers in a "gimme" gesture and Hayley held his mug tight against her chest. She didn't care if it was his; possession was nine-tenths of the law.

Hayley sipped again and, eventually and reluctantly, handed him his cup back, watching as his lips hit the spot where hers had been a few seconds before. Damn, she wished that he'd kiss her. He looked like he'd be good at kissing. And sex. Very good at sex.

Jackson's grin flashed. "I would love to know what you are thinking."

Not a chance. Hayley pulled the cup from his hand, conscious that her face was a few shades hotter than it was before.

"So, how goes dress shopping?"

Hayley frowned at his out-of-left-field question. "What are you talking about?"

"A dress for the gala? You should wear red, or aqua. Jewel colors would show off your amazing skin."

He thought she had amazing skin? Really? The compliment, issued in his come-to-bed voice, made her feel alive and pretty and rather wonderful and…yes, uncomfortable. So, because she didn't know how to deal with compliments that weren't related to her work, she scowled. "Thank you, Coco Chanel."

But he was right, today was Monday, the ball was on Saturday and maybe she should make an effort to find something. She was good friends with Natalie Valentine and knew that she carried a few designer gowns at her bridal shop. "I'm hoping that Natalie will have something for me to rent."

"You're going to *hire* a dress?"

Hayley lifted one eyebrow at the horror in his voice. Jeez, she hadn't said that she was going to beat a confession out of a suspect.

"Hiring dresses is what people who can't afford designer dresses do," Hayley pointed out.

"But you're Juan Lopez's daughter."

And he assumed that she had access to Juan Lopez's credit cards and bank accounts. "I fund myself, Jackson. And I have since I was eighteen."

"I heard that you left the family fold but I, sort of, assumed that your parents still helped you out."

As did everyone else. "You assumed wrong. I don't take a cent from them…for anything."

"Why not?"

He looked genuinely perplexed but not judgmental so, instead of telling him to mind his business, Hayley decided to be truthful. "I left home after an argument with my father—"

Why was she telling him this? She never spoke to anyone about her complicated relationship with her parents.

"I told him to shove it and that I would make it on my own, my way. So I moved to Royal, starting as a dispatcher at the station. I attended community college and saved up enough to train with the sheriff's department. I was promoted and a few years back, I started my law degree."

"All on your own?"

Hayley nodded. "All on my own." There were times when she ate ramen noodles for two weeks straight, when she slept on a blow-up mattress and nights when she came so close to calling her dad and throwing in the towel. But she was more stubborn than most and had too much pride for her good.

"In six years, I've set up a home, put myself through school, have enough for my needs." She wrinkled her nose. "But not enough to buy designer ball gowns." She tipped her head back and glared at the wide, winter sky. "If Natalie doesn't have a suitable dress for me to hire, I might just ask Sheriff Battle if I can attend in my uniform."

"And if he says no?"

Hayley shrugged. "No idea...*yet*." A plan could always be made. Hayley wrapped her hands around the still-warm coffee mug. "Are you going to the ball?"

"Mmm-hmm."

"With Cammie Wentworth?" Why was she even asking? His love life had nothing to do with her. But every cell in her body disagreed and she was one big nerve ending of overripe jealousy.

"Cammie is with Drake Rhodes," Jackson replied. "Besides, we never had any chemistry."

That was...*interesting*. Two of Royal's prettiest people with no chemistry. "Nothing?" she asked, sounding doubtful.

His lips quirked upward. "Nothing." He made an up-and-down movement, drawing attention to his ripped body. "I know, right? How can anyone resist this?"

Hayley immediately realized that he was making fun of himself. "Your lazy-ass body and ugly mug are easily resistible, Mr. Michaels." Liar, liar, pants on fire. Hayley decided to throw him a bone. "Though you do have exceptional taste in cars and coffee."

She wrinkled her nose, thinking of the ball and her mother's suggestions for a date. "So, how many women have asked you to be their date?"

One big shoulder rose and fell. "Eight? Ten? I haven't kept count."

"And why haven't you accepted? Surely there is one woman in the bunch you could tolerate for the evening."

"Sure, but I don't want to give anyone any ideas that the date might lead to something. It won't. I don't do relationships."

Hayley had no idea why his statement made her feel sad. She was overtired and, despite making inroads into his oversize mug, was undercaffeinated. That was the only reason why she was acting like a sap

"Why not?"

"My mom, who was incredibly demanding and difficult, left when I was ten and I remember how devastated and broken my dad was. He was never the same after that. I vowed I would never put myself in a position of loving someone that much." He looked, just for a second or two, vulnerable, then embarrassed. Then his expression smoothed out. "Besides, I'm busy. I don't have time for anything that distracts me from work. I can't give a relationship the time it deserves, and I can't commit to anything other than my career."

Fair enough. She didn't have the time or inclination, either. She had a law degree to finish, a bar exam to pass, people to help. A man would only slow her down and split her priorities.

"And you? Are you going solo to the ball?"

"I'm intending to, but my mother has sent me a list of men she's already spoken to, men who would be happy to be my date," Hayley told him, sounding bitter. "I wouldn't be surprised if I opened my front door on Saturday night and found a man standing there, waiting to escort me to the TCC Clubhouse. My mother is ruthlessly efficient, and she likes getting her way."

He stared at her and Hayley tipped her head to her side,

her turn to wonder what he was thinking. "What if we go together?" Jackson suggested.

Hayley slowly lowered the coffee mug. "Say what?"

"It makes sense. You need a date, I need a date but neither of us wants to find a date. We don't want to date anyone who has expectations of said date."

"I've never heard anyone use the word *date* so much in one sentence."

He waved her observation away. "C'mon, Hayley, it makes sense. It'll be a no-stress, no-pressure arrangement."

And it would get her mom off her back. Hayley thought about it, didn't see any immediate downsides and slowly nodded. "Okay."

"Excellent," Jackson said. He plucked his coffee cup from her hand and reached for the door handle of his superexpensive car. As he was about to open the door, Hayley placed her hand on his to hold the door shut. Her hand was half the size of his.

Jackson sent her a lazy smile. "As much as I'd love to stay here and shoot the breeze, I need to get to Dallas. I have an appointment I can't miss, and I need to leave now."

"Not without me giving you a ticket for your illegal U-turn."

Hayley fought to keep her face impassive, to hide her smile at his astonishment. What? Did he think she'd forgotten why she'd stopped him in the first place? Jackson shook his head, as if trying to make sense of her words. "But I gave you coffee!"

"So you *were* trying to bribe me with coffee, Mr. Michaels?" Hayley asked, tongue in cheek.

"Yes, no, yes. Shit." Jackson released the door handle and pinched the bridge of his nose. "Can you make it quick, *Officer* Lopez? I am late."

"It takes as long as it takes," Hayley told him, amused. She wandered back to her car, grabbed her book and took down his details, loving the smell of his cologne on the crisp morning air. She handed him the ticket and struggled to hold back her smile. "You're free to go. Don't get caught speeding."

Jackson folded the ticket and placed it into the inside pocket of his jacket. He ran his hand through his expertly cut hair before yanking open the door to his expensive car. He dropped into the seat and hit the start button and Hayley shivered at the sexy growl of the engine. The car turned her on. So did the man.

God help her.

"Pick me up at seven thirty on Saturday. I live in the… colorful house on Elm Street," she told him, bending down to look into his face.

"Colorful house? Can I have a bit more of a description?" Jackson asked, sounding irritated.

"You'll know it when you see it." Hayley patted the frame of his window before deliberately looking past him and frowning. As she expected, he turned his head to follow her gaze and, when he wasn't looking, she jerked the travel mug from his hand.

She grinned at him and lifted the mug in a toast. "Thanks. I'll get the mug back to you."

"What? No! Shit, Lopez! A fine and then you steal my coffee?"

Hayley turned her back to him and walked back to her patrol car, sipping his delicious brew.

Yep, when she was done drinking his truly excellent coffee, she might, maybe, be ready to face the day.

Jackson had expected to be back in Royal Tuesday afternoon but complications with his Palms Springs development had him flying east to attend a meeting with his contractor and his architect, who were arguing pretty versus practicality. Finding a solution that worked for both of them took more time than expected and after telling them to pick up the pace because the development was behind schedule, he flew back to Dallas to pick up ten garment bags that he'd carefully placed on the passenger seat of the Chiron.

Jackson steered his car down Elm Street and looked at the pretty cottages on the leafy street. It was after nine and fully dark but, so far, the houses were pretty standard, nothing he would classify as colorful. He crossed the intersection and, in his headlights, picked up a flash of purple. He drove a little farther and looked to his right, a smile stretching his lips. Her house was indeed colorful, a mixture of purple, ranging from light to dark. It was the only house on the street that could be termed *colorful*.

The house was whimsical and quirky and didn't suit his favorite, no-nonsense, can-do-it-on-my-own and don't-mess-with-me-I-carry-a-Glock cop. Still smiling, Jackson turned his head and looked left, seeing the pile of garment bags on his passenger seat. This was either going to be his best idea ever or he was going to go down in flames.

And that was why he liked Hayley. He couldn't predict how she was going to react. Yeah, she was thirteen or so years younger than him but she had the heart of a lion and the confidence of a much older woman.

He admired her independent streak and was reluctantly impressed by her determination to carve out her place in the world. He hadn't had that choice. At eighteen he'd inherited his father's huge real estate development company when his father passed away from a very unexpected heart attack. Barely an adult, he'd been faced with a hell of a choice: to sell the company for billions to a competitor and bank enough to last for several lifetimes or to take over from his dad and build on his legacy. It had been an easy decision to make and he hadn't once regretted keeping Michaels International. It was a connection to his dad, a link that death couldn't take away. Jackson also wanted to build on the great work his father had begun; he loved and admired his father and it was a privilege to pick up where he left off.

Oh, and he also freakin' loved his job.

Well, he loved it when things went well. His Stone Lake development was almost dead in the water thanks to a stubborn old man who refused to sell. After this damn ball was over, he could give the project his full attention, which probably meant arguing with Officer Lopez a lot more.

He looked forward to it.

But, tonight, he had to navigate her very tricky pride.

Picking up his phone, he pulled up her number—Bubba had given it to him after he uttered those classic words *call my lawyer*—and quickly typed a text message.

Have you found a dress yet?

Twenty seconds later, her reply hit his screen.

No. I've been busy. I'll get to it. Stop nagging.

Nagging? That was a bit harsh since he'd asked only one question. But her not finding a dress made his next task a little easier…

Open up, I'm coming in.

Jackson exited his vehicle, walked around to the passenger seat and pulled open the door. Grabbing the garment bags, he draped them over his arm and slammed the door shut before walking up the path to her shades-of-purple whimsical house. Her front door—the color of a deep, violet bruise—opened and she stood in the doorway, leaning against the doorframe.

"Those had better not be what I think they are," she told him, her eyebrows pulled into a deep scowl.

Jackson resisted dropping a kiss onto her temple, instead gently brushing past her to enter her hallway. He looked around, grateful to see that the interior was painted a warm cream, that her sofa and chairs were navy blue. There wasn't a hint of purple anywhere.

"Why on earth is your house purple?"

Hayley's eyes darted to the pile of garment bags he draped over the arm of her sofa. She shut the door behind her and Jackson took his first good look at her lovely face. Her hair tumbled over her shoulders and down her back, in beach curls just a shade short of true black. Her soft, loose sweater fell off one creamy shoulder, revealed a hot pink bra strap and draped over an amazing pair of full, high breasts. Her sweater ended at the band of her tight yoga pants, painted over her flat stomach and long, stunning legs. Damn, that ugly deputy uniform should be burned.

She looked luscious, warm and sultry and beddable. But too young, dammit. Far too young. When she was born, he was kissing Patti Smith behind the bleachers and trying to cop a feel.

God, he felt old.

"What are you doing here, Jackson?"

"I came to see you," Jackson replied, keeping his tone easy. He looked across the open-plan room to the kitchen. "Have you got any whiskey?"

Hayley rolled her eyes. "No, I don't have whiskey but I can offer you a beer. And while you're drinking it, I'll help you decide on what dress you should wear to the ball."

Jackson's eyes collided with hers. "Me?"

Hayley's smile hovered on the other side of savage. "It's the only reason I can think of for you walking into my house with a dozen or so dresses. You seem to be a smart guy and you have to know that if I won't accept help from my parents, I sure as shit won't accept it from you."

Yep, feisty. And a little exhausting. Jackson sat down on her sofa and pushed a tired hand through his hair. "I'm not looking for a fight, Lopez, so go get me that beer and we'll talk."

He saw the fire in her eyes and quickly realized his mistake. "Please will you get me a beer and I'll explain?"

"Voy a sarcale la sopa!"

Jackson watched her very nice ass walk away and grinned. While he wasn't fluent in Spanish, he could converse and knew that she'd just uttered a slang phrase, telling him that she'd get the truth out of him. And she would. But only after he finished his beer.

"Do you want a glass?" Hayley asked him, standing in front of her old fridge. All her appliances were old. So was her furniture, but her home was lived in and colorful—rustic chic, as his decorator called it.

"It's in a glass already," Jackson told her, unable to pull his eyes off her long, lanky, sexy frame. God, what he wouldn't do to pull her down onto his lap, to slide his hand up and under her sweater, down the front of her panties. He wanted to know whether she tasted as good as he imagined, like hot sunshine, spice, whether her skin was as luscious as it looked.

He wanted her. Too damn much.

Hayley nudged his knee with the cold bottle, jerking him out of his musings. He took the bottle with a quick thanks and took a long sip, sighing as the cool liquid ran down his throat. Not wanting her to see the desire in his eyes or the action in his pants, he sat forward and looked at the open books on her coffee table, flipping the cover of one to see that it was a thick law book.

He'd hated the few law courses he'd taken at school and admired her determination to get her degree. She was the first woman he'd met who was as driven as he was but in a completely different way.

"How's it going?" he asked, genuinely interested as she sat down on the chair opposite him.

"Slowly." Hayley wrinkled her nose. "I have an assignment due on Monday and I haven't even started it yet."

"Is that why you haven't found the time to look for a dress?"

Hayley rested her bottle against her forehead. "I wish. No, I've been a little busy trying to find the parents of baby Pumpkin."

Right. The TCC gala and the abandoned baby were the favorite topics of discussion in Royal presently, with the Royal Reporters—as his friend Brett Harston called the biggest gossips—embellishing the facts to make them more salacious.

Jackson was about to ask her for an update on the case when she nodded to the pile of dresses. "You'd better not have bought those, Michaels. I'm pissed off at your highhandedness already but if you spent money on those dresses, I'm going to kick your ass, *hard*. I don't take charity from anyone."

She could try to kick his ass but he was not only taller and bigger than her—hell, he had a hundred pounds on her, easy—but he had a black belt in judo and thought he could hold his own.

"I never bought the dresses. They are—"

A hard knock on Hayley's door interrupted his explanation. Jackson frowned and looked at Hayley, who scowled. "God, I never have visitors and now I have two on the same night. It's like Grand Central Station around here."

Hayley stood up and stormed to her front door, yanking it open without checking the peephole. Hell, she was an officer of the law. Shouldn't she take a few precautions? Who knew who could be on the other side of her door, an ex-con she arrested, a dope dealer…?

"Hey, sorry to call on you so late but I have news."

Jackson stood up and looked past Hayley to see a woman standing in Hayley's hall. He took in her basic details—Caucasian, petite, long blond hair, green eyes, pretty—and realized that she was exactly the type of girl he normally dated. But, compared with Hayley's warmth and vitality, she looked a little bland, generic.

The blonde saw him, and her eyes widened in surprise. "You're Jackson Michaels."

Yeah, he knew that.

"I'm Sierra Morgan. I'm a freelance journalist working on a story for the *Royal Gazette* and *America* magazine."

"And a huge pain in my ass," Hayley said, smiling.

Sierra laughed. She turned to Jackson, her eyes bright with amusement. "Hayley and I have a love-hate relationship. I hate it that she won't share any of the details of her investigation with me and I love it when I find something she doesn't know about."

Hayley immediately tensed, her eyes bright with curiosity. "What did you find, Sierra?"

"Give me a beer and I'll tell you," Sierra retorted.

"What am I, a damn liquor store?" Hayley muttered. But she returned with a beer for Sierra, another for him, and gestured for Sierra to take the corner of the sofa, sinking to sit next to the pile of garment bags. Hayley scowled at the dresses before turning her attention back to Sierra.

"What did you find?" she asked.

Sierra nodded in Jackson's direction. "Are you happy for him to hear this?"

Hayley swiveled her neck to look at him and Jackson held his breath, wondering what she'd say. When she remained quiet, he told her that she could trust him not to repeat anything he heard. He never ran his mouth.

"He won't leave until we've had a conversation about these damn dresses," Hayley told Sierra, irritation sparking off her. "If I hear one word of this conversation on the Royal gossip line, I will disembowel you with a blunt teaspoon, Michaels."

Feisty, fierce, fabulous. Jackson ran his hand over his face and told his body to stand down. He was here to deliver some dresses, to make life a little easier for this overachiever, not to get into her head. Or into her pants.

He wanted to but he wouldn't.

Hayley sent him another "behave yourself" look and he swallowed his smile, amused that she was ballsy enough to think he'd blindly obey her dictates. He only ever did what he wanted to, when he wanted to, but for now, he'd simply listen.

Hayley sent a glance at her pile of books and frowned. He'd forgotten what it was like to try to juggle work and studying and...well, life.

"So, I have news," Sierra stated. He saw the glint of mischief in her eyes as she looked from him to Hayley. "But if I'm interrupting something I can come back tomorrow."

"You are, you're—" Hayley blushed when Sierra raised her eyebrows and Jackson found himself charmed when she waved her hands around.

"Not him," Hayley corrected. "I meant... You're interrupting my study time. And so is he. Just tell me what you found, Sierra," Hayley said.

Bending to the side, Sierra pulled a file out of her enormous tote bag and flipped open the paper cover. "These are hospital intake records for Jane Doe, who is, unfortunately, still unconscious."

Hayley's expression hardened. "How did you get those?"

Sierra pulled a face. "Let's skip that question."

"Sierra…"

Sierra sighed. "Hayley, I'm a journalist. People give me stuff they won't give to law enforcement. So, let's not look a gift horse in the mouth, okay?"

Jackson watched as Hayley, internally, debated whether to walk away or to hear Sierra out. He bet that her innate curiosity and her desire to reunite the baby with his mother would trump playing by the rules and when she gestured Sierra to continue, he realized that he'd read her correctly. Hayley had a strong moral compass but was prepared to be flexible when the occasion arose.

Good to know.

"Jane Doe was admitted the same day baby Pumpkin was found." Sierra pulled a piece of paper from the folder and handed it to Hayley. "This is the form where the patient's personal effects are recorded."

Hayley read the form and when she tensed, Jackson knew she found something of interest. "It says here that a blue-and-white-plaid handkerchief was found in a pocket of her pants."

Sierra stared at her as if waiting for her to connect the dots and it didn't take Hayley long. "It's his burp cloth."

Right, he had no idea what a burp cloth was. "What are you talking about?"

Hayley looked at him and Jackson knew that her brain was running at Mach speed. "Mothers of young babies toss it over their shoulders to protect their clothing."

Okay, got that. But he didn't understand why it was so important.

Hayley reached for her phone on the coffee table, quickly scrolling through her picture gallery. She held up a picture of a sleeping Pumpkin and Jackson noticed that the kid was wearing blue-and-white-plaid pj's and a matching cap.

"It's the same pattern as the burp cloth," Sierra said.

Yep, he got that. But what did it mean?

Hayley looked from her phone to the form, her shoulders hunched. "We ruled Jane Doe out as Pumpkin's biological mother because she hasn't given birth recently. So, who is his mother and what is Jane Doe doing with this kid?"

"She could have stolen him, could have adopted him—the possibilities are endless," Sierra said, her expression troubled. "I'll nose around town in the morning and see if I can find anyone who recognizes Jane Doe. Maybe I'll get lucky."

Hayley pinned Sierra to her seat with a mock-hard look. "Hey, sunshine, that's my job! I'm the cop, remember?"

"It's also my job because I'm an investigative reporter, remember?"

Hayley closed her eyes, shook her head and released a long sigh. When she opened her eyes, Jackson saw the exhaustion in her eyes and a wave of protectiveness rolled over him. She needed a solid six to eight hours of uninterrupted sleep. She also needed to slow down, to relax, to have some fun.

But he knew that Hayley would think she was slacking if she took even an afternoon off.

Hayley rubbed the back of her neck and when she looked at Sierra again, Jackson saw the capitulation in her eyes. "If you find out anything, anything at all, you tell me, Sierra."

"And if you find anything out, you tell me."

"That's not how this—"

Hayley's reply was interrupted by Sierra jumping to her feet. When Sierra dropped a kiss on her cheek, Hayley looked stunned at the unexpected gesture of affection.

She rubbed her cheek with the back of her hand and glared at Sierra. "What was that for?"

"You are too precious, tough girl." Sierra pulled the file from Hayley's fingers and stuffed it back in her bag. "Don't bother getting up, I'll see myself out. And Hayley?"

"Yeah?"

"Get some sleep, okay? You look like hell."

A statement he completely concurred with. She didn't look like hell, he doubted she could, but she did need sleep. Unfortunately, he wanted Hayley to fall asleep only after he'd pleasured her. And, preferably, in his arms.

A thought that was, for a commitment-phobe, completely terrifying.

It was time to get out of here before he acted on his impulses.

He stood up and Hayley followed him to his feet, her expression inscrutable. "Where do you think you're going?"

"I agree with your friend. You need sleep."

"You're not going anywhere until you explain why there are dresses on my couch," Hayley informed him, hands on her curvy hips.

Right, the dresses; he'd forgotten about them.

"As for sleep, I can do that after I pass the bar," Hayley told him, draining her beer. "Explain the dresses, Michaels. And make it good."

Three

She had a baby's parents to find, assignments to complete, her hair to wash. But right now she had to deal with a Thor look-alike in her tiny cottage. Jackson dropped down to sit on her sofa, looking very much at home and like he belonged in her space. His big arms rested along the back, his long legs were crossed at the ankles and his eyes were deep, dark and mysterious.

And all Hayley wanted to do was to straddle those hard thighs, slam her aching core against his erection and ride herself to some mind-blowing pleasure. And, judging by the ridge in his pants, his thoughts weren't far off hers.

He wasn't her type…

Sort of.

Sure, he was gorgeous and ripped, and she wouldn't mind exploring the wonderland that was his body, but he wasn't long-term material. And Hayley wasn't a girl who jumped into bed just to scratch an itch… Hell, she had a vibrator for that.

No, if she slept with someone it would be because she thought their attraction had legs, that he had the potential to become someone very important in her life.

Her second lover was a cowboy she adored, someone she loved enough to introduce to her folks. She'd been thinking of forever, he'd been thinking about how to access her father's bank account.

But Jackson—older and hotter—didn't want or need anything from her or, more crucially, from her family. He didn't need her family's money, their contacts or their influence. Jackson had enough of that on his own. He just seemed to dig her. And while she might be inexperienced in seduction and attraction, she knew he wanted *her*.

And that was a hell of an ego boost.

Flickers of hot, prickly attraction danced up and down her spine as heat settled between her legs. Her breasts felt achy and heavy and all the moisture in her mouth dried up…

She wanted him and if he made the smallest move— a crook of a finger, a quiet suggestion of taking her to bed—she might just agree and consequences be damned.

They could argue about the dresses later. After he rocketed her to heaven and back.

Hayley jumped when Jackson uttered a sharp curse and watched him lean forward and start slamming her textbooks and notepads closed.

What was he doing?

"Uh—"

"I am not going to sleep with you and you're not going to study! The only place you are going is to bed. Alone."

Wow. And… What?

"You need to sleep. And I need to get out of here before I do something stupid." Jackson jammed his hands in the pockets of his pants and Hayley saw the tension in his jaw. He looked a little pissed and a lot frustrated.

Hayley felt like she was sitting in a plastic bucket on storm-tossed waves. When Jackson started stacking her books and notepads, she threw her hands up in the air. "Stop messing with my stuff, Michaels. And please tell me why you are acting like a crazy person."

Jackson stepped back and lifted his hand, leaving a small space between his thumb and forefinger. "I'm this close to losing it so don't push me, Hayley," he said, through gritted teeth.

Don't push him? What the heaving hell? "You are in my house, dumping dresses on my sofa, listening to private conversations, bossing me about and rearranging my stuff. And I'm the one who's being pushy?"

"No, you're the reason why I'm taking cold showers lately. And they haven't helped a damn!"

What was he talking ab—oh. *Oh.*

Jackson pushed both hands into his hair and tugged. "That pink bra strap is driving me nuts. I keep thinking about your amazing breasts under that silky fabric, how your ridiculously long legs would feel wrapped around my hips."

His words, uttered in that deep, sexy growl, dialed her heat factor back up to a thousand degrees. She had to be in his arms, she needed to have his lips on hers. She couldn't wait any longer to know how he tasted, whether reality came close to her imagination.

Jackson took a step back and raised his hand in a "stay there" gesture. "I'm going to go."

What? Noooooooo! Why? Things were just getting interesting.

"I thought you were going to kiss me," Hayley whispered, shocked to hear the disappointment in her voice.

Jackson scrubbed his hands over his face. "God, I want to."

"So what's the problem?" Hayley demanded, confused.

"You're...you're..."

If she wasn't so comprehensively confused she'd be a little amused at seeing the usually confident Jackson grasping for words. "I'm...?"

"Too young!" Jackson forced the word out. "Goddammit, Hayley, I'm thirteen years older than you. You're just a kid."

What? Oh, he didn't just say that, did he? He couldn't possibly be that stupid.

"I can drink, I can vote, I can hit the bull's-eye on a target at a hundred feet away. I'm a contributing member of society, a valued member of this community. I goddamn help people every damn day! I support myself with no help from anyone." Hayley felt her voice rising with every syllable, knowing that Jackson had hit her hottest of hot buttons. She worked her ass off every day to cultivate respect, to get people to see her as capable, so Jackson's statement was a knife blow to her heart.

Angry beyond measure—angry with him because he defined her by her age and not her capability and angry with herself because she felt rejected—she pointed to her door.

"Get out!"

"Hayley—"

"Swear to God, Jackson, get the hell out of my house or I might just call for backup and make you leave." She wouldn't. She'd never tell anybody about this but he didn't need to know that.

Jackson rubbed his forehead and slowly made his way across the room. He faced her again, his expression inscrutable. "I never meant to insult you, but the fact is, I'm in my midthirties and you haven't even hit your midtwenties yet. You are still establishing your career. Mine is rock solid. You are, I think, inexperienced in bed. I am not. Yes, I'm attracted to you, you're freaking beautiful."

Blah, blah, blah…

"But we're at completely different stages in our lives, Hayley." Jackson momentarily closed his eyes. "I don't want to take advantage of you."

Take advantage? Seriously, he was talking like she had no control over her body, like someone else made the decisions about her sex and love life. Holy crap on a rocket ship, she couldn't believe this was happening.

Nobody took advantage of her, ever. She was stronger and better than that. Making her own decisions, walking her own road was the reason she bucked her father's control, rebelled against her mother's wishes. She made her own decisions and lived with the consequences of them and Jackson's making assumptions on her behalf pushed every one of her buttons.

Hayley's hot look was intended to scorch. She allowed him to see her disdain before walking past him to pull open her front door. "As I said, get the hell out of my house. And, really, don't bother picking me up on Saturday night. Despite what you think, I am a big girl and fully able to attend a TCC gala without a big, important, self-important man on my arm."

"Hayley—"

She was done. Exhausted and disappointed and on the point of tears. She refused to let him see her cry. Nobody was entitled to see her tears. Her father and brothers never had, and Jackson was barely more than a stranger.

She had work to do, assignments to complete and a baby's parents to find. That was important work. Jackson Michaels, the billionaire buffoon, was not.

"Good night, Michaels. Don't bother dropping by unannounced again."

Hayley walked away, heard the door shut behind him and closed her burning eyes. Forcing them open, she looked over her sitting room and cursed at the pile of dresses on her sofa. She looked at the door, wondering whether she had time to gather them up and get them to him, and then she heard his car start and the engine rev as he pulled away.

She'd missed her chance. Maybe that was a blessing in disguise because when she next saw Michaels again, she wanted to be ice-cold, emotionally unavailable and ridiculously formal with a badge on her waistband and a gun on her hip.

Too young, her ass.

"Hayley!"

Hayley, standing on the porch of yet another house in her quest to track down baby Pumpkin's mother, turned to watch Sierra run up the concrete path to the house, blond hair pulled into a messy knot on the top of her head. Were those wooden skewers holding her hair up?

"Why do you have chopsticks in your hair?" Hayley asked, laughing, when Sierra reached her.

Sierra grinned. "I couldn't find any hair ties and these work." She shrugged. Then she frowned. "God, you look more exhausted, if that's even possible, than you did last night."

"I already have one nagging mother, thank you very much."

Sierra sent her a naughty grin. "So, was he good in bed? He looks like he would be."

Hayley slowly lowered her sunglasses. "What the hell are you talking about?"

"Jackson Michaels, of course. Judging by the electricity crackling between you two, I kept expecting one or both of you to spontaneously combust," Sierra replied. She leaned forward. "So who jumped who? Is that grammatically correct? Should I be asking who jumped whom?"

Hayley felt the beginnings of a headache at the back of her skull. "God, you're nosy."

Sierra didn't look chastised. "I'm a reporter. It's an essential part of the job. So, did he keep you awake all night?"

"No. And that's all I'm going to say," Hayley snapped, using the side of her fist to bang on the door.

"Pity," Sierra replied. "I think you two would suit each other."

When icicles formed in hell. She'd prefer not to hook up with a guy who thought he could boss her around. She was fully independent and didn't need an alpha male making decisions for her. And if she did, her father would be at the head of that line.

Hayley sent Sierra a done-talking-about-this look. Sierra smiled and, thank God, changed the subject. "What are you doing here?"

"Door-to-door canvassing," Hayley replied, knocking on the door again. "I checked the hotels and motels a couple of weeks back but someone somewhere has to have seen Jane Doe or someone with a baby. And why isn't Mrs. Kay answering? She never goes anywhere!"

Hayley heard movement within the house and faced Sierra again. "Why are you here?"

"I was asking questions, too, and someone steered me here, told me that Mrs. Kay was renting a room to a young female. I thought I'd come and check it out."

Hayley had to admire Sierra's persistence. And below her hardnosed reporter persona, she sensed that Sierra cared about Jane Doe and baby Pumpkin, that this was more than a story to her. She could respect that. She could even work with her, provided she didn't impede her investigation.

The door opened and Hayley smiled at Mrs. Kay, who,

with her snow-white hair, curved back and deeply wrinkled face, looked like she was 104 years old.

"Hayley Lopez, how nice to see you! And you brought a friend to visit with me," Mrs. Kay said in her high-pitched squeak. "Come in, have some coffee and a slice of pie."

Hayley's mouth watered. Mrs. Kay's pecan pie had won first prize at Royal's Bake Show for ten years running and it was bliss on a plate. But she had a million things to do today and couldn't afford the time to stay and chat.

"I'm here in an official capacity, Mrs. Kay, and we can't stay for coffee. This is Sierra Morgan, by the way," Hayley explained, stepping into her overdecorated hall.

Mrs. Kay folded both hands over the knob of her wooden walking stick and looked up at Hayley with troubled eyes. "I was considering calling you, you know."

"Really? Why?" Did she want to report her cat missing again? Hayley never minded responding to Mrs. Kay's calls about her missing cat. Joseph-John had a habit of hiding out under the porch and Hayley invariably found him there, and Mrs. Kay showed her gratitude by foisting something sweet on her.

Mrs. Kay's baking was a perk of her job.

"I was wondering how long I should wait to file a missing person report."

"Who is missing, Mrs. Kay?"

Mrs. Kay shook her head and looked stubborn. "No, no… You tell me why you are here first."

Hayley nodded, resolved to return to Mrs. Kay's concerns later. "There's an unconscious woman in the hospital and we are trying to identify her. We are also trying to identify the mother of a baby left in a carrier on Cammie Wentworth's car."

"I heard about that. Bad business."

"Sierra is here because she heard that you recently

rented a room to an out-of-town female," Hayley said. She lifted her phone and showed Mrs. Kay a picture of the unidentified, unconscious woman.

Recognition flared in Mrs. Kay's eyes and when Sierra tensed, Hayley knew that she saw it, too. They were on the point of a breakthrough and they both knew it.

"Will I get into trouble talking about her? Aren't there privacy laws I should be aware of?" Mrs. Kay asked, her expression troubled.

"We're trying to help her, Mrs. Kay," Hayley said, keeping her tone mellow. "Tell us what you know."

"The missing person report I thought about filing? It was for her. She paid me her rent up front, three months, but she never said anything about going anywhere and I haven't seen her in ages. But all her stuff is still in her room."

Hayley knew that Sierra was mentally doing a high five and, to be honest, so was she. "Who is she, Mrs. Kay?"

"Her name is Eve Martin. She said she's from Miami. She had the sweetest baby boy with her."

Progress, progress, progress!

"But that's all I know," Mrs. Kay stated. "She's a lovely girl but wasn't the chatty type."

And Mrs. Kay, lonely and long widowed, loved company and would pull anyone into a conversation at any time. Hayley reminded herself to talk to the town's social worker to see if Mrs. Kay qualified for any home help or programs to get her out of her house.

"Can we see her room, Mrs. Kay?" Sierra asked.

Mrs. Kay immediately shook her head. "Well, I don't know about that. I don't think that's right."

Hayley took Mrs. Kay's old hands in hers. "You know me, Mrs. Kay. I'm trying to help her. I really am."

Mrs. Kay considered her words and quickly nodded

her head. "Only because it's you and I trust you, Hayley Lopez. Let me get you the key."

When Mrs. Kay turned her back, Hayley held out her fist for Sierra to bump. They had a name for their unconscious Jane Doe and a probable connection to baby Pumpkin. Awesome news.

After searching the room, Hayley and Sierra decamped to Hayley's house to examine various items of interest they'd found in Eve's room.

Hayley led Sierra into her living room and scowled at the pile of dresses still sitting on her sofa. She needed to do something about them…

No, Jackson had brought them over without asking her. It was his job to take them away. Hayley told Sierra to take a seat and, after dropping Eve's bagged and tagged personal obsessions onto her coffee table, pulled up Jackson's phone number.

Typing quickly, she told him that she was home and that he needed to pick up the dresses. If they weren't out of her house by that evening, she'd donate them to the charity shop downtown.

Jackson's reply hit her phone ten seconds later.

Do you have a dress yet? Of course you don't, so for God's sake, pick one! And, no, I didn't buy them. A friend of mine owns a dress shop in Dallas and she's happy to take everything back.

Not being a child. I can find, and buy, my own dresses. Get them out of here by 5:00 p.m.

Hayley tossed her device onto the coffee table and slapped her hands on her hips. "Men. Can't deal with them, can't shoot them."

"Jackson Michaels?"

"Who else? And no, I don't want to talk about it," Hayley snapped. Wincing, she sent Sierra an apologetic look. "Sorry. Do you want coffee or something?"

Sierra shook her head. "No, thanks. I just want to look at her stuff." Sierra nodded to the evidence bags on the table.

Hayley looked up at the ceiling, looking uncomfortable. "We shouldn't be looking at any of this. We have no right to it and I will be taking it back to Jane Doe in the morning."

"We can have a quick peek, surely?"

"I'm just looking at her stuff so that I can find out who she is," Hayley told Sierra, thinking of the fine line between respecting Jane Doe's privacy and investigating. "I'm just gathering information."

Hayley opened a bag and pulled out Eve's ID, her eyes drifting over her fine features.

Who are you, Eve Martin? All she knew so far was her name and that she was twenty-eight and from Miami.

Miami was a city of close to half a million residents. Why couldn't she be from a small, Podunk town of five hundred?

Sierra pulled out a book covered in leather. She flipped it open and, glancing at it, Hayley saw the feminine writing. Was Sierra holding Eve's diary? If she was, then score! Diaries were great sources of information.

She wouldn't read it but Sierra could. Nobody, as far as she knew, had committed a crime so it wasn't evidence…

"What does Eve have to say? Does she mention the baby?" Hayley demanded.

Sierra shook her head, her eyes moving across the page. She flipped a page, then another and eventually looked up, her eyes puzzled. "This isn't Eve's diary, but her sister's, I think. She talks about Eve in the third person and…holy crap."

Hayley almost had to sit on her hands to stop herself from yanking the diary out of Sierra's hands. "What?"

"The baby's name is Micah. He is her sister's son."

Hayley took a moment to process that information. "Does it say why Eve has the baby?"

Sierra shook her head. "Not that I can see."

"Any mention of the baby's father?"

"Again, not at first glance." Sierra frowned at her. "Are you wanting to reunite the baby and his father?"

Hayley lifted one shoulder in a shrug. "I'd like to, at the very least, establish who the father is so that I can contact him. He might be going crazy wondering where they are, what's happened to them."

"Or he might not even know of the existence of a child," Sierra pointed out.

Fair point. "I'll need to head back to the station, see if anyone has reported Eve Martin or baby Micah missing. I'll also run a check and see if I can pull up details on who her sister is."

Sierra held the book up so that Hayley could see the front inside cover and the first page. Arielle Martin, Miami, 2020.

Well, then. That helped.

Hayley stood up and smiled as Sierra toed off her sneakers and lifted her feet, covered in bright red socks, onto her sofa, her nose buried in Arielle's diary. Hayley knew it was important that they discover who Arielle and Eve were but found reading the private thoughts of another woman disconcerting. But it was necessary and Sierra didn't seem to have any qualms so Hayley would leave her to it.

"Help yourself to whatever you need," Hayley told her,

picking up her phone. "Call me if you find anything interesting."

"I've found something interesting," Sierra stated, just as Hayley was about to open her front door.

Walking back into the sitting room, Hayley stood in front of her. "What?"

"There is one mention of Micah's father," Sierra said, finally lifting her eyes from the book.

"Well, who is it?" Hayley impatiently demanded.

"There isn't a name." Of course there wasn't. That would be too easy. "But she writes that he's from Royal and, drumroll, please…"

She was fond of Sierra but it had been a long day and she wasn't in the mood for games. "Sierra," Hayley warned.

"She says that he's a member of the Texas Cattleman's Club."

"Marvelous," Hayley sourly stated. "The TCC members are only the most influential, richest, boldest and most powerful men in the country, maybe even the world."

"But that's what makes it interesting. And fun." Sierra smiled at her, her expression impish. "I like ruffling feathers."

Hayley had noticed. Sierra was a bit like a large wave. Sometimes it was easier to go with the flow than fight it.

"Huh, that's strange."

Sierra held up the diary to show Hayley an almost blank page except for a name—Rafael Wentworth—bracketed by several asterisks. Cammie's brother? Rafael was the black sheep of the Wentworth family… Could he also be baby Micah's father?

"I need to start at the beginning and work through the diary systematically, making notes as I go," Sierra stated before placing the diary on the cushion next to her. She looked to her right at the pile of garment bags on that end of the sofa. "As we've already established, I'm incredibly nosy... Can I take a look?"

Hayley shrugged. "Knock yourself out. Jackson Michaels brought them over.

"He probably wanted to make sure I didn't embarrass him at the TCC gala," she added, her tone bitter.

"You're going to the gala with him?" Sierra asked, standing up.

"I *was* going with him. Now I'd rather stick hot coals under my tongue."

Sierra pulled down the zip of a bag and pulled out a soft gray ball gown. Pretty but a little dull. "What did he do?"

Hayley had a lot of friends but no one she was close to and, inexplicably, she needed to talk, to get someone else's perspective on last night's suck fest. "We have this weird attraction. All I can think about is jumping him. And I know he's attracted to me, too, but—"

Sierra opened another bag, saw the pink frothy material and immediately zipped the bag up again. Good call. She wouldn't be seen dead in anything that color. "But?"

"I, kinda, suggested that he should kiss me and he, explicitly, told me he wanted to but that I was too young."

Sierra frowned at that. "But you're in your late twenties, aren't you?"

Because of her height, people always assumed she was older than she looked. "I'm turning twenty-four in a few months."

"You're twenty-three? But you're so damn mature and together," Sierra spluttered, looking a little confused. She pulled out a red dress, laid it on the couch and slowly nodded. "I like it."

"I'm not wearing any of those dresses. They are going back to him, unused. I am not his charity case."

"Mature, together and very stubborn. And young," Sierra added.

Hayley threw up her hands. "I can't help my age, Sierra!"

"I know that, honey, but he is thirteen or so years older than you. And what would you prefer…a guy who takes what's on offer without a thought to the age and power dynamic between you or a guy thoughtful enough to consider the dynamics and the consequences of you hopping into bed together?"

Well, when she put it like that. "It's my body, I am fully able to decide if I want sex or not," Hayley muttered. "It's not like I asked him to marry me."

"Of course you are," Sierra told her. "And of course you didn't. But, as your friend, and we are on our way to being good friends, Hayley Lopez, I am happy to know that Jackson isn't the type to rush in and take advantage of someone a lot younger than him."

"He wouldn't be taking advantage. I want to sleep with him!" Hayley shouted, frustrated.

"Good to know."

Oh, Jesus, oh no. Crap. Hayley spun around, praying that she'd imagined his voice, that she was starting to hear crazy voices in her head and having delusions because anything would be better than having to face Jackson Michaels ten seconds after *that* heated declaration.

Sierra held her stomach, tears of laughter streaming down her face. Hayley glared at her and raised her index finger. "You know what you said about us being friends? Not gonna happen."

"Nah, it will," Sierra told her between laughter-tinged hiccups. She held up a silver dress and Hayley's breath caught somewhere in her throat. Despite feeling Jackson coming up to stand behind her, smelling his cologne and feeling his heat, her attention was snagged by the panels of fine silver silk. The neckline of the dress would end halfway to her navel, and the spaghetti straps were anchored to the draping fabric at the sides. The back would skim her butt and the color suited her complexion.

Yeah, she could work with the dress.

Straightening her spine, she lifted her chin, hoping her face wasn't still on fire. "I'm going back to the station." She pointed at Sierra again. "Go through the diary, let me know if you find anything."

Hayley turned to Jackson and lifted her eyes, slamming into all that purple-blue. There was amusement in those dark depths but she also caught a hint of remorse. He opened his mouth to speak but Hayley cut him off.

"Get those dresses out of here. But leave the silver one. I might—or might not—wear it. Text me the details of your friend in Dallas so that I can talk to her about buying it—" She saw him about to speak, knew that he was considering buying it for her and handed him a hard look that said don't even go there. Jackson's mouth snapped closed and she nodded. "Pick me up on Saturday night unless…"

She stopped talking and deliberately waited for him to prompt her to continue. "Unless?"

"Unless I'm too much for an old man like you to handle."

Jackson's mouth fell open, either at her insult to his age or the challenge, but she didn't care. He was caught off guard and that was the way she liked him. The man was far too confident and self-assured.

On Saturday night she'd blow all thoughts of their age difference out the window and they'd see exactly who could resist whom.

Guaranteed, she wouldn't be the one begging for a kiss when the night ended.

Four

Hayley had lived and worked in Royal for years and Jackson never noticed her before. But on this Friday morning, the day before the gala, she seemed to be everywhere. He'd seen her patrol car pass his offices when he walked into his building shortly before seven this morning, caught a glimpse of her talking to Sheriff Nate Battle on the steps of the courthouse earlier and now she was interrupting his lunch with Brett Harston and Clint Rockwell, old friends and fellow TCC members. To be fair, she wasn't interrupting per se—he was seated in a booth and she was standing at the counter ordering lunch to go—but she was the reason he'd lost track of the conversation.

When Hayley was around, hell, even when she wasn't, she tended to dominate his thoughts. And that had to stop. There were a hundred reasons why he shouldn't be thinking about her but the top three were that she was too young, too headstrong and too much of a handful.

He didn't have the time, energy or inclination to become emotionally involved, wrapped up in a woman, *any* woman. Even if he wasn't gun-shy after watching his mother make his father's life hell, he had a multibillion-dollar business to run, deals to strike, developments to build. His business required his time and focus and he owed it to his dad to carry on his good work and legacy. He just needed to get through tomorrow night and he and Officer Lopez could go back to being polite strangers.

He'd pick her up, escort her to the ball, be polite and then he'd drop her off and...

Leave.

"He wouldn't be taking advantage. I want to sleep with him!"

Her words reverberated in his head and Jackson sighed, telling himself for the billionth time that he could not take her up on her offer, that sleeping with her wasn't going to happen.

Too young, too headstrong, too unforgettable...

Brett snapped his fingers in front of Jackson's face. He jerked his eyes off Hayley's butt and back to his friend's face. He far preferred looking at Hayley; she was a lot prettier.

"Yeah, I heard that you are taking Officer Lopez to the gala," Brett stated, raising one eyebrow.

Jackson bristled. "So? Her parents wanted to choose her partner and every single woman in Dallas and Royal wanted me to be their date so it was a mutually beneficial arrangement."

"Every single woman? Exaggerating much, Jack?" Clint asked, amused.

Jackson, discreetly, lifted his middle finger. "You know what I mean... Hayley and me, it's an *arrangement*, not a date."

"Really?" Brett mocked him, "An arrangement? Do

you always bring a dozen dresses back from Dallas for a business arrangement?"

Jackson released a long groan. "Where did you hear that?"

Brett shrugged. "Dude, the Royal Reporters are on fire and you know that you are one of their favorite topics of conversation."

"Any way to shut them up?" Jackson asked, knowing it was a stupid question. Gossip was Royal's much-loved pastime.

"Get married," Clint suggested.

Jackson scowled. "Very funny, Rockwell." He'd rather put his head in a gas oven.

"Actually, it was a serious suggestion. Being happily married is a firewall between you and the gossips. The RRs don't find married bliss very interesting."

To be fair, it was a good point. Since their marriages, neither Brett nor Clint was the subject of gossip. Besides, he didn't care what people said about him. He was rich and powerful enough for that not to matter.

On the other hand, Hayley wasn't. She was a public servant, someone who needed the community's trust to work effectively. She'd hate being gossiped about…

And maybe he should have thought about that before he asked her to be his date to the ball, before he brought those dresses back from Dallas. Thanks to his wealth and power, he was insulated but she didn't need the town commenting on her life.

Jackson gestured the waitress over, asked her to fill his mug and looked across the table to his friends. "Officer Lopez is run off her feet trying to reunite the abandoned baby with his mother, and she has no time to go dress shopping. She heard I was going to Dallas and asked me to collect the dresses. Hell, if she had her way, she would go to the gala in her uniform."

Jackson gestured to the waitress to fill up his friends' mugs, as well. "I might walk in with her tomorrow, but after that, we'll go our separate ways. It isn't a date," he added, conscious of the server's flapping ears.

The waitress stepped back and Jackson smiled at her. "Thanks, Cathy."

Cathy left and Brett nodded, looking impressed. "Way to quash the rumors, dude. Your words, twisted and turned, will be all over town in—" he looked at his watch "—two hours."

Jackson looked at Hayley, his eyes drifting down her slim back. "She doesn't need to be talked about," Jackson muttered.

"Well, then I suggest that you take her eyes off her ass and stop drooling," Clint suggested.

Jackson immediately wiped his mouth with the back of his hand. His hand came away dry and he glared at Clint. "Not funny, dude."

"Actually, it was."

"Yeah, it was," Brett agreed, laughing. He looked at Clint and waggled his eyebrows. "Are you buying his early declaration that she's an arrangement, not a date?"

"Not even a little bit."

Jackson pushed his coffee cup away and tossed some bills on the table to cover his share of lunch. "I'm not looking to put a noose around my neck and she's way too young for me."

"Sarabeth is ten years older than me and it's not an issue," Brett pointed out. "It's not like Hayley is desperate to please. She's super smart, driven, community-minded and mature."

Clint sipped his coffee and nodded. "What he said."

"What is it with married people and their need to see everyone around them in front of a preacher?" Jackson demanded, standing up.

Clint shrugged and smiled. "We've found the one person we want to irritate for the rest of our lives. We want that for you, too."

His back to the room, Jackson raised his middle finger again and walked away to the sound of his friends' laughter. Assholes.

Leaving the restaurant, Jackson saw Hayley's squad car parked on the opposite side of the road. He shouldn't, it would cause more talk, but his feet refused to obey his brain's command.

Jackson crossed over and saw that she was steadily making her way through a huge helping of pesto-and-pasta salad.

"Hungry?" he asked, bending down to look into the open car window.

Hayley yelped and her fork wobbled and pieces of pasta landed on her shirt. Cursing him, she grabbed a napkin and cleaned herself up.

"Do not sneak up on me, Michaels."

"Shouldn't you be more aware of your surroundings?" Jackson asked her. "What if I were a meth head or a mugger?"

"Yeah, we see a lot of those in Royal," Hayley snorted as she snapped the lid onto the container. Her lovely brow furrowed and she wrinkled her nose. "Actually, we did bust up that meth lab a few months back and Candice Johns was mugged a few years ago." After placing the lid onto her salad container, she wiped her fingers and looked at him with eyes that held a touch of frost. "What do you want, Michaels?"

Her naked, her long legs around his hips or over his shoulders, his mouth on her… God, he had to pull himself together. "Seven thirty tomorrow?"

"I thought we already agreed on that," Hayley said, not letting him off the hook.

Jackson rubbed the back of his neck, amazed at her ability to cut through his bullshit. "Yeah, we had."

"So… What's the real reason you crossed the street to talk to me?" Hayley demanded.

"God knows," Jackson testily replied. "You drive me nuts. You know that, right?"

Hayley's grin was unexpected and as bright as the sun. "Yay, because you drive me nuts, too. Good thing that we won't see much of each other after tomorrow night, right?"

Yeah, it was a good thing. An excellent thing. Then why did his heart hurt at the thought?

Their eyes, brown and blue, connected and held and Jackson felt himself spinning down a vortex. He reached out to grab the window of her vehicle, trying to ignore the thought that these were the eyes he'd been waiting for, the face he could look at for the longest time, the body he needed to make his own.

He wanted her. A little less than he didn't want to want her.

"I should go," Hayley said, her voice soft and sounding, uncharacteristically, confused. She waved her hand at the notebook lying on the passenger seat. "I need to get to the hospital."

The mention of the hospital had the hair on the back of his neck lifting. "Are you okay? Why are you going to the hospital? Who are you going to see there?"

A slow, sexy smile lifted the corners of Hayley's mouth. "Why, worried that you might have to find another date for tomorrow night?"

Jackson did a mental eye roll. If only his life was that simple. "Explanation, Lopez. Now."

Hayley didn't look impressed at his command. "Not that it has anything to do with you, but I have to interview Jane Doe. I got word that she regained consciousness a few hours ago."

A troubled expression crossed her face and he wanted to wade into her life, sword swinging and mowing down anyone and anything that caused her a moment of stress and tension. *Overreacting much, dude?*

And Hayley was the last woman who wanted, or needed, the white-knight approach. Jackson opened her door and dropped to his haunches, resting his arm on his bent knee. *Can your savior impulse and see if you can help, moron.*

"Can you tell me or is it sheriff's department business?"

"It's official business," Hayley told him, her eyes on his face.

Damn, that was the answer he expected.

"But—" Hayley said as he started to rise. Jackson immediately resumed his position, prepared to listen to anything she was prepared to tell him.

"But I, for some strange reason, trust you to keep your mouth shut. I shouldn't but I do and I need—"

She stopped talking and Jackson wanted to howl. What did she need, how could he help her? He resisted the impulse to demand that she carry on speaking and, reining in his impatience, waited her out.

"I know her name, her real name. It's Eve Martin. I did a background check on her. She's from Miami and she's a suspect in a case down there."

"What did she do?"

"She, *allegedly*, embezzled a ton of cash from the investment bank she worked at."

"Are you heading over there to arrest her?"

Hayley shook her head. "The Miami PD are still building their case so no arrest warrant has been issued yet. No, I'm just going over there to talk to her."

Jackson placed his hand on her knee. "That sounds pretty straightforward, so what's worrying you?"

Hayley's slim shoulders reached her ears and confusion skittered across her face. "I just feel like... I have this intense...*crap*."

"Just spit it out, Lopez."

Hayley stared at his fingers on her knee. "It's silly, I'm just being weird."

"Let me be the judge of that," Jackson gently suggested, squeezing her knee.

Hayley hauled in a deep breath and for a moment, a quick flash, she looked a little lost and so very damn...young.

"I'm about to sound stupid and I hate sounding stupid."

Of course she did. Jackson smiled. "At the risk of repeating myself, let me be the judge of that, sweetheart."

Hayley looked like she was going to object to his endearment but caught her words on her tongue. She rested her head against the headrest, her eyes on his. "My *abuela*, my mother's grandmother—not the one who owned a cabin next to Bubba—"

Whoa, hold on. "Your grandmother owned a cabin on Stone Lake?"

Hayley nodded. "The Lopez empire started in Royal. Didn't you know that?"

He did not.

"I loved that house, loved spending time with my grandparents on the lake. It's another reason why I'll fight to keep it the way it is."

Damn, she was emotionally attached to the lake. It held memories that she didn't want to be tainted. From experience, he knew that the hardest people to sway were the ones who had a visceral attachment to the land.

But Jackson thought he had some valid reasons for developing the land. He'd yet to do a project in Royal, and he wanted something he could put his dad's name to. His projects provided jobs, stimulated the local economy and boosted municipal coffers. All things his dad approved of.

But he wasn't going to argue with her about the development now. "Tell me why you are feeling angsty," Jackson reminded her.

"Right. Well, my *abuela* had this uncanny ability to see into the future, to know when stuff was heading her way. She said that she felt like she was standing on the edge of a chasm, about to fall. The feeling of wanting to look over your shoulder, like you are waiting for the hammer to drop on your head."

"And you are feeling like that?"

Another shrug. "Sort of. I feel like I am setting in motion something that is uncontrollable, something that has repercussions."

"Are you talking about your professional or private life?"

Hayley lifted both shoulders to her ears. "I'm not sure…either? Both?

"I live an unexciting life, Jackson. I work and I study," Hayley added. "Occasionally, I talk to the less privileged about their legal rights, but always with the disclaimer that I'm not a qualified lawyer. But between Eve Martin, the abandoned baby, being an honoree at this damn gala and my sudden and ridiculously inconvenient attraction to you, I feel like I'm sitting in a leaking boat on a stormy ocean. I'm feeling…"

"What, sweetheart?"

This time, she didn't react to his endearment. Progress, Jackson thought.

"Overwhelmed," Hayley admitted. "And I hate feeling like that! It's not who I am. I control my thoughts and feelings, not the other way around."

He remembered being her age, remembered thinking

that as he was now an adult, he had to have everything figured out. But life was a constantly evolving process and once you have a handle on one thing, a dozen other issues always bubbled up to challenge your confidence.

"Hayley, take a deep breath. You don't have to have a handle on everything all the time. Just focus on what's directly in front of you, tackle that, and then move on to the next thing. You'll work out the rest."

"Promise?"

Jackson stood up and handed her a reassuring smile. "Go to work, tough girl." He saw the hesitation in her eyes and nodded. "You can trust me to keep anything you say confidential, Hayley."

Fire flashed in her eyes again. "If you don't, I'll just arrest you for obstructing an investigation."

He grinned, happy to see that she was back to being fierce. He tapped the roof of her car and stepped back. "Go to work, Officer Lopez. And I'll see you tomorrow night."

Hayley wrinkled her nose. "Schmoozing and smiling. I'm not looking forward to it at all."

She started the engine of her car and pulled off into the traffic. Thank God he had a fairly healthy ego or she would've destroyed *his* confidence several conversations ago.

Hayley walked into the Royal Memorial Hospital and headed toward the bank of elevators, jabbing the button with her free hand. Lifting her bottle of water, she sipped and considered the conundrum that was Jackson Michaels.

He was a tough and ruthless businessman, bossy as hell, but—for reasons she couldn't yet pinpoint—she trusted him.

And Hayley didn't trust easily.

Hayley stepped into the elevator and pushed the button for the third floor, happy for a few minutes alone to gather her thoughts. Maybe she found it easy to speak to Jackson because he was wholly unconnected to her day-to-day life. As one of the few women in law enforcement in Royal, she had to work twice as hard as her male counterparts and not give them any excuse to see her as weak or emotional or temperamental. She couldn't talk to her family because if she even hinted at any dissatisfaction with her situation—work or otherwise—they would use her words against her, insisting that she come home, get married, play it safe.

Like Sierra, Jackson didn't seem bothered by her smart mouth or independent streak, and when she was around him, she felt like she'd found her safe space, the place where she could be herself.

Why him and why now? He was a lot older than she was but that didn't bother her in the least. She could handle him…

But only when they were fully clothed.

He'd take control in the bedroom, of that Hayley had no doubt. He'd push her to explore her sexuality, to try new ways of making love, would introduce her to new positions, push her out of her comfort zone. *Comfort zone? You have to have a love life to have a zone, Lopez!*

Anyway, Jackson would be a demanding lover, someone who expected his partner to keep up with him. She wished she could say that she was sexually adventurous, but the truth was that she wasn't. At all.

She wasn't a virgin but she'd slept with only two guys. She'd taken her first lover to assuage her curiosity—and the entire act had been a disappointment of epic proportions. Her second foray into sex had been a bit better—no fireworks but better than blah. She'd taken him home, introduced him around, invited him to move in. One morning, after falling asleep with her head on her cowboy's chest, she'd woken up to an empty apartment and a note telling her he was out of there because her father refused to invest in his cowboy-themed bar.

Oh, and that he was going back to his wife.

His wife... *Dios.*

After that debacle—and months of sleepless nights worrying that she'd be cited as the other woman in a divorce settlement—she'd taken herself off the market and devoted her time and energy to her job and her studies.

But Jackson Michaels, older, hotter and experienced, was the first man in years who had her imagining what his body looked like under his designer clothes. She wanted to know whether his skin tasted a little salty on her tongue, to rim her tongue around his belly button and over his hard abs, to push her fingernails into his gorgeous ass.

She wanted him...

Dammit.

"Ma'am?"

Hayley blinked, realized that she'd reached her floor and that the elevator doors were open and a group of people were waiting for her to leave the space. Hayley strode out of the elevator, apologized and tossed her empty water bottle in a recycling container on her way to the nurses' desk.

Eve Martin had been moved to a private room and Hayley followed the nurse inside. Eve was asleep and Hayley moved to a position just out of the patient's eyesight and leaned her shoulder into the wall, taking a minute to inspect the woman who was at the center of her case.

With her golden-brown skin and long brown hair, she was beautiful, her Afro-Caribbean roots easy to see. Long eyelashes rested against her skin and her cheekbones were high and full.

But criminals could be beautiful, Hayley reminded herself. Monsters sometimes came in pretty packaging. It was her job to be cynical, to be unemotional, to find the truth.

The nurse woke Eve up, helped her sit up and took her blood pressure and her temperature.

When she was done, the nurse gestured to Hayley, who stepped forward. "Officer Lopez would like to talk to you."

Eve whipped her head around and big eyes, scared eyes, slammed into hers. "Are you here to arrest me? Where's Micah?" She immediately tried to get out of bed, reaching for her IV drip to yank it out of her arm.

Ah, confirmation! "Micah is safe," Hayley quickly told Eve as the nurse slapped her hand over Eve's to stop her from pulling out the needle.

"You regained consciousness a few hours ago, Ms. Martin, and you're not going anywhere," the nurse told Eve in a don't-try-me voice.

Eve looked at Hayley again. "Are you sure he's okay?"

"He is. He is staying with foster parents Cammie Wentworth and her fiancé, Drake Rhodes. They are good people. They didn't know his name, so they've been calling him Pumpkin."

"Can I see him?"

Hardening her heart against the hope in Eve's eyes, Hayley sat down in a visitor's chair and pulled her notebook out of her bag. "Let's get through this interview and then we can discuss your access to the baby."

Worry flashed in Eve's eyes and she pulled her bottom lip between her teeth. "What do you want to know?"

There was so much to discuss, and Hayley wondered where to start. Because she believed that you caught more bees with honey than with vinegar, she crossed her legs and leaned back in her chair.

"Tell me about yourself—what you do, where you are from."

"My name is Eve Martin, but I guess you know that already."

Hayley didn't respond and waited for Eve to continue. She picked up a glass of water, took a sip, and Hayley tried to hide her impatience. Eve replaced the glass and was about to speak when a knock on the door distracted her.

Hayley whirled around and rolled her eyes when she saw Sierra's face between the door and the frame. "Can I come in?" Sierra asked.

"I'm conducting an interview, Morgan," Hayley grumbled.

Sierra ignored her and walked over to Eve, her expression gentle. "Hi there, I'm Sierra. I'm an investigative journalist and your story has me intrigued. How are you doing?"

Eve simply shrugged and Sierra perched on the side of her bed. "You scared us," she told the wan patient.

"I scared me, too," Eve admitted.

"What happened?" Sierra asked.

It was a question Hayley wanted the answer to, so she decided to wait to kick Sierra out. "That's a long story," Eve said, sounding exhausted.

"And one we're both eager to hear," Sierra replied. "I've been helping Hayley with her investigation."

"Journalists don't help cops, Morgan," Hayley reminded her. Again. She turned to Eve. "I can make her leave if you want to keep this discussion confidential, Ms. Martin."

"Call me Eve and I've got nothing to hide so she can stay," Eve replied.

Okay, then.

Sierra left the bed, pulled up another chair and sat down. "We're listening, Eve."

Eve looked at Hayley. "So, I guess you know that I'm under investigation for embezzlement."

Hayley nodded.

"I'm surprised I haven't been cuffed to the bed."

"Miami PD hasn't issued an arrest warrant yet," Hayley explained.

"I'm being framed."

That's what they all said, Hayley thought.

Eve pushed her hair off her forehead. "I have an affinity for finance and numbers. Not to brag, but I've been called brilliant. I've been working as an assistant analyst in an investment bank in Miami and because my boss is a slacker, and because I'm good at crunching numbers and spotting trends, my boss entrusted me with passwords and account access."

That was the how. Now she needed the why, Hayley thought.

"Along with another analyst, I was up for promotion and I think she set me up to get me out of the promotion race. She's the type who would stab you in the back and climb over your still-writhing body on her way to the top. She did a damn good job of convincing the powers that be that I'm a thief. The bank laid a charge, I'm being investigated and they got a court order to freeze my bank accounts."

Wow, they weren't playing games, Hayley thought, making a note.

Eve stared at the wall beyond Sierra's shoulder, her thoughts miles away. "My life collapsed around me. Just a few days before I was framed, I received news of my sister's death. I was shocked and devastated. I wasn't surprised to hear that she'd named me as guardian of her son, Micah. I'm the only family she has…had. I watched Micah being born and now I have to raise him."

She released a tiny sob. "Do you know how much babies need and how difficult it is to buy stuff when most of your money is tied up in a frozen bank account?"

"Most of your money?" Hayley asked, picking up the nuanced phrase.

"I had money I kept at home," Eve admitted. "My grandmother gave me ten thousand in cash before she died and made me promise I wouldn't bank it. She hated banks."

A good move, as it turned out.

"What happened to your sister?" Sierra asked.

"She died of a heart attack," Eve replied, rubbing her hands over her face. When she lowered them, Hayley saw the distress and grief in her eyes. She was either a damn good actress or innocent. Time would tell.

But Hayley was leaning toward innocent; there was too much emotion swirling in her eyes to be faked. This woman had been through a lot, losing her sister, her only family. Hayley was frequently at odds with her family but they were all healthy, thank God.

Healthy, wealthy and successful. She had a lot to be grateful for.

"I collected Micah and met with a lawyer who said it looked bad for me, that the evidence against me was strong." Eve's tormented eyes met Hayley's. "I was scared to the depths of my soul. I took a good hard look at the crappy situation I was in and decided my only option was to run."

"Why?" Sierra demanded, leaning forward. "Why run? Running makes you look guilty."

"I was facing immediate arrest and I knew the moment I was arrested, Micah would be tossed into the system and I wasn't going to let that happen. So I packed a backpack for me and one for the baby and hopped on a Greyhound bus and headed here, to Royal."

"Why Royal?" Hayley asked.

Eve pulled her bottom lip between her thumb and index finger. "I found my sister's diary. It was in Micah's diaper bag. I read it because I needed information on Micah's father. I still don't understand why she wouldn't tell me who he is. She told me everything!"

Hayley exchanged a look with Sierra. Now they were getting somewhere. "Carry on, Eve."

"Yeah, you're doing great," Sierra told her, with an encouraging smile.

Good reporter, bad cop, Hayley thought.

"Arielle didn't name names, but she did imply that Micah's father is from Royal and that he has some connection to the Texas Cattleman's Club."

What was wrong with just writing down his name? Why did Arielle have to be cryptic about Micah's parentage? Were these people trying to make her job harder?

"What did Arielle do for work?" Sierra asked and Hayley admitted it was a good question.

"She was a photojournalist. She was really good," Eve wistfully replied. "Before she returned to Miami to have Micah, she traveled around and took odd jobs looking for interesting small-town tales."

"Her diary was mostly focused on her time in Royal, Texas, and a 110-year-old story with ties to the powerful TCC," Sierra said, looking down at her notebook.

Hayley waited for Sierra to look at her and when she did, she raised her eyebrows. This was information she hadn't yet heard and Hayley wanted to know why.

"I was going to tell you, I swear," Sierra told her, not at all chastised. She looked at Eve and shrugged. "I've been reading Arielle's diary, mostly to figure out who you, and Micah, are. But I am equally fascinated by the century-old mystery Arielle mentioned."

Eve smiled wanly. "She told me about it and I'm equally fascinated."

"It would help if I knew what you two were talking about," Hayley told them, too tired to use her scary-cop voice. It wouldn't work on Sierra anyway.

Eve looked at Sierra. "I'm tired. Would you mind explaining?"

Sierra stood up and started to pace the room. "Arielle, Eve's sister, worked as an aide in Royal's assisted living center and was transfixed by Harmon Wentworth's story."

"Is he related to Tobias Wentworth?" Hayley asked.

"A second cousin. Harmon was a hundred years old and he told Arielle a secret he'd never divulged before. Apparently, he was adopted and he always wondered who his birth mother was."

Eve picked up the story. "He was left on a doorstep in Royal, Texas, one hundred years ago without a note. Arielle's diary reveals that the long-ago baby was somehow connected to a feud between the Langley and Wentworth families at the time of the TCC's founding."

Okay, this was all very interesting, but all this happened a long time ago and Hayley had to deal with the here and now.

"We're getting sidetracked," Hayley told them. She looked at Eve and raised her eyebrows. "I need to know why you left Micah on the hood of a car in the middle of a hospital parking lot."

Eve's eyes held the sheen of unshed tears. "Not my finest moment."

Sierra was about to jump in and reassure Eve but Hayley caught her eye and shook her head. She wanted Eve's unfiltered reaction.

"As I said, I wanted to find out who Micah's father is. I wanted to leave Micah with him while I tried to clear my name. I came to Royal, rented a room and headed over here, to this hospital, thinking that I'd ask about DNA and how paternity tests worked. I was crossing the parking lot, holding Micah's baby carrier, when I felt incredibly dizzy. I thought I was about to pass out so I put the carrier on the closest car. I think it was a Mercedes, I'm not sure. I made it to the hospital entrance. Before I could tell anyone about leaving Micah, I blacked out."

"Do you know what caused you to lose consciousness?" Hayley asked.

Eve looked at Sierra. "Off the record?"

"Absolutely," Sierra responded.

Eve placed a hand over her heart. "Like my sister, I have a heart condition. I saw the doctor earlier and my heart problems will keep me in the hospital for a few weeks." Tears rolled down her lovely face. "I can't look after Micah and I don't want him going into the system."

Hayley didn't either so she pulled up Cammie's number on her cell phone and dialed, and a few minutes later she had Cammie's assurance that she and Drake were happy to keep Micah with them for the foreseeable future and that they would even bring Micah to see Eve in a day or two.

"I'll give you Cammie's number. She said you are welcome to call at any time," Hayley told Eve.

Eve wiped her tears away and managed a tremulous smile. "Thank you. Are you going to arrest me?"

Hayley shook her head. "Not today. As I said, there's no arrest warrant out but don't do a runner, okay?"

"If I do, I might pass out again," Eve told her and followed up her sleepy statement with a huge yawn.

Hayley used her index finger to tell Sierra that they needed to wrap it up and Sierra nodded. "I'm writing a story about the history of the TCC club, so can I dig into the story about the kid left on a doorstep a century ago?" Sierra asked.

Eve nodded. "Knock yourself out. Feel free to try and discover who Micah's father is, too, if you like."

Sierra nodded enthusiastically. "I like."

Hayley bid Eve goodbye and they walked to the door and slipped out of her room. Outside, they walked down the hallway toward the elevator banks, both of them deep in thought.

"Well, that was interesting," Hayley said.

"Very," Sierra said. "We need to discuss it a lot more. What about tomorrow afternoon while we get our hair and makeup done at the Saint Tropez Salon?"

Hayley sent her a "get real" look. "I don't have an appointment at the salon and, even if I did, I can't afford their prices. I'm on a cop's salary, remember?"

"A call came in on your answering machine when I was at your house reading Arielle's diary. Your mother booked the appointment and has paid for it. I called them and they are squeezing me in at the same time."

"Have fun on your own," Hayley told Sierra. She saw the small frown of disapproval on Sierra's face and shrugged. "Look, my mother is flying to Europe tomorrow and will never know if I make the appointment or not."

Sierra grinned. "Nope. According to her message, she's persuaded your father to delay their departure and intends to check on whether you are there or not. If not, she, and your dad, will fly to Royal and personally escort you to the salon."

Hayley tipped her head up to the ceiling and released a vicious curse.

"Don't you check your messages?" Sierra asked, curious.

"No," Hayley retorted, walking into the empty elevator. "And now you know why."

Five

It was official—he'd walked into the TCC ballroom with the most beautiful woman in the room.

Hayley was, possibly, the most gorgeous woman he'd ever encountered.

Standing by the bar, Jackson watched Hayley greet Cammie and Drake, her silver gown sparkling in the romantic lighting of the ballroom. The body-skimming dress highlighted her subtle curves, dipping deeply to show hints of her fabulous breasts. Breasts that didn't need any support. Her lack of a bra had Jackson wondering if she wore any underwear at all.

Eyes up, dude. Stop looking at her breasts, stop waiting for a peek of a luscious, bare long leg to appear between the thigh-high slit of her dress. The strappy sandals on her feet took her height to over six feet and her deep, dark lustrous hair was curled and parted to one side and swept over one bare shoulder.

Hayley in her cop uniform and wearing minimal

makeup was lovely but this Hayley, with smoky eyes and bold red lipstick, was knee-dissolving, dick-hardening, breath-stealing sensational.

He couldn't take his eyes off her.

Not that he wanted to...

Thanking the bartender for his whiskey, he picked up a glass of champagne for Hayley and walked across the crowded room to join her, Cammie and Drake. Hayley took her glass and thanked him.

"Who's looking after the baby, Cam?" Jackson asked.

"Ainsley," Cammie replied. She looked at Hayley. "She's Drake's stepsister. By the way, I love your dress, Hayley. You look sensational."

Hayley pulled a face. "I'd feel far more comfortable in my uniform."

Jackson didn't doubt that for a second. Hayley might look stunning but now and again she tugged at the neckline of her dress or fiddled with her hair. She far preferred to be complimented on her brains and her competency than on her looks, and Jackson, used to women who put a lot of stock in their appearance, found her attitude refreshing.

Jackson forced his eyes to move off Hayley and looked at his old friend, immediately noticing her tight lips and the worry flashing in her eyes. He sent Cammie a reassuring smile. "I'm sure Rafe will be here soon."

It was a lie. He had no idea whether Rafe was coming or not.

Cammie bit the inside of her lip. "I hope so, Jackson. Wouldn't it be awesome if we could all spend Thanksgiving dinner together?"

Right, Thanksgiving was in a few weeks. Not having a family, he usually joined the Wentworths for Thanksgiving dinner and spent the rest of the holiday weekend working.

If Rafael didn't come to this ball, then he'd head to Miami and kick his ass, Jackson decided, coming back to the subject they were discussing. Cammie had been devastated when Rafael left Royal, and his half-sister had nothing to do with Rafe's feud with his father. All she wanted was to get to know her big brother.

His eyes met Drake's and at that moment Jackson knew that Cam's fiancé would gladly accompany him to Miami to kick Rafe's ass if he disappointed his sister. It was nice to know that Drake had Cam's best interests at heart. Love and loyalty weren't always, as he knew from watching his mother, a given in marriage.

"Tobias is going to be making the big announcement soon. I hope he's here for that," Cammie fretted.

"Don't get your hopes up, darling," Drake cautioned her.

Jackson heard a buzz of excitement and, using his height, he looked across the tops of many heads to the entrance and his eyebrows lifted.

Well, well, well, the prodigal son had returned. No kicking would be needed.

"Cammie, he's here," Jackson quietly told her.

A huge smile split her face and she put her hand on her heart. "Oh, that's amazing. Where is he? I can't wait to see him."

Jackson looked across the room to watch Rafael and sighed. Rafael was wearing his poker face but Jackson immediately noticed his tight lips and tense shoulders and knew that his old friend was already regretting his decision to return to Royal.

"Don't rush him, baby. Let him come to you," Drake suggested.

Jackson nodded. "That's good advice, Cam."

"Officer Lopez."

Hayley whipped around and teetered on her heels and

Jackson caught her elbow to steady her. He shook hands with Nate Battle, Royal's sheriff, and greeted Amanda, his always lovely wife.

Nate turned to Hayley and lifted both eyebrows. "Who are you and what have you done with my boot-wearing, ass-kicking officer?"

Hayley narrowed her eyes at him. "Hey, I'm dressed up like this because you wouldn't let me wear my uniform." Hayley winced at her frank reply and hastily tacked on a "sir."

"I should've. That dress is ..." Nate waved his hands, looking like a distressed father about to order his teenage daughter to wear a much longer skirt.

"You look lovely, Hayley," Amanda jumped in, nailing her husband with a "shut it" look. "And who wants to be photographed wearing that ugly uniform?"

"Me!" Hayley and Nate Battle said in unison and their companions laughed at their mutual distress.

Amanda rolled her eyes. "Well, do try and smile when you accept your awards. No hard-eyed cop grimaces, please."

"I don't see why we even have to do this," Hayley grumbled. "None of us want recognition. It's not necessary!"

"The town is deeply appreciative of Nate's work during the tornado that ripped through here in 2013 and for your and your fellow officers' service during the COVID-19 pandemic," Cammie quietly stated.

Nate tugged at the collar of his white dress shirt. "That's what we do, what we signed up for. We don't need thanks."

"Well, thanks is what you're going to get so suck it up, cupcake," Amanda briskly told him before looking at Hayley. "You, too, buttercup."

Hayley narrowed her eyes at Amanda, who laughed.

"Oh, relax, Hayley! I've known you for far too long to be intimidated by your 'I've shot people for less' look." She patted Hayley on the arm. "Besides, you're not armed so I'm safe."

Amanda tugged Nate away to join another group across the room, and Jackson watched Hayley as she tracked their departure. Nate took two steps before retracing his steps back to Hayley.

"I meant to tell you that I took a call from a captain in the Miami PD earlier today," Nate quietly told her.

Despite her fancy dress and Hollywood hair, Hayley immediately morphed into cop mode, her lips flattening and her eyes narrowing. "And?"

"She's in the clear and they no longer consider her a suspect."

Nate's words were vague enough to sound ambiguous but Jackson knew enough from Hayley to assume they were talking about Eve Martin, suspected of embezzlement in Miami.

Hayley nodded. "Good to know. Thanks, boss."

Nate darted a look at his wife, saw that her attention was elsewhere and raised his eyebrows. "Tailored jacket, Glock under my arm. You?"

Before Hayley could reply, Amanda called her husband and Nate left without waiting for an answer to his question.

But Jackson needed to know...

He looked at her tiny clutch bag, thinking that there was no way she could've stuffed a weapon into a bag just big enough to carry her phone. And her dress was painted on her, falling into silver waves from her hips down.

No way was she wearing her weapon.

But the thought of her carrying made him hot. Seriously hot. Like take-her-out-of-the-room-and-run-his-hands-over-her-body hot.

Jackson placed his hand on the bare skin of her lower back and dropped his head to talk into her ear. "He was joking, right?"

Hayley looked up at him through extralong eyelashes. "Nope, I'm a cop and I always carry."

Jackson closed his eyes and shook his head. Man, she was something else. A curious combination of savage and sexy and stunning.

"I don't believe you," he said because, really, no way was she wearing a skimpy designer gown and carrying a concealed weapon.

Hayley sent him a low, slow, wanna-bet smile. "I have a Ruger LCP, very small and lightweight, strapped to my left leg. Unless I decide to do the cancan, nobody will know it's there."

Thank God. And all his angels and archangels. Then Hayley placed a hand on his lapel and her breath caressed the shell of his ear. "I'd offer to show it to you but…"

"But?" Jackson's one-word question came out as a strangled gasp.

Her bare, golden shoulders lifted in a casual shrug. "But someone very stupid said I'm too young for you so…"

"What an idiot," Jackson said, his fingers digging into her hip.

Hayley's red lips curved upward. "I thought so." She lifted her chin and gestured to the French doors leading onto a balcony. "Want to come to look at the stars with me?"

If she was old enough to wear a slip-looking dress and carry a weapon, he wasn't going to joke around with her. "If we go outside, my hands are going to be all over your body."

Hayley looked at him with those dark, dark eyes. "Screw the stars," she stated and walked toward the balcony.

Jackson, feeling a little disconcerted and very turned on, followed her.

* * *

Hayley stepped onto the empty-of-people balcony, walked down its length to where it was dark and shivered. Her thin dress was no barrier to the cold and her nipples instantly pebbled and goose bumps broke over her skin. But being a little cold was a price she was very prepared to pay if it meant being in Jackson's arms, having his mouth on hers.

Hayley heard the door close behind her and slowly turned, her breath catching at the sight of a tuxedo-clad Jackson slowly making his way to where she stood.

There was something about a man in a tux…

No, there was something about Jackson. Underneath his urbane, charming facade, Hayley sensed something untamed and a little feral and she wanted to taste that wildness on her tongue. She was tired of dancing around her attraction to him. She wanted him and, judging by the possessive look in his eyes, he wanted her.

This was chemistry, pheromones, desire…two healthy people who wanted nothing more than to know each other in the most biblical of ways.

She was still Hayley, she told herself, still independent and forthright, still her own person, and nothing she did with, or to, Jackson would change that.

Hayley felt a flicker of trepidation when the back of Jackson's knuckles drifted over her cheekbone, down her jaw. So sweet, so tender.

Hard and fast she could handle; sweet and tender scared her.

She was physically attracted to Jackson but she intended to remain emotionally detached. She had things to do, goals to reach. She didn't have the time or the inclination to dive into a relationship…

"A million thoughts are buzzing around your overactive brain, Hayley Lopez," Jackson said, placing his hands on her waist and nuzzling his mouth against her ear. "Why don't you stop trying to control the world for ten seconds?"

Hayley placed her hands against the lapels of his jacket, resisting the urge to sink into his body and his heat. "I'm not trying to control the world."

"No, you're just trying to control your reaction to me," Jackson murmured. His hand moved to her bare back and dipped down between her dress and her bare skin. "Don't. Be honest with me. Do you want me?"

She couldn't lie, not about this. "Yes."

"Do you want to want me?"

"No."

Jackson chuckled as he raked his lips up the side of her throat, before pulling her earlobe between his teeth. How could such a small area of her skin be so sensitive? How was it possible that she had a highway of lust running from her earlobe to between her legs?

Jackson's bare fingers drifted over the top of her bare butt and stopped when he found the very thin, almost invisible cord to her thong. "I was wondering whether you were wearing any underwear."

"Only panties," Hayley told him. Was she sounding breathless? That was new.

Jackson pulled back to look at her and his hot gaze on her breasts caused her nipples to harden. Haylcy watched, mesmerized, as his eyes darkened and he lifted his hand to run the tip of his index finger over her nipple. Hayley shuddered. He was only touching her with his finger yet every nerve ending on her body felt alive, like she was plugged into a universal source of energy.

"You are so incredibly beautiful, Hayley."

No, she wasn't, but right now, with his eyes on her, she felt like she was. Beautiful, strong, feminine, powerful…

Hayley lifted her hand to curl it around his neck. "Is that all you are going to do, Jackson? Touch me there?"

A small smile lifted the corners of Jackson's mouth. "You don't like it?"

"Oh, I like it. I was just wondering if there's more to come."

Jackson moved his finger to her other breast, rubbing the palm of his hand over her nipple and causing Hayley to whimper. "I want you, more than anything in the world. I want to take your mouth, kiss you senseless and dig my fingers into your hair. I want to skim my hands up your truly excellent legs and slide my fingers inside you and make you shudder in my arms."

Hayley felt her womb pulsate, her skin prickle. Oh, God, she couldn't wait. She wanted all of that, all of him. She wanted him on her, sliding his long length into her, filling her and completing her. And she wanted all of that…right damn now.

"What are you waiting for?" Hayley asked, her voice husky with need. Needing to show him that she was very on board with anything he wanted to do to her, she placed her palm on his long, rock-hard erection, curling her fingers as best she could around him. Jackson sucked in a harsh breath before releasing a low groan, pushing himself into her palm.

"In case you didn't get the message, this is me giving you the green light."

"Ah, honey…" Jackson dropped his face into her neck.

"Kiss me, Jackson."

Jackson lifted his head to look at her, deep blue eyes frustrated. "I'd love to but if I start, I won't stop and they are about to announce the honorees. I don't want to mess your hair and makeup and if I start kissing and touching you, I know I will."

"I can't tell you how little I care," Hayley muttered.

She didn't care about the award but she did care about knowing what it felt like to be on the receiving end of Jackson's bedroom-based skills.

"God, you smell amazing," Jackson said. "You always do."

He pulled back and lifted one hand to her face, his thumb lightly stroking her cheekbone. "When the gala is done, when you have seen and spoken to everyone, received your award and done your thing, let me know and I'll be more than glad to divest you of that dress and your weapon. Though we might keep those sexy shoes and the thong on. I'm going to make you scream, Lopez."

Hayley stared at him, her heart thundering in her chest. "You promise?"

"Yeah. You give me the word and we're out of here."

Hayley picked up his wrist, pushed back his shirt and jacket to look at his slim, elegant watch. Piaget? Good taste, Michaels. "It's eight thirty. We're out of here by eleven thirty, awards or no awards."

Jackson grinned. "God, you are the bossiest woman I've ever met."

Hayley's grin flashed, lighting up her dark eyes. "But you like it."

Jackson started at her for twenty seconds before he nodded. "Yeah, I do," he admitted. "But I have no damn idea why."

"It's because I keep you on your toes," Hayley told him, threading her fingers through his. She tugged him toward the doors. "Let's go back in and I'll find whoever is running this show and tell them to move it along."

Jackson's laughter rumbled over her. "Are you that desperate to get your hands on me, Lopez?"

Hayley spun on her heels to look him dead in the eye. "Yes, the sooner we sleep together, the sooner we can work each other out of our systems and get back to normal. Do you disagree or have a problem with that?"

"No. God, *no*."

Damn straight. She didn't, either.

Hayley thought that sleeping together would allow them to move on, but Jackson suspected it would just complicate the situation further.

Oh, he wasn't going to back out of their deal—he wasn't a fool or a saint—but he knew that there was a good chance that instead of being able to walk away with a brisk, it-was-fun goodbye, they'd find ways to justify their decision to keep sleeping together. Somehow, Jackson knew he would not be satisfied with a one-night stand, or even a one-week stand. Hayley provided too many challenges, excited him on a deeper fundamental level. She had depths to plumb, secrets to discover, and all of that took time.

And when he was done on his quest to explore Hayleyland, where would that leave him? Would he find himself even more entranced with her than he currently was, craving her with every beat of his heart instead of with every third beat? Would he catch feelings? Would she?

Jackson headed to the bar, rubbing his neck as he avoided various people wanting to speak to him. He ordered a drink from the bartender, took the shot and threw it down, gesturing for the bartender to pour him another. Deciding that he needed some air, he headed back toward the balcony, hoping that no one would follow him out.

He needed a few minutes alone, to think and regroup.

If something developed between him and Hayley, where would it go? Could it go anywhere as they were at vastly different places in their lives, in their careers? He was established, successful, while she was still trying to make her mark. She was feisty and challenging but she still had a streak of idealism found only in the still young, the ones who believed that they could make a difference. And Hayley probably could, if love and marriage and a relationship didn't get in the way.

Jackson leaned his hip against the railing and stared into the dark Texas night. Usually, he didn't give his relationships—okay, hookups—this much thought but he was coming to accept that Hayley was a bright comet in a sky filled with pinprick stars. And because she was different, he had to change his thought patterns and consider all his options.

And that meant admitting that Hayley—too young, too independent, too in his face—could be the one woman who could change his mind about remaining a bachelor. She was the only woman he could imagine having in his life on a long-term basis.

But their age difference could and would cause problems. When he was twenty, she was seven, for God's sake. She was building her knowledge base, still finding her feet in a career, and he could retire tomorrow without a second thought.

He was strong-willed and was used to calling the shots. She would never stand for him being who he was, a confident alpha guy who liked being right. They'd fight. They'd yell.

They were equally bossy and because he was older and had more life experience, he'd expect to be the one leading, Hayley a step behind.

He'd grown up in a house with two dominant personalities vying for control and he didn't want to put himself in that situation. Neither did he want to raise kids—God, he was thinking about kids!—in a war zone. Hayley wasn't a shrinking violet. Nobody who walked away from her rich, generous family to carve her path could be. But Jackson didn't think he could be with someone who would question his every decision, who was headstrong and willful.

His mother had emotionally shattered his father in her quest to show him that she was physically, mentally and emotionally tougher than him.

If he and Hayley started seeing each other, Jackson knew that they were walking into a field filled with quicksand and vents emitting sulfuric acid. Eventually, they'd start to dissolve...

So maybe it would be better not to get involved. Not to sleep together.

But that wasn't going to happen. He needed her and he intended to have her.

And this, Jackson realized, was how his father stepped onto the path of self-destruction...

"Evening, Jack."

A deep voice pulled him from his thoughts and Jackson lifted his head to see his friend Gabriel Carrington standing a few feet from him, a glass of whiskey in his hand. Jackson shook his hand and echoed his stance, leaning back against the balcony and crossing one ankle over the other.

"It's been a while," Gabe said, lifting his glass in a silent toast.

"I haven't been as active in the TCC lately as I should've been," Jackson admitted.

"Yeah, I heard you are trying to develop the land around Stone Lake."

Jackson heard a discordant note in Gabe's voice and frowned. "You don't approve?"

"Not up to me to approve or disapprove. But I do know that Bubba is not going to sell. Not now and not ever. He's a stubborn old coot and he's attached to his land.

"He lost both his sons, one in a car accident when he was a teenager and the other died in Iraq. They, and his wife, are all buried on that land, as are his daddy, momma and both sets of grandparents. The land has been in his family for four generations and he's determined to die there," Gabriel explained. He looked through the French doors and nodded in Hayley's direction. "Did Hayley not tell you?"

"I didn't ask," Jackson admitted, embarrassed. "But, to be honest, we're either fighting or fighting our attraction so we haven't had many conversations, either."

A brief smile hit Gabe's eyes. "She'll keep things interesting, that's for sure." Gabriel took a long swallow of his drink and nodded to the crowded room beyond the French doors. "I wonder what my male ancestors would think of the TCC today. So many members, African Americans and Latinos. Women members, too!" Gabriel mock-grabbed his heart. "Shock! Horror!"

Jackson recalled that Gabriel's great-great-grandfather was one of the earliest members of the TCC. "It's good progress, though."

"I agree. And my grandfathers can keep spinning in their graves."

Jackson turned his back on the ballroom and leaned his forearms on the railing off the balcony. He'd been hearing rumors about Gabe for a while and had been meaning to invite him out for a beer, wanting to give him a heads-up about what was being said about him in town. Gabe could choose to either quash the rumors or ignore them but at least he would know what was being said about him.

"The rumor mill is saying that you are looking for the perfect wife and that you have hired a high-profile international matchmaker," Jackson said, keeping his tone flat.

Jackson expected Gabe to immediately refute his words but he took a while to respond. He was about to reply when Brett opened one French door and told them to get inside, that the formalities were starting.

They moved toward the door and Jackson waited for Gabriel to confirm or deny the gossip. His patience exhausted, Jackson bumped his shoulder and frowned at him. "Well? What's going on?"

Gabriel sent him an enigmatic smile. "Have a good night. Let's get together soon. And good luck with the lady-cop. She's a firecracker."

Yeah, he was going to need it.

Hayley was both touched and appreciative of Tobias Wentworth's pledge to pay for the college education of all children of the Royal hospital workers and first responders, which included the members of Royal PD. She was a child of extreme wealth, and her father had already made provisions to pay for all his grandchildren's education, but Hayley appreciated the gesture. Her relationship with her parents was a minor war zone with both parties jostling for position but she knew she was still loved.

She frustrated her family and they frustrated her more but she was still a part of the Lopez clan. Two of her brothers were in attendance tonight and, apart from a quick "hi" and a hug, she'd, so far, managed to avoid a long conversation with them.

But she'd felt their eyes on her, seen their frowns when they realized Jackson was her date. Luis and Miguel occasionally cut her some slack so there was a fifty-fifty chance of them reporting back to their parents. She could only hope this was one of those times or else she'd be bombarded with questions from her mother first thing tomorrow morning.

Hayley, standing next to Sierra, looked across the room to see Jackson talking to some men at the bar and she sighed, wishing it was time to leave. She was sick of making small talk, her face was sore from smiling, and if one more person complimented her for doing her damn job, she might just whip out her gun and shoot herself, or them.

She wasn't a spotlight-y type of person. She just wanted to do her job. And nail Jackson.

Sierra jammed her elbow into her ribs. "Stop sighing, for God's sake!"

Hayley moved her plaque from one hand to the other, wishing she could toss it under the table and forget about it. "What time is it?"

Sierra looked at her bracelet watch. "A little after ten."

God, ninety minutes of torture left. *Aok.*

Hayley looked across at Jackson, saw him looking at her, and her entire body prickled under the heat of his gaze. His eyes moved down her neck, across her collarbone, across her breasts and slowly, oh, so slowly, drifted over her stomach and her lower body. Every inch of her skin heated and prickled and when his eyes stopped somewhere around her calves, he lifted one eyebrow.

Thong and shoes are staying on.

Hayley nodded in response to his silent order and Jackson's eyes heated with passion. Yeah, he wasn't as unaffected as he was pretending to be.

Sierra waved a hand in front of her face. "Can you two dial it down, please? You both just shot up the temperature in the room by a hundred degrees."

Hayley widened her eyes to look innocent. "I have no idea what you are talking about."

"Please," Sierra scoffed. "You are so getting lucky tonight."

Hayley laughed, unable to pretend. She placed a hand on her chest. "God, I hope so."

"Lucky bitch," Sierra said, without a trace of rancor in her voice.

"Who is the tall guy standing by the French doors?" Sierra asked, moving to stand between her and her view of Jackson. It was a good call on Sierra's part since she couldn't stop looking his way.

Hayley looked across the room to see Rafael Wentworth lifting a glass to his stern mouth, looking like he'd rather be facing a firing squad than hobnobbing with the great and good of Royal.

Hayley sympathized. "That's Cammie's half brother Rafael."

"Good-looking guy," Sierra said. Biracial, Mexican and Caucasian, he was tall and broad and broody. "Where is he based?"

"Miami," Hayley replied.

"Eve is from Miami, and so was Arielle," Sierra stated.

"The thought has crossed my mind more than a few times this evening," Hayley replied. "But it's a big city. The chances of them knowing each other are slim."

"She did write his name in caps letters on a black page in her diary," Sierra pointed out.

She knew that. "It's a long shot, Sierra."

"It's the only shot we have," Sierra insisted as they both watched Rafael drain his glass. A hovering waiter took his glass, spoke, and when Rafael shook his head, Hayley assumed he was refusing another drink. Did that mean he was leaving? And if he left and went straight back to Miami, she might not have another chance to speak with him, to read his body language, to look for cracks in his composure.

It wasn't the right time or place but it might be the only chance she had.

"Go talk to him, Hayley!" Sierra urged her.

Hayley looked around for Sheriff Battle, didn't see him and winced. This was a social occasion and Rafael wouldn't appreciate being ambushed, but what other choice did she have? Her window of opportunity was narrowing...

Shit. Hayley pushed her glass of champagne and award into Sierra's hands, picked up the hem of her dress and pushed through the crowd toward Rafael. When she saw that he was heading for the exit, she changed direction to cut him off before he got there.

Stepping out from between two groups of people, including some members of the Royal Reporters—i.e., Royal's most skilled gossips—Hayley pulled a smile up onto her face.

"Mr. Wentworth? May I have a word?"

Rafael stopped and frowned at her. "Who are you?"

"Officer Hayley Lopez, Royal PD," she automatically replied. She cursed herself for her instinctive reply. She'd all but announced to everyone surrounding them that she wanted to talk to Rafael in an official capacity.

"Can we chat, in private?" Hayley asked, forcing a smile onto her face.

The cold expression on Rafael's expression didn't change. "I think here is just fine."

Every ear in a six-foot radius was flapping. This was so not a good idea. Hayley shook her head. "Maybe we can catch up in the morning."

"I might not be available tomorrow so it's now or never—" Rafael's eyes skimmed her body to come back to her face "—*Officer.*"

Double, triple shit.

Right, she was going to have to be super subtle. Putting her back to their audience, she lowered her voice. "You live in Miami, right?"

Rafael lifted a shoulder in a casual shrug. "Mostly."

"I was wondering if you ever met two women in Miami, one Eve Martin or her sister, Arielle."

Rafael folded his arms across his chest and tipped his head to the side. "Why?"

Hayley knew that a few people had shuffled closer

and all the conversation in the immediate vicinity had stopped, the gala guests dropping all pretense that they weren't eavesdropping. Thanks to Royal's superhot gossip line, she did not doubt that everyone in Royal knew that she, and Sierra, were trying to track down baby Micah's father.

"There's a mention of your name in Arielle Martin's diary."

"And that means what?"

"Can we talk somewhere private, Mr. Wentworth?" Hayley asked, on the point of begging.

"No point because I don't know anyone with those names." Rafael's smile didn't reach his eyes. "If that is all?"

If she was in her uniform, hell, if they were anywhere else, she'd pull out her phone and show him a picture of Eve. But she was at a very upmarket gala, wearing next to nothing, and if she pushed harder, she'd cause a scene.

And then her boss would ream her a new one and she'd be riding a desk for the foreseeable future. Hayley nodded. "Thank you for your time, Mr. Wentworth."

Hayley stepped away, straightened her shoulders and took a glass of champagne from a hovering waiter holding a tray. Her duty was done. Now she could have some fun.

Turning to an elderly man wearing an exquisite tuxedo and a black Stetson, she asked him for the time. "It's ten twenty."

Crap, still an hour and a bit before they could leave.

Dammit, who knew time could move so slowly?

Six

Fifteen minutes until they could leave and Jackson could not wait. In twenty-five minutes, thanks to his stupidly fast Chiron, Hayley Lopez would be naked and he'd finally, finally know whether reality could compete with his imagination.

Knowing that he would be in control of one of the world's fastest cars, he'd opted to limit his alcohol consumption so when a bartender turned to take his order, he asked for a club soda.

Jackson took his drink, turned and noticed Rafael behind him. He smiled, genuinely pleased to see his oldest friend. "Rafe, it's good to see you. I'm glad you could make it."

Rafael didn't return his greeting and the handshake they exchanged was ultra-brief. Jackson frowned. Okay, he hadn't expected a manly hug but neither did he expect such a cold shoulder.

"Everything okay?" Jackson asked, keeping his voice low.

Rafael walked to the end of the bar and Jackson followed. Dammit, he hoped that Rafe and Tobias hadn't exchanged words on the first night Rafael was back in town, but anything was possible when it came to them. They were more alike than either cared to admit. If they had exchanged words, he hoped Cammie didn't hear them as her heart was set on a Thanksgiving family reunion.

"Everything okay, bud?" Jackson quietly asked when they had a modicum of privacy.

"Oh, peachy," Rafael retorted after ordering a double bourbon from the bartender. "After an awkward handshake with my father, witnessed by everyone in the room, I remembered why I hated being here. And everyone keeps telling me how wonderful my father is. And what's with his transformation into Mr. Nice Guy?"

"Danae's death did that, Rafe."

Rafael waved his words away. "And they keep asking me whether we've kissed and made up and whether I am staying in Royal."

"Are you?"

Rafael took a large sip of his drink. "I'd rather shove a branding fork against my cheek," Rafael shot back. "I've got Cammie constantly hugging me and looking at me like I hang the moon—"

"Drake does that for her now," Jackson quipped, hoping to break the tension with a joke.

Rafael did not look amused.

Okay, something else must've happened to throw Rafe off his stride. "What's going on, Rafael?"

"Well, apart from being the black sheep and everyone watching me to see whether I'm going to argue with my father, I had some woman publicly demanding to know

whether I met two women in Miami, sisters with the sur-
name of Martin."

"Who asked you that?" But Jackson suspected he knew.

"Young, gorgeous, wearing a silver dress. She said
she's with the Royal PD."

Jackson silently dropped a series of F-bombs. Dammit,
Hayley. What the hell was she doing questioning Rafael
Wentworth, one of Miami's richest men, at one of the most
prestigious events in Texas? Apart from the fact that there
was a time and place for everything, she was off duty.

"Then, in the men's room, some dude nudges me and
asks me if I'm the father of the abandoned baby."

Oh, shit.

"So, I've been back in Royal approximately four hours
and the rumors are already flying that I'm this baby's father. Goddammit, Jackson! Given the fact that I was all
but abandoned by my father, I would never be so careless
to get a woman pregnant and I would never, ever leave
her to fend for herself!"

Jackson looked around the room and took in the edgy,
vibey atmosphere. It wasn't difficult to miss the covert
glances, the whispers behind forced smiles.

And, with the blink of an eye, he was transported
back to parties his parents hosted or attended. His mother
had been a master of manipulation, able to turn a fun
party sour by dropping a couple of vicious comments.
She'd needed to be the center of attention and frequently
achieved that by spreading unsubstantiated rumors (some
about his dad) and by spouting off-the-wall and offensive
political and religious conspiracy theories just to irritate
the guests and to get a reaction.

Like his mother, Hayley blundered into situations without thought to the consequences.

And, like his mother, she was strong, independent and
forthright. *Uncontrollable.*

He should be running as hard and as fast as he could in the opposite direction. He'd watched this movie, and it always ended with blood being shed.

"I'll do what I can to quash the rumors but you know this town, the truth has never got in the way of a juicy bit of gossip," Jackson told Rafael.

Rafael raked his hand through his hair. "I shouldn't have come back tonight."

"I'm glad you did. And so are Tobias and Cammie," Jackson told him, briefly gripping his shoulder.

"I'm going to go," Rafael told him, and grimaced when he saw the still-crowded room.

"There's a door behind me. If you use it, it'll take you into a staff corridor. Turn left, left again and you'll hit the parking lot," Jackson suggested.

Rafael nodded. "I'd ask you to share a bottle with me but I'm in a foul mood."

So, suddenly, was he. "Thanks, but I have a fight to pick with a goddess carrying a gun."

Rafael's eyes widened and he lifted his hands. "I'm not even going to ask."

Over Rafael's shoulder, Jackson saw Hayley walking over to him, a small smile on her luscious lips. Out of the corner of his eye, he watched Rafael slip away and when Hayley stopped next to him, she placed a hand on his forearm and lifted to talk in his ear. "Ready to go?"

Yes. No. He didn't know.

He should be bolting, not wanting to kiss her senseless. She was trouble.

Everything-is-bigger-in-Texas trouble.

Not wanting an audience for whatever came next, Jackson gripped her elbow and led her through the door Rafael used a minute before. When they stepped into the narrow hallway, Rafe was gone.

"Was it necessary to ask Rafael whether he is baby Micah's father?"

Confusion flashed across her face. "What?"

"Everyone in there thinks that Rafe is Arielle's lover and that he abandoned her." He heard the harsh accusation in his tone and knew that he was using her questioning of Rafe to create some distance between them. Distance he desperately needed.

"But why?" Hayley asked. "All I did was ask him whether he knew the Martin sisters."

"You accosted him in front of a bunch of people..." Jackson trailed off, remembering that he'd seen Grant Webber in the group standing close to Rafael earlier. Grant hated Tobias with a passion bordering on pathological. And if he was in earshot of Hayley and Rafe's conversation, he could easily imagine him spreading a vicious, untrue rumor just to mess with Tobias.

"I did not accost him!" Hayley retorted, hands on her hips. "I asked him, very politely, whether he knew them.

"Before I mentioned the sisters, I asked whether we could meet in the morning, and he said he might not be here," Hayley added.

"Still, it could've waited!" he insisted, digging in his heels. Yeah, he could be stubborn, too. Why couldn't she be easygoing, lovely but uninteresting, unexciting? How could she, so young and so vital, tie him up in inescapable knots?

"In your opinion," Hayley whipped back.

"You caused a scene and you spoiled the Wentworths' evening!" Jackson stated, knowing that he was trying to pick a fight and not much caring.

"Wow, I did all of that with a two-minute conversation? I'm better than I thought," Hayley replied, her sarcasm levels sky-high.

"I was doing my job!"

Jackson scrubbed his hands over his face. "There's a time and a place for everything, Hayley, and tonight wasn't it. Rafael didn't want to be here in the first place and you harassing him has his temper fired up. If he leaves again, I'm going to blame you."

"That's not fair!"

No, it wasn't. But neither was it fair that he wanted to shake her as much as he wanted to kiss her, that he was as irritated as he was turned on. Women didn't get to him like this. He always managed to keep his emotions under control, preferring cold, hard logic to fights in corridors.

"The room is filled with some of the wealthiest, most influential people in the state, Hayley!"

"So?" Hayley asked, belligerently.

"So think before you speak!"

Hayley cocked her head to the side. "Are you done with the lecture?"

Yeah, he was done.

"I asked him a question, I didn't spread the rumor," Hayley told him, picking up the fabric of her dress to keep it off the grubby linoleum floor. "So you can take your judgmental attitude and shove it, Michaels.

"I don't care about wealth and status. I'm a cop, I do my job and sometimes that means inconveniencing people. Well, *tough*. I will always get to the truth, no matter how many toes, yours and your precious friend's included, I need to step on to get to the truth.

"I get enough lectures from my family and you are not my boss, so don't you ever lecture me again." Hayley grabbed the handle and pulled open the door. "And since you don't respect me and the way I do my job, you can go screw yourself."

Jackson winced.

"I'll find my own way home," Hayley said, back straight and her head held high. "I'd say thank you for a nice evening but it mostly wasn't."

At home, Hayley showered, scrubbed the makeup off her face and dragged her hair up into a messy up-knot. Wearing a tank top and loose pajama bottoms, she stomped into her kitchen and put the kettle on the gas stove. She needed to run, to pummel a punching bag, spar with her training partner, but since it was close to one in the morning, chamomile tea would have to do.

She doubted there was enough chamomile in the world to make her temper subside.

She hadn't done anything wrong! She'd asked Rafael Wentworth, a couple of times, whether they could talk privately, and when he refused to budge, she framed her questioning delicately. It wasn't like she demanded to know whether he was Arielle's lover using a bullhorn.

Okay, maybe asking him at the gala wasn't ideal but he *had* said that he might not be in Royal when the sun rose, so she hadn't much choice but to push him for answers.

It wasn't her fault that someone—and God help him or her if she found out who—started the rumor that he was baby Micah's father.

As for Jackson...

Hayley gripped the edge of the counter and stared down at her bare feet. He'd overreacted, and immediately chosen to believe the worst about her without hearing her out. He immediately aligned himself with the Wentworths, his loyalty to them unquestionable and absolute.

But his actions did tell her that when the chips were down, that when she was backed into a corner, she couldn't rely on him for backup or for him to even consider her point of view. She was, as she always was, alone.

Her head pounding, Hayley dumped boiling water over a tea bag. Her family loved her but she didn't have their unqualified support. They loved her but would love, and like, her more if she came home, pursued a career within the Lopez group of companies, found a nice man to marry, had a couple of babies.

But Hayley had this strange and weird conviction that, as their daughter and sister, she should be loved no matter the path she chose to walk.

Love and acceptance should not be subject to whims and conditions.

Hayley picked up her cup and walked over to her sofa, curling up into the arm and tucking her feet under her butt. She knew she wasn't easy to love. Sometimes she thought she wasn't even easy to like. She was headstrong and opinionated, impulsive and determined and fully accepted that she wasn't everyone's cup of tea. Hell, she'd far preferred to be a handful of people's whiskey anyway.

But she was intensely disappointed that a two-minute conversation with Jackson's friend blew her plans for the evening out of the window. If she hadn't confronted Rafael about Arielle, she could be rolling around her bed right now, writhing under Jackson's hands, exploring his big, masculine body. If she had taken a moment to think, her evening would have ended with joy and not a joust.

But she couldn't get past the fact that all she'd done was ask a question…an innocuous one at that.

Asking a question shouldn't be a hanging offense; neither should it be a barrier to some bed-based fun.

Stupid man. And stupid her for sitting here, second-guessing herself and wishing she'd done something different…

Hayley heard a light knock on her door and she sat up and placed the cup on her coffee table, her head cocked. She heard another light rap and, without putting on a light, walked over to her door and looked through the peephole to see who was standing on her porch at 1:20 a.m.

Because Jackson was so tall, all she could see was the bottom part of his face, but she instantly recognized his sexy mouth and stubborn chin, the small scar on the corner of his bottom lip.

Hayley took off her chain, flipped her dead bolt and pulled open the door to her very late-night visitor. She wished she could say that he was unwelcome but, because she always tried to be honest with herself, he wasn't.

Hayley ignored the open collar of his shirt, his short stubble and his sensual scent, leaned her shoulder into the frame of the door and crossed her arms against her chest. "What do you want?"

Jackson's eyes flicked down her body, all the way to her toes, lingered on her tight nipples—it was cold, and she was wearing a skimpy top—and returned to her face. "You."

Yeah, right. Hayley lifted her nose in the air. "You should've thought about that before you picked a fight with me earlier."

Jackson sent her a brooding look but didn't bite her baited hook. Damn, she was so tempted to just grab him by his jacket lapels and drag him into her hall.

And then she'd jump him...

Talk about being impulsive...

Hayley fought to keep her spine straight, to keep up the act of being a tough girl. But she was tired, and a little sad and a lot lonely. And horny, God, so horny. "Why are you here, Michaels?"

"I'm here because I always, always, keep my promises."

What was he talking about?

"I promised to make you scream and I want to keep that promise," Jackson calmly stated, his face impassive but his eyes a whirlpool of need and passion. "I'm pissed off, annoyed, beyond confused but I still want to take you to bed."

"Oh."

Oh? Was that the only word she could find? Apparently so since her brain just completely collapsed.

Hayley released an unhappy sigh. "How is it possible that I'm desperate to jump you? You're absolutely infuriating!"

A hint of amusement lightened Jackson's eyes. "I know that you hate it when I reference our age gap but experience has taught me that angry sex is a great way to release frustration and to deal with adrenaline. Anger can also work as an aphrodisiac. Science says that it gets your blood flowing and increases your heart rates and blood pressure."

"Thank you, Dr. Know-It-All," Hayley retorted.

Jackson stepped closer to her and curled his hand around her neck, dropping his forehead to rest against hers. "I'm annoyed with you and you're, obviously, still pissed at me but I swear on everything I believe in, that I'll make it good for you."

His honesty was refreshing and deeply appreciated. If he'd tried to BS her or sweet-talk her, then she would've kicked him to the curb.

"Yes or no, Hayley?"

Hayley was still in the process of nodding when Jackson wrapped his arms around her hips and hauled her up against him, his mouth instantly finding hers. Hayley framed his face with her hands, and poured herself into that kiss, trying to tell him that she needed more, that she needed every part of him, in her, around her.

Their tongues danced and dueled, fought and frolicked, and from somewhere far away, Hayley heard her front door slam shut. But all she cared about was that Jackson's erection was hard and wonderful and pushing into her stomach, that her nipples were rubbing against his chest, that her body was on fire and her heart felt like it was about to burst…

And she was okay with that.

Jackson pulled back to look at her, his eyes bright and intense. "You are so goddamn beautiful, Hayley. And you smell delicious. I can't wait to kiss you, taste you…"

But he'd already done that…*oh.* "Yes, please."

Jackson carried her into the lounge and laid her down on her sofa, the cushions sinking under their combined weight.

"This is my favorite fantasy coming true…" Jackson murmured.

Hayley lifted her mouth to capture his and their tongues clashed, fighting for control of the kiss. Bubbles of heat exploded in her belly, under her rib cage, in her soul, and her skin prickled with anticipation.

"Jackson." Hayley gasped his name, lifting her hips to push her mound into his steel-hard erection. "We have too many clothes on."

"Patience, spitfire."

Jackson pulled down her tank top with one finger, revealing her breasts, and he gently blew on her nipple and rubbed his stubble across the sensitive point. Hayley writhed beneath him and he finally, finally, took her into his mouth, alternatively lapping and sucking. This was pleasure, proper pleasure, Hayley decided as he switched to her other breast.

Her back arched and she released a series of disconnected words demanding more.

"Jackson, I need you." In case he was having trouble understanding her, Hayley decided to make her desires known. "I need you to put on a condom and come inside me."

Jackson released a little huff of laughter. "So bossy.

But not in the bedroom, sweetheart. Here I control the pace. Be patient, Hayley-mine."

Jackson sat up and pulled her tank top over her head and took a minute, and then another, to look at her. "Perfection, Hayley."

Hayley, unable to look away, ran her thumb over his jaw, down his thick neck. "I want to touch your amazing body."

"And you will…sometime." Jackson eased his fingers under the loose elastic of her pajamas and pushed the material down her hips.

"How am I supposed to take it slow when you look like this?" he asked.

"You're the one controlling the pace," Hayley pointed out a little crossly. "I'm ready for you and I need you."

"But you deserve more than a quick bang, sweetheart. Let me love you the way I want to. Please?"

How could she resist him? And why should she? Hayley dropped her hands to her sides and made her sigh overdramatic. "If you must."

Jackson's smile flashed on his face and in his eyes. "Oh, I must."

His hand trailed down her body and landed between her legs, and he unerringly found her happy spot. Hayley sucked in a harsh breath and clenched her legs against his fingers, wanting more but not sure she could bear it. His clever fingers explored her folds, sometimes just brushing her clit, sometimes rolling it in his fingers. Hayley pushed her head back into the cushion, her breathing harsh in the quiet air and broken only by her calling, *begging* his name. Jackson slid a finger inside her, then two and he lifted her higher, faster, encouraging her to fly.

This was pleasure that she'd never experienced before and it would be so easy to fly solo, to crash on her own, but she wanted Jackson with her, sharing this with her.

Jackson pulled back, quickly shed his clothes, and Hayley had a quick view of his ripped body—the man had muscles on his muscles—before he bent his head and placed his mouth on her, causing her to slam her eyes shut and release a series of joyful whimpers.

Hayley writhed on the cushions, her head whipping from side to side, and she knew she was close to an earth-shattering orgasm.

Putting both her hands on Jackson's shoulders, she pushed hard, forcing him to lift his head to look at her. His expression was feral, his eyes a deep, dangerous blue, his cheekbones flushed with desire.

"Are you asking me to stop?" Jackson demanded in a low growl.

As if she could. Hayley squeezed his shoulder. "No, God, please, don't. I'm so close but I want you to be inside me when I come. I want to come with you, on you."

Jackson knelt on the sofa, knees on either side of her, and reached down to grab his jacket. He pulled a strip of condoms from the inside pocket and ripped one off with his teeth, allowing the rest to fall to the floor. With a quick, practiced motion, he sheathed himself and, keeping his eyes on hers, positioned himself at her entrance.

Hayley waited a moment and when he didn't slide into her, waited some more. Placing her hands on his waist, she lifted her knees and wound her legs around his hips. Looking up, she lifted her eyebrows. "I might not be very experienced but even I know that this is more fun if you come on home, Michaels."

Jackson's soft laugh accompanied his quick, hard thrust. She expected a little pain, some discomfort—he was big and it had been a while—but all Hayley felt was a sense of rightness, of completion.

And pleasure. Mind-numbing, toe-curling, knee-dissolving pleasure.

Hayley released a moan but Jackson captured it in his mouth as his hands slid under her, lifting her slightly. Inside her, he hit a spot that made her hips rock and it felt like she was on a spaceship flying up, about to break through the fire-hot atmosphere. Jackson increased his pace and Hayley hurtled into another dimension, disintegrating as she hit that wall of pleasure.

Jackson pumped faster into her and she heard, sort of, his shout of pleasure, felt his body contract under her hands. While she attempted to find the scattered pieces of her body and soul, dismembered by her soul-shaking orgasm, he tensed and dug his fingers into her butt cheeks, before slumping on her, pushing her weight into her cushions.

Hayley turned her head and buried her face in his neck, breathing in the intoxicating concoction of his cologne, sex and pheromones. Lots and lots of pheromones.

She'd heard that sex could be addictive and now she, finally, knew why.

She was hooked.

Dammit.

It was Sunday morning, and Jackson was still asleep in her bed. Unfortunately, she wasn't on duty today so she didn't have the excuse to run out of the door...

Hayley had no idea what to do, how to handle the whole morning-after awkwardness.

Hayley stood in the doorway to her bedroom, shuffling from one foot to the other. The sex had been...*wow*... amazing, utterly mind-blowing. Jackson showed her how to enjoy her body, how to release her inhibitions, encouraged her to tell him what she liked—everything—and what she didn't—nothing.

Hayley felt like she'd attended a master class in making love, but class was over and she wasn't sure how to act.

Why wasn't there a handbook for these sorts of situations? And if there was, where did she find it?

"This isn't complicated, sweetheart." Jackson's growly voice drifted over to her. "You can either come back to bed or make coffee. I vote for the first."

Jackson lay on his stomach and Hayley's gaze fell on his broad back, her eyes tracing the indentation of his spine, the bunched muscles in his shoulder blades. Jackson took care of himself, of that there was no doubt.

"How do you keep in shape?" Hayley asked him.

Jackson cracked open one eye, yawned, and his eyelids drifted down again. "I run, swim, gym. Exercise is my way to combat stress." He rolled over, the sheet bunching tightly across his hips, showing an impressive amount of morning wood.

Yum.

Jackson pushed himself up into a seated position and ran his hands over his face. "God, I'm exhausted."

"Can't keep up with me, huh?" Hayley teased him. "You are a great deal older than me, you know."

"Come over here and I'll show you old," Jackson told her on a lazy grin. "And I'm sure it was you who told me that you couldn't come again, that you were too tired."

Hayley blushed. She had said that and she had been tired but then Jackson placed his mouth between her legs and had her begging for more.

She'd love to crawl back into his arms but she needed some space, some time to collect her thoughts and get her rampaging emotions under control.

Jackson ran a hand through his hair. "I like where your thoughts are going, Hayley, but maybe we should talk about last night."

Hayley wrinkled her nose. "Our fight?"

"Yeah. I'm not someone who sweeps things under the carpet, so let's clear the air." Jackson placed his hands behind his head and his biceps bulged. He looked like a cover model for an erotic romance novel and Hayley wanted to take a bite out of his big arms, to nibble on his neck.

She couldn't possibly think straight with him sitting there, naked under her covers, looking all scrumptious and kissable and well, fu—

"I'll meet you in the kitchen. And, depending on how that conversation goes, we can decide on how to spend the rest of the day," Jackson told her, tossing back the covers and standing up, gloriously naked and utterly unselfconscious. He didn't need to be. He was, frankly, beautiful in a way only a rugged, masculine man could be.

Hayley nodded, forced herself to turn away and, wearing just a tank top and a pair of panties, walked to her kitchen and put the kettle on the gas stove. After pulling mugs out of the cupboard, she spooned in coffee and impatiently waited for the water to boil.

If only she had some food in her empty fridge. She hadn't eaten anything last night and she could scarf an entire box of doughnuts.

The kettle started to whistle as Jackson walked into her kitchen, dressed in his tuxedo pants and his unbuttoned dress shirt.

He dropped into one of her mismatched chairs at her wobbly dining table and took the mug she held out to him. He sipped and grimaced. "God, this is…"

Hayley raised her eyebrows. "What's wrong with my coffee?"

Jackson took another sip and tried to hide his distaste. "It's…"

"Cheap," Hayley interjected, pulling out a chair and lifting her heels onto the seat. "I'm on a cop's salary, remember?"

Jackson tapped his finger against the handle of his

mug. "Why is that, by the way? You're an heiress, the only daughter of one of the richest men in the state. Why aren't you working in Dallas, working in your dad's company, enjoying the Dallas social scene?"

Hayley pulled a face. "Can you see me working crowds and fake smiling?" After sipping her coffee, she wrapped her arms around her bent legs. "That's exactly what they wanted me to do. I was supposed to go to college, do a degree in business marketing and run the PR side of Lopez Inc. My father had it all planned out, with all my brothers holding important positions in the company. He wanted me to join the family company, as well."

"And that wasn't what you wanted?"

Hayley sent him a scathing look. "No, I did not want to be their make-it-sound-pretty mouthpiece. I wanted to, I still want to, make a difference. I always wanted to study law and my father said he'd pay for my studies, provided I committed to working at the company, in PR and not in the legal department, for five years after I graduated, or until I got married and had kids."

Jackson's eyes flew upward. "Wow. That's pretty old-fashioned."

"My father is an old-fashioned guy." Hayley gathered her hair at the back of her head, twisted it into a knot and pulled it over one shoulder. "I told him to shove his offer and that I'd do it my way without his help."

Hayley picked up her mug and blew across the surface before taking a sip. "I know that he loves me and wants to protect me, but I will not let anyone dictate what I do and how I do it, not even my father." Hayley looked at Jackson, hoping he'd understand. "If I worked for my dad and with my brothers, I would be protected and cosseted, and have a firewall around me. I needed to know if I could do it on my own, stand on my own two feet."

"Okay, but why did you become a cop?"

"After the blowup with my dad, I came to Royal—
my grandparents lived here—and I managed to get a job
as a dispatcher in the sheriff's department. Nate Battle
helped me get into training. He hired me on the proviso
that I keep studying.

"I grew up privileged, Jackson, so privileged, and I
want to make a difference. I want to give back. It's important to me. Look, we all know that Royal has a lot of
wealthy residents. But beyond the big mansions and the
ranching and the independent shops, some people live
close to the breadline, lots can't find permanent work.
Thousands of immigrants live in fear of deportation and
there's a growing problem with drugs and gangs. These
problems are easy to ignore but I see and meet with the
people who are faced with those realities and I try to help.
I *need* to help. I can't turn a blind eye."

Jackson leaned back and stretched out his long legs. "I
admire your drive and your ambition, Hayley."

And here it came, the criticism. "But?"

"But you need to be able to read the room, sweetheart,"
Jackson suggested. Because his tone lacked the bossiness
and annoyance from the night before, Hayley's hackles
didn't fly up.

"What do you mean?"

"I understand why you wanted to talk to Rafael. Something about him being mentioned in Arielle's diary?"

Hayley nodded.

"Okay, so if you'd taken the time to get some background intel on Rafael, you'd know that last night was the
first time he set foot in Royal since he was seventeen. He
and his father, Tobias, have a very strained relationship,
one which Cammie and I would like to see repaired."
Jackson pushed his still-full coffee cup away. "Rafe is also
the type of guy who takes his responsibilities very seriously. Firstly, he would never put himself in the position

of fathering a child, but if that pregnancy happened, he would never, ever abandon his child. Your accusation—"

"I didn't accuse him of anything," Hayley hotly replied.

"Fair point," Jackson said, placing his forearms on the kitchen table, "but you questioning him in such a public setting raised questions and started rumors. Those rumors might be enough to make Rafe leave Royal."

Hayley pulled a face. "Isn't that a little, well, cowardly to be chased out of town by a few words?"

Jackson's hard eyes nailed her to her chair. "You weren't there to see the wounds that were inflicted on him so you can't judge his actions, Hayley."

Hayley winced, acknowledging the hit. "You're right, I wasn't." She still didn't think she'd done anything wrong last night. "I asked him a simple question, Jackson. Did he know the Martin sisters or not? The rumor was not my fault and it was unfair of you to accuse me of that."

Jackson stared at her and finally nodded. "You're right, I was out of line."

Judging by Jackson's lack of enthusiasm, he hated apologizing almost as much as she did. God, they were a pair.

But he had a point about gathering intel before she dived into a situation. "But I hear you on reading the room. I'll try to do better in the future. I can't promise but I will try."

The corners of Jackson's mouth lifted. "Good enough."

Hayley looked at his satisfied expression and hoped that Jackson didn't think that he had her under control because he'd made her beg, weep and scream with pleasure and because she'd conceded this particular battle. She didn't want him to think that she would always be this easy to deal with because she frequently wasn't.

"I don't take orders well, Jackson."

"Yeah, I know. You've made that abundantly clear."

Hayley waggled her index finger between them. "I

don't want you to think that anything has changed between us because I slept with you and because I was reasonable about your friend."

"What are you trying to say, Hayley?"

Hayley pushed aside her jumbled thoughts. "You were angry last night, but I got the feeling that not all of that anger was directed at me. I think it's fair to say that you overreacted, especially since I'm not your wife or even a girlfriend. So, what's up with that?"

Jackson took so long answering that Hayley didn't know if he would. "I like you, Hayley. I love your balls-to-the-wall attitude and I admire your ambition. I love making love to you—"

"But?"

Jackson hesitated again and Hayley wanted to shove her hand in his mouth and yank the words off his tongue.

"But you're not what I need, or want, long-term."

His words stung, a lot more than they should. Pride had her pushing her shoulders back and lifting her chin. "Damn, and here I thought you were about to offer me marriage."

Jackson looked a little green at the thought.

"Relax, Jackson, I'm not looking for anything long-term, either."

And she wasn't. She had things to do and goals to achieve. Work and studying and finding little Micah's father. But any girl in her position would feel a little, well, pissed off at his blunt words.

"That being said, would you mind telling me why I am such a bad bet?" Hayley's tone was polite but she was pretty sure Jackson wouldn't miss the underlying sarcasm.

Jackson stood up and wrapped his fingers around the back strut of the dining chair. "What do you know about my mother?"

"I know that she died when you were young. More than that, nothing."

"She didn't die. She left my dad and me," Jackson explained. His voice was devoid of emotion but his eyes reflected his distress. They were dark blue pools of unwanted memories, unresolved hurt and a whole lot of anger. "I saw her occasionally when I was a teenager but I haven't spoken to her since I was eighteen. I think she's still in New York City."

Wow. That was a long time to be estranged.

"My mom was, is, incredibly smart and ambitious. She was a Wall Street trader when she met my dad. When she got pregnant with me, my dad persuaded her to marry him and to move to Royal.

"She was miserable and she hated her life here in Royal. And, to an extent, she hated me because I was the reason she sacrificed her career, left the city, lost out on making a pile of money."

Hayley lowered her feet to the floor and watched Jackson pace her small kitchen. "She told you that?"

"I heard their yelling. She never wanted to be a mom, to be married. She wanted to be free to live her life on her terms. God, she was stubborn and so damn independent."

Ah, the dots she needed to connect were flashing like Christmas lights. "And you think I'm like her?"

Jackson's miserable expression was answer enough. "She was headstrong and thoughtless, completely convinced that she was right. You're not as hard as her but you are as ambitious, as willful."

"You didn't answer my question," Hayley stated, wondering why she was pushing him. Was she trying to drive a wedge between them because he scared her, emotionally? Because she knew that becoming involved with a man like Jackson, *with* Jackson, would mean having her wings clipped, being grounded, unable to be wholly herself?

Was she looking for a way to extract herself or to protect herself? Both?

"I like you, I do, but…long-term? We're oil and water."

Hayley nodded. "You're controlling and I'm uncontrollable.

"You want someone who is biddable and placid," Hayley added, surprised at the bitterness in her voice. She knew that theirs was a physical connection but the idea of not being what Jackson wanted hurt her, far more than it should.

"I saw what the fights and the arguments did to my dad, how he drew in on himself, how he second-guessed himself all the time. I vowed never to give a woman that much power over me, ever. And if I ever commit to a woman, which I doubt will happen, she'll be easy-going, someone who'd stand by my side and not compete with me."

She won't be you…

Hayley heard his unspoken words and added a few of her own. Jackson wanted someone who wasn't ambitious, who wasn't forthright, someone to stand in the shadows while he absorbed all the sunlight. Growing up in her family, she'd been pushed toward the shade, told that the light was too bright for her, that she had no place there.

If she married, if she ever even committed to someone, she'd choose someone who'd allow her to stand in her own beam of sunlight, someone who would help her fly to the sun, not keep her away from it.

It was obvious that Jackson wasn't, and never would be, that person.

And the realization made her profoundly sad.

Hayley rolled her coffee mug between the palms of her hands, thinking about how to extract herself from this conversation with as much grace as possible. Unfortunately, grace wasn't one of her strongest qualities.

She forced a smile onto her face and lifted her head. "Well, good thing I only want to have fun with your body, Michaels."

Jackson released the grip on his chair and flexed his fingers. He stared at her as if trying to read her thoughts. "So, you'd be prepared to do this again, without strings and expectations?"

Honestly, she'd far prefer to kick him out, tell him to go to hell and lick her wounds but her damn pride wouldn't let him think that he'd hurt her, even a little bit.

She didn't want a relationship, especially one with an alpha male like Jackson, so why was she feeling a little emotionally battered and bruised?

"Let's play that by ear," Hayley told him, standing up. She glanced down at her tank top and wished that she was wearing more clothes. This wasn't the type of conversation one should have half-naked.

Jackson stared at her, searching her face for something, but Hayley kept her smile on her face, refusing to show him that she was upset.

Would anyone, ever, just love her for who she was, warts and all?

It seemed not.

Hayley forced herself to move toward him, to stand on her tiptoes to drop a kiss on the corner of his mouth. "Thanks for a fun night. I'm going to shower while you get dressed. Please flip the lock on the front door on your way out." Hayley walked away and she was about to step into the hallway when Jackson said her name.

Hayley slowly turned and lifted her eyebrows.

"I…" Jackson rubbed his hands over his face. When he dropped them, she saw the confusion on his face.

Good. Being kept off-balance would probably do him

the world of good. "I'll see you around," he finally said, buttoning his shirt.

"See you around," Hayley blithely responded, concentrating on not bolting from the room.

Seven

Jackson drove away, his gaze frequently returning to the rearview mirror to look at the silly, shades-of-purple house.

Oil and water...

Wanting control and being uncontrollable...

Jackson steered his car around the corner, Hayley's whimsical house fading from view.

They'd both used the right words, said what they needed to, and now they both knew where they stood. They might, or might not, hook up again in the future, but there was no chance of a deeper connection forming between them.

They were on the same page...

But Jackson couldn't help thinking that the conversation had hurt Hayley, that she was hiding her pain behind her tough-girl facade. He'd caught flickers of anguish in her eyes, seen it in the tightening of her lips, the tension in her shoulders.

And the thought of someone hurting her—even if that someone was him—made him feel sick to his stomach. Nobody was allowed to do that, especially not him.

Jackson braked and considered spinning his car around and heading back to her house to apologize, or grovel, or to kiss her hurt away.

Pulling over to the side of the road, he rested his forehead on the steering wheel, wishing he didn't want her so much, that he could stop thinking about her.

He'd told the truth when he said that he liked her. He did. He enjoyed her sharp mind, her sassy mouth, her independent spirit.

He adored her body, loved hearing the sounds she made as he pleasured her...

Their bodies fit together like they were carved from the same jigsaw pattern. She was soft where he was hard, her skin silky smooth and scented. Sliding into her felt like coming home...

But these were, undoubtedly, the same feelings his dad felt on first meeting his mother. The chemistry between them had been, so he'd heard, electric.

Their fights had been equally combustible...

Jackson lifted his head and flexed his cramping fingers, annoyed that this woman, so much younger than him, could tie him up in so many knots. He hadn't given anyone this much headspace since high school and he didn't like it.

Hayley Lopez was not going to derail his perfectly ordered, smooth-sailing, calm life. He was perfectly content with charting his course, adjusting the sails when the wind changed, and he liked not having to ask anyone's opinion on how and when to do that.

Jackson did not doubt that Hayley, like his mother, would try to take the helm.

Jackson started his car and pulled off, wondering if

he was being fair comparing Hayley to his mom. Yes, they were both driven and ambitious but Hayley wasn't as intractable as his mom, not really. After their tempers cooled—extinguished by incredible sex—she'd considered his viewpoint and conceded as much as she could. His mom would never admit to being wrong or to making a mistake and had been convinced of her moral and intellectual superiority in every situation.

His mom didn't know how to capitulate, to back down or to apologize. Hayley, it seemed, did.

Hayley might be ambitious and forthright but she wasn't cruel or selfish. Her desire to make a difference, to change people's lives, was on display for anyone to see.

His mom had been the ultimate victim, convinced that life had handed her a terrible hand. According to her, because of her pregnancy and marriage, she'd been deprived of the job promotions, the huge salary and the year-end bonuses. Despite being married to a billionaire, she felt that the only money that counted was the money she made, the only opinion that mattered was hers.

His mom had been a classic narcissist and the ultimate control freak.

Hayley was a strong woman, he knew that, but she wasn't a selfish monster.

But that didn't matter. Nothing mattered but his need to keep her at arm's distance, to not allow himself to feel more for her than he should. He'd loved his mom, as much as she allowed him to, but her leaving had been a relief for him and complete devastation for his dad. He'd watched his father's heart break, and he would never allow that to happen to him.

Hayley Lopez, young, gorgeous and determined, might just have the power to do that to him so he needed to put an enormous amount of distance, physical and emotional, between them.

He knew what he needed to do but never expected it to be this hard.

A few days later, in his man cave—a separate building to the left of his lap pool—Jackson sat at his custom-made poker table and pushed a pile of chips toward the center and lifted his beer bottle to his lips. Brett scowled at him and glanced at the cards in his hands before tossing his cards facedown on the green baize.

"You suck, Michaels," Brett told him as Jackson raked the chips toward him, adding to his very impressive total. Brett Harston, along with Nate Battle, Daniel Clayton and Clint Rockwell, were his poker opponents tonight but that could change next week, depending on who was around and available.

Clint dealt another hand and Jackson looked around his man cave, remembering that his father used to hold monthly poker games in this room twenty-five-plus years ago. Back then it used to be a storeroom attached to the pool house. His dad and buddies sat at plastic tables and pulled bottles out of an ice chest because Hazel hadn't approved of his gambling and refused to allow his child-hood friends, and their smelly cigars, into the house.

Jackson knocked down the old pool house years ago and directed his designer to create a man cave of epic proportions. The long room, with a wall of glass looking out onto the pool, hot tub and landscaped garden, held a six-man poker table, a bar and a hundred-year-old billiard table.

Two pinball machines sat at the back of the room, sandwiching an old jukebox. The first deer his dad ever shot—relegated to a storage room because his mom hated it—was affixed to the end wall, a University of Texas scarf wound around its neck.

He loved this room. It was one of his favorites in his extensive mansion on the outskirts of Royal and he loved it best when it was filled with his close friends and cigar smoke.

Clint picked up his cards and moved them around. "How's the Stone Lake development progressing?" he asked.

Jackson saw that he held two aces and not much else. "It isn't," he answered Clint. "Most of the owners have expressed a willingness to sell but I can't do anything until Bubba agrees to sell his land. His property is the centerpiece of the development and without it I might as well shelve the entire project."

"Is that what you are thinking of doing?" Nate Battle asked him, leaning back in his chair.

Jackson shrugged. "Bubba won't sell so I might as well." It burned his ass to walk away from such an exciting project and he genuinely thought it was a good development for Royal. Apart from the work it would bring in, there was a shortage of property and he'd fulfill that need.

"He's a stubborn old goat," Nate commented.

"Not helped by your deputy who keeps telling him not to sell until he's good and ready. And that Royal doesn't need a development at Stone Lake."

Nate grinned at his sour words. "Officer Lopez is entitled to give an old man her opinion if he asks for it," he calmly replied.

"She gives everyone her opinion all the time," Jackson grumbled.

"Hayley isn't scared to wade in," Nate said. "With three bossy brothers and a very controlling father, she's had to defend her corner."

"Who's met her father?" Jackson asked, knowing he was opening himself up to being ragged on by his friends.

"Why? Are you trying to figure out how to ask him permission to date her?" Daniel demanded, his eyes filled with amusement. Daniel was one of his oldest friends and, like the others, lived to rag on him.

"As if," Jackson retorted. "She's too young and…" Too sexy, and too intriguing and too smart and…

Shit.

"I've met Juan Lopez," Nate said, tossing his cards away. "His parents owned a holiday cottage on Stone Lake when Hayley was a kid. She spent a lot of time with her grandparents, especially over the summer holidays. Her parents also used to visit for two weeks every July."

"I heard that Juan was hard and demanding and has, or had, a hell of a chip on his shoulder. He kept those kids on a short leash," Brett stated. "All hearsay. I barely know the guy."

Nate picked the label off his bottle, his expression pensive. "I think that's what he wants people to see. In Juan's mind, people respect a man who is strong and tough. I'm not sure that's who he really is…"

His cards forgotten, Jackson leaned forward, intrigued at this window into Hayley's life. "What do you mean?"

Nate thought for a minute before speaking. "One summer, the Lopez boys were teenagers, the oldest must've been sixteen, so Hayley must've been about ten. I caught them car surfing—"

"What's that?" Clint asked.

"It's where one person gets on top of the car and holds on while someone else drives the car down the dirt road, trying to fishtail them off," Daniel explained.

He and Dan were once the undisputed kings of car surfing. "Standard small-town fun," Jackson said.

"But still dangerous," Nate said. "But I did it and hundreds of teenagers before and after me did it and I've never heard of anyone getting hurt." He shrugged. "But God protects the stupid.

"Anyway, I caught them. Hayley was in the back seat, her eyes as wide as saucers. I pulled them over and did what we always do—"

"Handcuff the perps, threaten to take them to jail and lecture them before calling the parents," Jackson interrupted Nate, remembering his encounter with a Royal sheriff's deputy. These days, certain members of the force were a lot prettier and filled out their uniforms a lot better.

"I did all that and their old man arrived at the scene," Nate continued. "When the boys told him that I'd threatened to take them to jail, Lopez told me to lock them up for the night."

Jackson lowered his beer bottle, astounded. "Was he being serious?"

"Nah, he was just trying to scare some sense into them.

"Lopez lined them up in a row and started rattling off in Spanish. He tore fifty strips off them, telling them that they disgraced his name, embarrassed themselves, how disappointed he was in them. I watched them shrink in on themselves and thought that he was what everybody said he was…a hard man with huge expectations and little room for compromise."

Nate smiled. "Then Hayley, her hair in two braids, started yelling at her father, telling him that he was being unreasonable, that her brothers were just having some fun. I'll never forget that kid, so full of fire, standing up for her much-older brothers."

Jackson could see it. Hayley, when faced with injustice, would always wade into the fight.

"She and her father got into it and Hayley refused to back down."

Interesting, Jackson thought. That went a little way

to explain Hayley's tough-girl, I'm-good-on-my-own attitude. When one grew up in a tough environment, one could either bend with the wind, ride out the storm or face it head-on.

"In the middle of arguing with Hayley, Juan threw up his hands, walked off the road and disappeared behind a bush. I was standing off to the side, could see him, and the guy bent over and tossed his cookies. When he stood up straight, I could see that he was shaking, and was as white as a sheet," Nate explained. "It hit me he was bone-deep terrified of something happening to his kids, and that, maybe, he was such a hard-ass because he loved them to distraction.

"I think Hayley was his favorite kid by a country mile," Nate added. "When she was defending her brothers, he looked almost bemused, like he was trying to figure out where she came from. When she stomped off to the car, he smiled, and I saw the love and pride in his eyes. To my mind, that kid was—probably still is—the reason the sun rose and set for him."

"But she left home at eighteen, and doesn't have much to do with her family," Jackson countered.

"Probably because she's as stubborn and contrary as her old man and won't allow anyone to tell her what to do. They might not talk much, but there's love there," Nate replied.

Lots to think about, Jackson thought as he inspected the cards he was dealt. He started to ask Nate another question about Hayley and realized he was opening himself up to a round of ragging and a great deal of speculation.

No, his questions could wait until he got Nate alone or—here was an idea—ask Hayley herself. After a few minutes of trash talking each other about their shitty hands, Brett returned to the original subject of his dead-in-the-water development. "So, are you going to dump the project?"

"Probably," Jackson replied, resting his forearms on the table. "The hand I'm holding isn't good. Bubba has an emotional attachment to the land. His sons and wife are buried there—"

"I'd forgotten that," Nate said, nodding.

"—and he places a lot of stock in Hayley's opinion." Jackson grimaced. "I can't afford to waste any more time and energy on something that probably won't fly."

"Years ago, I remember a proposal coming up before the city council to build a bike, jogging and walking path in that area," Daniel said before taking a sip from the glass of red wine at his elbow.

"We need something like that in Royal," Brett agreed.

"We do and Stone Lake is a pretty venue," Clint agreed. Of course it was pretty, Jackson thought. He wouldn't build a multimillion-dollar development in a dump.

"The residents would love it, especially if someone established a restaurant at the site, built boat ramps and Jet Ski launches and developed a picnic area," Dan added.

Jackson saw that all eyes were on him and he squirmed in his chair, waiting for someone to spit it out.

Clint was the one who found his balls first. "You should build that, Jack."

"No profit in it," Jack automatically replied.

"You are wealthy enough to forgo the profit on this one project, Michaels."

Jackson squirmed under Nate's hard look. Yeah, he was. Of course he was. If he never raised another building again, he had enough to last him several lifetimes.

"A project like the one Dan is suggesting would generate a lot of goodwill, and weren't you looking for a way to honor your dad? You could name the venture and venue after him," Nate suggested. A sneaky smile crossed his face. "And it would get a certain woman off your back."

He'd far prefer to have her on *her* back... *Focus, Michaels.*

Jackson tipped his chair back so that it rested on its two back feet and looked at the ceiling and considered the suggestion. He already owned a few properties around Stone Lake, pieces of undeveloped land he'd either snapped up years ago or inherited from his dad. It wouldn't take much to convert the land into picnic areas, to build boat ramps and, possibly, buildings to house a casual restaurant.

It was an idea...one he needed to give a lot more thought.

Jackson dropped his chair down and picked up his cards. He saw that his friends were waiting for him to speak, and he shook his head.

"I'll think about it," he told them. He looked from one trusted face to the other, keeping his scowl on his face. "Do not breathe a word about this to anyone. If someone hears about this idea, the town will take it and run with it and I do not need to be harassed by the Royal Reporters or the general public."

His friends nodded and Jackson knew that nobody would breathe a word. His friends were crap poker players, but they knew how to keep their mouths shut.

A month later Hayley, sitting in her patrol car a half mile down from Bubba's driveway at Stone Lake, yawned and tried to keep her eyes from fluttering closed. It was Saturday but she was on duty, huddled into her car on a chilly fall day. She'd had a hell of a week, frustrating, annoying and unexciting.

Eve was still in the hospital getting her heart checked out, Sierra was still researching the story of the child abandoned over a century ago, Micah was still living with

Cammie and she'd made no progress to find the baby's real father. Rafael Wentworth was in town but refused to talk to her or anyone from the Royal sheriff's department. She was late with two assignments and her professor was getting antsy.

In law enforcement parlance, her week had been a shit show.

Oh, and her mother was demanding her presence at her always over-the-top Thanksgiving dinner in Dallas. Hayley would far prefer to spend the day eating junk food and binge-watching Netflix

But she'd skipped Thanksgiving last year and made only a brief appearance for Christmas, skipped Easter and ducked out of their Fourth of July party with a have-to-work excuse.

If she told her mother she wouldn't be home for Thanksgiving, she could expect a SWAT team to haul her back home.

She could push her mother only so far…

She'd also spent too much time thinking about Jackson, wondering when he would be back in town. Before he left Royal over a week ago, they'd managed to have dinner twice, and to catch a movie once—always ending the night with earth-moving sex. In between their "dates," they'd also snuck in a few late-night, hot-as-hell hookups.

Despite her outwardly casual attitude, Hayley felt branded by him, like it would take her a long, long time to move on from him. If she ever could.

There was something about him that her entire being—heart, body and soul—responded to. He was the first man who'd not only made her body sing and her soul sigh but he seemed to, on a cellular level, get her. Something about him made her think that if she could break down her wall around her heart and hand it to him, he'd take care of it.

That was if he wanted to.

Which he didn't.

As a result, she was, as she was every day, feeling horny and irritable and the emotions had yet to dissipate. Knowing she wasn't fit to be around people, she routinely volunteered for the horrible jobs that would take her, and her bad mood, away from her colleagues and out of the public eye. So far this week, she'd searched for records in the dusty basement, driven to Dallas to deliver a packet of evidence that needed to be forensically examined and spent time on the computer updating their records.

This morning, knowing that her serotonin levels were still low, she'd volunteered to monitor one of the more desolate back roads into Royal for two hours, in a ridiculous attempt to do vehicle checks and catch speedsters. Nate just shook his head and told her not to look at any dairy cows as she might curdle their milk.

Her boss thought he was a comedian.

But, in his way, Nate was looking out for her. He knew that the traffic on this back road was minimal and in the half hour she'd been here, she hadn't seen one passing car. Being stuck on the side of the road also gave her a couple of hours to do some work, to catch up on her assignments. And that's what she'd intended to do but thoughts of Jackson kept strolling into her brain, plopping down and making themselves comfortable. She remembered the way his lips curved against her skin, his big hand running down her hip, his delightful belly button and his equally delightful…

Hayley was jerked out of her sexy daydream by someone tapping on her half-opened window and her hand instantly flew to the handle of her weapon, pulling it out and up and into…

Jackson's face.

Perfect.

Jackson pushed away the barrel with one finger, the

anger in his eyes unmistakable. Hayley couldn't blame him. She wouldn't want a gun in her face, either. Hayley placed her weapon in her lap, rubbed her hands over her face and finally looked into Jackson's still-angry face.

"You scared me," Hayley told him, her tone fractious. "You shouldn't sneak up on me."

Jackson opened her door and gestured her to get out. When she was on her feet, he pointed at his enormous pickup truck. "It weighs two tons and isn't quiet. You were zoned out. Jesus, Hayley, you are a sheriff's deputy! What the hell were you thinking?"

That I miss you, that I want to be with you.

"Sweetheart, this is the second time I've caught you unaware. You got to know that you put yourself in danger when you don't pay attention to your surroundings. And that scares me," he told her, sounding annoyingly reasonable.

She wanted to argue with him, she did, but she didn't have a leg to stand on. She'd messed up. "Are you going to tell Nate about this?"

"No, I'm not a snitch. But you can't keep doing this. Why are you doing this? What are you doing here? Why weren't you paying attention?"

She heard the worry in his voice and sighed. Hayley left her car and rested her butt against the back passenger door, crossing her arms. "I'm here because I have an attitude problem. I have had one all week."

Jackson looked around. "But why here?"

"Nate knows that it's an empty stretch of road, that I'm behind in my assignments and that being here is a good chance for me to catch up."

"Yet you weren't working when I arrived," Jackson pointed out. "I see no open books, no laptop."

Hayley lifted her chin and her eyes slammed into his.

"No, I was thinking about you and what you did to me and how much I wish you'd do it to me again."

He stared at her, the blue in his eyes deeper and darker than ever before. He raised his hand and clasped her face, his thumb sliding across her bottom lip. "I haven't stopped thinking about you, either."

"You said that this can't work, that it won't work," Hayley pointed out.

"It won't. But that doesn't mean that I've stopped lusting after you."

Oh, man, she wished he wouldn't say things like that. Words like that made her think of his mouth on hers, his hand on her breast or down the back, or the front of her pants.

"Can you take a break from your busy schedule of thinking?" Jackson asked.

Hayley heard both amusement and a trace of sarcasm in his voice. She glanced at her watch, saw that it was close to lunchtime and nodded. Picking up her radio, she told the dispatcher that she was taking a break and would return to duty in an hour. "I'm just going to take a walk by Stone Lake, clear my head."

"Copy that, Lopez."

Hayley looked at Jackson. "I'm off duty for the next hour or so. What are you thinking?"

"Many, many things," Jackson replied. He looked down the deserted road, then up. "How many cars have used this road this morning?"

"None," Hayley told him. "Most of the cabins out this way are holiday cottages and are all currently empty. Of the year-round residents, only Bubba uses this road and his car is in the shop. So, no, I'm not expecting a lot of action on this superbusy highway."

Jackson's expression held a hint of daring. "Want to do something?"

There was something in his tone, in the quirk of his lips, that had her skin tingling and her nipples tightening. "Like what?"

Jackson took her hand, led her to the passenger side of his car. He opened the two passenger doors, back and front, and Hayley realized that the tall doors made a little cage, and no passing traffic could see what they were doing.

Not that she was expecting anyone on this lonely road.

Jackson rested his forearm on the vehicle above her head and stared down at her. Hayley knew what he wanted and God, she wanted it to.

"I could get fired, Jackson."

"For indulging in a kiss on the side of an empty road while you're off duty? I don't think so," Jackson responded, nuzzling the side of her mouth. "I've missed you, Hayley. I've wanted you in my bed and my arms every night since leaving you."

"You know that we can't be—"

Jackson covered her mouth with a quick, hard, toe-curling kiss. "I don't know what we can or can't be. All I know is that I need to kiss you, to have you kiss me back."

When he put it like that, she couldn't say no. Hayley peeled her hands off the truck and placed them on his chest, slowly moving them up to his shoulders and around to the back of his neck. "You confuse and frustrate me but when I'm with you, I can't think," Hayley told him.

"Well, then don't think, just feel."

Okay, then.

Jackson shivered when Hayley's fingers speared into his hair and her tongue wound around his. His cock hardened, pulsed, but instead of anticipating what was to come—and there was no way he was taking her on the side of a country road—he sank into the passion, allowing it to flow over him, letting each wave go. For now, he was content to explore her mouth, to run his thumb up and down her slender throat, to inhale the citrus scent of her body lotion. Stepping closer, Jackson felt her breasts push into his chest, his erection into her stomach, and his breath hitched and his heart stuttered. This woman, the way she felt, smelled, kissed, touched… He was addicted to her.

Jackson pulled her bottom lip between his teeth and nibbled gently before lifting his mouth off hers, needing to look into her dark, fabulous eyes, struck by the thought that it was no coincidence that he'd found Hayley on the side of the road. He was starting to think that he'd always find her, that his heart and body would always want and need to know where she was and what she was doing.

He was also starting to accept that he was put on this earth to pleasure Hayley. That making love to her was what he was best at. Promising himself that he wouldn't take this too far, he skimmed his hands over her body, frustrated by her jacket and the thick material of her uniform. With growing impatience, Jackson unzipped her puffy jacket and immediately went to work on the buttons of her shirt until he had enough space to slide his hand inside and cover her breast with his palm. Needing to taste her, he pulled her bra cup away and swiped his tongue over her nipple, reveling in her sexy moans. He felt the weak sun on his shoulders, heard the sound of a distance *killy!* call of a kestrel.

As long as he didn't hear the sound of an engine or tractor, he was good…

"You are so perfect, so sexy. I've missed you so much."

"Jackson…"

Jackson pulled her shirt out of her pants, undid her button and eased her zipper down. A slight breeze picked up as his fingers skated over her muscled stomach, under her panties and down into her strip of hair, parting her folds, finding her heat. Hayley groaned his name as his fingers probed her, his thumb caressing her nub of nerves, making her shake.

"Open your legs a little, Hayley-mine," Jackson gruffly told her, smiling when she immediately obeyed his instruction. Hayley didn't take orders but when he touched her, she was more than happy to comply. When she got more confident in herself and in her lovemaking skills, that would change. And God, he hoped he'd be around to be the one taking orders instead of giving them.

He couldn't think of anything hotter...

Jackson slid his middle finger into her, then another, and Hayley stiffened, caught up in her pleasure. His cock was hard and ready to rock and roll but that wouldn't happen. This was all about her.

"This is madness, Jackson. What are we doing?"

"If you don't know, then I'm doing it wrong," Jackson told her, smiling.

Jackson tapped a spot deep inside her and Hayley's fingernails lodged themselves in the muscle of his shoulders, perfect pinpricks of pain.

"Am I making you smile yet, sweetheart? Banishing your blues?"

Hayley looked heated and harassed, exactly like a woman on the edge of orgasm should. "You're driving me insane, Michaels."

Hayley moved her hand, skimming his lower abdomen to find his hard cock. She palmed him and Jackson hauled in a harsh breath, wishing he could strip her down, wind her legs around his waist and plunge.

Her hand on him, her thumb rubbing his length, tempted him to do exactly that so Jackson picked up her hand and told her to keep it flat against the vehicle.

"If you don't, I'll stop," he warned her, brushing his thumb against her clitoris.

Hayley had just enough gumption, enough sass left to toss her head and lift her chin. "Then stop. I can cope."

He played with her clit again and spread his fingers wide inside her and smiled at her deep whimper. "You sure about that, Hayley? Do you want me to stop?"

Hayley shook her head but her eyes remained defiant. Needing her capitulation, needing to know that she wanted him and his touch, Jackson lifted his other hand to grip her jaw. "Tell me what you want, Hayley."

Jackson saw Hayley's attempt to remain unaffected, but within a few seconds her defiance disappeared and lust, animalistic and uncontrollable, flashed in her eyes, skimmed across her face. "I want you inside me, I want your mouth on my breasts and I want to come."

"I can't be inside you but I can give you this."

Jackson increased the friction on her clit, pumped his finger, and Hayley whimpered into his neck and begged for release. She dropped her face to place her mouth on the bare patch of skin between his open collar and his throat, sucking on his skin, panting in pleasure as he mimicked the sex act with his fingers. She arched her back, demanded that he kiss her, but Jackson wanted to watch her as she disintegrated in his arms, wanting to see if she could look even more beautiful than she already did.

Hayley's eyes closed and he knew she'd stepped into the world he'd taken her to, lost in the way he made her feel. He was a guy in his midthirties. He'd had many lovers, probably too many, but none were as responsive as Hayley. None of them made him want to forgo his pleasure to make her feel desired, lovely, indescribably feminine and a little wicked.

He'd always remember this moment. How the wind pulled tendrils of her dark hair from her tidy bun, the way her eyelashes rested on her cheek, the soft sounds she made as she climbed higher and higher. The weak sunlight, the sound of the wind in the trees, the smell of dust and citrus and Hayley's light perfume.

Jackson pulled back farther to look at Hayley, noticing that she was close, about to lose herself to pleasure. He stilled his hand, wanting her to wait, needing to watch her a little longer, to see her brown-black eyes widen, the way pleasure danced over her skin, painting it with a pink sheen.

He kissed her mouth, needing the connection, the intimacy of the act. Because kissing was intimate, sometimes even more so than sex itself.

Hayley writhed and her moans became louder and her demand for release more intense. Pulling his fingers out, he pushed them back into her slick channel and dropped to his knees to cover her clit with his mouth, teasing the bud with his tongue.

Hayley released a loud yell as she bucked against him and he felt her channel clench around his fingers, her fingers pulling his hair as she bucked against his mouth. She banged her head against the car, once, twice, her pants splitting the silence of the country air.

After a minute, maybe more, her breathing slowed and she relaxed, softly murmuring his name. Jackson stood up and, after gently pulling her pants up and closing her zipper, knew that for as long as he lived, he'd always remember Hayley standing in the space between his car doors, the rays of the sun deepening the golden tint of her skin, her ugly uniform covering her gorgeous curves. Her hair was half falling from her bun but her lips were curved with feminine satisfaction. Best of all, under his hands, she still vibrated from the violent orgasm that he'd given her.

He didn't want to move, to break the spell.

So they stood there for a while, her one hand on his hip, her other hand still resting against the door, her head tilted to the side, their eyes locked. Then Hayley moved and she wrapped her arms around his neck and buried her face in his neck, her lips on his skin.

It was curiously intimate, strangely and compellingly sexy, standing on the side of the road in the middle of the day with a woman whom he had no business wanting, her body tucked into his.

This mattered. She mattered.

And he didn't know where to go from here.

Eight

Sitting in her car, Hayley watched the dust that Jackson's car kicked up dissipate, trying to make sense of the last twenty minutes. The facts were undisputed: Jackson had rocketed her to an orgasm on the side of the road during her lunch break.

Hayley released a loud groan and dropped her forehead against her steering wheel. She was pretty sure that their little tryst was totally against regulations and that if anyone found out, Nate would fire her ass.

Breathe, Hayley. No one had passed them, she didn't intend to divulge any information and Jackson wasn't the type to kiss and tell.

But the fact remained that she'd taken a hell of a risk. Should this get out, she could lose her job.

What the hell had she been thinking?

She hadn't been and that was the problem. Whenever Jackson Michaels was near, her brain shut down and her libido took control and made her act like a feral, wild woman. What was it about this man who could upend her entire world?

His looks aside—and they were great looks and an even better body—she liked the man. She liked his sly sense of humor, his decisiveness, his way of cutting through frivolities to get to the heart of the matter. She liked his loyalty to his friends and family, his honesty and his forthright way of speaking; she always knew where she stood with Jackson.

He was strong and sensible, ferociously intelligent. He was ambitious but he wasn't egocentric. He was also demanding and bossy and commanding, but having more than a fair share of those negative traits herself, she didn't hold his flaws against him. Their age difference was irrelevant. Guys her age were, well, annoying. They were still, for the most part, trying to find themselves, were insecure or conceited, and mostly irritating.

She preferred the company of older men, always had, and she loved being with Jackson more than anyone else.

Hayley lifted her head off the steering wheel and picked up her water bottle, taking a long sip. Wow, she was thinking of the *L* word, considering the concept. She didn't know what falling in love or being addicted to someone felt like but if it meant not being able to stop thinking about Jackson, wishing she were with him, needing to connect with him, then there was a good chance that she was there.

No, no, no! She didn't want to be, *couldn't be*, in love with him. It was too soon, they hadn't spent enough time together, hardly scratched the surface of what made each other tick.

And she had things to do, her job, people to help, a life to create, a law degree to complete. She did not need the distraction of a man in her life.

And, let's not forget that she was exactly the type of

woman Jackson didn't want and wasn't looking for. He'd stated his preferences. He wanted someone placid and easy-going. She was mouthy, in your face and assertive. As his girlfriend, he'd expect her to toe the line and not rock the boat, but that wasn't her style. Hell, at eighteen, she'd defied her powerful and domineering father and she would never regret making the break for freedom, for being in control of her own life.

She would not give up her independence for love. She couldn't. It wasn't part of her psyche.

She and Jackson might share combustive chemistry but, if this situation was a poker game, she was holding a pair of twos. He was attracted to her, but he couldn't deal with who she was, at her core. She was attracted to him and she refused to be someone she wasn't to be loved by him.

Rock, meet Hard Place.

On leaving her, Jackson told her to come to his place after work, no doubt to take up where they left off minutes ago. And yeah, she wanted to be with him, to love and be loved by him, but could she sleep with him, knowing that there could never be more between them than chemistry and desire? But the hell of it was that as soon as she saw Jackson, the minute she looked into his eyes—she didn't even need him to touch her—she'd start shedding her clothes. Or his clothes.

You're heading for heartbreak, Lopez, and you know it. You know that if you allow this thing between us to grow legs, to become brighter and bolder, that you will end up trying to glue together pieces of your broken heart. This is not going to end well, you know this.

Walk away now...

I can't...

Hayley slapped the steering wheel, feeling frustrated and impatient and confused. This wasn't who she was, what she did. She had goals and worked out what steps she needed to take to reach those goals. She was disciplined and thoughtful and determined and decisive.

Jackson made her feel like she was a turtle trying to swim its way through a lava flow. Scorched and bewildered and uncertain and scared.

Hayley cursed the burning sensation in her eyes and swallowed back the tears gathering in her throat. *Wonderful.* No man, ever—not even her father or the unfaithful cowboy—made her cry and she hated that Jackson could.

Hated wanting him so much, hated feeling like she was flying apart.

Hayley opened her glove box, pulled a tissue from the box inside and wiped her eyes, calling herself a fool for being weepy. She blew her nose, breathed deeply and tried to pull herself together.

So far today, she'd accomplished less than nothing. Her assignment was untouched, the road was empty of traffic and she'd simply wasted a few hours. And that was unacceptable.

Thinking that she'd check on Bubba before heading back to the office, she started her engine and did a quick U-turn. She pushed her car faster over Bubba's pitted road than she should and pulled up in front of his cottage with its spectacular view of Stone Lake. Her father sold her grandparents' cottage after their deaths and Hayley deeply missed them and being able to hang out by the water.

She'd been happiest here, during those long summers she spent on the lake, boating and fishing.

Hayley exited her vehicle and called Bubba's name, wondering why the elderly man hadn't stepped onto his porch to greet her. Ignoring her little kick of worry, she climbed the steps of his porch and rapped on his door. When the older man didn't answer, she frowned. It was lunchtime and Bubba was always at home at this hour. His car was in the shop. She'd seen it there when she passed the other day. So where could he be?

Hayley walked around the corner of his wraparound porch and looked out onto the blue waters of the lake. It was too cold to swim now but she recalled swimming out to the red buoy that bobbed in the wind chopped water. Hayley saw a figure in the distance, squinted and recognized Bubba's hunched back, his whiter-than-snow hair. He was quite far down the rocky beach and it would take too long to walk to him so she decided to call him later to check on him.

Hayley walked back around to the front door and glanced down, frowning when she saw the white business card on the wooden plank. She picked up the card, her heart thumping when she saw Jackson's name under his company logo. Turning the card over, she frowned at his block print writing.

Bubba, the documents are ready to sign. Please contact me so that we can finalize this matter. JM.

What the hell?

Hayley stared down, not wanting to acknowledge the fact that he'd done it, he'd persuaded or, more likely, bullied Bubba into selling his property so that he could develop the area around Stone Lake.

That's where he'd been when he came across her on the side of the road. He'd been out here, wanting to talk to Bubba.

And, judging by his message, they'd struck a deal. Bubba hadn't called her or asked for her input or advice. And that hurt. It shouldn't but it did. Maybe she, or her legal skills, weren't needed in this town as much as she thought.

Her heart aching, Hayley placed the card on the small corner table, securing it with a ceramic pot holding a cactus with a pink flower.

Bubba's capitulation to Jackson, another win for corporate America, stung. Her lake was never going to be the same again. This vista would change and not for the good. And all because Jackson-damn-Michaels wanted another sprawling development with his name on it.

She couldn't possibly be in love with a man like him, a man who couldn't appreciate nature, who'd pestered an old man into finally selling his beloved property, who didn't care for the opinion of the community he lived in. She would not be in love with him. Any feelings stopped here, right now.

She was put-a-fork-in-her done.

Hayley pulled her cell out of her jacket pocket and dialed his number, impatient for him to answer.

"Sweetheart, everything okay?"

Stupid heart for bouncing off her chest, crazy that her womb clenched at the sound of his voice. Her attraction to him was very damn inconvenient.

"Where are you now?" Hayley demanded, ignoring his question.

"At my house."

"Stay there, I'll be there in ten."

"Can't wait for later, huh?" Jackson purred, his voice deepening to a darker, sexier tone. It sent prickles up Hayley's spine and all over her skin, causing her to close her eyes.

"I've just showered but that shouldn't be a problem," Jackson murmured.

It took Hayley a while to make sense of his words and when she did, she blushed. And then the images of Jackson's strong hand on his shaft, his wet head tipped back to rest on the tiles, eyes closed as he pleasured himself, crashed over her and she had to place her hand on the wall of the house to steady herself.

That was an image she didn't need…

Hayley gritted her teeth, annoyed to feel the heat between her legs. "As I said, I'll be there in ten."

She made it seven and a half.

Hayley wasn't coming over to pick up where they left off.

Somehow, because life was a bitch, something had gone badly wrong in the half hour between his leaving her on the side of the road and her tense phone call.

Hell, would anything ever be easy with this woman?

Jackson dressed quickly and ran a towel over his wet hair, before raking it back with his fingers. He glanced in the mirror above his sleek credenza and grimaced at the crow's feet at his eyes, the grooves by the sides of his mouth, the flecks of gray he could see in his hair.

Thirty-six years old and he'd just taken an unexpected shower, spent some time with himself to take the edge off, to get through the day. No woman, ever, had forced him into an afternoon shower to find some relief. Insane that it was a twenty-three-, almost twenty-four-year-old who'd fractured his control.

There was something very wrong with this picture. He'd tried to ignore her, deny their chemistry, but she was a force of nature, someone he could not ignore. And God knows he'd tried.

Jackson left his bedroom and ran down the stairs to the hallway, trying to figure out why her *I-want-you, see-you-later* wind had changed direction. He'd left her flushed, glassy-eyed with pleasure, and he'd thought, at the minimum, that they had a fantastic night of hot sex ahead of them. What on earth could've happened between then and now to cause the frost in her voice?

This was why he stuck to one-night stands, weeklong flings, Jackson thought as he strode into his barely used gourmet kitchen. If you didn't give women time to get their panties in a twist, then you didn't have to deal with the drama. And Hayley Lopez was drama personified. She was challenging and frustrating, hot and fiery and...

And he wanted her in his life for the longest time.

Jackson yanked open his fridge and stared at the mostly bare shelves, desperate to deny the thoughts that wouldn't fade. That he wanted her, that he felt more for her than he should, that all he wanted to do was to pull her into his arms, heart and life and keep her there.

Jackson slammed the fridge door shut and rested his forehead against the cool metal door. No, God, *no*. There was no way he was in love with a strong-willed, determined, opinionated woman. He'd seen what loving a willful woman did to his dad. He'd always vowed to not let the same thing happen to him.

But it had and while he had no problem following in his dad's footsteps, he'd always refused to make the same mistakes with his relationships as his dad did.

That plan hadn't worked out so well.

Jackson rubbed his hand over his jaw, reluctantly admitting that he was deep under Hayley's spell, that, if he didn't slam on brakes and skid to a halt, she had the power to emotionally destroy him. Just like his mom destroyed his dad.

Jackson was almost tempted to take that risk.

"Michaels!"

He heard his front door slam and the sound of her boots crossing the hallway. Jackson rolled his head to relieve some tension in his neck and rolled his shoulders back. For the first time in ages, possibly the first time in his adult life, he didn't know how to deal with a woman. And the fact that she was more than a dozen years younger than him pissed him off.

He should have this under control...

It was, he decided, the Hayley Effect.

Jackson walked from his kitchen into the hallway and sighed when he saw Hayley's cold, hard face. Yep, she was in cop mode.

Awesome.

"Hayley," Jackson said, gesturing for her to enter the smallest of his three reception rooms. This house was stupidly big for one person but it was his home and it held the best memories from his childhood and teenage years spent with his dad. With its six bedrooms, theater, gourmet kitchen, study, home gym and steam and spa rooms, he rattled around in it but he couldn't bring himself to buy something smaller and leave the memories behind.

Hayley, because she was intractable, didn't move from her spot in the middle of the hall. "This isn't going to be a long conversation, so we don't need to sit." Her eyes flicked over the larger-than-life portrait of his dad that dominated the hall, her eyes lifting ever so slightly. Did she approve? Was she curious? And why did he care?

"Care to tell me why you rushed over here?"

Hayley's hand snapped up and her palm faced him in a "just stop" gesture. "I'm not here to pick up where we left off on the side of the road!" Her nose wrinkled in distaste and Jackson sighed. *Right. Got it.*

"I never said that you were," Jackson replied. Irritated that he felt so off-balance, he jammed his hands into the pockets of his pants and stared at her. "Are you going to tell me why or am I supposed to play guessing games?"

"You bullied or bribed or harassed Bubba to sell you his land."

Wow.

"That's what you believe?" Jackson asked, feeling the first bubbles of cold anger pop in his stomach.

"That's what I know," Hayley retorted. "You left him a business card on his porch, asking him to come in and sign some papers."

"I did."

"You're not even denying it?" Hayley demanded, slapping her hands on her hips.

So far, she hadn't stated anything but the truth so Jackson just shrugged.

"I thought you heard me when I explained how important the lake was to me—is to the community! I thought that you'd shelved the development, that you'd left Bubba alone!"

"On your say-so?" Jackson raised his eyebrows. "Isn't that a little arrogant?"

"I—"

He didn't know where this conversation was going, or whether they had any type of future—he was beginning to think that they didn't—but he might as well face this issue head-on so that there would not be any future misunderstandings.

"Let's make something very clear, Hayley. You don't get to decide what I do with my business and how I do it!"

Hayley's eyes flashed with anger and disappointment. "I thought we had an understanding about the lake, Jackson. I thought you understood how important it was to me, to the community, that it stays as it is. These days, corporate entities have to be socially conscious and have respect for the environment!"

"Did you pick up that phrase on a website geared toward spoiled millennials?" Jackson sarcastically asked. "Or did you find it on a TikTok video?"

"Don't throw my age in my face!" Hayley stated through gritted teeth. "I would be this angry if I were thirty or sixty! You've no right to force Bubba out of his home! Royal does not want or need a development. And if you plow ahead with your project, the entire community will lose respect for you!"

He'd heard her, heard the feedback, and had tailored

his plans accordingly. The fact that Hayley was quick to think the worst of him scorched his soul.

Hayley held out her phone. "Call Bubba, tell him that you've changed your mind."

Jackson glanced from her phone to the tight expression on her face.

"And if I don't?"

Hayley stared down at her feet, her shoulders lifting up and down in a tired shrug. He could, maybe, dismiss her words but that shrug ignited something within him. It was the same gesture his mom used to convey her frustration and distaste, and a red mist formed in front of his eyes.

"Please call Bubba, Jackson," Hayley quietly asked him, anger fading from her eyes and expression. Sad walked on in, as well as disappointed.

He could just explain but he was damned if he would. He didn't owe her any explanations, and she had no right to question him, his motivations or his decisions. And if she couldn't trust him, if she was continually going to second-guess him—just like his mother did his father—maybe they should call this over. Right now.

They were done. They had to be.

And really, they were both insane to think that a relationship between a jaded capitalist and an idealistic do-gooder could ever work.

What the hell had he been thinking?

Jackson abruptly turned and opened his massive front door and gestured for her to leave. "I think we're done."

Surprise and indecision flickered across her face. "Jackson—"

"You said what you came here to say," Jackson said, using his don't-mess-with-me-I'm-in-charge voice.

"Can we not talk about this?"

Now she wanted to talk? Jackson handed her a hard stare. "Maybe you could've led with that instead of storming into my house and laying into me," he suggested. "I've wasted enough time on this so…please go."

Hayley planted her feet and scowled at him. "What is it with you alpha males? What gives you the right to decide when a conversation is done? My father does the same thing and it's freaking annoying!"

"No, annoying is dealing with someone who doesn't have all the facts but throws temper tantrums anyway!"

Hayley's hands bunched on her hips and her scowl deepened. "That's not fair, Jackson."

Jackson gripped the bridge of his nose. "Just go, Hayley. I can't deal with this."

Hayley released a tiny hiccup, a cross between a sob, a snort and a laugh. "Of course you can't because men like you can't deal with strong women, women who have opinions, women who refuse to stand in the shadows." Hayley walked past him on her way out the door. She turned to face him and shook her head. "I'm not scared to leave, Michaels. I walked away from my father and I'll walk away from you, too. I've never been afraid to be the only one eating at my table."

Jackson watched her walk down the steps to her patrol car, parked under his portico behind his pickup truck. It looked right there, like it belonged. He shook his head and tamped down the urge to call her back, to explain, to make her his.

If he did that, he was delaying the inevitable. It might hurt a little today—or maybe a lot—but if they deepened their connection, bound her more tightly to him and he lost her, he'd fall apart. He'd seen his dad do that and he had no intention of following in his footsteps.

Jackson, unable to watch her drive away, closed his door, leaned his back against it and closed his eyes.

Alone, again.

The way it should be.

Nine

For the past week, since storming out of Jackson's house, Hayley felt like she'd been repeatedly punched in the stomach, over and over again. She recalled being eight, running into a pole and having the air knocked out of her and this felt the same, sort of, but much, much worse.

Hayley stood in front of her fridge and scowled at her shelves. Heartbreak was also the best diet. She hadn't eaten a proper meal in days. She knew that she couldn't afford to lose any more weight but neither could she make herself eat...

So she didn't. Hayley slammed her fridge door closed, figuring that she would, eventually.

Hearing her doorbell chime, she felt her heart rate kick up before cursing herself for being stupid. It wasn't Jackson; it would never be Jackson again. Besides, she'd heard he was out of town.

For the first time since she could remember, she was lonely, and she missed him with every strand of DNA in her body. The thought of never seeing him again, not ever being held by him, kissed by him, hearing his voice, made her want to weep.

She'd shed enough tears to make Stone Lake overflow…

And she was the girl who never cried.

Hayley wrapped her arms around her torso, feeling both hot and cold and shaky. Man, how long did hearts take to heal? Would she be feeling like this next week, in a month or a year? At some point she had to start to function again—she had a job, a law degree to finish, people to help—but none of that was currently possible.

She was a wreck and despised herself for letting a mere man make her feel this way. But, Dios, what a man.

Her doorbell chimed again and Hayley sighed, resuming her walk to her hallway. She caught a glance of herself in the mirror to her right and grimaced. Lank hair, sunken cheeks, deep stripes under her eyes. She looked like something or someone Dracula had used, abused and tossed aside.

Yet she didn't care.

Pulling her door open, she stared at her parents standing on her doorstep, her mother's hand on the perfectly matched strand of pearls she habitually wore, her hair and makeup perfect. But her lips were flattened and her perfectly shaped eyebrows were pulled together in a deep frown.

Even her father looked less than debonair. His thick hair was a little ruffled and he looked harassed and worried and very unlike her normally impassive father.

"What are you guys doing here?" Hayley asked, stepping back to let them inside.

"Why aren't you answering your phone? Why aren't you checking your messages? Sheriff Battle says that you haven't been to work." Her mother touched the back of her hand to her forehead and pulled down her bottom right eyelid. "Are you sick? What's wrong? Why aren't you answering my questions?"

"She would if you gave her half a minute to do so, Inez," Hayley's dad told her before placing a kiss on Hayley's forehead. Hayley couldn't remember when last she received any affection from her dad and she stared at him, her eyes welling.

"Oh, crap, she's crying!" Juan said, placing his hand on Inez's back and pushing her forward. "You never told me there would be tears. I can't do tears!"

Hayley wiped her eyes with the ball of her hands and pushed back her shoulder blades and straightened her spine. Leading her parents into her sitting room, she told them to sit and offered them something to drink, hoping they'd refuse because she wasn't sure she had anything to give them. She'd been short of food before Jackson kicked her to the curb and she hadn't ventured near a shop, or anywhere else, since.

"I want you to sit down and tell me what's going on!" Inez told her, patting the couch next to her.

"I'm fine, Mom."

"Of course you are," Inez scoffed. "Your clothes aren't falling off you, your hair isn't a mess, your complexion is dewy and your cheeks are nice and plump. Try again, Hayley Sofia Maria Lopez."

Wow, she was using all her names. Her mama wasn't playing. Hayley didn't want to do this, not now or not ever. Her mom wasn't the sympathetic type and instead of listening and consoling her, she'd tell her she should've dated the men she tried to set her up with, that she knew best.

She'd rub salt in an already oversalted wound.

Hayley wanted to curl up into the corner of the couch, she wanted to sleep, she wanted to sob. What she didn't want to do was try to be brave in front of her demand-ing parents.

Maybe she could claim a wicked dose of flu. Or a strange virus…

"I can see you trying to find a way to get rid of us and it's not going to work, not this time," Juan told her, placing his still-thick forearms on his thighs, his expres-sion intent. "I know that we've had our disagreements, sweetheart, and I drive you as nuts as you drive me, but you are still my daughter and I can see you are hurting. So, who must I kill?"

Hayley stared at him, completely shocked at his state-ment. "Dad! I'm a cop. You can't say things like that!"

Juan shrugged. "It'll never be traced back to me."

Hayley rubbed her temples, both pleased and scared at her father's ferocious expression and the anger in his eyes. For once, he wasn't mad at her but incandescently angry at the person who'd hurt her.

And his statement was, strangely, comforting.

Hayley watched as her mom perched on the sofa next to her dad, dark eyes boring into her. They weren't going anywhere, not until they knew why she was upset and whether she was okay.

She wasn't okay.

Hayley chose her words carefully. "I've been seeing this guy," she said, pulling her bottom lip between her teeth. "I thought we had something, but it turns out we don't."

Inez released an exasperated breath. "You're moping over a boy? I never thought I'd see the day. Maybe if you'd dated one of the boys I suggested, you wouldn't be sitting here looking like death on a plate." Inez dug in her phone for her bag, pulled it out and started squinting at the screen. "I will set you up with someone right—"

"Inez, *enough*."

Hayley stared at her father, unable to believe his harsh command. Her dad was a tough man, alpha to the max, but her mom was his soft spot and he never spoke to her with anything other than affection and reverence.

Inez looked equally shocked and if she wasn't feeling so broken, she would've smiled at her mom's fish face.

"This isn't the time, or the place, *mi alma*. Hayley needs us to listen, not to solve this for her," Juan stated, his voice firm. "As she's shown us, she's very capable of running her own life."

They both stared at him, unable to believe what they were hearing because Juan Lopez was known throughout the state, possibly the country, as being the ultimate problem-solver and trouble-shooter. He got things done...

Who was this man and what had he done with her controlling father?

"Tell us what happened, Princesa," Juan softly asked.

Right, okay. "As I said, I was seeing someone—"

"Jackson Michaels." Juan nodded.

"You knew?"

Juan shrugged, as if her question were a stupid one. And maybe it was. Her parents liked to know what their brood was doing at all times. And she was the youngest of said brood...

"I thought we had something. It turns out we don't."

"What's the problem?" Juan asked and Hayley couldn't believe that she was discussing her love life with her normally irascible father.

"What *isn't* a problem?" Hayley asked him, sounding bitter. "Firstly, he thinks I'm too young for him..."

"Pffft." Juan waved her words away. "I'm eleven years older than your mother. That's inconsequential. What else?"

"He's not interested in a relationship and if he were, he wants someone he can control and I'm uncontrollable,"

Hayley told him, feeling exhausted. "I'm too bold, too outspoken, too independent…"

"Too much like me," Juan added. He smiled and lifted one shoulder, his usually stern mouth lifting into a smile. "Why do you think you and I clashed so often? Of my children, you're the most like me, poor child."

Juan patted her knee before taking her cold hands in his. "Love isn't easy, *mi vida*. It's messy and hard and sometimes horrible. But it's always worth fighting for."

Hayley shook her head. "I won't beg him to love me, Dad. I…can't."

"Because if love is coerced and demanded, it's not love," Juan softly replied, understanding in his eyes. "You're right, of course you are."

"You'll be fine in a day or two," Inez told her, still looking ill at ease. Her mom was great at the practical aspects of life but struggled to express empathy or deal with emotion. "This will blow over."

Oh, and she was a terrible cheerleader.

Juan caught Hayley's eye and she thought that she caught the tiniest roll of his eyes. "*Querida*, I am very sure Hayley has no food in this house. She never eats when she's upset. Why don't you run down to the store and pick her up some food?"

"No—"

Juan silenced her protest with an I've-got-this look. He then spent the next two minutes ushering Inez out of her house, handing over keys to his beloved 1967, fully restored to original specs Ford Mustang.

When he heard the Mustang pull off, he looked at Hayley and held out his hand. "You and I? We're going for a drive."

Sick of his own miserable company, Jackson rocked up on Cammie's doorstep, hoping to share a glass of wine with his best friend after a series of shitty days. He stepped through her kitchen door—the entrance for friends and family—and lifted his eyebrows at the ultra-messy kitchen.

Cammie was the most organized person he knew and the stacks of dirty dishes, baby bottles and tins of formula scattered over every conceivable surface surprised him. He'd heard that kids could upend one's world but this was insane. Drake employed a housekeeper. Where the hell was she?

"Cam?" he called.

"Coming."

A few minutes later, Cammie, looking like she'd been pulled through a bush backward, walked into the kitchen, baby Micah resting in the crook of her arm. "Jackson? What are you doing here?" she asked, looking surprised.

"I thought I could grab a glass of wine with my best friend," Jackson suggested, noticing the stain on her long-sleeve T-shirt and that her yoga pants were splattered with a white residue.

"Six o'clock in this house is murder hour," she told him, swaying from foot to foot. "Find the wineglasses and open a bottle of red. I'll have a glass or four hundred."

"Everything okay?" Jackson asked her, his expression doubtful.

"Micah is colicky. He screams…a lot," Cammie told him. "I think I got about an hour's sleep last night, two the night before. I have never been so tired in my life."

"Where's Drake?" Jackson asked, opening a cupboard door and taking out two wineglasses.

Cammie sighed. "He's away and will be for a few more days. Mrs. Hampton's daughter had a baby, so she went to Dallas to meet her new granddaughter. But Ainsley will be home around eight. Hope I can make it that long. I never knew babies could take up so much time." She plucked at her shirt and wrinkled her nose. "I desperately need a shower but every time I put him down, he screams."

Jackson crooked his finger. "Hand him over and go take that shower."

She stared at him, astounded. "Have you ever held a baby before, Jack?"

"No, but I have held a football. How hard can it be?" Jackson told her, walking over to her. "Take a break, honey. I can look after the little guy for a little while."

She still looked undecided but transferred the small bundle into the crook of his arm, told him to support his head and bolted for the hallway before he could change his mind. A few seconds later, she came rushing back in. "If he starts to cry, there's a bottle in the warmer over there."

"I've got this."

"Or you can just pat his back…"

"You're going down the hall, not to Outer Mongolia," Jackson told her. "Go away."

Cammie narrowed her eyes at him. "And when I've showered and feel marginally human, we will discuss why you look like hell."

Jackson turned his back on her and walked Micah over to the picture window in the kitchen, to look out onto the landscaped garden. It was cold and overcast today and the weather perfectly reflected the state of his soul.

Without Hayley in his life, he felt cold and wet, denuded. He wasn't much interested in his business, he couldn't be bothered to exercise, he felt lethargic and…blah.

Lonely and lost.

And all because a dark-eyed beauty had dropped into his life like an F-5 tornado. She'd displaced his heart, rearranged his organs, messed with his mind.

He'd been right to call it over. They didn't have a future. They were at vastly different stages of their lives: Michaels International employed excellent people and if he wanted to take a six-week trip around Europe, he could. Hayley couldn't just up and leave whenever she wanted to. And, he presumed, she used her vacation time to study.

He was wealthy and could buy, and did, whatever his heart desired. She couldn't afford designer dresses or to buy decent coffee. She had a degree to finish, her career as a lawyer to start...

And he hadn't even started to consider the difference in their personalities. Did they even matter? He was starting to think that they'd hyped their different styles to find a reason to stay away from each other, to protect their hearts.

Well, he was done doing that. Life was meant to be lived and he wouldn't be able to live his life without Hayley in it.

Jackson looked down at the bundle in his arms and looked into the pair of deep, dark wise eyes dominating Micah's little face. His skin was sallow, his tufts of hair dark and his mouth a perfect rosebud.

This was what Hayley's baby would look like...

Jackson felt his knees wobble and he tightened his hold on Micah, causing the baby to release a little squeak. Jackson ran his free hand over his face, unable to get the vision of Hayley holding a baby, his baby, off the big screen behind his eyes. He could see her, standing in his kitchen, wearing one of his shirts, legs and feet bare, hair tumbling over her shoulders and down her back, holding his child.

And it felt so damn right.

So, they'd fight. She wouldn't always agree with him, and he certainly wouldn't with her. He'd try to tell her what to do and how to do it and she'd tell him to shove it. He'd want to protect her and she'd remind him that she was the one who carried a gun...

But in between the fights and arguments, they'd laugh and talk and make sweet, sweet love and hopefully, in time, babies. She'd look at him with eyes the same shade of Micah's—big and bold—and he'd do anything, be anything for her. She'd fill his big house and his life with love and laughter and color, and his heart with joy.

He wanted to be there when she graduated from law school, support her through the grueling bar exam. He wanted to be the one who put a ring on her finger, who stood between her and her demanding parents. He'd catch their babies and, if Hayley's career took off and she wanted to work full-time, he'd cut back and work from home to be there for their kids.

He could do anything, be anything, as long as he had Hayley—his bold and beautiful butterfly—in his life.

Hayley pulled up next to what used to be her grandparents' cottage on Stone Lake, pulled her keys out of the ignition and turned to look at her father, who sat in the passenger seat.

"What are we doing here?" Hayley asked him.

Juan gestured to the silver-blue lake stretched out in front of them. "You always liked this property, liked being here, at the lake. I thought we could take a walk along the shore."

"Why?" Hayley demanded. It was cold and miserable on the other side of her car window and she didn't want to walk. She wanted to go home, binge a fantasy series and eat chocolates and chips. Because wasn't that what brokenhearted people did? She wasn't sure, she'd never been in love before, neither had she experienced such emotional pain.

She didn't have a manual telling her how to act, what to do next.

Juan exited the car and Hayley shrugged. What the

hell, they were here, her father wasn't shouting at her, so she'd take the moment.

Hayley followed him down the path to the lake and when she hit the rocky shore, she jammed her hands into the pockets of her puffy jacket, feeling the cold wind on her skin.

After walking for ten minutes in silence, Juan spoke. "I know that you and I have had our differences, Hayley, but I am proud of what you've done and what you've achieved."

Caught off guard, Hayley darted a look at his stern face. "You are?"

"Sure. None of your brothers would've, or could've, struck out on their own and succeeded, no, flourished."

Hayley wasn't completely sure she was hearing him right. He considered her career as a cop and her studying law a success?

"Do I wish you were working for me? Of course I do. I love the idea of having all my kids under one roof, working together to expand my company.

"I'd love you to be in Dallas, to see you more often. I'd love to know that you are safe, that you live in a nice apartment, drive a nice car and wear nice clothes."

And here came the lecture…

Hayley braced herself for her father to embark on his familiar campaign to get-Hayley-back-home. Until she was back under his wing, he wouldn't be satisfied.

Hayley brushed tendrils of hair off her forehead and, instead of shutting down his suggestions, she simply shrugged. For the first time in six years, leaving Royal was a reasonable alternative. Oh, she didn't think she'd go so far as to accept a job within the Lopez group—ugh—but the nice apartment or the nice car sounded… nice. She could still be a law enforcement officer in Dallas, she could keep studying there, and Dallas had its fair share of marginalized and underprivileged people to help.

Royal wasn't the only place that needed her skills. Or her future skills.

And if she moved, she wouldn't keep running into Jackson, wouldn't be continuously slapped in the face with something she couldn't have.

"I'll think about it, Dad," Hayley told her father.

Juan laughed and put his arm around her shoulder, tugging her into his stocky body. "But you know what I want for you, Hayley?"

"For me to marry and have kids," Hayley muttered.

"No, that's your mother's dream. Believe it or not, I want you to be happy. And I don't think moving back to Dallas would make you happy. I think you need to stay here and find a way to make it work between you and Jackson," Juan told her. "I think he's a good man and someone strong enough to handle your—*our*—fiery temperament."

"Well, that's a fine idea, Dad, but he doesn't want me," Hayley told him, her voice rising. "He wants someone else, something else, but not me!"

Juan was about to reply when they saw Bubba step onto the lakeshore from the path from his house. He turned to look at them and raised his hand and waited for them to reach him.

Juan shook his hand and Hayley kissed his leathery cheek before sending him a sad smile. "I'm sorry I couldn't help you stop Jackson Michaels from developing here, Bubba. I don't know what he said or did to get you to change your mind, but nothing is legal before the papers have been signed. Have you signed his papers, Bubba?"

Bubba frowned at her. "Well, yeah."

Hayley winced. "Why didn't you talk to me first? We could've tried something else to get him off your back.

It's your land. You didn't have to sell, and he can't force you to!"

Bubba looked at her like she was a mutated alien. "What are you talking about, Hayley? And why wouldn't I want to sign the papers?"

Was the world completely mad today? "Because you didn't want to sell!" Hayley yelled.

Bubba looked at Juan, lifted his hands and turned his attention back to Hayley. "That's not what happened... exactly."

Hayley rubbed her hands up and down her face, unable to keep track of this conversation. "You said you signed some papers, Bubba, papers that Jackson gave you."

Bubba nodded. "Okay, I did sell, sort of. Jackson bought my property, for a ridiculous amount of money. But I get to stay here until I die, and after that, the land will be donated to a trust Jackson set up."

A trust? "What?"

Juan rubbed his hand up and down her back. "Jackson set up a trust, Hayley. All the land he's acquired on the lake will be donated to the trust and the trust will be a public-private partnership with various partners, including the Royal municipality. He's building a running and cycling path next to the lake, upgrading the picnic and camping facilities, building decent boat ramps. The only stipulation was that the park will be named after his dad and that no new houses can be built on the shore."

Hayley felt like she was existing in an unfamiliar and strange alternate reality. "I don't understand," she told her dad.

"Jackson won't be developing the land, Stone Lake will stay the same and Bubba will get to live out the rest of his days in his cottage. When he dies, Jackson will own another cottage on the lake."

"Another cottage?" Hayley demanded.

Juan smiled. "He bought your grandparents' cottage from me a week ago."

Hayley wasn't sure how much more she could take in. "You own, owned, whatever, the cottage? I thought it was sold!"

"I bought it from my parents' estate," Juan told her. "I thought that someone, at some time, would want to develop this area so I held on to it, thinking I could sell it for a huge profit. Which I did."

Holy smoke bombs, it was all too much.

Jackson had been planning on developing the area around this lake. Now he wasn't. He was now going to build a biking and cycling path for the residents to use and name the park after his dad? Not that she had any problem with that. His father, as she'd heard, was a wonderful man who'd done a lot for the residents of the town.

No, what she was having a problem with was Jackson's swinging from one position to another, him changing his mind so rapidly. When she left his house, he'd been harassing Bubba to sell his land…

Or was that just what she'd assumed?

"When did you speak to Jackson about him buying your property but allowing you life rights, Bubba?"

Bubba wrinkled his forehead in thought. "Ah, two weeks ago?"

Before he found her on the side of the road, before she found his business card and jumped to the wrong conclusion.

Hayley stared down at the rocks beneath her feet, wondering if she'd subconsciously sabotaged their…whatever they had. She'd been so quick to jump to conclusions, it was almost as if she wanted to find fault with him, to find a reason for him to fail. Had she been trying to protect herself because she knew that Jackson could hurt her?

It was possible. No, it was probable.

And hadn't she just shot herself in the foot? Because, despite trying to protect herself, she was still carrying around her sliced-and-diced heart.

And the reason Jackson could hurt her was that she was utterly, completely, horribly in love with the man. He was the man whose face she wanted to wake up to, whose laugh she wanted to hear, whose arms she wanted to rest within.

He was the father of future babies, her lover and her best friend.

Hayley had a million doubts about their suitability, didn't know if they could live together, knew that they would argue—a lot—but her heart wanted what it wanted and what it wanted was him.

Jackson...

But there was a good possibility that she'd blown all her chances.

"You need to talk to him, Hayley, work it out. Everything can be worked out."

Hayley lifted her eyebrows at that scorcher and Juan winced. "Everything eventually works out," he amended. "I might've taken a while to come around but here I am."

Hayley had to wonder if they'd still be having this conversation if Jackson wasn't in the picture. She folded her arms across her chest and raised her eyebrows.

"And how do you know so much about Jackson Michaels, Father dear?"

Juan simply smiled. "When your brothers mentioned the chemistry between you and him—they saw you interact at the TCC gala ball—I decided to keep an eye on the man. It's been an interesting few weeks."

"And have you been keeping an eye on me, too?"

Juan nodded and slung an arm around her shoulder. "Of course. Watching over you is what I do best."

"You've been spying on me?"

Juan rocked his hand from side to side. "*Spying* is such an ugly word."

She'd take that as a yes. Hayley rolled her eyes. "And will you ever stop?"

Juan looked at Bubba. "At what age do you stop worrying about your kids, Bubba?"

"Only when you're dead," Bubba replied before turning away and ambling off.

Hayley turned to Juan. "I'm not happy with you and we will be having a conversation about boundaries, Father."

Juan waved her words away. "So, what comes next? Are you going to visit with Jackson and ask him for an explanation or do I need to visit with him and remind him that I own a shotgun, a shovel and sixteen backyards where I can bury his dismembered body parts?"

Hayley tipped her head to the side and hoped that her father was kidding. She was 99 percent sure he was...

She also needed to apologize to Jackson, to beg his forgiveness. For doubting him, disbelieving him, for being so damn quick to believe the worse of him.

She thought she was so damn brave, thought that her actions of walking away from her wealthy family and striking out on her own had been so courageous, but she'd always known, in the back of her mind, that she had a safety net, that she could always run home to Mom and Dad.

Going to Jackson, apologizing and telling him how she felt, would take more courage than she had, but what was the alternative?

Hating herself for the rest of her life for not taking the chance, being unable to look in the mirror because she didn't want to confront her cowardice or face her regrets? She might be young but she wasn't dumb.

What was that old saying? That, in life, we only regretted the chances we didn't leap at, the relationships we didn't make and the decisions we waited too long to take?

Ten

It would've been more romantic if she'd just rushed from the lake to Jackson's house but first Hayley needed to re-unite her dad with her mom—she loved her parents but she loved them more when they stayed in Dallas and let her be—and she needed to take a shower as her hair desperately needed to be washed.

Hayley powered through her shower, hurriedly swiping a razor under her arms and down her legs, and tossing shampoo and conditioner into her hair. In her bedroom, she pulled on some fresh lingerie—she desperately needed to do some laundry—and looked for a pair of clean jeans. Pulling on a black pair, she found her left Ugg boot but the other was not visible. Dressed only in jeans, one boot and a bra, she knelt to look under her bed, desperately hoping she had a clean top to wear.

She kinda thought she didn't…

And where the hell was her other boot if it wasn't under her bed?

"Now, that's a hell of a view..."

Hayley jerked her head up at the deep voice and her forehead skimmed the ledge of the side table. She yelled, slammed her hand on her head and released a series of the more colorful curses she'd heard over the years, taught to her by veteran cops.

And criminals.

Leaning her back against the side of her bed, she looked up to see Jackson standing in the doorway to her bedroom, big arms folded, hair mussed.

"How did you get in?" Hayley asked him, pulling her fingers off her forehead to see if there was blood. There wasn't, thank goodness.

"Ah... I arrived as your dad was leaving," Jackson explained, his eyebrows pulling together. "He greeted me and then muttered something under his breath about a shotgun and a shovel?"

Nope, that didn't sound right. Mostly because her father was as subtle as a Sherman tank. "I think he was more direct than that."

Jackson winced. "Yeah, he told me that if I hurt you again, he'll blow my head off and bury me so deep that even Satan couldn't find me."

Yep, sounded like her dad.

Jackson stepped into her bedroom and held out his hand so that he could haul her to her feet. Hayley put her hand in his, and he jerked her to her feet with no effort at all. He immediately dropped her hand and Hayley felt a knife tip enter her heart. If he couldn't even hold her hand, what hope did they have?

Jackson kept his eyes on her face but waved his hand in the direction of her chest. "Get dressed and we can talk."

Hayley started to object to his peremptory command and then noticed the hot flicker of desire in his eyes, the way his eyes kept dropping to her chest. It was obvious that he was finding it difficult to concentrate and the thought charmed her...

Jackson brushed past her and picked a shirt off her bed and thrust it in her direction. "Put it on. I'll see you in the kitchen."

Jackson didn't give her a chance to respond but whipped around and left her bedroom, his footsteps heavy on her wooden floor. Tossing the shirt—she'd worn it days ago and it was less than fresh—she walked over to her closet. She flipped through her hangers and found, by some minor miracle, a white silk T-shirt. She pulled it over her head and wondered why she never wore it until she looked at herself in the mirror affixed to the inside door of the closet.

The shirt was one size too small and clung to every curve, making it look like she'd painted on the fabric. The V neck showed her cleavage, and when she lifted her arms an inch, it showed off a strip of her belly.

Hayley grimaced. Loose and dirty or tight and clean? Tight and clean won this round.

Hayley took a minute to towel dry her wet hair and another to run a comb through the long strands, flipping her head over to scrunch her curls.

You're wasting time, Lopez, trying to delay the inevitable. Get in there, apologize, tell him you were scared because you like him more than you should, and then take his rejection on the chin.

You can do this, you have *to do this.*

Walking down her short hallway, Hayley rubbed her palms on the seat of her jeans and stepped into the kitchen to see an unfamiliar bag of coffee standing next to her cheap coffee maker. "And that?" she asked, nodding to the black-and-blue bag.

"Decent coffee," Jackson said, handing her a cup. "It's

too early for liquor and I need to do something with my hands."

Touching her would be good…

Stop it, Lopez.

Jackson sent her tight shirt a sour look before lifting his cup to his lips. Hayley followed suit, sighing at the rich, dark taste. She could become addicted to the good stuff…

Just like she was addicted to Jackson.

"I was on my way to see you but why you are here?" Hayley asked him.

Jackson put his cup down on the counter and gripped the edge of the counter behind him. His gaze sharpened and his body tensed. "Why were you coming to see me?"

"Why are you answering a question with a question?" Hayley demanded, shifting from foot to foot. When Jackson didn't answer her, she released a frustrated huff. "If you must know, I was coming to apologize."

Now that she was standing in front of him, she wasn't feeling quite as brave as she did earlier, doubts washing over her in a relentless series of waves. What if he rejected her? What if he said that there was no chance? What if the sky fell in?

Hayley scratched the side of her neck. This was why it was so much easier to be single. You didn't have to second-guess yourself on a day-to-day—or, in her case, minute-to-minute—basis.

Oh, she hated apologizing. Had she mentioned that? "I wanted to say I was sorry for jumping to the wrong conclusion."

"And what conclusion was that?" Jackson asked her, sounding super polite.

Man, she'd rather walk over a bed of hot, spiky coals. "I assumed that you forced Bubba to sell you his property," Hayley admitted.

"I wish I had the skills you think I do. My job would be so much easier," Jackson said, sounding a little sarcastic.

"I saw your business card, read the message and jumped to the wrong conclusion," Hayley reluctantly admitted. "I'm sorry I didn't ask you to clarify the situation."

Jackson folded his arms across his chest and looked broody and simply stared at her like he was trying to figure something out. When he didn't speak and the silence turned uncomfortable, Hayley jumped in with another question. "My dad told me that you bought my grandparents' cottage from him?"

His eyebrows lifted and surprise jumped into his eyes. "You two are speaking?"

"Apparently so," Hayley admitted, still bemused by her dad's compassion earlier. "He and my mom came to check on me this morning because they are worried about me."

"Why are they worried about you?" Jackson demanded.

"When I'm upset, I tend to act like a turtle. I pull away and hide out."

"Why are you upset?"

"What are you going to do with my grandparents' cottage?" Hayley countered.

Jackson's harsh curse bounced off the walls. Her eyes widened as he sprung away from the counter and captured her face in his hands, his mouth covering hers in a harsh, demanding kiss. It was a take-no-prisoners kiss, a "you're mine" kiss, a kiss that belonged between the pages of an epic love story, on the silver screen.

It sent tingles to her feet and made her stomach wobble and her womb throb and her heart ache.

Hayley couldn't tell if it was the end or the beginning of something. But she did know that she didn't want it to end. Jackson's strong arms wrapped around her back, holding her so close to her body that a piece of paper wouldn't find space to slide between them. But she did know that she didn't want his kiss to end, that in his arms was where she wanted to be…

Hayley wrapped her arms around his neck, tunneled her fingers into his hair and wrapped her tongue around his, using all her senses to imprint this moment on her psyche. The coffee taste of his mouth, the muscles in his neck under the tips of her fingers, the sound he made at the back of his throat as he took their kiss even deeper, she loved it all. She loved him…

Jackson palmed her butt and lifted her into his erection and Hayley wrenched her mouth off his and breathlessly suggested that they take this to her bedroom. They were useless communicators and were so much better at showing than telling.

Jackson squeezed her butt cheek, swiped his tongue against hers and then retreated, pulling back from her to run both hands through his unruly hair. "No."

"No?" Hayley repeated, dumbfounded. "Don't you want me?"

Jackson glared at her. "That's a stupid question. You know I do."

Hayley tipped her head to the side and eyed him, noticing the frustrated expression of his face, his flushed cheeks, his blazing blue eyes. The huge erection tenting his pants. Okay, he did want her…

"If you want me so much then why did you stop?" Hayley asked.

"Because we can't keep putting off important conversations because we get distracted by sex!" Jackson growled.

Hayley reached out to play with a button on his shirt. "Okay, then let's make it quick so that we can go to bed. You go first."

Jackson pinned her to the floor with intense eyes. "Okay, but on one condition…"

Hayley swallowed. "What?"

"After we finish a sentence, we each get to choose a piece of clothing that comes off. I bought the cottage and put it in your name. I want you to have a place of your own, somewhere you love." Jackson gestured to her chest. "Take off your shirt."

Hayley was still playing catch-up. "You bought a cottage for me? Why?" she demanded.

Jackson pulled her shirt up to her chest and over her head. "Because you love the lake and I thought that if you didn't like my house, we could live out there. Or we could use it for a weekend house. Or you could rent it out. Whatever you want to do with it, it's yours."

"I don't know what to say to that," Hayley admitted, knocked sideways. She felt a spurt of excitement at the idea of waking up in her grandparents' bedroom with its astounding view of the lake and distant hills. "Except that you can't buy me a cottage, Jackson. That's crazy."

"It's my money and I can do anything I want," Jackson told her, running his finger down her chest to hook in the front clasp of her bra. "Your turn."

"Why didn't you tell me that you were thinking of turning the land by the lake into an area the community could enjoy?" Hayley asked, tugging his shirt from the band of his pants.

Jackson shrugged. "I was going to, along with a lot of other things, the afternoon we ended things."

Jackson put his arm behind his head, grabbed his collar and pulled his shirt over his head. Faced with all that tanned skin, Hayley immediately placed her lips on his chest, needing to taste him. When she tried to skim her mouth across his skin, Jackson's hands on her shoulders gently pushed her away.

"Your turn to confess," Jackson gruffly told her.

"I was looking for a reason to put some distance between us because you scare me," Hayley admitted. "That's why I didn't want an explanation of your message on the business card you left Bubba. I was looking for an out."

Jackson gently undid the front clasp to her bra and Hayley sighed when his big hands covered her breasts. "Why do I scare you, sweetheart?"

Hayley went to his pants and slowly pulled his belt from its buckle. "Because I feel so much for you, Jackson." She dropped the belt to the floor. "Your turn."

"You scare me, too, by the way. This thing between us terrifies me," Jackson admitted, his voice rough with emotion.

Hayley held his hips and forced her words out. "Because I am so much like your mom?"

Jackson stared at her, his eyebrows lowering into a frown. "What? No! Well, sort of."

"Well, that clears it up," Hayley wryly responded.

Jackson moved his hands from her breasts to clasp her cheeks, his thumbs gliding over her cheekbones. "You are like my mom, in some ways. You are intelligent, charismatic, forthright as hell. But, unlike her, you are not self-absorbed or demanding or manipulative."

"Good to know," Hayley murmured, relieved.

"You terrify me because you force me to be more, to not to settle for the mundane, the quiet, the easy. Because nothing about you is easy, sweetheart. A life spent with you will be a wild ride as opposed to a gentle cruise."

Did he want a life with her? Really? Hayley wanted to do a happy dance but managed to resist the temptation. Just.

Hayley dug her fingertips into the bare skin of his hip. "Do you really want a life with me?" she whispered. "I thought you didn't want to commit to anyone."

Jackson handed her a wry smile. "I've spent the last week feeling like a walking corpse. I've missed you intensely. At my lowest point, I even considered doing another U-turn on Main Street to get your attention."

"Pathetic," Hayley teased him.

"I am." Jackson dropped a kiss on the side of her mouth. "Did you miss me, Hayley-mine?"

The time for teasing was over and she needed to put up or shut up. Holding on to his wrists, she nodded. "I was coming to you tonight to firstly tell you I was sorry for being a complete bitch and secondly to ask you if there was a chance that we can make this work. I'm so in love with you, Jackson."

"I'm in love with you, too."

Hayley dropped her forehead onto his chest, overwhelmed and completely relieved. Then Jackson wrapped his arms around her naked torso and cuddled her close, his lips in her hair. Hayley breathed him in, took the moment before pulling back to look at him. The love in his eyes nearly dropped her to her knees.

"You do love me…" she said, her voice tinged with awe.

"More than I thought possible. And I always will." Jackson dropped a kiss on her nose. "You're it, for me."

"So, I'm going to be your date for any future TCC galas?" Hayley teased him.

"And for everything else," Jackson stated, opening the button on her jeans and pulling down the zipper. "Hopefully, you'll be my date for our wedding."

Hayley slapped her hand against his, her eyes wide and astonished. "You want to marry me?" she squeaked.

"That's what 'you're mine' means, sweetheart." Jackson pushed her hair off her forehead with one finger.

"Uh…huh…what?" Hayley felt the room spin and she wasn't sure why she was feeling so off-balance. She was feeling ecstatic, and scared, and wonderful, and utterly overwhelmed.

"Hayley, look at me," Jackson commanded.

Hayley's eyes met his and she saw both amusement and determination in those amazing eyes and her heart rate started to slow. "I am going to marry you, Hayley, at some point in the future. I hope we will also have children together—"

"If we don't, my mother will kill me," Hayley told him, her voice faint.

Jackson grinned. "I'm taking that into consideration." He gripped the back of her head and tilted her head up. "Marrying me doesn't mean that you have to stop being you, Hayley. I'd hate that because then you wouldn't be the woman I fell in love with. I might not be able to wait to marry you, to make you mine, but I think babies can wait for a while, don't you? You still have a law degree to finish, a career as a Legal Aid lawyer to establish. Being with me doesn't mean that you have to stop being you, sweetheart.

"From now on, we're a team and we're in this together," he added.

Hayley felt tears well and then slide down her cheek. He got her, he did. "I love you so much, Jackson."

Jackson dropped a kiss on her temple. "Excellent news. Can we get back to our game now of getting us naked?"

Hayley stepped back from him and grinned, joy invading every atom of her being. "I love you. Drop your pants."

Jackson pushed his pants down his hips and they pooled on the floor. "I love you and get those gorgeous legs out of those jeans. What plans do you have for Thanksgiving?"

"To spend it with my family. But I'm not going if you don't come with me," Hayley said, shimmying out of her jeans. "Did you really buy me my grandparents' house?"

"I did. Anything else you need? And that's a seriously sexy thong, sweetheart."

Hayley looked down at her emerald green panties, stepped out of them and swung them around her finger. His eyes deepened and she swore she heard him growl. Sexy man. "Thanks. No, I don't need anything else, just you with me. Drop those briefs, Jack."

Jackson, too slowly for her liking, pushed his hands under the band of his briefs and started pushing the fabric down. Hayley decided that if he didn't hurry up, she'd do it herself.

"I was thinking that I could buy you a truck, or you can just have mine."

She didn't care. She just wanted him naked and preferably inside her…

Wait, *what*? He wanted to buy, or give her, his limited-edition Ford 150 pickup? Her instinct was to say no, to refuse, but she knew if she did, she'd hurt his feelings. Jackson wanted to share himself with her, all that he was and all that he had, and that included his money.

If she was going to marry this man, and she sure as hell was, she'd have to put aside her independent streak and get used to his generosity. As he said, from now on they were a team.

"We have many, many, many things to discuss, including you buying me a car and me driving your Chiron, darling. But can we please do it later?"

"We can and we will. And no, you can't drive my Chiron."

Hayley pouted, knowing that her request was a long shot. "Because it's super expensive and ridiculously rare?"

"Because it's super fast and super powerful. I don't care about the car but I do care about your safety," Jackson told her. She was a protector but he was her protector, the man who would always make sure she and the kids were safe. She couldn't argue with that…

"I couldn't handle it if anything happened to you, Hayley-mine."

She was his, just as he was hers. The thought made her want to do a happy dance on the spot. "I love you so damn much."

Jackson's eyes flashed with pleasure and passion as his briefs hit the floor. And there he was, physically and emotionally naked and all hers. God, she was so incredibly lucky.

She held out her hand to him and threaded his fingers through hers. Hayley lifted his knuckles to her mouth. "I can't wait to share my life with you, to plan the rest of our amazing life together but—"

"But?" Jackson asked as she led him out of the kitchen, down the passage and into her bedroom.

She turned to face him and stood on her tiptoes to drop an openmouthed kiss on his mouth. "But right now, I need you to make love to me."

"I can do that," Jackson assured her. "Today, tomorrow, as often as I can for the rest of our lives."

It was a beautiful promise at the start of a beautiful life…

* * * * *

COMING SOON!

We really hope you enjoyed reading this book. If you're looking for more romance, be sure to head to the shops when new books are available on

Thursday 1st December

To see which titles are coming soon, please visit
millsandboon.co.uk/nextmonth

MILLS & BOON

THE HEART OF ROMANCE

A ROMANCE FOR EVERY READER

MODERN

Prepare to be swept off your feet by sophisticated, sexy and seductive heroes, in some of the world's most glamourous and romantic locations, where power and passion collide.

HISTORICAL

Escape with historical heroes from time gone by. Whether your passion is for wicked Regency Rakes, muscled Vikings or rugged Highlanders, awaken the romance of the past.

MEDICAL

Set your pulse racing with dedicated, delectable doctors in the high-pressure world of medicine, where emotions run high and passion, comfort and love are the best medicine.

True Love

Celebrate true love with tender stories of heartfelt romance, from the rush of falling in love to the joy a new baby can bring, and a focus on the emotional heart of a relationship.

Desire

Indulge in secrets and scandal, intense drama and plenty of sizzling hot action with powerful and passionate heroes who have it all: wealth, status, good looks…everything but the right woman.

HEROES

Experience all the excitement of a gripping thriller, with an intense romance at its heart. Resourceful, true-to-life women and strong, fearless men face danger and desire - a killer combination!

To see which titles are coming soon, please visit

millsandboon.co.uk/nextmonth

JOIN THE
MILLS & BOON
BOOKCLUB

* **FREE** delivery direct to your door

* **EXCLUSIVE** offers every month

* **EXCITING** rewards programme

Join today at
Millsandboon.co.uk/Bookclub

MILLS & BOON

Desire

Indulge in secrets and scandal, intense drama and plenty of sizzling hot action with powerful and passionate heroes who have it all: wealth, status, good looks…everything but the right woman.

MILLS & BOON

MODERN

Power and Passion

Prepare to be swept off your feet by sophisticated, sexy and seductive heroes, in some of the world's most glamourous and romantic locations, where power and passion collide.

MILLS & BOON
MEDICAL
Pulse-Racing Passion

Set your pulse racing with dedicated, delectable doctors in the high-pressure world of medicine, where emotions run high and passion, comfort and love are the best medicine.